The Styx

Dear Ricky
Come on U Irons
X

Matt White

M White

Bloomington, IN
authorHOUSE®
Milton Keynes, UK

AuthorHouse™
1663 Liberty Drive, Suite 200
Bloomington, IN 47403
www.authorhouse.com
Phone: 1-800-839-8640

AuthorHouse™ UK Ltd.
500 Avebury Boulevard
Central Milton Keynes, MK9 2BE
www.authorhouse.co.uk
Phone: 08001974150

First published by AuthorHouse 12/21/2006

ISBN: 978-1-4259-6587-7 (sc)

Printed in the United States of America
Bloomington, Indiana

This book is printed on acid-free paper.

DEDICATION

To my family for all their love and support.

ACKNOWLEDGMENTS

Special thanks to Jason White for his brilliant editing skills.

Thanks to my parents for absolutely everything.

Thanks to Johnee, Dawn and Lol for all their input.

Thanks to my great friends from Hall Mead School and Derby University for the inspiration.

Additional thanks to my ex colleagues at PWS and Scotts Primary for their support and also to everyone else that knows me. This is for you.

"For the seventeenth century German nature mystic Jakob Boehme, the power source of magic was the life force in nature"

PART ONE

PROLOGUE
DOOM'S DAY APPROACHES

1008 AD
'By God's mercy.'

Curses of Robert Cranley. A friend missing, three days now. Full attendance at the manor showed the situation's severity. Normally court would be held once a month, maybe seventy percent of the village would show. With people living in fear, the Lord had called upon an emergency hearing. Everyone was present.

It wasn't just the disappearance of Roger Brooks that created concern. The decapitated head of a deer on the parish steps, blood smeared haphazardly across the doors. Pig skins draped over the priest while he slept and harsh storms had all blown terror across the inhabitants. A village disturbed. The King would be notified. Reinforcements sent for. No one knew how long it would take. No one wanted to wait.

Now the solemn figure stands alone. Court ended over an hour ago, yet Cranley didn't want to return home. Lived all alone. Sleep becomes difficult when no one's around to delay imagination. Knows he should turn back soon however. Even his lonely cottage stands as more comfort than the forest when nightfall arrives.

Counts his blessings though, he saw Brooks' wife earlier. Must be terrifying. Her world far more desolate now. Shakes his head. The woman frightened, yet unprotected by those in charge. They're more concerned with livestock and deer than the life of a lowly serf. Some even hold her responsible. An argument between the couple causing heads to turn, tongues to wag. Brooks marched into the night. The last interaction she would have with her husband. Still no return. If it wasn't for her he'd still be here now...

No. Cranley knows something more sinister loomed over their village. He would have come back. His friend was not one for straying. A hard working serf, provided well for his woman. Besides, there was no life elsewhere. Just the forests.

Storms damage crops, dampening spirits. Weather, another receiving blame for the missing person. A charge also dismissed by Cranley. The rain was bad, but floods had not occurred. Shelter stood all around.

No. Something was out there. Could feel its presence now. Must move away. Not safe here.

Folds his arms and turns toward home. Another downpour brewing, a chill wind sweeping through the royal forests and beyond. A further sensation creeping its way beneath the man's ragged clothing. A shiver. Someone walks over his grave.

I'm battered. If I keep blanking out like this I'm never gonna make it back upstairs.

Cranley takes one last look back at the vast expanse of trees, beginning to shake and sway as one. Their sound an intimidating hum. So tall and proud. The mystery of nature. Gigantic shadows form a black. Vision into the trees now impossible. Mind races at the content of this other world. Something so magical, yet daunting. He abhorred to be near it. Not even in broad daylight. The task of cleaning the boundaries for cultivation was left to other serfs.

Preferred to work within the village. Chopping trees seemed sacrilegious. The sound when it hit the floor sent a rumble through the ground. Groans of discomfort. A warning. Echoes of his overactive mind

Something is looking back at him. Convinced, Cranley turns his focus to the walk home, picking up his pace. Wants to be inside when dusk settles. Alone there, far more comforting than solitary here. Safe from whatever connected his friend's disappearance to the darkness amidst the trees. That thing encased in black...

Arrives at his cottage, swings open the door.

This time he is not alone.

Two figures stand in the centre of his room. Cranley, heart pounding already from the conjures of his mind, lets out a yelp. With this they turn, instantly calming. The faces belong to his friends Hevey Little and Wadard Mooning. Hectic thoughts had got the better of him once again.

Little and Mooning were also serfs in the manor. They too concerned with their friends vanish are convinced the King's help will arrive too late, if at all.

Taking the law upon themselves now. A search for Roger Brooks. A group of five to delve into the unexplored section of the forest. Deep within. Their only chance will be at night, knowing hefty punishment awaits any absence from work.

Wandering through chasms of unthinkable ingredients?

The thought terrifies Cranley to his very soul. But this was a friend. If Brooks was in trouble, something had to be done.

Reluctantly he agrees.

CHAPTER 1
THE MAGIC NUMBER

2008 AD

'Christ on a pony.'

If only for a second me feet hit the ground, then I'd sort this mess out. Clocks running an hour slow, a pornographic mind, sweat drenched hair, ears ringing, beef soup armpits, two twisted mates, beercans, ashtrays, empty wraps and a broken glass. Until morning I'll ride this wave though, if I have to. Such is life. Littl' Leg and Moon are well fucked. I'm absolutely battered meself. The coke's banging round me system like I don't fucking know. Like some kind of lightning train on the underground. Hits every stop at once. Fucking journey that'd be. We'd lost Tin Lid about 1, surprising? No. A Wendy Hughes knockback, collapse at the bar and the geezer was Frank Bough early again.

'What ya doing Crane?' Littl' leg's voice interrupts my train of thoughts. I realise I'm stood in the doorway of my room, clutching three beers, just staring at my two friends.

Moon's skinning up. Beautiful.

'Leg.' I throw him one of the Stellas I chaffed from me Dad's stash in the garage.

'Cheers geez.'

'Moon.'

'Can you jus' put it down there for a sec?' Says Moon navigating his way through the most intricate part of the reefer construction phase.

'Are yous as fucked as me?' I ask needing reassurance

'Why do you think I'm building this joint?'

'Yeah man look at me legs...' Littl' Legs' legs are bouncing around with no particular rhythm, to absolutely no sound of music. '... I' jus' got that fucking stupid *Mylo* song banging round me 'ead.'

'Shall I put some moosic on?'

'Moosic?' Moon laughs

'Fuck off Moon.'

He's taking the piss. At least I think so. This is all a bit much.

'Yeah whack on that fucking, what is it? Shit rap moosic.'

As he says this I stare at Little Leg through wide pupils: cocaine inflated eyes. No wonder he pulled tonight, he has this confidence in his appearance that I can only dream of. Full stubble at eighteen. When I try and grow anything like that, it makes me look like I've got downs syndrome for fuck's sake. He never has to spend hours over his hair like I do either. His big frame suits his skinhead. I'm not jealous though, because despite his abuse, all I can think is that he's well cool. I love him... he's taking the piss, but I love him.

'You're well cool Leg.'

He gets up and gives me a hug.

'I luv ya too man.'

An amazingly drug inspired show of affection from two blokes who've had a good night. He had the better one though. Bastard!

'That bird you pulled was alright, weren't she.' I tell him.

'She was minging.' Moon butts in. That geezer's never content with a mate getting one up on him. We ignore the cunt.

'Yeah I'd 'ave tried to get 'er 'ome, but I'd never've got it up.'

'I thought 'er mate was up for me at one point, till she strolled off with that trendy cunt.' I add.

'Well you was both blonde and you know what they say? Two blondes don't make a right.' Leg laughs, Moon tuts.

'Who gives a fuck though when you're on this shit?' Not me boy.

'Exactly.'

I suggest *Panic! At the disco*

'Oh 'ello sailor.' Goes Leg, camping it up. Hand on hip and shit.

'What the fuck's gay about *Panic*?'

'I was joking about the rap mate. Go on put your *Will Smith* on. Anything but *Panic.'*

'*Panic's* cool man. How's it gay?' I say maybe a little too defensively, the coke's doing a Liam Gallagher on me. Littl' Leg senses this and quashes it instantly.

'Cor I've reeled you right in. Moon got any more bait mate? The fish are really biting 'ere.'

I laugh. Realise I've been had. Hook, line and fucking sinker.

I go to me Hi-fi to put on some sensible hip hop, beginning I think with a classic; *Dr Dre: 'Chronic 2001'*. Finally a rap album that got me mates appreciating a bit of hip hop, back when Oasis had taken over their lives. The intro receives nods of approval.

Moon lights the reefer. Instantly the room begins to fill with smoke. The stench of weed overcomes my senses as *'The Watcher'* kicks in.

"*Things just ain't the same for gangsta's...*"

This is controversially my favourite song on the album. Real laid back stuff. Dre mumbling about all he's done for rap, but not getting appreciated. I bang the volume up a couple of notches 'cause me parents are away for a long bank holiday weekend. A peaceful fishing trip to escape life's tribulations.

I need some more coke. I pull the bullet from me pocket. This beautiful contraption only cost me seven notes. That's value for money. Now I can bang any stuff up me nose without the hassles of cubicles, credit cards or bouncers. I'd whacked a gram and half a' Charlie in the little bottle at the start of the night. Inspecting it now, I find I've got about half a' g left. I'd done half a' gram of speed in *Time* too, just to make sure of a top night.

'Anyone fancy a bang?' I ask, waving me best purchase ever, bar me Fila*s,* in the air.

'Nah mate, I'm still flying off that speed, I'm trying to bring meself back to earth with this fucker.' Moon answers showing me the spliff before moving it on to Leg.

'Me too, I'm gonna be up all night as it is.' Leg says gratefully receiving the joint.

'Well fuck me, if it ain't all turned gay in 'ere.'

I laugh, then realise the contradiction. They don't seem to notice. Was it a contradiction? Was what a contradiction? Oh for fuck's sake, I dunno anymore.

Just have another snort Crane. I tip the bullet upside down, then turn the nozzle to the right. This brings the coke up to the small tub within. Tip it straight, move the nozzle up, simple as that and sniff...

Whoa, fuck me. Did I feel that!

Have to go over and sit on the couch to steady meself. I crack open me Stella and thankfully Leg moves the joint on to me.

'It's good what ya done wiv ya bruvver's bedroom geez. It's like a living room now.' goes Moon.

'Yeah man, the lads can 'ave a proper smoking session in 'ere now.' Leg says laying back, feeling the effects of the herb, but still shaking his right leg as if it ain't part of him.

I take a couple of quick puffs. The gear immediately mingling with the Charlie...

Start to black out a bit.....

* * * *

I can see my room. See the transformation of my brother's old bedroom. That was my old bed, that sofa we sit on now... Away from the dream now, take the top mattress away and put the cover on the bottom one will you. Come on Mum, help by making huge cushions, big blue pillows that I can drown in. Sinking through to a deep sea. When did the mirrors arrive? Oh them, they don't work no more.

"Just remember that you're fucking with a family man, I gotta lot more to lose than you, remember that."

No one like *Dre*. He's in my Hi-fi now. I see my Hi-fi, placed in the centre of a stacker. Dad could you help me shift this cupboard? Yous two can help too. We'll be finished in no time.

What lies within? Something hideous? What else could have sent these appalling warnings?

Shh!... Listen a minute. The rain's getting in. Climbing through the window. It's coming in. Stop it from getting in my room...

'CRANE.'

Where the fuck am I?

'You alright mate?' It's Moon. My eyes flicker.

'Did I just say something then?'

'Nah, but you nearly left us there. Shit man, the reefer's gone out.'

'You better take it a minute.' I say to Moon, wondering what the fuck I was just thinking about.

'Give it to Leg a sec. I'm rolling you a small joint for after we've gone.'

'Wicked! Cheers mate.'

Starting to come round again. The coke and speed take hold of the reigns. I prefer this for now, far too early for that weird slumber fuckedness.

I look at Littl' Leg. He's decided to get up and wander aimlessly round my room. He lifts an ashtray, looks at the underneath, then puts it down. He picks up one of my football trophies. Doesn't even read the engraving, just looks at the underneath and puts it down.

'What you doing Leg?'

'Fuck knows.'

Moon passes me my joint for later, then takes the one on the go from Leg. It's like pass the fucking parcel in here...

I don't grasp what he's saying at first, but I think Moon's definitely on one. I think he's saying that all history is bollocks, just an increased exaggeration as time goes on.

'You think about it, a couple of weeks ago Leg said 'e done a couple a' grams a speed, a gram a' bugle and an acid. I told Brooke about it, who then told Beeke that leg 'ad done shit loads a' drugs. So when I spoke to Beeke, 'e expected that Leg 'ad done five grams a' speed, two g's a' coke and two acids. Whereas 'e'd only done two grams a' speed, a gram a' coke and an acid.'

"ang on a minute, that's 'ow much I said I did.'

'Shut up Leg, this is important. I'm trying to explain it to Crane.' He turns back to me, but I'm fucked if I know what he's talking about. I've only just realised I've got the reefer back.

'Right so now you think about the war...' Moon continues '...and 'ow it gets reported as worse and worse over the years'

'Does it?' Leg asks

'LEG, for fuck sake man…' Moon pauses, look of discontent. '… Well what I think is that there was only about five geezers who actually died in it. It was probably just a really 'arsh argument or some'ing.' Moon finishes and looks at us both. I start to grin, so does he.

I can feel it. Here it comes... Start giggling like a fucking schoolgirl. Increasing in volume 'til I'm leant back, erupting into Littl' Leg barbecue style laughter, just knowing he's gonna have a thousand of these fuckers.

'The plague was just one geezer with a right itchy mosquito bite.'

'Christ Moon.' Littl' Leg gives up on his examination of my room and sits cross legged on the floor. I pass the joint to him, laughing too much to smoke it.

'The great fire of London was a bonfire what gotta bit outta control in me Grandad's garden.' Moon's grinning inanely, looking at me with half open eyes. He ain't stopping now.

'Sweeney Todd drew a bit of blood from a nick on someone's cheek; and Jack the Ripper used to rip peoples 'eads off with 'is bare teeth.'

'What?' I'm really confused now, but no sensation can make me laugh more

'Shut the fuck up Moon you bell end.' Leg tries to show he's not cracking up on the inside…

Sinking back, listening to their argument about Moon talking bollocks. Moon's not having it.

It ends the same way every Thursday night. I fucking love it!

Trust in it... Live for it... **Live for the rain in the sky. Completely skied. Yes sirreee, fucked and loving it**…

'Bollocks, wha's time Crane?'

'What?'

'Fucking 'ell geez, you're losing it.' I come round to Moon's voice.

'I know, I need another snort.'

I work my magic bullet shaped wand.

'Anyone else?'

'No. I just wanna know the fucking time ya muppet'

'Err, five past three.' I finally answer after a huge struggle to focus on my watch.

'Well Littl' Leg man, I'm feeling mighty fine after that joint. I'm still buzzing, but at least it's taken the edge off the rush. So let's fucking adjourn so I can take the 'ead off it, before it starts pissing down.' Moon sounds like a train when he's talking.

'You're not wrong Moon, we can stop at the garage and pick up a couple of Frankie's on the way'

'I love the way you think Leg, 'ow about you Crane? Trip to the garage?'

'Nah geez, I've got enough material 'ere to last me a lifetime. Tonight anyway.'

'Yeah I'm sure you'll manage...' -I know I will, Gabriella awaits. '...Right Leg you lucky kappa-slapper dog pulling mother fucker, let's do one.'

'Done my son.'

'You can both stay over if you wanna miss the rain?' As much as I love 'em, I'm hoping they say no. I'm getting the proper horn now.

'You're not turning the way of Beeke are ya?...' Laughs moon, meaning our poof, I mean 'gay' friend. I fail to answer. He continues. '...Nah nature's calling geez. I must bash one out.'

'Fair enough, me too' I say; and sure enough:

'Me three.'

'Shut up Leg you moron.'

'You can talk, how many GCSE's you get?'

'Oh 'ello, listen to the old 'I got a flukey C in 'istory, now I'm a right smart cunt' Littl' Leg.'

'Well it's one more C than you got innit Moon.'

'Yeah who earns more money then Leg you peasant?'

'You only got that job cause ya brother's a director ya mug.'...

I just know these two'll be slating each other all the way home. I love Littl' Leg, Moon as well. He don't pull as much as Leg 'cause of his trainee beer gut at only 18, but he does have you in stitches. That gets him a few half decent birds.

Back in the days of The Styx we used to call ourselves The Magic Number, after the *De La Soul* song. We didn't tell the others of course.

CHAPTER 2
3:27

Brooke's eyes snap open . Two seconds and the rain slamming itself against the window helps him realise why he woke. A crash of thunder that follows moments after confirms it.

'It's fucking pissing it down.' He groans with a whisper.

Whilst waiting for the inevitable lightning, he feels the warmth of the naked body lying against him. Tightens his grip, seeking comfort. Never felt safe in the dark, especially so when a storm blows outside. Fights hard not to recall a scene in *Poltergeist*, but loses the mind's battle as another roar sounds outside;

'one one thousand'

'two one thousand'

'three one thousand'

the room illuminates causing Brooke to tense, half expecting a tree to come crashing in and grab him.

Nothing.

Blames a friend for this over active imagination. Every time he and the rest of The Styx would end up at Crane's after *Time*, all feeling the intense height of an acid trip, the host would put on horror films such as *The Evil Dead* or *Amityville* for "background viewing". Yet nothing's background when you're tripping. By the end they'd all be staring intently at the screen waiting for the terror to cease. All except Crane that is. While the rest told him to turn it off, he would just sit laughing, showing unhealthy immunity to the immense bloodshed and gore.

In preparation for the storm's next clamour, Brooke seeks solace. Starts by getting his head into a position that the lightning strike may reveal his girlfriend's face. As far as he knows she is sleeping through this deluge, just as she sleeps through everything that has before left himself tirelessly tossing and turning.

Then the rapid developing noise of thunder rattles through the room. Just can't help himself.

'one one thousand'

'two one thousand'

'thr...'

It comes. Flashes of blue light shoot through the gap in the curtains and the room brightens instantaneously. The face staring back at Brooke belongs to his friend Sloo and it twitches with anger.

'Get a grip son.'

Quickly shuts his eyes and tries to steady the heavy thumping in his chest that pumps raw confusion to his mind. He knows Sloo wasn't really there. Surely?

Static lightning. The room continues to glow a deep blue. Eyes reopen to steady vision.

There she is: Gemma. His Gemma, his restful Gemma. Not Sloo at all. Just the beautiful woman that, maybe, Brooke could settle down with. She is everything he wasn't looking for, but everything he wanted. There she is, here, curled up peacefully next to him, oblivious to the episode of imaginary demons going on inside his mind.

Is glad she doesn't know he was like this at night. Turning his face back toward the ceiling he whispers with relief

'Fucking fruitcake.'

He knows it's not all Crane's fault. Brooke was tormented like this as a kid. Spent many sleepless nights laying dead still, completely convinced there was a clown lurking beneath the bed. Had got over it though, that was until he discovered drugs. The chemicals once again opened his mind to the possibility that anything could happen.

Surprised at how quickly he managed to fall asleep tonight, what with the rain starting just as his girlfriend curled around him and their conversation ceased. Normally would stay awake waiting for the storm to get in full swing, then have to see it through 'til day light arrived. Yet with her he felt comfortable, safe in bed. It was never like this with the girls before. They were just a release of sexual tension. After climax he'd either go home or lay awake wishing that were the case.

No girl prior Gemma found it possible to get on his wavelength, but she could tap into his feelings whenever she liked, with no effort whatsoever.

It was over two years before he met her, that he discovered a skill of channelling girl's thoughts. Brooke could then play them to their strengths and weaknesses. It just took their body language to decipher whether they fancied him, wanted one night stands or simply didn't want to know. He had them down to a tee, or at least he thought so. Until she came into his life.

Nearly a year ago Tin Lid obtained invitations for a party at a college friend's. The Styx arrived in their usual drugged and drunk state, except Brooke, who for maybe reasons of fate, had taken it easy. A few dabs of speed, but nothing overboard. House parties to him were the best opportunity to meet girls. One thing he wasn't expecting however, was to meet the woman of his dreams.

Half hour of lingering in the kitchen the boys forced themselves toward mingling. Then Gemma entered. From that very moment Brooke turned from the man in control, to a standard nervous seventeen year-old, clueless about female complexities. She noticed him too, as close a look-alike of Johnny Depp to be found in Essex. As the young lady walked through to the garden, she flashed him a smile and flicked back her long copper red hair. Brooke, momentarily disorientated by her large green eyes, made her his mission for the night.

Eventual success. Having spent an hour building courage to approach, he earned the girl's phone number. Yet only after numerous dates did she finally sleep with him. Something totally unheard of for Brooke. No pressure on Gemma though. Sex wasn't important. Her conversation swamped his interest. From then on attempts to decipher what she wanted failed. He discovered her far too complex for his usual mind reading tactics. Factors bemusing him into finally respecting a girl. She was an enigma he became completely engrossed with. As time passed he found, and still does, infatuation.

He knows what she wants from him now of course... At least the belief lay at the surface.

The freak weather continues, more loud claps of thunder, Gemma budges. She gives a slight murmur of approval as he moves his right arm down her back, bringing her even tighter against him. Doesn't wake though; even with the rain still determined to break its way through the window.

Thoughts return to his friend Sloo and The Styx. The ironic vow they all made at the age of ten. Reminisces the seven of them sitting at the camp, all agreeing against their own secretly kept wills to never allow women in the way of their gang. What were they to know? All Brooke understood at the time was admittance of a crush for Katy Davis could prove disastrous. There would be undoubted dismissal from the group, not to mention the piss taking; he'd have to talk his parents into emigration.

A few of the others suffered the same dilemma. He appreciates this now. Not about Katy Davis, but some other girls they felt pre-pubescent love for.

So they all agreed, substitute The Styx for a girl=result: death. None of them knew how exactly, fatality would decide. Sloo's rule. Brooke determines Sloo's instability was as rife then as now. Then remembers how the edict was tested when they reached twelve and senior school.

The Christmas disco laid groundwork to the damage. A life altering event involving mistletoe and hormones. Somewhere the boys first explored their attraction for the opposite sex.

Can't forget *Atomic Kitten's*: *'Eternal flame'* kick starting numerous boys into such painstaking tasks as having to ask the girl they've secretly desired to slow dance. Brooke's choice was Georgina Kellet. Most of his naive feelings for Katy Davis having been washed away with the move to upper school and the wider range of girls to choose from.

The dance floor loaded with pubescence sufferers slavering over each other as if drowning in saliva. With Littl' Leg and Moon achieving their first full snogs in the corner, he and Tin Lid desperately wanted part of the action. So Georgina and his friend's choice Beverly became targets. Without persuasion the girls obliged and were soon to become their first true girlfriends. Strangely enough he paired with Beverly while Tin Lid took out Georgina; the couples having swapped kissing partners when *Westlife* replaced *Atomic Kitten* on the talent-less DJ's turntables.

That was the uncertain way when you're twelve, creating the platform for The Styx's childish rule to be constantly tested. None of them were too dismayed by that fact. Except maybe Beeke. Brooke has not enquired if his friend discovered homosexuality at that young age.

And Sloo.

Lifts his head for a better view of the clock situated at the other side of the bed.

3.27...

The storm continues...

It looks like another one of those long nights...

* * * *

Sloo wakes with a start. That dream again. Some sticky liquid resting on his lower stomach now spreads and mingles with the sweat on his duvet cover. It takes a few moments but soon he notices the storm raging outside. Bedroom windows rattle, frightening him to jump from bed and bring light to his surroundings. Calms him slightly, able to sit back down amid damp entangled sheets.

Tries to shut them out, but cannot stop his thoughts returning to the disturbing recurring dream. Sickening images that all seem too real, re-gather in his mind as repelling visions.

They start in a forest, the exact haunt in which The Styx set up their camp many years before. Sloo is riding the BMX he remembers having at the same time. He isn't eight anymore though and his big frame causes difficulty in keeping the small bike stable, until eventually the two collapse.

Two hundred metres from the camp. Hears The Styx cheering and laughing there. Picks himself up. Looks around, but as always the bike is nowhere to be seen. He must set off on foot toward the site of his friends.

Then the moment arrives in which the dream turns to nightmare. A darkness forms, not from the sky, but from everywhere encompassing. His bearings are now confused, a feeling of uneasiness creeps over the whole setting. Warnings of approaching horror.

Begins to run. Too petrified to look back for the origin of resonant footsteps amalgamating with laughter from the camp. Closer and closer they get. Hears snorts of heavy breathing from behind. Nearer salvation. Can now distinguish the figures of Crane, Littl' Leg, Brooke, Beeke, Tin Lid and Moon. Yet they are not laughing or shouting. Each of them have solemn and lost expressions. Sloo realises now that the laughter originates from surrounding trees. Life has been afforded to them, they taunt his effort for escape.

He gets to fifty metres from his friends.

Thirty-five

Twenty

Ten…

Then the hand grabs his shoulder.

Sloo is swung round to face his assailant his face to round swung is Sloo.

A large cloaked figure stands before him. Fear rises to such an intensity he understands to kneel in respect before it.

Looking up as the semblance raises a hand to the hood of its covering. Watches as it draws it back.

Turns away at first, too scared to see what has been revealed. Yet he is too compelled. Has to see what is there. Slowly he moves his gaze back to the apparition.

There is no face, but a mirror sits on top of the large body. It begins to loom over 'til he can finally look into it.

demrofed dna deregna tub flesmih fo si noitcelfer eht.

Blisters cover the blood splattered face, some burst with semen that smear the vision. Sloo can still make out the mouth. It opens with a scream flooding the air. Birds attempt to scatter from trees, but branches reach up. Arms gripping, caught in mid flight. Squeezing them tighter and tighter until eye sockets release. Veins burst, showering the earth with blood once more.

The howling ends. The speech begins:

'NATURAL LIFE SLOO, THE END FOR THIS WORLD. DESTROYER OF MANKIND, EXCEPT HERE. BRING THEM HERE AND BE SAVED WITH ME FOR ETERNITY.
LIVE BY OUR OWN NATURE.'

A calm arises. Colour returns.

The young boy dazed, still kneeling, opens his mouth. The figure reaches inside the waist area of its cloak. Sloo lets the snake slide into his throat. A never ending flow.

Finds himself sucking. Desperately trying to reach the end. Keeps inhaling harder and harder. Static, no end.

The laughter returns. Even more fierce and tormenting.

Looks back up. No longer faced by the mirror. Instead witnesses Beeke smiling down at him. Extreme pleasure written over his expression as Sloo sucks on his penis. Rising enthusiasm. Pulls out his own organ to masturbate. Assiduous he tugs, licking and slurping. More enjoyment, more, more.

The semen flows down Sloo's throat, soothing, reassuring. Stronger he yanks. Feels it coming, coming, coming...

... Sits, head in hands. The thought of giving Beeke oral sex resulting in a wet dream, the most sickening fact. That is not natural, not allowed.

Anger rises. No thoughts of cleaning the mess of his bed.

Instead he trembles with rage. What does this all mean?

'NO, I'M NOT BENT AND I FUCKING HATE THAT LITTLE CUNT BEEKE FOR BEING A DIRTY FAGGOT. I'M GONNA SMASH HIS FUCKING STUPID CUNT FACE IN.'

Beeke sits by his window. Staring out amidst the rain crashing almost antagonistically upon the street. Concentrates more determinedly.

Looks further than the modern well maintained houses opposite. Ever distant past high trees, no longer standing proudly tall as the wind pushes their peaks to the right. He sees deep into the night, sensing the darkness, the unknown it holds. Doesn't like the visions.

3.27. Sleep disturbed by a shuddering roar of thunder. Normally would have rolled over, attempted a return to slumber, but tonight a shiver ran down his spine. Not caused by the sinister sounding weather. There was something else.

Unable to explain the eerie feeling, Beeke had got up feeling uneasy and very alone. Hadn't ventured out with the others as was usual for a Thursday night. Eighteen, already perceiving himself too old for party night at *Time's Out*. The failing numbers the club drew under the title Hollywoods made its revamping essential, but only led for more overcrowding of eleventh years and girls as young as fourteen.

The real reason for his absence however, poisons his mind now. Two weeks ago he told his friends he was gay.

Started out a standard Thursday evening. The Styx heavily under the influence of drugs and alcohol before even departing Crane's house. A Playstation FIFA tournament in full swing in Crane's bedroom, the host took on Brooke in the first semi-final. Next door Moon tore into Tin Lid for his failed attempts at pulling Wendy Hughes.

'What d'ya expect ya mug when you're that pissed? All right Wendy d'ya fanshy a shnog?'

Narcotics abuse, character assassination and console competitions had become an integral ritual before setting out. Although each knew maturity should replace the excitement shown in the football game, none were prepared to give up the tradition. Realising most people their age warmed up festivities by socialising in pubs didn't matter, they remained comfortable with this environment. Good times of previous years undertaking this exact performance fresh in their memories, they feared an outing would be jinxed if they weren't here. Subconsciously however knowing none of this ever decided the occasion's standard. The vast amount of drugs they consumed, or attracting women, really created that special night.

This was just the warm up.

Beeke was inebriated, having polished off almost a litre of vodka mixed with Metz. Such a vulnerable state distracted Moon's attention from Tin

Lid. Fresh meat for the torrent of jibes he enjoyed aiming at friends. All good natured, but with the topic of Beeke's recent lack of female involvement, the instigator had hit a nerve.

'You're probably queer innit!'

An extreme secret holding him back for years. The drink, dabs of speed, his hidden affection for Sloo, suddenly the burden became a lead weight he could no longer bear to carry. Beeke provided an affirmative answer without hint of sarcasm to Moon's exclamation. A look of eventual post confession horror, the others could ascertain their friend wasn't playing along with a prank...

Couple of moments of silent shock, then Littl' Leg came up on acid he'd swallowed half-hour before. Started to giggle profusely. Everyone stunned as Leg tried to suppress laughter. Tin Lid finished a can of Bud, Moon took several quick puffs on a joint. Sloo sat silent...

Suddenly there was a shout from the next room.

'Ah you jammy cunt Crane.' Brooke came storming in, complaining he'd been knocked out the FIFA tournament by a fluky late goal. A display of ignorance in Brooke's arrival, despite the shocking revelation that had quashed the atmosphere, sent Moon, Tin Lid and Littl' Leg into hysterics.

Ease of tension, Beeke remembers a desire to laugh himself, first he wanted to see the reaction of...

Too late.

Sloo had stormed from the room.

A loud clap of thunder jolts Beeke from his mesmeric trance, also reinstating dejection he'd experienced with Sloo's response.

The person he craved a most positive reaction from, but realistically knew would give the more negative. Had become attracted to Sloo more and more over the last few months, an affection destroying his life. Was the best friend he had. Remembers Moon once joking about the closeness of their companionship...

''e only likes ya so much coz you aint broke that fucking "no girls in front of The Styx" rule.'

Then there was Crane's comment straight after:

'Yeah, why ain't we all died yet?'

Pictures everyone laughing, except Sloo. The supposed friend didn't even raise a smile.

It wasn't that the two had never kissed a girl, this was a large factor of school discos and parties, but neither had maintained a relationship long enough to claim a girlfriend. Beeke knew his own reasoning behind this; a fight against reality. Despite all efforts he hadn't discovered the attraction of the opposite sex, in turn enthusiasm to find a female partner dwindled. Sort of hoped this was Sloos reason as well, yet the possibility that his friend was still sticking to a childish vow could not be ruled out.

Sloo was like that.

He also hadn't properly spoken to Beeke since the coming out. There was a few encounters at college or whilst out, they'd still greet each other, but no longer shared meaningful conversations. Beeke longed for Sloo to return his affections, yet not foolish enough to believe these would be openly admitted. Not from the self proclaimed toughest member of the group. Despite the rest ridiculing this leadership arrogance, Sloo knew none would rile him far enough to test his belief.

Crushed at losing his friend in this manner. Views the continuous downpour, the strong wind delaying a fox's route home. Wishes he could return to that night and react differently to Moon's outburst. Life would revert to normality, he would have just got in from a night out. Happy. Not feeling like the person who wrecked everything.

Life would never be the same again.

* * * *

It's not only Beeke failing to rid his memory of that night. The same storm passes by their windows, similar thoughts cross their minds. Sloo stares through the darkness, recalling the moment that tore his gang apart.

BACK

Not waiting for the aftermath of Brooke's sloppy entrance, Sloo stormed downstairs. Needed to get his head together in Crane's bathroom. Fortunately he had brought his gram of speed along and swallowed it on arrival.

Mind come alive.

Don't fucking believe it, the cunt's ruined everything. We had it sorted, had a fucking good group there. Now it's fucked. How could he do it? I thought he was the best. Given us no trouble before. Followed the rules better than any other. There's been a few adjustments, but now this. Fucking bent. No way. What are the others gonna think of me now? I spend the most time with him. Ah MAN THIS FUCKING AIN'T HAPPENING. WHAT A CUNT. THAT FUCKING BENT CUNT'S GONNA PAY FOR THIS...

...Sloo, calm, we need him for now, he has not given his dedication to you yet. With this news he'll be the easiest. When we get his pledge we'll deal with him there and then. Then the others will not be harmed by his sickness. You always lose one to the cause. We'll still be strong with six. Bide your time. The moment will be with us soon.

COMFORTING

Sloo stared at his reflection in the mirror, heard the soothing voice again. He will wait, but feels unable to face Beeke until... until he can make him pay for this disruption to the plans.

FORWARD

That time has not yet arrived. So still he suffers tormenting dreams and the clogging of his thoughts with Beeke's queerness. It is why he sits awake now, gibbering, plotting revenge whilst enjoying the weathers disturbance to the street and houses outside.

There was one aspect he knows worked to his advantage that night. The bad effect upon his 'beloved' group his attitude caused after they left Cranes'. He scared them in a way considered unhealthy for a person to do unto friends. They must fear him to follow. Respect is vital, it was for their own good.

The rest of that night was tarnished with the tension created by Sloo. The others tried to continue the best they knew how, but with acid being dropped the whole evening became a complete downer. Littl' Leg's bad trip started on the bus taking them to the club in Romford. He sat and watched Sloo silently carve his name with a key in to the upper decks front window.

This was the last time Sloo would take drugs.

He was ready.

The others would have to take more and more chemicals to deal with this whole situation.

That was the plan...

* * * *

I don't want the night to end at a quarter past three. Without this line there's a slight chance it might.

So I chop and chop at the small white powdery lumps. Push it all together, a nice fat line stretching for a couple of centimetres, beautiful. Deciding to tip the remainder of coke from my bullet and do it the old fashioned way is a great idea. I know this will prolong my night further, hopefully an extra hour or so.

What am I talking about? I'm fucked here and this is shitloads left. I could still be going for another two hours without any more Charlie, this will turn it into an all nighter. God my brain must be fried, rationality out the window please, we're going for it.

I'd be letting everyone down if I left a little bit of coke like this for tomorrow. It's an all or nothing situation.

I roll up a Bobby for the first and last time tonight. Quick glance at the clock: **3.25**.

Moon and Littl' leg have been gone about quarter of an hour. By the sound of it, they've been caught in the downpour on their twenty minute plus stoppages trek home.

I get the note just right. A wide-ish hole tightly wrapped, beautiful. This should be a clean hit. I bend over the line and breathe out away from the gear. Careful not to destroy my work like I've done on numerous occasions before. I take the note in between me thumb and forefinger, then put one end to me right nostril. Sharp movement of the old head to the right. Line disappears. Job done.

Stand straight, take the feeling in. I can already tell it's not been the good hit I thought. It'll be a few minutes before Charles gets right up there. Me nose is packed to fuck already.

A large crack of thunder scares the shit outta me...

Steady Crane. I look at the bookshelf for the leftovers. Wipe any remaining powder with my index finger then rub it over me gums. Take another big sniff, try and dislodge something.

I find my beer and sit on the sofa. The upstairs of the house became all mine after me brother moved out. I turned his bedroom into a type of living room. It's large enough. Decorations include posters of Uma Thurman as *Black Mamba* equipped with sword, all ready to *Kill Bill.* There's Paris Hilton in full blow-job pose, Carmen Electra looking fit as fuck and the legend that is Paul "the konch" Konchesky.

The sofa's situated in the left hand corner of the room as you walk in. This faces a reasonable standard Telly connected to me X box, so I get by for entertainment. There's me sound system next to me as well. I turn to it and, still sniffing encouraging the gear to hit the back of me throat and start its work on my blood, put on *R.E.M.*'s '*Up*'. I flick straight to no. 3 '*Suspicion*', my favourite song on the album.

Two birds with one stone, I can lean back and enjoy the music whilst tilting me head skywards opening the runway.

We're about to take off.

The song starts, drowning out the rain I've noticed getting heavier by the second.

"Now my suspicion's on the rise,"

Tonight was a goodun, even though only four of us made it to *Time.* It seems Beeke's coming out's been a major crossroad in our lives. Not that most of us really cared that he was gay.

"I have known, I have known your kind."

You could tell Sloo did though, last week at college was right tense. He hardly spoke to Beeke at all.

"Please don't talk"

Forcing one of the big drug takers out of our weekly ritual. Three weeks running now. Pretending he was ill! Even with Sloo backing out anyway.

"don't make me think,"

The third blow out was Brooke, who now more than usual spent the night in with his bird. Can't fucking blame him with that Gemma though.

"order up another drink,"

That left The Magic Number and Tin Lid to represent The Styx tonight. We did us proud, taking vast amounts of drugs and dancing the night away.

"let me let imagination drive."

Tin Lid didn't hammer substances though. Yet the half acid and twenty gallons of alcohol made up for it.

"Can't you see"

I wasn't dancing as much as Moon and Littl' leg tonight. Jesus, three grams of speed each. I had half a g` of Billy. Fancied a bit of a change.

"I need"

I've partaken in the odd sniff of coke before, but never a whole gram in a night.

"nothing"

Decided I might as well tonight after winning 130 quid on an horse today.

"too deep?"

So Thank You True 9 for doing the business. 12-1, beautiful. Now I know the real high of rich man's drugs.

"Imagination"

This is a fucking buzz. Really hitting me now. Just wish I still had someone to talk bollocks with.

"come alive."

Judging by the time now, Moon and Leg must've been back here about three quarters of an hour before setting off for the post party ritual.

"Suspicion"

They've definitely failed an attempt to stay dry on their trip for porn. They'll be soaked when they're wanking themselves silly.

"tonight, I'll dream tonight."

Wanking don't seem too bad an idea...

I go back in my bedroom. A smaller room containing a wardrobe, a bed and me record breaking collection of porn.

Have to delve deep in the large cardboard box behind the bed. Dig me way through old 'Match' football magazines and copies of 'Sunday Sport'. Eventually here it is. My pile of treasured rag mags. Although my dick is pretty numb and lifeless my brain's still buzzing, so the last thing I wanna do is try and sleep. So I search through the material and my fried memory to remember which ones have the most quality birds in them. I come to a 'Club International'. The first piece of porn I ever bought, well bar those shit erotic playing cards I got on a school trip to France. This edition's got a special place in my heart, because within the pages is... Gabriella. Her long dark curly hair, tan skin, perfectly sized and formed tits, succulent big red lips and long legs. The look similar to a girl I used to lust after at school and fantasy knocked one out over regularly. A resemblance strong enough for me to bash one out over Gabriella, what must be a thousand times now. The best ones being six hour speed enhanced tugs that blistered me nob for days.

I also wanted her now, with a passion you just can't comprehend. Suffice to say it's such a potent sexual urge that if she, either Gabriella or my school boy crush Tanya Allen, was here now, then I'd have the closest experience of heaven humanly possible. Even if me dick has shrunk to the size of a cocktail sausage. Gabriella always sorts me out. If anyone can get me hard again, finish me off, it's her.

I open to page 52, a little too easily perhaps. Gabriella's spread-eagled on a bed wearing only a white bra, the cups pulled down revealing her amazing tits and erect nipples. Her body's slim, her hips are wide. I spy your bikini-shaved pussy Gabby, all open, showing me your wet pink clit. Ccorrr Fuck.

I pull down me trackie bottoms and boxer shorts, take me penis in thumb and forefinger and start to tug.

* * * *

Tin Lid opens his eyes. The whole room spins. Struggling to focus, knows there's only one way to settle this. Turns slowly feeling his head reverberate with the shift.

The digital clock on his dressing table reads **3:26**.

'Oh fuck.' He murmurs. If it weren't for the storm he would have been passed out 'til morning- then he could handle a hangover.

Now though has to stumble out of bed, incessantly attempting to swallow the sick sat waiting in his throat. Climbing to his feet, clings to the wall, guides himself to the bathroom where he collapses on arrival. Despite having to crawl the final couple of feet, Tin Lid managed to lift himself from the floor and now knowingly faces the expectant porcelain God.

Remembers little of the night except the usual: getting far too drunk and...

Making a fool of himself in front of Wendy. Realisation creeps in. The fifth week running, still no success. He'll have Crane on his back. Equalled the record his friend set in his obsessive Claire Delaney days. Left early too...

Now the memory of three Aftershocks he downed at *Time* pulls the vomit trigger. Putrid showers flow from mouth and nose, lining the toilet with blood red splats.

The Aftershock he hopes.

Thunder answers the bathroom silence.

* * * *

Two figures sit in the sheltered doorway of Upminster Hall, a refuge from the heavy surrounding rain. The building has stood more than a thousand years, paying sight to centuries of change. Witnessing numerous human extremities, from hard working serfs to drugged and drunk teenagers.

Can it tell the difference?

The hall has altered. Once it housed members of royalty, used as a church for inhabitants of a tiny village. Now a large modern building frequented as a club house by golfers.

One thing which hasn't changed is the history the Hall persevered. Now it's recording of the events of *time* were about to be replayed as the circle of existence meets its starting point once again.

''ow's the *Men Only* shaping up?'

'On first sight, pretty fucking good geez.'

'I'm sure that paki in the garage's gonna start asking our names soon, we must be 'is best customers.'

'Every Thursday night. 'ow's the *Two Blue*?'

'Fuckin' A. I just can't wait for this pocsy rain to calm down so I can go 'ome and do me beans all over Nicola. Just look at that.'

Littl' Leg's trance breaks from his own pornography. Now has to view centre spread of a beautiful blonde wearing nothing but stilettos, in Moon's magazine. Her legs spread wide apart whilst she makes facial expressions that would suggest a well-endowed invisible man lay above.

'Oh beautiful!'

'I know. Wha's time?'

'Coming up to 'alf three.' Littl' Leg's answer is drowned by raucous thunder, swiftly followed by a flash of lightning illuminating the Hall and its adjoining land.

'A?'

"alf three. Repeats Littl' Leg.

'D'ya know what I think Leg?'

'What?'

'You know when the sun comes up in the morning?'

'Mmm.' Littl' Leg is back in the possessive hold of *Men Only*, sizing up who will be his chosen lady for the evening.

'Well I think it should come up with a bit more of a bang, know what I mean? Like just fucking zip up in the sky as if to say "right you cunts, its fucking daytime so you better get the fuck out of bed."'

Littl' Leg looks up at Moon. Feels that uncontrollable desire to laugh build within.

'Yeah, and the moon should be up there at night with a huge blifter.' He blurts out with giggles.

'Come on de world, take it easy Mon. It's bedtime what's de rush?' Moon says in a convincing Jamaican accent.

Two friends now in fits of laughter outside the Hall doors. Their night together coming to a close, yet separately they will be awake for approximately five more hours. Both masturbating profusely, wishing they had girlfriends to perform the act instead, then realising this was the exact behaviour which left them single.

All this whilst a storm rages over the South of England. The thunder sounds around every corner, while the sky becomes a flashlight for the indescribable.

Each spark of brightness revealing events far across the park.

Long Ago.

The houses of River Drive will glow like the searching fires of before.

Then into the woods.

Further…

Further

into Camp Styx.

Where the boys started their gang almost a decade earlier.

Under a storm of thunder and lightning.

The same conditions suffered nearly a thousand years ago. Not by those who remained safe and dry under the trees. People protected against the harsh nature of slavery, believing that their salvation had arrived.

Three days later the slaughters began.

Lightning.

The blade lopping head from shoulders.

Lightning.

A raised arm, hand clasping brains. Devouring, celebration. It would all begin and would always return in preparation for this day.

The storm that pushed William Smith into Ingrebourne Brooke. The force like a hand upon his head. Breathing the water, lungs filling, hands flailing. No time.

Warning.

Lightning.

Running scared, is there a way out of these woods?

Figures dash between trees. Entangled feet, stopping progress. Captured. The shadow looms.

Legs ripped from sockets. Trails of blood, innards scraped around the ground. Bodies hanging from trees.

Robert Shelley 'the bird scarer' shouldn't have entered the forest during storms. The flow of water. Dam bursting, hitting body with such force stomach pushes up. Out from the mouth, hanging by intestines. Mess washed back to the farm.

Lightning.

Pigs, sheep drowning. Floods, animals gasp, choke, deafening squeals.

No chances.

Squeal, no one to hear you. Severed limbs. Death. Warning. It's back, ten years since the promises.

They only felt it then. That presence, something feeding off their oaths, turning vows into sacred pledges. Soon they would know it.

This is no adventure. Nor fantasy.

The storms reign again.

* * * *

Flicking back and forth through the pages for about half-hour now. Gabriella has instigated a passion within me, so exaggerated and fired up by cocaine that just wanking has become insufficient. I need the real thing and bad.

No Crane. Not prostitution again.

Been down that road once, or twice, about eight months ago. The burdens were away for the weekend then too. I say "or twice" 'cause it was on the same night and I spunked, no I mean blew, hundred and seventy quid on two separate whores. The result was: Whore 1: Couldn't shoot me load. Whore 2: Couldn't even get it up.

The first bird was at least a good effort, I'd had a couple a' lines a' Charlie, and nearly a gram a' speed. More than anything I needed company at half four in the morning. So when she arrived I spent about ten minutes of me allotted half hour just chatting to her. I felt like Nicholas Cage in *Leaving Las Vegas* or something. She eventually said "shall we have sex then?" I said "yeah" and reckon I did a pretty professional job on her, as did she. I mean I could've sworn she was actually enjoying it, but no matter how much I wanted to, I just couldn't offload me beans. I pleaded for more time, she refused. Her driver was waiting outside, apparently and she had to leave.

I got a nice compliment when she was leaving though, something I'll remember for the rest of my life: " I always get the nice blokes after four in the morning"

A tad unexpected, seeing as I put '*Funny Man*', this real shady horror film where a deformed jester mutilates people, on whilst fucking her.

With one down I decided on another line and half-hour break. Restored energy, I called the second lucky applicant for the job of extracting come from my dick.

Number 2 advertised herself, quite reasonably, as a Whitney Houston lookalike. For her I put on 'Enter the 36 chambers' by Wu Tang. I felt for some maybe unintentional, institutional racism type thing that she would like it, but then I wanted to fuck a black bird and half me music collection's hip-hop, so I'm definitely no fucking Adolph.

Whitney was more forthright with her actions. She began stripping off straight away and ordered me to take my boxers off. I obeyed, then started the most humiliating 30 minutes of my life. With one look she began to giggle and asked "What is that?" pointing towards my shriveled penis. At the time though I laughed along, admitting to an excess of liveners. She said if I put some porn on she'd try and suck me to life.

I got one of me dvds down. Unfortunately when I turned the film on, it was exactly at a point where some black geezer with an absolutely humungous cock was busy filling the mouth of a bewildered blonde bint.

The irony!

Still, all the porn and all the sucking in the world could not revive my boy at that moment. After a valiant effort she apologised, so did I, then she gave me the opportunity for a discount if I called her again. I never did.

Tonight however, I reckon I could go round three.

NO.

The temptation's becoming unbearable.

My body's tingling. The thought of touching bare flesh and fucking someone gorgeous is... Shit, I'm gonna do it.

I take my hoody and *Echo* trackie top off, which for the life of me dunno why I've still got on. Everything's off bar me boxers, which I pull up and go downstairs.

The all too familiar hunt through our newspaper cupboard, then I find the otherwise useless local *Recorder*. Searching through, I catch stories of sponsored charity leg shaving by local male teachers and something about a hero that saved his dog from some swamp. Yet no amount of human kindness can conjure any guilt in me for my next actions.

I'm hell bent for fucking.

Finally the personal ads. Now the massage services - all discreet and personal.

Right, I need someone fit. I scan the adverts 'til I come to one that says I can have a massage girl from 18 to 30, looks and size of my choice, beautiful. This is the one. Oh fucking yes. I get me *Sony Ericsson* and dial the number. Getting a bit nervous, but still confident I'm doing right.

Cocaine mean Bad Crane in control...

A man answers.

"ello can I 'ave a girl please?'

'Sure can I take your name please?'

'Yeah it's (I almost say Crane) Steve.'

'Alright Steve, what type of girl d'ya want?'

'Err... can I have a blonde?'

'Sure and what size?'

'Err... about ten'

After a moments extremely awkward silence.

'Yeah we can manage that..." Fuck me how many birds has this place got? '...It's gonna be about seventy-five quid, is that ok?"

'Yeah wicked.'

I give me address details. Then me landline phone number for some reason, before signing off with a deluge of gratitude.

`Beautiful.

Now just to find seventy-five squeeba...

Returning to my room I rake together fifty sheets of me own money, some left over from the night and the last of me bet money. This means I've already done a ton tonight on drugs, drinks, club entry, taxis and lending Leg an Ayrton.

I've got a bit more time to spare before I have to find the rest, so I search through some more mags. I come across a fucking beautiful blonde bird called Holly in September's edition of the Canadian mag: *Friends and Lovers.*

I get going again…

Back in my sleazy world, staring at Holly, believing she wants me too. Each picture becoming part of an imaginary scenario building in my head. Except in my fantasy my dick is hard and long and Holly just can't get enough of it. All positions. FUCK. FUCKING HELL –MOVEMENT. Jesus prostitute you are gonna get it soon.

I turn pages back and forth, trying to put Holly's different levels of nudity in some sort of order. It starts with her in a white blouse, black skirt, stockings. Looking all sort of business like. Then the blouse is off. A black bra contains huge tits. Now the skirt is off, black knickers, black stockings and suspenders. Now I get a peak of her nipples as she lay back on a bed. Bra off, knickers come down. Shaved pussy shows. Stockings round her ankles, legs raised. Now from behind. Her on top. Every way Holly, until by the centre spread you're butt naked, me on top, giving you what for as you scream: "GIVE IT TO ME CRANE YOU FUCKING STALLION, FUCK ME, FUCK ME, YOU'RE SO GOOD." AAH FUCK. TAKE IT HOLLY YOU KNOW YOU WANT IT YOU…

The phone rings making me jump and almost belt at the same time. That was close.

I check the clock, half four. Fuck me that was quick. I have to pull me boxers up and run downstairs pointing my direction. I grab the phone on the sixth ring, cursing why I didn't give out me mobile number.

"ello.'

'Is that Steve?' It's a real sexy voice; I don't even think it's being put on.

'Yeah, yeah it is.'

'Hiya I'm Louise, I'm afraid my driver's a little lost at the moment darling, we're at Hornchurch station. Could you tell us where to go?' Me hard-on's being maintained just listening to this bird, knowing that she's nearly here. Yes.

'Yeah, yeah you're not far. Go past the station down towards the Town centre, then you do a right and keep going straight up. Then it's fourth road on the right.'

'Ok my love, I'll be there soon.'

'Err… you've got the 'ouse number yeah?'

'Yes thank you dear – be ready.' Click.

Oh beautiful.

It registers I still need twenty-five notes from somewhere, so I venture pretty guiltily in me parent's bedroom, vowing to repay the money tomorrow. I'll have to. I don't switch the light on, in case any of our nosy neighbours are spying in, even at this time at night. Drug paranoia. The light from the hallway's enough to guide me in opening a few drawers. The first reveals my Mum's make up. The second her underwear – still I'm not turned off. Then the third drawer reveals a brace of Ayrtons.

'Solid.'

There's some spare change in there as well, but only three pound coins, a couple of fifty's, four twenty's and two ten p's can I muster. Not that impressive, but at least now I can actually afford this whore.

I must have a couple of minutes left, so I run upstairs and back to Holly. This time I'll be horny enough to come if it fucking kills me. Seeing as I've had a hard-on for about half-hour now, the signs are good.

4.45.

The doorbell goes. I'm hard. I rush to put me boxers back on, but fuck me *Echo* off. Then scramble back downstairs.

Open the front door. Face to face with a beautiful blonde, shoulder length hair, full-length fur coat. Possibly imitation, normally I'd care, but I can safely say at this moment in time, I really don't give a fuck.

I let her in, it's fucking brilliant to have the rare, well let's face facts, nigh on extinct chance of shagging someone that could be a model.

She declines my offer of a drink, so I lead her straight to the downstairs lounge. I feel like one of those snobby upper class geezers, leading a lady of honour into the drawing room for caviar and champagne. The reality being: I'm a sex starved junkie student chav, who's not wearing a smoking jacket, but instead just me pants, leading a hooker to be shagged in the room where me Mum and Dad sit watching TV, whilst eating their tucker.

Still I'm flying though, and Louise is cool with it... I think

I turn and face her. She smiles as if taking the role of a newly met girlfriend coming back to mine for the first time. Then she looks confused and asks.

'Have you been snorting coke?'

'Err... Yeah, sorry I can still do it though, I've been in preparation' Oh my God, why did I just say that?

'You look fucked.' She's smiling again, but in a motherly sort of way. I definitely don't fucking well need that.

'You sure I can't interest you in a drink?' Trying to get away from thoughts of Mum and how fucked I look.

'Yeah go on then. You look like you need one as well.' I bet I do. I must look like fucking C3PO or something.

'What d'ya want?'

'You got Bacardi?'

'I think so.'

'Not your house then I take it?'

'Err... no. Me parents are away.' Smooth operator.

'Go on I'll have a Bacardi and Coke if you've got it. If not, anything strong really.' I must be doing well.

Thank God the nicety's are over. I wander off to get the drinks, noticing for the first time that I'm wearing me disgusting Paisley boxers. Good God Crane.

Returning with a strong Bacardi and Coke and an even stronger JD and Coke for meself, I take a sip of mine and sit beside her. I haven't bothered with any music or dvd's this time. I must keep full concentration on the job at hand.

'Thanks.'

'How old are ya?' I wanna get all the relevant details sorted for future head material when I'm bashing one out over this moment.

'How old do you think?'

'Err... about twenty-five.' She starts to giggle, then replies:

'I'm only nineteen my love.' Oh Leave it out, she's only a year older than me. That's gonna put some fucking pressure on.

'You really do look a lot older...' My God '...'ow comes you're doing this?' I hope she don't take offence to my questioning. I really do respect the work of a whore, but I can't control me mouth at the minute.

'I'm down from Sheffield at Uni. in East London. I can afford it this way.' She doesn't

'Excellent, I really respect that.' I do.

'You're quite nice looking you are.' She smiles towards me. Ego boost. If only other birds found me as good looking as prozzies have, then I'd be laughing.

I could definitely fall in love with this bird. My future wank scenarios are gonna be based on her giving up prostitution for me, 'cause I was such a good bunk-up.

'Do you want sex now?'

'Err… yes please.'

She stands up and takes her coat off, revealing black lingerie barely covering one fit body. Move over Gabby and Holly.

'What do you think of my tan?'

'Fucking wicked for April. ' I answer eyeing her with awe.

'Thanks, I go to a tanning salon... Right I'm gonna need the money now.'

'Oh yeah right.' I've got a semi as I collect the money from the coffee table. The pieced together change makes her smirk, but she don't look bothered as she bundles it in her purse.

'Right now take your boxers off.'

Yes Ma'am. I obey her orders willingly. As she removes her stockings and suspenders, my boy rises to its height, unfortunately about five inches at present.

'You know we can't kiss and you can't finger me don't you?' Who says romance is dead?

'Yep.' I smile, probably inanely.

She reaches round her back, unclips her bra and maybe too swiftly takes it off. They're not Holly's tits, a little saggy for nineteen, but they're tits. Then she pulls down her knickers. This is much better. A lovely blonde trim pussy. Beautiful.

She goes back to her purse, pulls out a Johnny and removes it from its wrapper.

'Right I'll put this on with my mouth.' Yes. Come on Louise, come to Crane.

She straddles me and grabs me cock while thrusting her titties in me face. I take her right nipple in mouth. Now all my education in pornography can come to the fore. Grabbing her arse I move on to her other titty, enjoying her soft hand caressing me dick. Come on Cranie, concentration. Enjoy it, not too much, don't wanna finish your load straight away, just enough to keep it up.

With the hand that's not wanking me, Louise positions the condom in her mouth so that when she goes down on me it'll roll straight on. She begins the process.

Oh my life.

Even with a Johnny on, this is the best of the seven blow-jobs I've ever received. I watch her lips go up and down me nob, while her hand stays at the bottom caressing my balls. I can feel it good now, I sit mesmerized by her head bobbing movements.

Oh man, this is too good.

Then I feel it. Oh shit, there's definitely something happening too fast in me balls. I think I'm gonna come already. I tug lightly at her armpits gesturing her to stop, gotta try and prolong this a bit. Louise only takes it as a signal to rise on top of me and shove my dick straight up in her. As it sinks in she grinds her lower body in a way that makes my head lose control over my balls. I know I'm about to lose me beans. There's no point stopping her now, ejaculation would be wasted. Here it comes…

Aaah Fuck. Jolting. Fuck. AAAH. As the jism streams out, I grab Louise tightly...

A few blissful seconds...

...then the embarrassment begins to swarm over me.

I can't understand it. Last time I couldn't get it up, now I've survived about ten of me allotted thirty minutes. Nine of those involved talking and the making of beverages.

She's saying not to worry, it happens to a lot of her clients or something. I'm not really listening. Still tell she's surprised it's happened to me though, what with all the coke that should have disconnected interaction from head to groin. She wants to see what I can do when I ain't got any substances in me.

I knew I'd got too worked up over Holly before Louise arrived. What a prick. I ain't said nothing yet. Leaving the Johnny on, I lay back on the couch and watch her get dressed. I gurn and tense up me fingers as another rush hits me.

She takes a large gulp of her drink before leaving. I say 'bye', but don't bother to see her out.

After a few more seconds I've gone fully limp, so finally get up to clear me mess. Seventy-five pounds, my winnings, and more have all gone...

Fuck it.

CHAPTER 3
CAMP STYX

Out in front Kevin was peddling hard, leading his six friends to the place he'd relentlessly talked about that day at school. The trail took them right across the park, their usual destination, and further on up Station Lane, until they came to a No Through Road on their left-hand side; **RIVER DRIVE**. Kevin made a sharp left turn, eager to show his mates the perfect hideout for their gang. Behind, the others took the journey a lot easier, practicing wheelies, talking about football, not minding a great deal that the guide was soon waiting impatiently at the foot of the road.

The seven children occupied the same class nearing the end of its second year at Upminster Junior school. They'd first met at age four and were soon best friends, sharing the tough growing experiences suffered in early education. Their link and understanding of each other grew strong over four years and culminated in the highest accolade of all; they were the playground football side everyone wanted to beat. Followers came in the guise of girls, who at break times displayed interest by performing cheer-leading routines in their honour.

Other second year boys were jealous and tried desperately to join the crew. Their rejection invoked attempted jealous backlashes, but none could ever get one of the seven alone. Plus no other gang in the school could match them. They were powerful, even the older children left well alone. Kevin was apparent leader and arguably strongest of the group, although this was never confirmed as under no circumstances would they fight amongst themselves. The factor that led to his appointment as chief decision maker was his victorious tussle a year before that stayed fresh in the others memories.

A couple of sixth years had one member of the gang, Adam, cornered in the playground. They heard he was in possession of an acclaimed `seventy-fiver` conker and were attempting to prize it from him. That was until Kevin ran over and landed his fist in the back of a head, sending one bully crashing to the floor. The other boy turned in surprise, but before he'd any chance to defend himself, took a strong blow in the stomach. These were no wayward kid punches either, the ones that mostly found the air. No, Kevin landed strong and calculated blows.

Once the second boy buckled with pain, Kevin grabbed both sides of his head and slammed a knee square into the face. Nose broken ejecting blood, the injured boy released intermingling tears with the red. If the assailant's other five friends hadn't arrived in time to hold him back from landing a kick to the first child's face, they may not have seen him at school again. As it was the two victims were scared to admit Kevin's responsibility to those in authority. Fear of the crazed attackers revenge, led them to claim they'd fought each other. From that day on the young gang were deemed untouchable.

Everyone there would remember the haunting anger shown in Kevin's features as he tried to continue the demolition of two elders.

The reason that one year later it was he who led his six mates to the woods. Preparing to reveal the place he'd picked as their secret camp for the coming years.

Having locked their bikes against railings, they entered into the trees. Marching through branches and over muddy ground before eventually arriving at a tiny clearing deep into the woods.

Kevin stopped, the others copied.

'Nearly there.'

'Dib, dib, dob.' Someone behind joked, raising a laugh from everyone bar the leader who resumed the trek by turning left. He brushed aside obstacles of twigs and headed further into thicker growth. They eventually arrived at a second clearing where Kevin halted and waited for the group to gather. When they were all standing before him, he pointed to the left.

'There…'

The boy's heads turned in unison to face a row of four trees, beyond these was a ditch. They trudged through boggy earth towards it. Each of them knew, but didn't admit, that their parents would be far from amused when they arrived home dirty later that day. It had been a wet March and the April showers were really beginning to fall. The weather forecast for the next week didn't report an improvement, so it would certainly be deemed unintelligible to set up camp in woods. Yet, when they drew closer the group noticed that the four trees in front of the ditch rose and entangled with four trees at the other side, forming a near perfect arch. This created a decent shelter that stretched about eight foot long and four foot wide.

Kevin ducked and pushed up some branches, this made an entrance for himself to descend into the would-be camp. The rest followed.

'What d'ya think?'

Many voices were heard in the reply, it was 'great', 'cool' and 'perfect'.

'There's an old rug a bit further up there as well. We could spread it across the floor 'ere, and I thought if we bring some posters and stuff it's gonna look pretty cool. No-one ever comes down this far either.'

All in agreement that it was the ideal set up for the forthcoming spring and summer holidays. Here they could chat, mess around and most importantly be away from moaning authorities. And so they began to construct plans for the site.

The previous evening Kevin had phoned them all to arrange the meeting time for this day's venture. He also told them, "without question", the name he had made up for both their gang and the camp: '**The Styx**'. He also informed the other boys they needed nicknames acquiring to this moniker. "*Put a word in front of Styx and that'll be your name.*" He hadn't made the spelling clear, didn't want to at that point, so he expected their connection would be with sticks. Had already devised what the rest were to be called.

So under protection from increasing rain and darkened skies, the crew deciphered nicknames that would remain with them for many years to come.

'So what name did you come up with Steve?'

The boys had taken place along banks of the camp's hollow. Three sat on each side, while Kevin stood in the middle controlling the conversation.

'Me? ...err well I thought of Drum as me Mum made us chicken drumsticks last night.' Steve said a little nervously, the golden haired boy being the quieter of the bunch. His answer raised a few giggles from his friends, but only of excitement. They all recognised the benefits that being part of this popular group had brought them. With the introduction of nicknames and headquarters it had become more official

'Hmmm...' Kevin looked thoughtful for a moment and paced as much as he could in an eight by four foot ditch, then shook his head.

'Nah, I was thinking more along the line of Crane for you, 'cause you're quite tall.'

'Crane sticks, what the fuck are those?' Interrupted Brad, who sat two along from a rather confused Steve.

'You know, the extendable parts of a crane that pick things up.' Answered Kevin.

'What?' Was the general response, except from Steve who didn't want to cause a major fuss. His lackadaisical agreement ceased the clamour. From then on he would be called "Crane".

The first deal done.

Kevin moved quickly on to prevent any renewed protest from the others. Yet none of them seemed bothered. Short concentration spans of eight year olds, they began making noise amongst themselves, much to the leader's annoyance. He moved along the line. Next to Crane sat Adam, who was inspecting the bottom of his trousers and the mud that encrusted them.

'Adam...' The tubby boy looked up in a start '...what have you got for us?'

'I was gonna say Drum as well, but I thought of Match just now when you told Steve that he couldn't be Drum. Or can I be Drum if Steve's not?'

'Crane.' Kevin answered

'Eh?'

'Crane, his name is Crane... his height... Crane sticks!'

'Oh right yeah, I forgot.' Adam's lack of memory that had seen him fall behind at school did not desert him outside the classroom either.

It was only the aforementioned two that paid attention to Kevin as he revealed the next new name.

'Tin Lid? Uh?' Crane and Adam looked at each other in bewilderment.

''Ere Brad, 'e wants to call me Tin Lid.'

Upon mention Brad turned towards Kevin and drew the attention of the rest with him.

'Are you alright Kev?' Brad was the gang's only member who had the front to challenge Kevin's leadership. His confidence to speak out in such situations far exceeded the norm for an eight year old.

'Yeah, Tin Lid Sticks is the name of the people who make the biscuits me Mum eats, and I thought it would suit Ad, as e is a bit of a fat bastard.'

The others roared with hilarity at Adam, who could only mumble for them to 'shut up'. Kevin had smartly taken re-control of the situation again. Due to the overweight jibes amusing the rest so much, they accepted the new name of "Tin Lid". Everybody was in agreement of its intelligence, which helped contradict the fact they had never even heard of the fabricated *Tin Lid Sticks*.

Kevin was beginning to enjoy giving these inventive and cryptic names for his friends. Gloried in his domination. To him, this was how it should always be.

With his confidence flourishing he could sense that outside inspiration breathing in.

The second deal was done.

'The second deal is done.'

'Wha?' Crane questioned.

'Nothing. Now Brad.'

'I can't wait for this, just give it to me Kev, it's not worth me saying anything, you'll only change it.'

'I thought you could be Moon.' Brad faked a laugh and for effect held onto his stomach as if his sides were literally about to split. The loudest of the group and a similar build to Kevin, was less fearful of his friend than the others secretly were. This still didn't mean that he wanted to take the place as the hard man. He was the gang's joker and found the leader's lust for power amusing, a good source for some of his ribbing. Enough sometimes to quip him as 'sir', which Kevin privately enjoyed.

'Moon Sticks.' Brad continued to giggle and its infectious nature spread to the rest.

'S'better than Tin Lid.' Tin Lid joined in, instigating more humour.

'They're those lollipop things. You get 'em in Martin Mccolls.' Kevin tried to claim regarding his *Moon Sticks* invention.

'Wha's that gotta do with me?' Brad asked

'S'your big round 'ead.' Tony, Brad's best friend and apprentice wag, grinned.

'Exactly.' Kevin agreed

'What ya saying? You're 'ardly normal Kev or should we call you crazy sticks?' Didn't gain expected mirth Brad intended. The boys were defending Kevin, they envisioned a chance to witness Brad take the proverbial sip from his own medicine.

Wind ups continued into a football style chant at him. The gang repeatedly called out his new name "Moon" in unison as he tried desperately to muster words of revenge for each. This time however, the commotion against far outweighed his higher level of wit. With additional shrieks clogging the air, his mocking replies were left to evaporate into the darkened skies that signified an increasing April downpour.

333

'Tony.' Kevin cried above the bedlam.

'Yes sir.'

'Or Little Legs.' said Moon. Within seconds everyone convinced Kevin that this new name was imperative. The leader was ready to insist on his own idea of 'walking' sticks, yet a voice told him to abstain from the argument. Moon's concept followed the plan, a cunning foresight to leave the rest believing they had some contribution that day. Both names could be deemed equally as clever, Tony did have small legs, the youngster found it hard to keep up with the others whether running or walking.

Despite Little Legs sticks being as fictitious as Kevin's earlier constructs, Moon's input brought more amusement to the gang. Tony became "Little Legs". The e at the end of little and the s in Legs would eventually be dropped a couple of years on. Littl' Leg considered it cooler.

NUMBER 4

The rain fell heavy around the shelter. A tree twitched. Whispers, echoes of the past. A place corrupted by scenes of long ago. Torture creating evil. Familiarity of a daunting episode. The woods craved more horror. The trees wanted life. Crane turned his head sharply. He could have sworn someone said 'number four' in his ear. Yet Tin Lid talks to someone else.

A shiver, someone walks over the graveyard once again. A naked soul trudging. Ever nearer to the twitching body. Out to play with a dismembered corpse.

A presence loomed over the pawns. Each moment followed the plan.

Soon after the fifth person was named.

'What's wrong with Candle anyway?' Andy pleaded.

'We can't go around going 'Oi Candle' all the time can we? And I wanted to 'ave something that involved our camp.' Kevin included, referring to Ingrebourne River which flowed as a stream by the edge of the woods. Alternates that had not excited the boy in charge either. He was told Brook would be far more masculine. Somewhat ordered.

'But Brook 'asn't got anything to do with sticks.'

'We've played Pooh sticks down the river though ain't we?'

'So we should call 'im Pooh then.' Laughed Moon.

'I don't think no one wants to be called that.'

'Or River?'

'Brook's better.'

'This ain't making no sense any more.' Said Crane shaking his head.

'Look it's all connected, it's just a bit different, you know, a bit original.'

Kevin knew his names were distancing themselves from the word "sticks" more and more. It didn't matter to him. These titles were all pre-planned, there was no intention of listening to his friend's ideas. Just let them think they had a little participation toward the gang. Minor concern to the others anyway. Priority of wonder was why Kevin had even asked for their input. Clearly he was not interested in using their choices.

'Yeah I suppose Brook is better than Pooh.' Brook conceded.

'There it is then.' Concluded Kevin. And it was.

"Brook" would become the group's womaniser and add an e to his name when Little Legs decided to drop his.

THE FIFTH HAD OBEYED.

Tears from the skies covered the woods like a blanket. Forlorn angels cried, a witness to the beginning of the most feared return. The harder the grief fell, the more the river could flow. Yet The Styx stayed miraculously dry under their shelter, ignorant to the distant choruses of thunder that concealed the whispers around their camp.

Where the fifth deal had been made.

Kevin decided to interrupt the naming session. An attempt to disguise irrelevance. He wanted to discuss, no, tell the others about his spelling alteration for the name of the camp.

'For a bit of a difference. I think we should spell it S T Y X.'

'What's that mean though?' Asked Tin Lid.

'I'm not sure...' Kevin lied, '...but it sounds cool though, don't it?' Yet he knew exactly what it supposed. Had been visited again, within dreams. The shadowed figure explained all. Souls travelled safely along the River Styx in their transportation to the other side. Use of this handle for the gang's home would also ensure their protection. Kevin didn't want to mention it then however, the others were too young to understand. Had also been sworn to secrecy by his guest. Until the time was right.

No argument was received. With this the leader could continue. Turned his attention toward David.

'I can't think of anything else, I was going to 'ave Drum or Match meself, but it don't seem to matter.' The next in line shrugged.

'So can I name you then?' Kevin asked.

'Thought you would anyway.' David didn't really care what his best friend called him, he knew a derogatory moniker was unlikely.

'I thought of Beak for you, what d'ya think?'

'My God, Beak sticks, let's 'ear this one.' Once again Moon became involved. With this followed intrigue.

''e likes his bird spotting don't 'e and they carry sticks and twigs and things in their beaks. Just reckon that'd be good.'

At the time, David's parents were still together and the child enjoyed Essex countryside outings with his father. Always excited at the prospect of viewing varying species of birds. The splendour of the creature's colours was exhilarating to someone so young. Consequently his new name was fitting, suiting his lifestyle and chirpy character. Beak compared far better than Moon or Little Legs too. There was no ridicule aimed against him. Everything was complete.

'Yeah that sounds good to me.'

The others had grown restless of the activity, just as eight year olds would, so the queries into Kevin's inane notions dwindled.

7 **6** 8

"Beak" would eventually translate his own name. Preferred Beeke for reasons that only he knew. No one asked him why.

The sixth deal had been made. The woods stood patiently and waited for the leader to enroll himself into its hold. Open the path for the second chance. The second coming.

S

'So Kev, can we name you?' asks Moon **E**

'Nah, I 'ave to be called Sloo.'

'So wha **V** t the fuck are Sloo sticks then?' Little Legs asks.

'That doesn't matter, I 'ad this dream that I was 'ere and I could hear these voices. They kept saying "*Sl*oo" over and over, as if they were calling to me.' **E**

that's right SLoo,, Dream on and on. Then I can enter.

The boys stared to the unknown. Thoughts of their friend's insanity written across faces. Even as their laughter ceased, the tone of happiness continued. Mingling with whispers throughout the surrounding area. All The Styx could hear was the escalating storm. This was making them feel uneasy enough. Wanted to be home, safe and warm. So without argument:

'I am SLOO.'

N THE TRANSITION WAS COMPLETE.

Thunder rumbles. Children remember the threat: stay away from trees under these conditions. Yet here they were dead in the middle of woodlands. None of them knew it then, but they shouldn't have panicked. They were being kept safe despite the havoc being played throughout their setting.

For Now.

-L I G H T N I N G

Flash. Torn limb from limb. Blood soaks Sloo. Standing before his lifeless friends. Tongues cut from their mouths. No argument now. Visions

Flash.

They sit and chat, normality.

THUNDER. Rushing through the trees. Shattering speed. Cackles spitting blood. Turning the sky red. Darkness covers. Lightning FLASH.

Sloo feasting on Brook's brain. Membrane dripping from his chin. Just an aperitif. Still a main course of Crane intestines and Moon liver to go. So hungry, feeding time. There for a photographic second.

FLASH.

I'm coming to rip you up, dumb children. Revenge will be sweet. You thought escape was a possibility. No it's just a delay. Soon I'll be back for good. Not one of you stands a chance. Death is everywhere. I watch you now. You can see me, but you don't know it. I AM THIS STORM. Cutting into your hearts. Give me blood.

THE FEAST IS NIGH.

FLASH, anger travelling away. The boys could return home relatively dry.

First the vows though Sloo. I will remain till they obey.

Vows that should never be broken on punishment of...

'Death, why who's gonna kill us?' Moon asked.

'I dunno the God of broken promises I suppose.' Sloo proposed

'This is all getting spooky...' Beak '...We should 'ave gone to Sloo's, look at that weather.'

The rain continued to sweep through the woods and despite gaps betwixt hovering branches, somehow The Styx were dry. No one questioned it.

Sloo pulled out a folded piece of paper.

'I wrote this last night, after I had that dream. It woke me up just before half three.'

"ang on a minute. I woke up then as well.'

'Yeah me too.' Sustained agreement from others. Had all shared the occurrence.

All been disturbed.

Sloo silenced them.

All of the boys, even Moon, listened intently. Their mischievous nature and indeed that of most eight year olds disappeared.

Sloo would take full control.

'This is what we must follow.'

A tree crashed not far away. Too new.

No one heard it.

It ripped through their souls instead. Shivers. Cursed home, a plague waiting to spread. An outside world oblivious to the waking cemetery within the woods. Souls clamber on board. Vicious faces, previous guise discarded. Reversing the journey, the time is near. *Lightning.* The Styx glow. Burning. WATER

FALLS to wash away their skins.

The Seven Commandments

1. **No one can put girls above The Styx.**
2. **No one can fight with another member of The Styx.**
3. **The Styx must stick together.** Come CRASHING in on your world.

4. **The camp Styx must remain a secret.** Time to fear all that is natural
5. **The Styx must return regularly to the Camp.** You can't hide
6. **No one will leave The Styx.** fall at my feet and believe
7. **Sloo's word is final.** in me.

I AM HERE in the clouds
IN THE RAIN.
CAN YOU HEAR ME
SURROUNDING yOU

'It's an electrical storm.' CRASHING
'I hope the boys are safe.' IN

THEY'RE SAFE. The weather is only entering their minds.
THE POSSESSION BEGINS.

'YES SIR.' The Styx rose to salute Sloo...

Pause of understanding...

Concentration then broken.

The boys burst out with laughter.
Even Sloo was cackling.
'Now, do you agree to the commandments?'
'Yes our master.' Said Moon. Looks at the others, each boy repeats. It would soon be time for the real work to start. For then though peace could prevail. Juveniles could be eight again.

All seven of them were piled on the floor, jumping on top of each other, practicing wrestling moves and being inherently their age.

The storm calmed. The rain ceased to beat, settling for a patter. The earth was cleansed that time.

Later the storm will not pass.

CHAPTER 4
TAKE ME BACK

The room gradually comes into focus…

I'd gone there.

Man my fucking head. It feels like someone's took me brain out and carved a small section off with a Stanley knife. Then shoved it back in using a shoehorn or something. All whilst I've been asleep.

They might as well have, what with the amount of brain cells I must have fucked over last night. Reckon I've slept a couple of hours, at the most.

Last thing I remember is sitting up watching Friday the Thirteenth part Two, drinking strong Whisky and Cokes. Wanted alcohol to take over the sleeplessness of cocaine. Eventually worked. Must have.

Dunno if the film was scary, more messed up really. Images of decapitated heads and spazza's getting pick-axed in the back fucked with me head enough to stop me going upstairs to bed anyway. Kept saying to meself it's only drugs paranoia Craney. My own little calming method I've developed for those scary scenarios that leave me terrified at night.

Someone told me they knew this woman who stayed at a hotel once. The owner told this woman it was haunted, but only in a presence sense, whatever the fuck that means. Anyway this bird was just getting settled in bed, her eyes were closing, slowly drifting... drifting... losing herself in the land of nod...

Suddenly she hears this noise in her room. Opens her eyes and staring back at her was this ugly grinning jester. Man the amount of nights that story kept me awake.

When I think about it and I'm trying to sleep I say to meself shut your eyes Crane, I do. Right now don't open 'em again 'til morning. But with me eyes closed all I can picture is this fucking jester dancing about me room. It drives me mad. I think I've gotta look, so me heart starts really pounding and I'm sweating like a bitch... then I look. Nothing. One of these days the fucker's gonna be there though, right enough.

I tell meself its all drugs paranoia. All in your head son. When I look on it like this it eases me through these tough nightmarish occasions. Which are especially rife the nights after big sessions. Like the time I dreamt I was blagging Madonna. Then the bitch turned into Tin Lid while I was doing her.

So saying it's 'drugs paranoia' to meself only seems to work when I'm not high as a kite on the fuckers. Just like I was last night.

Seems I eventually passed out on the sofa. TV's still on, displaying the crackling Black, White and Grey of the dvd channel that shows no film.

Grab the remote and switch over to BBC One and get confronted by a large choir singing miserable hymns. Now I remember; it's Good Friday. What an irony. Still, it's a day that I can write off and just piss about on. Only half way through me Easter break. Me Mum and Dad won't be back from Aylesbury 'til Monday and West Ham's on live this weekend.

My sudden rise in optimism is met by the recollection of last night's prostitute...

Oh God, don't let that bring you down now Crane. It's fatal to start making yourself feel depressed with cocaine hangovers just around the corner. But bollocks, seventy-five sheets on one minute. I've gotta bit of dough thanks to me Mum and Dad's increasing wealth, but I'm spunking it too fast. Now I'll have to walk all the way to the bank if I'm gonna afford to eat and drink later.

Or I could always...

'Leg, its Crane.'

A noise comes through the phone that can best be described as a feeble attempt to say "hello". Or maybe "what?" or anything really. Whatever it was, pathetic mumble comes to mind. 'Done your load yet?' I ask, but once again get the same grunt of a reply. Backing up what I already thought. Leg is not yet in the mood for small talk and must be well pissed off that I'm calling at ten in the morning. Best put this next bit forward carefully.

'Listen, I'm sorry geez, but I'm gonna need that Ayrton back later and just to take the piss, d'ya reckon you could sort us out an extra Lady and, maybe 'alf a gram a' Charlie. I'll pay you back next week?' Well done Crane. Subtle Simon.

'Mmmm.' He goes.

'You can bring it round 'ere if you want. Grab some beers then we can just chill.'

'Yesss.' At least this time Leg finally forms a word. Though the extended s sound tells me he wants me to piss off so he can finish wanking or something.

'Cheers I'll see ya round one then?'

'Mmmm.' Again.

'Cool, see ya mate.' No answer. Phone goes dead.

Deep down I know he's well up for coming round later. A chance to hit Colombia's finest. He'll not want the speed comedown and definitely won't want to be hanging around his family all day.

Leg, along with Moon, are the only ones out of us with full time jobs and cars. They both work for Insurance Companies in Fenchurch Street and have done pretty well for themselves since school. Not like the rest of us college lay-about wankers. Well bar Sloo I suppose, he helps out at some garage where he got himself a reworked old Ford Cortina. That piece of shit sounds like a plane taking off though. And Brooke works at that bar alongside doing his GNVQ, so we're not all useless.

It was from his job that Leg became our best source of drugs. One of his work mates, we call him 'The Geez', got into one of those conversations with him saying he could sort him out anything. Good shit as well, and pretty cheap with the bulk we normally buy in.

Leg had got quite a bit of coke in for this weekend, a big one for him and Moon. It's pretty normal for me, I never do fuck all from Friday to Monday every week, so all Thursdays I go overboard. But you don't get much time off working in the city, it's why they did extra speed last night. Must be their first Friday off since about Christmas and they've still got three more days to go mental on Coke.

With the amount he bought, I reckon I'll get sorted out a freebie later. Of course I'll offer to pay for it, but once I tell him about the events after he left last night, he'll probably be so proud I'll get half a g' for diddly. He loved it when I told him about the previous two whores I fucked up.

He'll fetch Moon on his way round. Expect they'll probably get here about an hour late. There's always a lot of shit to do when you've just finished your speed wank. Gotta let yourself drift off for at least half an hour, or there'll be paranoia/ confusion hell for the rest of the day. Then there's the hiding of all pornographic evidence and putting the penis cooling cans of beer or jars of mayonnaise back in the fridge. Then they've got to shower, wash away the evil odour of sweaty speed. Once dressed they gotta pretend they're interested in what the old folks have to say before they can finally fuck off.

That's even if they've finished knocking one off yet.

My plans for the day are to sit veg-ing in the front room watching a David Lynch film or something. Some footy's on later and there has to be an episode of 'The Simpsons' on Sky or Channel Four at some point today. Soon it will be the three of us sniffing coke and avoiding food like the plague. That's the best way I can think of in preventing comedowns. Well till tomorrow at least, but we'll cross that bridge when we come to it. I should be a tad more concerned today really, what with me A levels just around the corner.

Fuck, forget about that. I've still got a lot more enjoyment left this weekend to start letting little things like my future get me down.

I switch over to ITV, a weather report. The geezer says it'll be sunny today, but expect downpours over the next week. Big fucking surprise. That was some storm last night. England's weather really pisses me off.

Fuck this shit, I need a livener.

Go into the kitchen and pour meself a sherry. Another of last night's discoveries concealed in me Mum's drinks cabinet. She's not an alcoholic, but does enjoy a bit of Sherry now and again. There's no doubt about that.

Back in the front room, memories of me Leg and Moon - The Magic Number come flooding back. I smile at the childishness of it all. The Styx and how us three had our own little pact at the age of ten. We used to be round each other's houses a lot of the time playing computer football games together. There we'd have the chance to complain about Sloo and his bossiness and how he used to sulk if he didn't get his way. At the time we agreed if Sloo ever started on any of us, then we'd join together and do him over instead.

We never told this to the rest of The Styx. They might have felt we were going against them as well, or they actually liked the geezer or something and told him. Plus we did like Sloo ourselves really. Together with the fact we was in the most popular group at school; we didn't want to cause a rift or nothing. So we kept it quiet, but each of us knew there could be a point sometime in the future where Sloo could easily turn. He hasn't yet of course. May have got angry with us if we took the piss or something; or didn't make it to his stupid camp for the day, but most of us just laughed it off. Plus we had Commandment number 2 on our side: **NO ONE CAN FIGHT WITH ANOTHER MEMBER OF THE STYX.**

Yet I've never seen Sloo so pissed off as when Beeke came out the closet a couple of weeks back. Seems to have lost the spirit of passing things over, coming out and taking lots of drugs. Enjoying himself again with the rest of us. It was actually that night when he last took anything I think. Really changed him. There was no dancing wildly and smiling with the rest of us to cheesy songs like YMCA. No, this night he sat in the corner, eyes closed, protesting that the speed weren't working and he'd had a hard week...

Later in the night though I noticed his pupils and you could tell he was as fucking trolleyed as me. He was just trying to cover the drugs joyous ability with sulking. What a waste of gear.

The other difference was his not speaking to Beeke at all that night. Normally at any point where they were both off the dance floor they'd be together like glue.

Sloo would have a go at Brooke a lot, saying he should be more like Beeke, and not spend so much time concentrating on girls. The rest of us were proud of Brooke's womanising; he's the only one who regularly got birds since our group's notoriety dwindled over the years at senior school. To us he was a legend, a hero, something we strive towards. I mean it's not as if The Magic Number and Tin Lid never pulled at all. Littl' leg came a distant second and we all had our fair share of girlfriends, it's just that none of us could make it last. Our ex's would tell us we spent too much time taking drugs with our friends. Apparently we ought to have grown up.

Yet Brooke still never totally blew us out for birds. He may have done last night, but that was rare for a Thursday. And you can't really blame him with the way things have been over the last couple of weeks.

Gemma's a fit bird as well. Brooke the lucky cunt with his Mediterranean, Johnny Depp good looks and floppy dark hair. It makes him look about twenty-five and sends out some sort of magnetic force to girls. If I, or any other member of The Styx, was out on the pull with him, then we had to accept he always got the looker while we got her dodgy, plump mate.

Not that I ever complain. They all count.

It just makes my track record of eight fucks now, look a little flattering. Four were fat mingers, one was all right and three were struggles with whores; and one of those shouldn't really come into the equation.

Brooke's differing success makes him ooze with confidence. Never acting childish or foolish like us. We spent our night at *Time* jumping round like little kids on the dance floor, annoying girls rather than impressing them. He'd just hang round the side checking out who he wanted later, ninety per cent of the time he'd get 'em as well.

All this understandable attention towards women means that Sloo's a bit funny with Brooke, but we all know him as a good mate and put it down to Sloo being jealous. Brooke never completely put a bird above The Styx.

My staring and train of thought gets broke. I've just remembered that Moon skinned me up a small joint before he left last night.

Fucking beautiful...

I run upstairs to get it, deciding I'll smoke it in the conservatory. Then I can sit with the door open and not create a huge smell of weed for me Mum and Dad to return to. It's finally a nice day after a week of rain that erupted into that fucking immense storm of last night. It must have raged till about six o'clock, adding to my nervousness created by Jason Vorhees and his variety of weapons. Not to mention the paranoiac effects of taking too much speed and cocaine in my life. Drugs.

I settle in the conservatory and watch as the sun brightens the back garden. It's all beginning to bloom with spring, fantastic. There's butterflies and some other insects buzzing around as well. Like a picture. I love nature like this, brings me a sense of calm and feeling of togetherness with the outside world. Sit back and stare deep into our long, well kept garden and plan to reminisce about a great time in my life. A feeling, that along with this spliff, I really do need right now.

Put my feet up beside an ashtray on the coffee table. There's a lighter at hand so I spark at the end of the joint till it's ready to begin puffing.

This is what I call life; nice weather and drugs.

The fumes of the weed start to fill the air and the smoke partly covers my vision. I whiff a familiar feeling of smell de-ja-vu. Drifting me back to Littl' Leg's barbecue on a summery Sunday evening nearly a year ago.

Twas last year's Easter Bank Holiday weekend, so Moon and Leg had the next day off. Me, Sloo, Tin Lid and Beeke had invited some of our friends from college along to get completely plastered. It'd already been a huge weekend.

I remember it especially as I'd pulled on the Thursday before with definitely one of the best looking birds ever. Louise Burns, I knew she was at my college as I'd seen her there, nay idolized her there, from afar. This pull came surprisingly in the days that I sported an awful attempt at Adidas stripes in me Barnet. Shocking. It was only the fact I'm blonde, which meant it barely showed, that saved it. But I looked far from adult and this is what made the whole event somewhat unbelievable.

For the life of me, to this day, I still can't remember how the hell I actually got to snogging her at *Time's Out*. It was probably 'cause I'd only taken a quarter a gram a` speed that night, so I weren't buzzing out me nut like I normally would be. Plus I was sufficiently tanked up on alcohol. The fuel that makes me a thousand times more confident. The whizz had banged out that stupid cunt drunk edge of being pissed up.

After numerous snogs I got her number and arranged to meet her on the following Saturday, again sadly at *Time.* But that Saturday was the night of all nights. Oh yes.

I remember that The Styx were round mine before hand, surprise –surprise; and I was getting wasted on Whisky. Was well nervous about meeting such a quality bird that evening. I mean I weren't used to it. I'll never forget Sloo's speech before we left for the club:

'Now don't forget who your mates are...' He went '...Just don't forget we'll always be here for ya, will she?'

Just what you need before a monumentous occasion like that. Anyway at some point on the bus from my house to the club, someone managed to get me on acid. No one to this day admits who it was. The fact is I was so drunk and couldn't remember taking it, spelt **T r o u b l e**.

Luckily, it didn't take control for some time and surprisingly Louise was all over me when I got there. I can still visualise that, but what happened next was very much a blur. I found meself at the back of the club, with two girls I used to know from school. Don't remember exactly how the fuck I'd lost Louise. Then not so much out of character, as never had such a delightful opportunity before, I found myself getting off with one of these birds. Then the next thing I know I'm snogging the other one. The really fucking weird thing was these two birds were absolutely blinding looking as well. All of a sudden I'm the fucking Don Juan or something.

Dunno what happened to me that weekend. Must have had some sort of Brooke aura rubbing off on me. I wouldn't say I'm ugly or nothing, but I'm not overly familiar with three stunners up for it on the same night I can tell ya...

Take another toke, me head starts to feel very light. Now me body feels like it's floating away. If only life could be like this all the time.

Fucking good weed.

…So when I stopped snogging with this second bird, I turned around and there was Louise's best mate standing there watching me. Unsurprisingly I got a slap.

"You're well out of order, Louise saw that." She gives it.

"Saw what? I ain't done nothing." Denial that continued for about five minutes until absolutely amazingly, after being watched by two people snog two separate girls, one straight after each other, I had Louise and her mate apologizing and kissing me on the cheek.

Then again I am a fucking good liar. It's a trait that's seen me out of some scrapes before, especially with the old dear. Like that time I passed out with me trousers and boxers round me ankles in her front room. I'd done some speed and wanted a wank. Whilst I grabbed me porn upstairs, I decided it'd be a great idea to have three huge tokes of skunk on a pipe. I'd passed out before I could even reach the sofa. She came home from some family do with me dad about four. Me old man was pissed so went straight to bed not wanting to know. There was me with me little todger out, a porn vid set up, tissue in hand, absolutely sparko. She'd woke me up with some smelling salts she had. Straight away I realised the predicament and goes:

'Mum, thank God you're home. I've had this pain in my side, I've been crying with it and everything. I must've passed out it hurt so much.' Then I faked another huge pain, started screaming and everything. Two hours, suspected appendicitis and one confused emergency doctor later and the whole thing went too far for me Mum not to believe me. Even with the gear making me babble constant shit at her, I told her it was only because speaking helped me forget the pain.

I have a little chuckle to meself which makes me choke on the joint that's now smoking along nicely. I'm getting pretty stoned here. The buzz when this happens gets the hairs on my arms standing on end. It almost seems as though I can feel the blood running through my veins. What?

What was I thinking about? I wanna get to the end of this... Oh right Louise Burns.

Later that Saturday night, apparently, I was jabbering on to Moon and Littl' leg that I couldn't find me sheep anywhere and if you played the pinball machine it made you feel as though you was in space. I do recall the end of the night when I was snogging Louise up against a wall. Probably for about an hour or so. Fuck knows, it don't really matter. We was waiting for a cab we eventually shared with her mate Anna and some geezer. I was the second person to be dropped off. It was at the top of my road where I finally realised I was on acid. The colour of everything changed rapidly as I made me short walk home. Lampposts flashed green, purple, blue, red. Me neighbour's front door, originally white, was suddenly yellow, then blue and even black. At home I spent some considerable time staring at an *R.E.M.* cd cover. It took me ages to figure out why Michael Stipe was talking to me. Eventually I discovered I had the 'Shiny Chatty People' interview cd on.

So somehow that night I managed to hold it together. The next night I struggled to maintain this form. Big-time.

I'd spent the day listening to me Mum's 'Love Moods' album which showed, as per usual, I'd already fallen head over heels in love with a girl I'd known for three days. I should've known then that when this happens it's usually the signal for me to begin fucking things up. This I did royally on that fateful night on Barbecue Sunday. Along with a little help from my good friends Littl' leg and Moon of course. Oooh I get by with a little help from my friends.

Take another huge lug. Can no longer keep me eyes open to look at the beautiful scenery outside. Could probably sleep again now. Seems like a good idea. Could do with some more kip before the others turn up and we start getting high again. I'll finish this joint first, not a lot left. Sink further into the armchair, spread my legs and with me head-spinning conjure the events of the sacred barbecue. There's not much.

The Magic Number decided to kick off early. Guests were not due till eight, but we began drinking at six. I had a bottle of *MD 20/20* and a four pack of Fosters to get through. Moon had brought the smoke, Littl' Leg the quarter gram capsules of speed and six tabs of Acid.

Before I started drinking I vowed to only take speed and definitely not the acid; and then only after we'd eaten. That way I could enjoy the barbecue fully. It is a food party after all, for fuck sake. The plan before the guests arrival was: we'd play some cards, have a bit of a drink and smoke maybe two joints. Tops.

The reality however: I ended up drinking the whole bottle of sickly Strawberry *20/20* cordial and was on my third can of Fosters when the first visitor arrived. Add to this five joints and a gram and half a' speed between the three of us and you've got the recipe for disaster. So from very early on me memory was in serious fucking jeopardy. I can remember the first guests vaguely, yet I was almost certain Louise was not one of them.

That was it. From eight to what must've been about four in the morning, I couldn't and still can't remember one slightest detail of that night. This wasn't due to being flaked out in some corner paralytic somewhere though. No, I was awake and apparently active for the whole eight goddamn hours and can't remember one fucking minute.

But I was told though, oh yes I was told. Not from Moon or Littl' Leg though, they've only slightly more recollection than I do. It was that man Sloo who couldn't wait to phone me the next day and give commentary on my stupidest night yet.

I had spent the post-party hours staying at Littl' Legs and judging by our actions was hundred percent sure that at some point in the night we had both taken acid, but at what stage? And what happened with Louise? That's what I really needed, or didn't need to know.

Sloo couldn't tell me every detail. Weren't with me all night. He did tell me he arrived at nine at which point I was standing outside drinking Hooch. Where the fuck I obtained this shite I do not know. Apparently I'd finished the fourth Fosters by that time, so I was already adding more alcohol to my system. An increasing amount that would normally see me through a whole night at *Time*. He said I was in the garden for about half-hour not even touching the food. Following this he saw me on four separate occasions.

The first was at about ten. Sloo had knocked on the bathroom door to receive a simultaneous reply of 'Who is it?' from Littl' Leg, Moon and myself. On hearing it was Sloo; we let him in to witness what was going on, just in case he thought it was something dodgy or something. Well I suppose it was something dodgy really. Sloo said we were sucking fiercely on acid, then we followed that with a shot of speed from a Nurofen capsule straight down our Gregorys. Sloo said it was like we were all possessed. He can talk.

The second time he allegedly saw me, was in Littl' Legs little sister's room, reading her a bedtime story. Now Littl' Leg's parents had gone for a swanky meal in London and off to a posh hotel for the night. Something Leg got enough shit for:

"Your burdens off for a night of hardcore fucking to rekindle that old flame eh Leg?" Moon kept going.

This left Leg in charge of his eight year old sister, a good girl who didn't kick up any fuss about this hush-hush barbecue. How, and if, she managed to sleep with all the racket I will never know, especially with me acting like a maniac in there.

When Sloo heard my voice he was concerned about what I was doing in Leg's sister's room. Though surely he knows even if I'd done a fucking shipload of cocaine I wouldn't think about that sort of thing. Despite me jokes that wind up Leg.

Sloo said he peered round the door and saw me sat beside her bed reading one of her books to her. Reckons I was more engrossed in this children's story than she was. Me eyes were staring incessantly at the book and when he looked at the pages nothing matched what was actually coming out me mouth. Said it was meant to be about some shoemaker and these elves or something. Yet there was I talking about some young ice maiden that wouldn't make beans on toast for her sausage dog. Sloo told me he was worried about me. Tried to get me to go with him, but I couldn't be persuaded and Leg's sister seemed to be enjoying the attention, so he left us to it.

"That girl's brain's probably messed up for life now because of you." I remember him moaning on the phone.

So continued the tale of disaster. He didn't see me for a good hour after that incident. Was too busy laughing at Moon and Littl' Leg who were trying their arm at garden hopping. Apparently they only succeeded to make it next door, deciding that would do. Leg lived at the end of his street and the only neighbours were halfway through a vacation in Majorca. This made the barbecue so convenient.

Anyway, not intent on climbing back to the party, Moon and Leg began setting up garden gnomes into some sort of disco scenario around a big bird table. Once they felt the rave looked perfect they started to dance round it themselves singing Prodigy tunes. It was at that point when someone caught Sloo's attention at Leg's upstairs window. He looked up and saw it was my face appearing all cum-shot like. His initial thoughts was that I was getting a blow-job off Louise or something, but upon looking round the garden he saw her chatting to some other bloke... And that they were talking very closely.

I remember being on the phone to Sloo, the smug cunt, at this point, heart all sinking like, knowing I'd truly fucked it up once more. Crane's drug habit strikes again.

He continued that his second thoughts then, were that I was getting a blow job off Littl' Leg's sister!

I remember being on the phone to Sloo, the sick cunt, at this point and nearly throwing up. You must understand, I'd swallowed a huge concoction of drugs by this time and when my memory goes then... No I just couldn't...

So typically Sloo felt he'd better go and investigate, make sure I wasn't being too corrupt. He found me in Leg's bedroom kneeling on the bed, just bouncing up and down. Next to me was Louise's mate with her tits out. She had begun throwing up over a pillow. Beautiful.

To this day I wish I could remember what happened leading up to that moment, but nothing has come back. At the time Sloo asked if I was alright. "Yes..." I apparently replied "...I'm watching the gnomes 'aving it large".

Fuck I must have been totally skied.

The fourth and final time that Sloo crossed my path, was right near the end of the party just when he was leaving. Said he came in from the garden and saw me rolling round the floor in front of everyone's exit. Told me I was completely covered in dog hair, had pissed meself and was in bits even though no other fucker was in the room.

Apparently Louise followed him through shortly after, just as he was trying to get me to my feet, calm me down and such. But all I could do was fall back down again in heaps of laughter. Kept saying that the washing machine couldn't cope with the amount of folders someone'd put in it.

Sloo said Louise just stepped over me tutting and walked out without her friend. No one knew what happened to her mate, or what I did to her. No one's seen her since.

I have seen Louise out and about, she says hello to me now and again. I don't think she quite realised at the time, what sort of fuckwit drug addict she'd got involved with. Well I call meself an addict, but that's a little harsh. I know there are millions of people out there a lot worse than me, I think. Anyway it was acid and that shit's nasty when you get a strong one.

Or two as Littl' Leg had worked out the next day.

Now feel sleep fully knocking at the door. The sofa in the front room'll be far more comfortable, so I stub the joint out and stagger back to lie down.

Get into relaxed mode and use the remote to take the TV off stand by and tune into TMF. They're showing that old *High* song by *James Blunt*. The video shows him running through the forest...

I watch the leaves and trees...

get lost...

and memories of Camp Styx...

Crystal lake,

Styx come to me as I Crys...

drift off to the land of heavy drug induced unconsciousness that Styx Lake takes me back to the river which flows through the forest and runs red with the blood of the men that once roamed the Camp, with Jason shedding the blood and Sloo with his scythe, lopping heads, spurting blood taking the camp apart and stripping it dry of the freedom it once had.

Further... taking me back and back to a man who stands in front of me as I fly through space and *time*, he looks solemn and pleading, take me back before the rules and tyranny and we can all be saved again, save the future and the past. It will soon come he will soon return watch those who are closest to you....zzzzzzzzz.........Or gooooo zzzzzzzzzzzzzzzzzzzzzzzzzzzzzzzzzzzzzzzzzzzzzzzzzzzzzzzzzzzzzzzzzzzzzzzz zzzzzzzzzzzzzzzzzzzzzzzzzzzzzzzzzzzz

REMEMBER THE DEALS HAVE BEEN MADE THAT CAN NEVER BE CHANGED. THE THREAT IS OUT THERE. NO ONE IS SAFE. RETURN TO THE CAMP AND BURN IT. BURN IT DOWN TO THE GROUND..

....

....

....

....

....

....The doorbell snaps me out of a very strange slumber.

Good the sleep's taken the edge of me cocaine and booze hangover. The weed is now banging round me system.

What was that about burning camps down to the ground? Man I've gotta calm down on the narcotics. Still, more chip, chip, chipper now.

Check the clock **1.30**.

Wicked this must be Littl' Leg and Moon at the door. Here with more drugs.

Long may this weekend continue.

CHAPTER 5
TAKE ME FURTHER

1008 AD

Insane snaps, the forest at night. Spectral sounds highlighting the obscurity of deadly surroundings. An animal darts, twigs crack. A devil that grinds his teeth. Owls hoot, the siren of unearthly occurence. A branch crashes to the ground, the crumpling sound of a friend captured and dragged away.

All sounds portray anything when you cannot see them being made. The imagination of a five man hunt runs wild. None more so than Robert Cranley's, trying to shut out an ever increasing terror. The forest he so fears, the growth that held unspeakable monstrosities. Here he was deep within. Pitch black. Wishes he was in his retire. Safe and warm. Unwatched by the surrounding presence he visualises impending upon him now. His every move a step towards whatever it wants. All part of a hideous trap he walks into head first. Yet what choice? Roger Brooks was out there somewhere, can't leave him to suffer alone within this undiscovered cemetery. His friend would do the same if Cranley was in the ungodly position. He knows that. Must face up to his deepest darkest phobia, push the horror to one side. March on with love for a companion.

The search had so far proved fruitless. A daunting trek for five unwitting men willing to put their lives at stake. Though none had a great deal to survive for. Hevey Little limps behind, a disability acquired from gruelling labour demanded by the manor in which he lived. All for the benefit of the Lord and priest, now his hindrance classified him as near worthless to the powers that be. The small hovel where he resides a complete misrepresentation of the arduous work he partook. All too ready to face the danger of the forest. What was there to lose?

Alfred Beech misses the warmth from his fire, yet even the flickers taunted the obvious absence from the man's side. Alone he spent nights. To wonder why exist, a terrible trick of insomnia. Why not head of in exploration of evil? No one in the village will miss his disappearance. Roger Brooks was a close friend, someone who took his mind away from celibacy and poverty. Now the man was gone. *Time* to bring him back.

The men continue further, deeper they delve. Brushing aside the poking fingers of perennial plants and snapping twigs underfoot. Tree upon tree loom ominously over them. Each tower creating an impression of an entity watching and waiting for the hunters to fall into a perfectly set trap.

Wadard Mooning leading the pack. Bravery setting aside the trepidation of being first caught. Time after time this man would put friends first. Providing Hevey Little from his own small helping of food, preferring to go without than see a comrade suffer. In the same position now. Ready to put life at risk if he could save that of another. The perfect guide also spent long hours in the forest borders, collecting wood for the village and guarding his habitat against wildlife. Before they set off he guaranteed the pack a safe return. Believed in his ability, despite the journey's blindness, to maintain a straight path. Confident that he could count 5,000 steps deep, far enough to search without danger of entrapment by the forest itself. If by that point they had seen no sign of Brooks they would turn directly around and head straight back. Something that they would all be very willing to do right now. Mooning's counting continues. Undisturbed by silence from the following serfs. Sensible reasoning of safety, to remain inconspicuous. Whatever accursed quantity that held Brooks should not be disturbed. Every hundred steps would call out the suspected captives name. This was the only risk he took, in hope the searchers would receive a friendly reply and not the unwanted depravity they believe had enslaved the friend.

Following close behind the leader, a spirited Adam Tilnid. A man accepted as a valued acquaintance despite his difficulty in speaking. Total absence of education leaving the poor man clueless of the events of village life. Lives mainly in silence and wonder. Understands he faces trouble, does not care.

Darkness. Enveloping black. An expedition into the night's possession. Was the only option. The manor had forbidden a search of the forest until gratification from the King was received. By then the five serfs knew it would be too late. Two days without action already. More sheep and pigskins decorated cottages. Further blood sprayed over the parish doors. Enough was enough, the whole village knew now there was more to the forest than meets the eye. So under disguise of night the lower members of society sneaked past the manor and into terrifying wilderness.

Exadurated uneasiness, trudging slowly between dark wooden columns. Their only beacon the candles each person carried. A dim light insignificant to calm their shoddy nerves.

Appalling images cloud each man's mind. As if evil literally provided food for thought. Yet they all know there is no alternative. Brooks was out there somewhere. Have to help.

Partial blindness to their surroundings enforced the knowledge; no matter how brave, this was an ignorant quest. Nothing would be discovered within these forests without actually tumbling over it. With each step Mooning half expects to trip over the corpse of his friend.

Suddenly the guide halts…

His suppression signals the rest to copy.

'Does anyone smell that?' Mooning whispers as he turns to his followers. A faint smell of fire lines the air.

Each serf looks round as if expecting to see flames dancing, circling and entrapping them. Cranley sniffs, this was the moment he knew was coming. Something was about to happen. Desperately tries to detect the origin of the scent, before it distinguishes them. Smoke thickening within their lungs. Candles are raised yet none can locate this supposed worsening hazard…

Silence surrounds them. The small light they have created together shows no blaze. No sparkle amongst the trees, nothing. A forest fire would be unlikely, Little unspeakingly reasons. Heavy rain today had continued as drizzle overnight. Surely no flame could withstand the recent constant downpours.

Fumes become more dense by the second, yet still no heat is felt from a suggested approaching inferno. Increasing panic crawling in. Five men stand as rooted as encompassing trees. Only their heads turn to desperately locate the creator of this smoke. Cranley's head in a spin, vision clouds. Doesn't want to lose his friends.

'We must join hands. We have to stay close.' Waving hands to seek out a partner to grab. Soon form a chain. Still Mooning refusing to continue the journey. Smoke would completely finish the losing battle they had commenced.

'It must be remnants of a fire, the rain is probably still extinguishing it.' Beech calls. Settles the paranoia, slightly. Little has another idea that may calm them further.

'Or it could be...'

A loud crack fills the air. The shrillness echoes through each man's heart. That could be no branch falling, no wild animal getting caught by another. That wasn't the standard noise of the forest. Each member of the hunt senses something far more petrifying baring down upon them. Closing in on its prey. Whatever had captured their friend. The thing that delivered skin and blood to their village doorstep was near.

Robert Cranley can feel it. Stomach rising, forehead sweating, hand shaking. This was no longer intuition. Something was here. Here to verify their worst fear...

b l a c k

Confirmation. A startling cry from out front

'Oh please God no, what is that? It's coming towards us'...

THE BIBLICAL DIRECTORY
(i)

'Take a seat.'

The mad librarian geezer's led us through to a room at the back. We're the only people in the whole building and the three of us have gone into this tiny box. It's painted this horrible lime green colour. There's only one window to let daylight in. But there's none of that going on out there, so he switches the light on.

Doesn't exactly reveal a great deal. All that's in there is this old school-desk type table. On it is some old looking books and bits of paper. Two chairs one side and one the other. The rest is empty...

That's it! I get it now. When the geezer sits down I finally figure out what's going on here. This is some sort of frigging lecture. Man this girl is something else. She's heading for an A if she does this sort of thing every Sunday. Whilst I'm on the fast track to a fucking F. If I'm lucky! Still I suppose if this geezer knows what he's on about, I might learn something. Just in *time*.

It's been too big a fucking weekend for all this though. Had about four hours sleep since Thursday's drunken unconsciousness. I'll be gone in no time.

Tina makes herself comfortable then continues to smile at me. Makes me feel that everything's alright. I'll put up with anything to be with her.

Having put me parka over the back of the chair I sit next to her. The weird thing is nobody's said shit about what's going on here. Not even an "oh by the way, this is a private lecture". It's surreal man. Hope there's no kinky weird shit going on. I mean I said I'd do anything for this bird, but I ain't gonna involve meself in a spit roasting session with this old cunt.

'CRANE.' Ooh ya bastard. Made me jump that. I'm almost asleep already. Hang on a minute.

''ow do you know I'm called Crane?' Don't even remember telling Tina me nickname. Or did I? I look at her, still grinning away at me. Man I'm a sucker for it.

'There's going to be a few things that I say which you'll not understand. Stories that defy belief or even comprehension, but I'm sure we're gonna get there in the end.'

'Listen. Can we get a few things straight 'ere. I don't really understand anything to do with Sociology; and I'm sorry if this upsets anyone, but I don't even find it that interesting. So let's not start sugar coating it up.' I don't wanna get all narky here, but lack of sleep and all that.

'Well young man, this is nothing to do with Sociology. Or of some sorts at least.'

Oh fuck, it is kinky.

'What's this all about then?' For crying out loud.

'This is about God.'

'Oh I do get it now.' I drop me head and let out a laugh. Bible bashers. Tina here must be into her church and shit. Now she's having it away with me, she wants to get me on side.

'Get what?' He asks.

'Listen, I don't mind all this. As I said to Tina earlier, I'd do anything as long as it's with 'er. Even if that does mean church and all that shit, sorry...stuff. I'll go. Just don't expect me to formulate much of an opinion. I don't really 'ave one of those about anything.' Tina giggles and takes hold of my hand. Gratefully received. Even the librarian nutjob's having a bit of a chuckle. I don't care. Just relieved this geezer ain't trying to spread me arse cheeks.

'By the end of our time together Mister Crane, you will believe in everything that is holy. I can assure you of that.' That's it, lap it up.

'Alright, well let's get cracking anyway, no offence but I ain't spending me whole day 'ere... I've got revision to do.' I crack up at this one, but it ain't gone down as well as I thought. Champion.

'Right, we'll start at the beginning.'

'Sorry to interrupt again, but really, 'ow do you know I'm called Crane? And you don't 'ave to call me Mister or nothing.'

Tina squeezes me hand a little tighter as if to say "don't butt in". But come on…

'I will come to that, all in good time.'

'Cool.' Not that bothered now anyway.

'First there was God…' I'll let him waffle, but it'll soon be time for Mr Craney's brain to switch off. I'll pick up on little bits. Try and chuck a 'yes' in here and there and we're laughing. Anyway if you don't know about all the creation bollocks you must be some sort of flid.

'…You know the story of Adam and Eve, correct?' Ooh caught that bit.

'Yeah Adam and Eve. Garden of Eden. That snake that give 'em the apple. Then they realised they was starkers and God done his nut. Yeah I know that.' Sit back all proud of meself.

'Good, basic summary, but… well without worrying about the ins and outs…' Bet there were a few ins and outs with them two. Corrr. '…Firstly, I'll try and put this in ways you may understand. The 'snake', as you say, had legs, so in fact it was a serpent. Secondly, it was a forbidden fruit; and not an apple, but that's by the by. It's not all important, but it's good to have a healthy understanding.' Woah, slow down there egg head!

'The serpent had illegally removed this fruit from the tree of knowledge. Which will become important later.'

'Ok.'

This is gonna be a long day Mr Crane. If only the lads could see me now, they'd be absolutely pissing 'emselves.

'For the serpent's misdemeanour it received punishment from God. Some say it had its legs removed and became the snake, but that's a little unfair on snakes don't you think? Ha ha ha.'

Tina's pissing herself, but I thought me revision line worked on so many more levels.

'This is what actually went on…'

CHAPTER 6
I LOVE SATURDAY

I look round the Bridge House and wonder how much money it must be making today. The Saturday of a bank holiday weekend and what with the Hammers match live on Sky, the landlord must be creaming in our pints at the moment. Lucky I organised a few of The Styx to get here early for our regular seats at the back.

None of the other fuckers would sort it this well.

Although I'm going off the footy a bit, we get a good view of the big screen here and it keeps the lads together. The screen's blank at the moment, we've still got two hours to kill and I've gotta suffer chart music bullshit 'til West Ham starts.

That Robbie Williams is a cunt. Fucking entertain me, you couldn't fucking entertain Beeke with your cock, you queer cunt.

I was the first to arrive as usual, but fair play to Tin Lid and Brooke. They weren't long after. We've been moaning about the others lateness and though I'm really pissed off with 'em, I hold it down well. It's not those three I've got the problem with. I'm just tired cause of that arse wanker Beeke. His evil dreams have fucked up my sleep this weekend. I've had all sorts of visitations and everything, and it's all that cunt's fault.

Annoyed with Brooke's lack of appearance for a beer last night, but he's making up for it today. Last night was a bit of a blow out anyway. It was only Lid who turned up early on. Crane, Moon and Leg didn't get there 'til about half nine and they was all fucked off their heads on coke anyway. I swear they only turned up 'cause they got bored with

TV and didn't want to waste good gear staying in all night. Still I suppose I'd have been the same a while back. No more though, I gotta stay with it, make sure they don't branch away from us.

Don't wanna get left with a faggot, an alky and a bloke who can't be arsed to go out 'cause of his bird. Mustn't let The Styx fall apart, I know that now.

To be fair Brooke don't always blow us out; he still remains faithful to The Styx. I'm satisfied that Commandment 1 ain't been broken.

Quick check of the old watch. Experiencing some anger at those fucking junkies who still ain't turned up yet.

Calm down Sloo, they're all good lads really.

Just that wanker Beeke that's let us all down. Lucky I've stopped taking drugs now. I'm in control. I'll make sure The Styx don't start straying and have ideas above themselves. Thinking we can all split up. Just wish I'd added a couple more commandments that day at the camp: No excessive drug taking and definitely no fucking well being bent.

You're the leader, remember commandment 7, you can alter them.

No the others would think I'd gone loopy... give me time. No-one has done anything wrong yet. No-one need die.

Sloo get a grip you've lost all plot of the conversation. Pick it up.

* * * *

'So leg went up to 'er and goes "get ya coat luv you've pulled" and the cunt only gets away with it and that...' Tin lid tells Brooke regarding Thursday night '...She goes "why where we going?" and he goes that corner for a snog.'

'Can't believe 'e pulled 'er with that line, she must 'ave been a right dirty old bint.' Muses Brooke. A person in the know.

'You're telling me, she was dressed like a right slag and that. I reckon she'd've been game on for a right good nailing too, but that cunt'd taken so much speed 'e never'd got it up, so once 'e'd finished snogging 'er and feeling 'er up, 'e says see ya later and goes off and starts dancing with Moon and Crane. That's about the time I fucked off and bollocks knows 'ow I got 'ome.'

Brooke laughs with recognition at the traditional events in Tin Lid's recap.

'But it was a good night though, yeah?' He asks.

'Yeah not bad from what I can remember. I spent the early hours throwing up all this red shit and that.'

'What was it?' Sloo finally returns to the conversation with a rising interest.

'I'm 'oping it was After Shock.'

'You fucking monster, still d'ya fancy another one?' Brooke offers.

'What ya mean, After Shock?'

'No you tosser, beer?'

'What do you think?' Tin Lid laughs

'Yeah, suppose it was a stupid question, Stella?'

'Aye.'

'Sloo?'

'I'll 'ave another Guinness please mate.'

'What about a Whiskey chaser too?' Tin Lid enquires.

'It's a bit early for all that innit? We still got four hours 'til the footy finishes.'

'Yeah, I suppose.' Tin Lid shrugs. Two bottles of cheap French lager 'liveners' he had whilst getting ready put him comfortably ahead anyway...

'Come on you Irons.' Littl' Leg arrives with Crane in tow. Both proudly sporting the colours of their team.

'Where's Moon?' Asks Sloo.

'Lightweight's sleeping off the drugs. Reckons 'e wont be long... Oi Brooke two Stellas mate.'

'There's a good lad.' Crane jokingly backs up Leg's request having spotted Brooke at the bar.

'So what d'ya reckon then Liddy boy, gonna do the Mancs or what?'

'Man, three-nil at least.'

'Wicked, I've got a sov on three-nil.' Crane smiles

'Nah mate, two-one, Matty first scorer.'

'You got a quid on that then Leg?' Tin Lid asks.

'Gimme some credit geez. I'm not a student bastard like you commie cunts. Gotta tenner on it.'

'What odds?'

'Twenty five to one…' Littl' Leg answers, then notices Tin Lid's expression as he desperately tries to calculate the winnings.

'…That'll be two-sixty back to me you daft cunt...' Helps Tin lid, then turns to Crane '...What do they teach you at that college?'

'Giz 'and at the bar Sloo ya lazy git.' Brooke calls, waking Sloo from another stare…

'Where's Beeke?' Littl' Leg asks Tin Lid once Sloo has gone.

'Dunno, I spoke to 'im this morning and 'e said 'e's gonna try and get down 'ere later, but I reckon 'e's worried 'bout Sloo and that.'

'Still not over it yet eh?' Asks Crane.

'D'you think 'e ever will be with that cunt around?' Laughs Littl' Leg gesturing toward Sloo…

Sloo returns with the first two pints. Brooke follows shortly behind with another two, before returning to the bar for the settling Guinness. Both receive a cheer from the seated trio all set for an afternoon and evening session of drinking.

Crane sits calm, had tidied his house this morning in case of a surprise visit from a brother or Nan whilst he was out. Also clearing any sign of drug abuse before his parents get back. Armed himself with an Air Freshener and black bin liner for the arduous task. Despite having two days till they return, the youngster wanted to be safe over sorry. That included replacing the money which funded the prostitute in the exact way he thinks he found it in his parents drawer. Had thanked God for Leg's 'life saving' visit yesterday.

Makes to talk, then stops himself. Decidedly a little tentative as to whether admitting his escort activities to Brooke, Tin lid and Sloo was such a great idea. It would only mean more people to take the piss. He'd told Littl' Leg and Moon yesterday, but he knew they'd respect him for having the guts to do it. They'd not said anything to Sloo last night, perhaps the state they was in made them forget. Brooke would probably find it impressive, but Tin Lid's inexperience and Sloo being a virgin would raise question. Most likely respond with grumbles that they would never do such a thing, then Crane would argue they'll probably never do it with anyone… and so on. Resolves it best left unsaid.

'Guess what this fucker done on Thursday night?' Leg decides otherwise!

The others look interested, full encouragement for Leg to begin an in depth report about a night of prostitution, lust and cocaine...

'Well at least I weren't just bashing one out over a mag all night like you.' Crane retorts having heard Leg mention the word desperation in his speech.

'You told me you did...' Laughs Littl' Leg. Crane realises he should have known better than to become entangled in a war of words with a master. '... before the brass showed you was wanking 'til about five in the morning and then 'ow long did you last with this prozzy then eh?' Leg starting to enjoy the obvious upper hand. Has his friend on the ropes. Can see a subject change desire in the eyes.

'Go on then Craney, 'ow long mate?' Brooke Joins in.

'Ten minutes.' He murmurs.

'That ain't bad.'

'Nah, that's 'ow long she was there for, 'e only fucked 'er for a minute.' Leg disputes, causing an eruption of laughter louder than trees from their table. Turns many a head in the pub...

Shortly after Moon arrives. Wearing sunglasses to cover deeply sunken and blackened eyes. Black hair not its usual tidy self. Experiencing a little insecurity for a change. Paranoia already making him believe he should have stayed home. No he'd never do that.

'Get the beers in then.'

'I just did you wanker... 'ere there's three quid, get it yourself.'

'Cheers Brooke. 'ere 'as Leg told you 'bout Nicholas yet?' Moon asks gesturing toward Crane.

'Yeah, but why Nicholas?' Brooke asks

'Nicholas Cage, *Gone in 60 seconds.*' Moon walks proudly, if a little off balance, to the bar having produced a bigger laugh than the one heard when he entered.

'Cor dear did you see the state of 'im?' Asks Littl' Leg, once the hilarity had subsided.

'Yeah almost as bad as that bird you pulled Thursday.' Crane finally pleased after producing a somewhat stylish comeback.

'It's not what you said the other night, when you was all loved up. Ooh Leg I lurve you and you're bird was so beautiful.' He mimics

Ribbing continues, but it's all good natured. Sloo starts to think how at home they all seem; without Beeke. Moon soon arrives back with his beer, feeling no improvement to his health. His friends don't help by mocking his appearance.

''e looks worse than Lid did that morning in Ibiza.' Says Brooke.

'whooooah there. Dunno 'bout that.'

IBIZA

(The Styx first holiday together, the summer previous.)

First night here, can't deny how fucking excited I am. Ibiza, this is where it's at: The epitome for drug users. The pinnacle of our short careers. Managed to persuade Moon and Littl' Leg to have on me Ibiza rap cd: *'Crane's Rap 2007'*, that I spent hours enthusiastically putting together before the holiday. I take the cd out the case and notice some wanker has added an extra C to the title. Obtained the other's agreement for this musical choice only because I put the few hip-hop tunes I knew they liked on it, beginning with B.O.B. by Outkast - a banging Drum and Bass type number with rapid lyrics.

Open up a bottle of San Miguel on the edge of the balcony wall. As we've got no fridge we had to leave a few bottles in cold water in the sink, but as I swig it I see it's not helped it from tasting piss poor. *Time* to start getting dressed. So fucking hot, just out the shower I'm already sweating. Sharing the smokers room with Moon and Littl' Leg - The Magic Number together. Sloo, Brooke, Beeke and Tin lid are all next door. Brooke'll be in soon to get some of Moon's spliff, but the others ain't really interested in the herb he smuggled over.

The room's pretty shit. There's hundreds of these mini ants crawling all over the fucking shop, and the toilet don't even have a seat. But we're on holiday and I'm away from the parents and college for a couple of weeks, that's all that really matters. Well apart from drugs, but even they're sorted after a surprisingly short ecstasy search today. So we're well stocked up. We got hundred Mitsubishis for starters off this cool geezer from Romford of all places. He's gonna come and visit us at the hotel in a week, in case we've run out. There's a serious fucking chance of that. Reckon this is gonna be one huge holiday.

Moon's just had his towel whipped off by Leg on his way out the shower.

'Leg you cunt, give us it back will ya?' Moon's moaning, covering his pride with both hands.

Quite pleased that this seems easy for him to do, despite knowing we've all had a couple a` lines a` speed.

Leg's name was drawn out the hat to smuggle the speed over from England. Moon's came out second to smuggle the puff, though having met our ecstasy supplier today neither crime was necessary. Still at least we know it's our shit; and good, but I would say that, the fortunate one who had no potentially prison-bound tasks to complete.

'Come on lover boy show us your willy.'

'Fuck off little boy, that should be your name; Little Boy, not Littl' Leg.' Moon's laughing now, decided to give up on his towel and put on some boxers

'You're no fun any more.' Leg goes over to Moon and starts caressing his body. Moon just grabs him and pushes him on his bed. Then he drops on him with a wrestling move, invented I think by Jake the snake Roberts. They start grappling. I'm over hyped meself and decide to jump on screaming 'BUNDLE'... It's instigated the lads next-door to come flying through and join in.

The Styx bonding like never before.

Tussle continues for a few minutes 'til we realise we've all just had showers. Getting all sweaty again's probably not the best idea if we're gonna be on the pull tonight.

Me and Moon decide to get on the pills early doors, we wanna be well up as soon as we get out. I've always been told it's not worth taking E whilst drinking as it takes away the true effect of the drug. I disagree, my theory is: the drink before you go out helps ease you into the night's festivities, making you well up for it. Then once you're feeling merry and excited, that's when you pop the pill. In half hours time the whole world is your friend and you find yourself with the most extreme confidence to talk to anyone, especially the birds. One minute you're standing at the bar, the next you're chatting to some bird you've never even met before, telling 'em how great they look. Well this is what I'm hoping for later. The only mistake we're making is doing one before we've even left the hotel room; and then bringing three along for the ride. We've only recently discovered there was this wicked drug that wasn't acid or speed. In theory we're E amateurs. I've only ever taken two in a night before. Probably gonna end up gurning in some corner of a club, not having a clue where the fuck I am. Beautiful.

On our way out, we meet up with the others and pop down to the hotel bar for a sharp one. Soon as we walk in, Brooke's already on the pull with the fit barmaid. We order a variety of drinks: ranging from my Bacardi and Coke, where the measure's gotta be quadruple, to the Tequila Sunrise Beeke's ordered. Despite our piss taking Beeke's felt confident enough to come out in a tight luminous orange top, but to be fair he suits the life and vibrancy Ibiza offers. Only a week ago he bleached his hair for the holiday.

It's about half eight, we decide to sit on the sun beds around the hotel pool to see out the very warm August evening. I've sunk two San Miguels whilst getting ready. The second beer nearly made me fucking puke with every swig. Pill ain't taking effect yet, but it's only a matter of time. We've left Brooke to it at the bar, the rest of us discuss where we're gonna go tonight. Littl' Leg has the ideas:

'A geezer I work with reckons a good place to kick off is this bar called Kings. Then we just work our way round some other bars for a bit and end up at a smallish club for our first night, just to get a feel for the place, find out what's good. If we remember fuck all.'

'What are the big clubs called again?' I ask. He's told me several times before, but me memory's shot to shit with all the drugs I've been taking recently.

'Well 'e said that we should go to Manumission on Monday, but it does cost about thirty-five notes.'

'That's alright. We gotta try everything once we're 'ere ain't we?'

'Too right. Then there's Es Paradis on a Wednesday and Space any morning when we're fucking off our tits and can't be arsed to go 'ome'

'So most mornings then.' I add.

'Waa heyyy!' Moon and Beeke seal this with their approval.

'But tonight it's all about the birds.' Littl' Leg goes.

'Yeah and getting completely obliterated.'

'Trust you Tin Lid, what is that your drinking anyway?' Asks Sloo.

'Large Whisky and Coke.'

'You're a fucking beer monster Liddy boy.'

'But we don't care.' Sings Moon, instigating all of us to finish the chorus:

'Coz you're Tin Lid,
Super Tin Lid,
Super Tin Lid,
from Cranham.'

Beeke takes out an E and pops it.

'Is that your first one?' Asks Leg.

'Second.'

'Fuck me, I better get started, ain't you fucked yet?' Leg goes, pulling out a pill of his own, swallows it with a swig of Heineken.

'Nah, I've only just taken the first one. Wanna get fucked quick.'

''Ere 'ere.' Shouts Tin Lid.

'Well lads 'ere's to The Styx.' Toasts Sloo. We raise our glasses and all shout 'The Styx', before downing as much of our drinks as possible without gagging. That's pretty hard for me considering the shit I've gotta swallow. Sloo bangs on the window of the hotel bar and Brooke turns to see him raising his glass. We hear Brooke shout 'The Styx'. Then he finishes his bottle of Bud, slams it on the table and turns round to start snogging the barmaid.

We wait about thirty seconds more for him to come outside.

'We off then lads?' He says to our applause, geezer's off the mark already.

Finally ready to set off. I take me drink with me, feeling sure the hotel ain't gonna miss the fucking little shitty paper cup they give it me in...

We reach Kings when I feel the pill start giving me head-rushes. Got an urge to love building inside. Put me arm round Littl' Leg.

'You alright geez?' He can tell I'm coming up, got that knowing smirk on his face.

'You know that Leg.'

Memory patchy, trying to focus on Moon. What's he saying to me? Fuck me...

We get another large variety of drinks from the bar. Spot Beeke on the dance floor. It's only about half nine and he's already giving it some. This is not the last time we'll hear this *Bob Sinclair* song over the next two weeks. Bar's a bit cheesy, perfect for us lot I suppose. Birds everywhere, most of them wearing next to nothing.

Head-rushes again. Spinning. Have to exhale. Breath seems endless. Gotta spark a fag.

Sloo's propping up the bar with Tin Lid. Moon and Leg are pissing 'emselves about something, but I'm not interested yet. This pill's really gonna fucking hit me, any second now. I mean I'm fucked already, but I'm still waiting for that feeling you get when it totally blows you away. You know as if some bloke comes running up and smacks you with a baseball bat.

THWACK

...I'm in another clubby type bar, just stepping back to reality.

Ain't got a fucking Danny where the other boys are. I'm standing with a couple. Geezer looks about twenty-seven and judging by his tan has been in Ibiza for a while. Looks as though he's on something too, so does his bird. She looks a bit younger and has that frizzy blonde hair I go for in a big way. Both seem friendly enough. Probably 'cause their pilling too, but they're handling it much better than me. Reach into me jeans pocket. Only one banger left in there. Brought three out with me as well.

'You alright now Steve?' The geezer goes.

Obviously felt fit to lose me nickname to these strangers. Gets me out of The Styx explanation. Far too long a story; and fucking ridiculous.

'Think so.' Still trying to get me proper vision back. Must've been walking around fucking blind for ages.

'You were well gone there weren't ya?'

Breathe a heavy sigh, beginning to wonder where the fuck I am. The bloke sounds like he's from London so I can easily understand him. Not like some of the Yorkshire slags we met on the plane.

'Do you know the time?' I ask the girl. Came out like I was speaking to a foreigner. Didn't mean to.

'One o' clock.' She answers smiling from ear to ear.

'Fucking 'ell, you ain't seen any of me mates 'ave ya?'

They both have a little giggle at this. Not sure why. Probably chewing me face off.

'Nah mate we found you on your own outside, jabbering on about drumsticks or something.' It's comforting 'cause he looks proud as he's telling me.

Seems like I've made a bit of a miscalculation with the drinking and E. Totally blown me theory out the water. Should have a couple of beers to ease you into the takeover, not the mind-blowing Bacardi I had. That's the danger. When the pill hit me it took away all me senses. Chopped three hours of memory from me brain. With no mentality either, not had the option to stop at one 'cause I was battered off it. No, I swallowed a couple more instead, probably without realising. So far must've done three. It's led me to here. Lost me mates. Fucked in some strange unknown nightclub. Talking to two complete strangers. Beautiful.

'Sorry, but I ain't got a clue what I'm doing.' I tell 'em.

The geezer laughs again. The bird gives it a sympathetic 'ah' then gives me a hug. Much appreciated too.

'I've told you about seven times, but I'm guessing you don't remember. I'm Andy and this is Rachel.'

'And where are we?'

'This is Kaos, we brought you in here about half-hour ago. You was in a bit of a mess out there. We got you a bottle of water to try and sort you out a bit.'

'Cheers.' I just realise I'm holding a bottle of water. Have to take a swig. Not really enjoying this sudden consciousness. Scary actually being aware of not knowing what you're doing. Decide I'm gonna go to the toilet and take me last pill. Hopefully I'll bump into one of me mates, as I'll not have a fucking Danny Lareu how to get home.

I thank Andy and Rachel and say that I'll be back shortly then start me search for the bogs. Have to navigate me way through a bustling crowd. Not easy as my balance is fucking way off. Keep falling into people and have to apologise. Only just realising how fucking loud the music is in here. It's making me feel sick, need calm, but with the amount of people actually in this place I don't stand a Morris dance. Reckon it'd be wicked if I weren't so wired though.

Brain can't handle the sudden distortion it's just been through. Wanna get it back to the fucked up condition it was in about five minutes ago when I was unaware of my being. Know deep down this is probably a big mistake, but fuck it I have no other choice. Can't stay like this can I? I need to be awake and out for another few hours in the hope I do bump into one of the lads. Paranoia grip is taking effect. Feels as though everyone's looking at me and laughing. In fact they are.

Realisation. I've come to a complete stand still and I'm holding onto a pole. Thought I was walking just then. Fucking hell, I give a lopsided smile as if to pretend I know what I'm doing.

The toilets must be about ten miles away, and the clubbers laughter shrills through me like it did that day at The Styx. What? what am I going on about? Fucking get a grip Crane, Steve, Crane. Who the fucking hell am I?

BLANK

I'm in a cubicle, a little shaky. Rest me hand on the back wall, hang me head as I struggle to get me nob out. Think I need a piss, but various colours start flashing round the pan. It's putting me right off. Probably not a great idea for me to do this last E. In fact I'm fucking certain it's not, but I need to be at one of the extremes innit. Either completely up and fucking out of it again, or feeling normal.

Normality won't set in for at least another hour and this ain't no state to be in. Although fuck knows where I'll be in half-hour from now. Fuck it, here goes…

Pop me final pill of the night. Still clinging to the bottle of water, take a swig, swallow cleanly.

It's done. Sit down on the bog in the cubicle for a bit. Gotta build me confidence to hash me way through the crowds to find Andy and Rachel.

Hang on a minute. Swear I can hear some familiar voices outside.

Step out the cubicle and there's Littl' Leg standing over a urinal, his head resting on the wall. Moon's here too, looking deep into a mirror over the sinks. Thank God, I'm saved.

'YESSSSSSS!'

They both turn towards me.

'Fucking 'ell Crane, where 'ave you been?'

'Fuck knows, I'm completely wankered.'

'You're telling me, I'm in a mess mate. Can't believe they even let us in this place. We've completely lost it.' Says Littl' Leg shaking his head, mouthing every word as if they were vital to a plot.

'It's these pills man they're well strong, I've only 'ad two.' Moon joins in.

'I've just taken me fourth.' I tell 'em.

'What?'

'No fucking shit?'

'Did you not see Beeke earlier when that third one 'it 'im?'

All these questions man. Can't deal with it.

'Listen I don't remember nothing lads.'

''e was in a right mess geez, clinging onto some bloke and shit. Reckoned 'e was gonna stay in Kings with 'im on the pull for some birds. We've been a bit worried in case e's got 'imself caught up with some faggot or some'ing. Didn't think it through at the time, too fucked.' Leg goes.

'When did you lose me?' I ask, balancing against the sinks.

'Fuck knows! We was walking along together, six of us, suddenly it was just me and Leg.'

Moon answers, looking trolleyed…

'We're gonna 'ave to look after you mate.' Littl' leg finishes his piss. He's right, can already feel myself flying again.

'Don't know 'ow Leg, I'm fucking struggling enough to look after meself at the moment.' Says Moon.

'Who d'ya get in with?' Leg asks me.

I try to um... swallow and steady me focus on Leg. Can see him staring at me as if he's right worried. I'm swaying from side to side I think. Feel like me moment of consciousness back then was only the eye of the storm. This next pill's gonna hit me too then I'll be totally bangered. Beautiful.

'Andy and Rachel.' I manage a reply. Reckon I'm grinning like a cunt.

'Can you remember what they look like geez?...' Moon squints at me all serious looking '…Coz maybe they can look after all of us."

His lips make an upside down banana frown. Can't stop meself from giggling. I lean back away from something, dodging it. Shrug, can't form words no more or thoughts... Can hear Leg in the background fading away

'Come on Moon giz an 'and, we'll get 'im...'

'Eh?'

BANG

I'm sitting out in the open, it's starting to get light. Clenching someone's hand. Turn sharply to me left. Thank God Leg's there.

'You back with us son?'

I look at him in bewilderment. His face looks all twisted.

'Where's Moon?' Lick me lips. In a kind of drunken state. My guts feel acidic and the rushes to me head are banging. The lights from all the clubs change colours. Or maybe they are already? Man fuck this.

'e's behind you.' Woah! Who is? Turn in fright and see Moon sitting up against a pole. Phew! Geezer's just staring at something on the ground.

Lots of people are making their way out of clubs; real zombie like states. Pissed up groups of lads sing footy songs. See a girl comforting her mate who's throwing up in the road. The junkies are not out yet, well bar us- fucking lightweights. Still those pills are fucking mental. Never had nothing that strong. Could do with me bed now. Wanna lie there and stare at a wall. This is gonna be a heavy come down. Don't think we'll be going back to the hotel to carry on the drug taking. That was the plan if we didn't pull, but judging by the state of me and Moon there's no fucking way.

I stay holding onto Leg's hand. He seems all right at the moment, as if he's waiting for us to snap out of it so we can make our way back.

'So much for the birds.' I manage to form. Leg looks at me and laughs. Think it was fake. Did I even say it right? Probably just gibbering shit.

'Moon.' He calls.

Take a look behind me. Moon's looking at us with half shut eyes. Now he's gradually pulling himself to his feet. Takes a little while. Staggers over to us.

I know I'm still fucked, still tripping out me nut and that, but at least I'm almost back on planet Earth after that last blank out. Don't really wanna know what happened yet. I'll save it for the talk around dinner tomorrow.

'Come on we've got a bit of a walk ahead, if we start now I might be able to get us back by tomorrow night.' Leg goes...

Apparently Leg took his other two pills in the club. Tried to get to me and Moon's level, but they didn't hit him as hard. That's the way it goes sometimes, the luck of the draw. He's still fucked, but more dazed and tired. It's lucky, imagine the three of us like it. I mean how the fuck would we have got back? On the way home me and Moon get the giggles and piss ourselves at everything standing. The distorted figures of people. When they speak they sound like mice squeaking. Leg has the mission of getting us back to the hotel safely.

What a way to kick off our first holiday together...

Didn't get much sleep last night and when I did my dreams just woke me straight up again. Kept drifting off to unconsciousness. Felt as though I was flying through the air, above the world, above the trees, being carried along with the wind. Then BAM an aeroplane or some shit'd hit me and I'd be wide awake, heart beating like a fucking drum.

By the sounds of it I think Moon and Littl' Leg had pretty sleepless nights too. I don't remember getting back from the club, but I'll be surprised if we didn't have a reefer to knock us out. So why weren't I out cold? Probably those fucking pills, must have had all sorts in 'em.

Can hear Littl' Leg roaming around. It's fucking unbelievably hot. Rowdy people outside tells me the life ain't gone out of Ibiza like it has with me. It's those fucking wanker reps trying to organise pool games or something. I've only been properly abroad for one day in my life and already I can't stand 'em. They should just fucking leave it well alone, the cunts. This place would be shit hot if it weren't for fucking reps.

Me head feels like a bitch, desperately need some water. As I get up I glance over to Moon who's looking up at me all wounded puppy like.

'Water?' I ask. He nods, can tell he's not ready to speak yet. We've kicked off our holiday fucking big style. I vow to stay away from the E's for a couple of nights now. Honest.

It's then that I remember them telling me about Beeke and how he got left behind. About the only fucking bit I do recall. Gotta go and check on the situation next door before I can settle.

I walk in their room and Sloo's the only one who's moving. He's making tea in the kitchen area of their room. I call it a kitchen area, but it's just a fucking hob and a sink. Poesy place.

I check the beds. Beeke's there, he looks in the same state as Moon, he forces a smile. Everyone's condition here makes me feel proud of meself. I did more drugs yet still look the best the next day. Apart from Sloo that is, but I doubt he did four pills. Tin Lid's still fast asleep and already looks white, I dread to think how he's gonna feel when he wakes up. Maybe he's already awake, but hasn't plucked up the courage to open his eyes yet. It's only Brooke who's missing.

'Tea Craney?' Sloo asks.

'Love one geez. Where's Brooke?'

'Guess.'

'Fucking 'ell, 'e ain't shagging already is 'e?'

'Yep.'

'Lucky Bastard! What's she like?'

'She was alright.' With Sloo answering this question you never know what the truth is. He says every girl any of us has pulled's "alright" or "minging". None of 'em are ever stunners, even though Brooke's had some right shags.

''ow are you Beeke?' I ask turning my attention to the wreck tangled up in his bedclothes.

'Fucked mate.'

'Good, good. 'as anyone got the time?'

Sloo looks at his watch.

'Just gone two.'

'Oh fucking 'ell, I wanted to go out and get tanned.' Says Beeke leaning up in his bed.

We hear a murmur of disapproval coming from Tin lid, obviously now awake and not appreciating the noise around him. At this point Brooke enters the room behind me. Sporting a cheesy grin and despite being out all night still looks as smart as he did when he went out.

'Lads.'

'You spawny git! Who was she?'

'The bird at the bar.'

'Her? Sloo why didn't you tell me it was 'er?"

'Thought I'd leave it to Brooke, 'cause I'm sure we're gonna 'ear enough about it today.'

Sloo shrugs sounding less bothered with Brooke's exploits than he is jealous.

Sloo's a virgin, when anyone begins to talk about sexual experiences he tends to shy away. Beeke ain't done a bird either, but at least he still congratulates Brooke as the God lies down. Our own Essex Hugh Hefner. Arms behind his head, laid outstretched, tapping one of his feet side to side. The manner of a geezer with every reason to be totally chuffed with himself.

Suddenly Tin Lid struggles up out of bed then staggers to the bathroom closing the door behind him. We're all laughing as we hear the unmistakable sound of retching and heaving and splashing of puke.

'You better clean that up afterwards.' Warns Sloo as we continue to giggle.

Despite the heat I'm starting to feel a bit better. Me heart's beating like a maniac cunt though, but I'm beginning to look forward to hitting the bar and steadying it with an intake of alcohol.

It's not long before Littl' Leg and the slightly more refreshed looking Moon joins us.

'Where the fuck's my water you cunt?' Moon complains at me. Before I can answer the bog door unlocks. Everyone's in time to witness the emergence of Tin lid. The look of hurt in his eyes and the green shade of his cheeks shows us he's really struggling here. There are tears coming from his eyes and everything. You can tell his focus is all out of sync as well. He's standing there one hand clasping his head.

'Come on lads, let's hit the bar.' He bleats before collapsing on his bed. With this The Styx are fucking pissing 'emselves.

Fuck me, this is gonna be some holiday...

* * * *

Me, Lid, Moon, Crane and Leg all staggering out the pub at closing. West Ham done Man City 2-1. Etherington scored first too, so Leg's bet came through and he paid for most of the post match beers.

Tin Lid's having serious trouble speaking. The same goes for Crane trying to walk.

This was fucking wicked. Just the six of us out drinking, all having a laugh together, watching the footy. Brooke left a bit early to go see Gemma, but he stayed for the best part of the day. Good lad that Brooke, he knows the score. I'm pissed off that he needs to see his bird and blow us out so much, but he's turned up today.

That was important.

But Beeke... that fucking useless queer ain't shown his face in a while. He's breaking the rules and good riddance.

I think it's time for him to go.

CHAPTER 7
SO WHAT HAPPENED TO BEEKE?

Slouching on the edge of my bed, head in hands. Tension between me and Sloo's become unbearable. Missing Easter weekend. Always massive, I was so looking forward to it.

Why the fuck did I have to tell everyone I was gay?

What was I thinking? That everyone was gonna except it and reach for me with open arms? I can't be that dumb, can I?

At first I thought it'd pass, even thought Sloo might accept it. Practically fantasised him coming to me and admitting his own homosexuality. What an idiot I must be. Sloo the hard man, the leader.

Leader, for Christ's sake. Everyone takes the piss behind his back, I know that. He thinks they need him to guide them through life as if he's some kind of father figure.

A general or some sort of overlord.

He'll still say hello at college and acknowledge my existence, I mean too much to him for total exclusion from his life. I am a member of his stupid beloved Styx after all. The rest of us have a laugh with it.

"What was we like when we were younger?" We'd say, all ironically like. It was just kid's stuff you grow out of. Sloo hasn't.

Our names have just stuck, I mean I don't go birdwatching anymore, I haven't done in God knows when. That's another thing, Moon he can crack a joke about it:

"You used to really like birds as well." Everyone, including myself laughed. Sloo didn't. Treats it as though I've let everyone down. As if

I chose to be this way to fuck up his stupid gang. The others couldn't give an arse about the gang no more. We're eighteen for Christ sake.

Sight's gone all blurry. Tears welling in my eyes.

All I want is Sloo back as a friend, that's all. I miss him. Remember all the chats and laughs we used to have together. Suppose I used to find his stubborn ways well funny. The way he hated being called Kevin and the pride he took in his creation of The Styx. How he always wanted to be our protector. At *Time* if any people got pissed off with Moon, Crane or Littl' Leg being off their faces on drugs, acting all stupid, Sloo'd be there. Hanging round like their minder. Or if Brooke pulled a girl that some other bloke was after then Sloo'd be there. If Tin Lid fell into someone or spilled their pint, Sloo stood by him. It was as though he looked over us, our guardian. I respected that he loved us all, we were like a family, now I don't feel part of that anymore. I've stepped outside the circle, broken the rules.

Without him… somehow I don't feel safe any more.

Had to tell everyone I was ill, well everyone except Sloo. Unsurprisingly, he hasn't bothered to phone me.

They all know I'm lying. Ill for Christ sake. Wish I was ill. Ill enough to die and get off this fucking planet.

What happened? Why am I gay? Or at least why did I say anything about it? I've done wrong in that. I saw all these outed gays on TV, like George Michael and Will Young, saying how much better they felt after admitting it. So why don't I? Why do I still feel like shit? Been like this since Ibiza. It's nagged at me ever since that first night. Kept it to myself for long enough. It ate away at my stomach, destroying me, making me feel constantly sick. Now I've let it out I feel even worse

Feel like just fucking off somewhere. Getting away from this piss hole.

BANG

Fucking hell, that third pill's hit me hard. This is 'DJ Sammy' for Christ's sake and I'm dancing to it like some kind of nut case. Just can't stop myself from moving.

Neither can this bloke I've noticed moving nearer and nearer to me. Not that I mind, he's gorgeous. Reminds me of Sloo, faint goatee beard and the same sort of tidy short brown hair. Yet he's the more bronzed and slightly slimmer version. He keeps glimpsing over and smiling at me. Didn't realise how camp I must appear for him to think he could pull me. What with the pills though, gotta remember he could be mashing himself and is in that over-friendly mood. It's taking me a while to work out, but I'm pretty sure he's not with anyone.

Oh my God I really want him to come over, it would be perfect. Here in Ibiza I don't feel scared anymore. All the confusion and heartache I've been suffering these last two years trying to deny it, it's all disintegrating away. The girls I forced myself to snog in the hope of making myself straight seems stupid, why don't I just fucking admit it? I'm gay for Christ sake. I find the company of Sloo more arousing than any bird I've ever met.

BANG.

He finally came over to me and introduced himself as Ricky. Now he's offered to get me a drink, so I walk over to the bar with him and discover Moon and Littl' Leg balanced up against it, both looking well out of it. I introduce them, but they don't seem too concerned that I'm with this stranger, they've got their eyes on these two girls sitting in the corner. I know they're too wasted to get anywhere, but that ecstasy confidence must be obliterating their own doubt.

Before long Crane returns from somewhere even he don't remember. Looks well worse for wear. Moon and Leg decide against going for the kill. Three blokes trying to pull two girls is gonna be unfair on one of 'em. So like the good mates they are, they give up the ghost and go staggering off with Crane in search of a group of three.

This leaves me alone with Ricky and after he gets two tequila cocktails we spot a free table. We go over and sit down opposite each other and soon become engrossed in conversation.

Turns out he's on the little chaps 'an all, so isn't turned off by my gurning and excessive nature, despite his confident control over his own. I find out almost everything about him over the next hour or so.

Time is lost here...

My mind's completely blown by this gorgeous man. Find myself almost ignoring the rest of the lads, who after about every five minutes come to say they're leaving soon.

Not even the presence of Sloo puts me off, well maybe it does a bit, but the pills and I've already decided. This is the night I wanna lose my virginity. I just want the rest of 'em to go now and leave me to it, but they've already lost Brooke and what with Moon, Leg and Crane totally out of their boxes, Sloo's keen on me coming along. At any other time I would go immediately on his request, but I know he's still got Tin Lid with him, even though that boy looks like he's only got a few beers left in him. I know that nothing will happen between me and Sloo in the next five years, let alone this holiday and my hormones are firing.

Keep telling the boys I'm alright, but can hardly stand after all that dancing. Takes a hell of a lot of convincing, but eventually they believe I'll be o.k. here and that I'll meet them in Kaos later. The clincher was saying me and Ricky had noticed a couple of birds giving us the eye, so we were staying to go on the pull right here.

A half truth, they definitely don't need to know we've already pulled each other.

So Sloo reluctantly leads the others from Kings onto the next bar. His annoyance at me staying here gives me a hopeful notion, maybe he's jealous. This kind of turns me on and now I'm finally left alone with Ricky this feeling heightens. Wanna grab and snog him right here, but figure this could be a little dangerous. Some don't take too kindly to this sort of behaviour. Even in Ibiza? Fuck knows, not worth taking the chance.

Decide I'm gonna invite Ricky back to the hotel. The others wouldn't get back for hours and I reckon we could maybe have sex then get back out again. Whilst I'm thinking of a way to slip this into the conversation he says:

'Listen I've got a room to myself just round the corner, I think there's a couple of beers in the fridge, if you want we could go back there. I'm pretty fucked and I don't think I can put up with this music much longer.'

I agree to this, having had enough of the typically tacky holiday music which has now turned to *S Club 7*. We finish our drinks and leave Kings. On the way back to his hotel I find out that although he does have his own room, he came to Ibiza with his older sister and her friend, who are apparently out on the "last night pull". He has little doubt they'll succeed and not return 'til morning. We also bring up my friends. He's trying to politely pry into whether there's anything between me and Sloo, without making it too obvious of his own intentions, or his suspicion of mine.

I find this great, he suspects something of me and Sloo!

'He seemed very concerned about you.' He tells me.

'He's just a very good friend.'

We turn down a street taking us further away from the thumping beats of the island's main square. The E is sending a buzz down my spine forcing me to appreciate my surroundings. We're walking along a cobbled road and it's funny, I feel like we've gone back in *time*. Scattered houses and small hotels in amongst strangely peaceful wastelands and the white of these old buildings makes them stand out in the black of the night. It's mysterious but seems so familiar, like I know what it's like to live in such a town. It's a beautiful place, I'm with a beautiful man.

'Listen David... There's something I have to say...' Ricky breaks my reminisces and as soon as he speaks I know the time has come. My nerve begins to break, my heart speeds up an ear-worm rhythm in my head, causing my whole body to shake. Could this be the turning point in my life? Where I finally release the feelings that before I have bottled, for fear of my society's reaction?

'...This is my last night here...' A distortion in his voice disclosing his own fear at the situation helps me settle.

I'm beginning to think of Ricky as a Godsend. I could get away with this, it's just a one night stand. There would be no complications of meeting him later on in the holiday and getting caught out by Sloo or anyone. Then I could spend the rest of the holiday concentrating on drugs and booze and have this massive weight taken off my shoulders. This is gonna be my deciphering moment, it'll confirm the sex with which my true feelings lie.

'...it's all right...' Dunno if it's the pill or what, but suddenly I'm the one in control. I wrap my arm round his waist. '... I know.'

We walk and talk for about 5 minutes more, feeling extremely relieved that everything's out in the open, before arriving at his apartment. He lets me through the door and at first sight I'm fucking glad I didn't take him back to the *Hotel Samfora*, to share my single bed with twenty ants.

'We only got the holiday a few days before we came out. How lucky are we? This is a cancellation, apparently. A family had booked it.' He tells me.

The first room I have walked into is a living room for god's sake. It's got sofas, a coffee table, it's even decorated with pretty pictures. My god, we booked ours a year in advance, this is an absolute joke. I now start to wish he was staying longer and I could spend my two weeks living here. The front room is not all. There's a separate section for the kitchen which includes a fucking breakfast bar. Plus the last thing I expect to find is stairs, but, there they are!

'They lead up to the three bed rooms...' He goes before winking and saying 'Mine's the one with the double bed...'

Despite my obvious interest, I'm thinking not just yet and my reaction suggests I really do need another beer before we make the ascent. I need to curb the power of these E's or fuck knows what I'll only nearly manage up there.

Ricky as if reading my mind walks in to the kitchen and grabs two cans of Fosters from the fridge while telling me to 'take a seat'.

'Fosters ok?'

'Perfect.'

He throws the can to me before reaching into his pocket and taking out a small wrap.

'Not quite.' He laughs waving the small package at me. I laugh too, suddenly realising that this must be heaven. Here's this man I've met on my first night, supplying me alcohol and cocaine in his, compared to our hotel, mansion.

Got this feeling he knows I'm a virgin, so he's trying extra careful to be sensitive.

Haven't had coke for a while, being a student means the drug is a bit of a luxury designed for birthday celebrations.

Ricky puts on some old dance anthem that I remember as a kid. *Stretch and Vern*, I think:

'I'm alive, the man with the second face and I'm ready yo, to rock this place.' Then settles beside me to prepare two lines of Charlie on the coffee table. I listen intently and knock back my beer as he tells me about his recent split from a long term boyfriend back home. How he came to Ibiza to get away from the situation for a while.

I know the time can't be far off now and once again my body starts to tremble. Ricky is very comforting, but no one can be prepared for a moment like this, gay or straight. Just hope the coke can restore my confidence in this decision I'm making.

Ricky hands me a Euro note and asks me to take my pick. Both are huge so I don't look for the largest. I take the one nearest me and it goes up sweetly. Continue to sniff whilst closing the other nostril to make sure it hits me quickly. The drugs I've already had were only for the headstrong. Never had pills like 'em. Let's hope this coke will be as potent. Brooke told me that sex was fantastic on pills, he said he shagged some girl for three hours once without coming. I'm not sure that'll be good with my predicament, three hours in the arse has gotta be painful. Don't know how this whole thing works.

My earlier panic subsides and my balls are really tingling. As Ricky finishes off his line I draw closer to him. We both have a final gulp of beer and place the cans down.

We're looking into each other's eyes and I notice how bright and green his are. They're almost hypnotic, I'm being pulled in by them nearer and nearer till our lips finally touch. Put my arms around him. As our tongues meet I feel the hair round his mouth brushing up against my chin. This is weird. I have only kissed six girls before, but already know I prefer this. We begin to clutch each other tighter as the rising love effect of the pills takes full hold

Ricky knows what he's doing and soon starts to move his hand down to my groin. He rubs at it, causing the numbness around the area to evaporate and I start getting hard. He feels this and automatically moves up to my belt to release my dick. First the belt goes, then the buttons start to come undone. His kiss with mine becomes harder with the passion flowing through us. He soon has all the buttons open and he slides his hand into my boxers. His hand is cold and I shudder slightly, but soon feel the warmth as he starts to tug softly at me.

My thoughts jump to a Jerry Springer show I once saw. He interviewed several gay people who all argued that the best sexual pleasure for anyone would come from a partner of the same sex. They would have far better knowledge in what the other person likes, having had plenty of practice on themselves. At this moment I agree. Ricky's pulling smoothly and at times pushes his hand down further to give my balls a slight rub.

I want him to go down on me, so I lift my head up for him to kiss my neck. He responds and is soon lifting up my shirt. I take it off for him to lick round my chest, then stomach. Lower,

Lower HIGHER This is Ecstasy
Lower I have waited my whole life
Higher for this and now as it happens
nothing seems real. I'm
floating in the
Higher clouds wanting to scream to the sky that
I've finally arrived. This has got to be the
drugs as well, surely no feeling can be this good.
My God, fucking hell, fucking hell, fucking hell!

I look down at the back of Ricky's head bobbing up and down. The sight amuses me, he's sucking my cock. The first time anyone has ever done it and it's fucking brilliant. Gotta calm down here. This has got to go all the way. Don't wanna come down his throat then get all scared and bottle out of this.

I stroke his hair, and he gets the message, he rises back up and we're kissing again. He pulls away.

'I think we're ready to go up now, don't you?' He laughs.

Our passions have been rising like fuck, this small break gives me reason to laugh with him and hold him.

'I'm ready.'

'Do you want to take another pill with me? I've got some poppers as well. I know this is your first time and I want you to really enjoy this.'

'Is the pope queer?'

BANG

The smell of Amyl lifts me up to the sky once more, each sniff is like a mini ecstasy rush. Keeps you at the top for how long you want to be there. With this pill I want to be here for ever. My god. This is ... What... yes THE *TIME* IS NOW.

'What the song?'

'What's that love?

Ricky looks up at me, my God he's sucking me off again. This is a different room, we're on a bed.

'Nothing that pill's really fucking hit me.' pffff

'That's good, are you losing yourself in the moment?'

'Am I baby? Am I? I'm so there. WOOOO' I lay back and feel my head fall straight through the mattress for a search of below...

'I think it's *time.*'

Was that Ricky that just said that?

BANG

Holy fuck. My mind's just been in a state of fucking disarray. I dunno, Lakes and Logs,,, maybe. Now I'm actually fucking someone. Ricky is out in front of me. Naked and on all fours. Like a dog, he he heh he heee

I'm fucking someone. It's going in ok. Is it going in? Fucking hell I don't know how I got here, BUT IT'S THE PLACE TO BE.....mAN hEREEEEE WWE ALLL GO AGAIN...

BANG

yeaaah I'm biting the headboard, actually fucking biting the headboard. I was worried this would hurt, this is not painful at all. Ricky puts the poppers under my nose....wwwwweeeeeeee.

BANG

As I look back at Ricky his face twitches and shakes as if he's having a fit. I can almost make him look like Sloo.

Fuck, IT IS SLOO.

Shit this room's fucked up. I can't make him out. HE'S COME UP MY ARSE.

BANG

Sloo stands in his room, drunk after the hefty session in the Bridge House. He has taken out The Styx commandments from inside a children's book *'Professor Brainstorm up the pole'*, hidden under a loose floorboard. It was his favourite read as a child, since then it has become the wallet for the safe future of his friends. Felt it made sense to keep the commandments in what was his own bible at the time they were made. To Sloo the commandments were sacred and had been kept for these last ten years in perfect condition.

He reads the bottom of the page.

SLOO'S WORD IS FINAL.

The others had agreed to this in the camp. So he had the power to change one commandment to:

No member of The Styx is allowed to be homosexual, by punishment of death.

BANG

I'm coming back round again. Still hard, Ricky's sucking me off. Think I've just been to heaven and back. It's been one fucked up trip I'll probably not remember a lot about tomorrow. Only that it's been good. Fucking good. Oh yes that's it. Fucking god good.

'uhh, fuck, uhh.' I'm coming.

BANG

Sloo takes a pen from his bedside cabinet and studies all the commandments. No can't change No. 1: **No one can put girls above The Styx,** that would mean Brooke could blow them out for Gemma all the time. Would not be having that.

No. 2: **No one can fight with another member of The Styx,** no, he knows they must all be loyal to each other in this time of crisis and it would affect

No. 3: **The Styx must stick together.**

No. 4: **The Camp must remain a secret.** This is a possibility. It's hardly as if people wouldn't have stumbled across it. No it could be important. Wait.

No. 5: **The Styx must return regularly to the Camp.** Now that can definitely go for now, they stopped doing that when they were about twelve. Well at least all the others grew tired of it, for the need to play constant football. Sloo however, kept check on the headquarters ever since. The old rug was still there and so were a couple of the posters. Despite the rotting and yellowing he kept them safe there, they reminded him of that day nearly ten years ago.

Sloo takes his pen and draws a line right through commandment No. 5 and in the space underneath it, writes:

Alteration; 5. **No member of The Styx is allowed to be homosexual, by punishment of death.**

BANG

It's after half five. I walk across the beach in the glorious morning sunshine of Ibiza. Completely dazed by my experience, but also unbelievably happy. I hold in my hand a piece of paper with Ricky's name and address on it. I read it over and over, doubting that I'll ever write. He'll probably get back together with his boyfriend. This was a holiday romance after all, but at least the option's there, and I've fucking done it. I can't believe I've finally done it. I wish I could tell my mates the truth, but I'll just have to head back now and turn Ricky into Vicky or something. What a night, what a fucking night.

BANG

Since the night of his coming out, no one had asked Beeke if it was Ricky that he'd spent the first night in Ibiza with. He presumed they'd all guessed and supposed they didn't really want to know either.

Even though most have accepted his queerness and had been very supportive, he was sure they were not in full approval. Before his admittance, when The Styx phoned him and he said he wasn't going out that night, they would badger him until he said otherwise. Yet today's outing to watch the football was different. When Beeke had said he didn't feel like going, both Moon and Littl' Leg had said "fair enough" and "I'll probably see you in the week then yeah?" Beeke continues to cry. He feels like the outcast of the group and decides maybe he should get away for a while.

His parents had split when he was four. Beeke was their third child. The hope was for a baby to bring them close again, but it only drove them further apart. Eventually his father got a job in Cheshire and moved away leaving Beeke with his mother and two sisters. The absent parent still remained in contact and regularly sent money, so the boy never hated his father for leaving. Beeke often paid visits up north to see him and feels it could be time to do so again, maybe next weekend.

That was it. He'd tell his Mum tomorrow and arrange it with his Dad as soon as possible.

* * * *

Outside, for the third night in a row, a storm begins.

The branches of trees shake with the gale of laughter swirling about the air.

The deal had been done and due to Sloo's intervention a commandment broken.

As Sloo puts them back in their safe place, he begins to consider what he has done. His conscience comes alive and a feeling of guilt stirs his stomach causing a sickening realisation of what his actions mean. Beeke has not broken any of the previous seven commandments and should have been forewarned about any changes that are made. That way he could have changed his ways and saved himself.

Then another voice enters Sloo's head.

'It's too late now Sloo. It is done, the commandments have been altered and the punishment has to be laid down.'

Sloo doesn't know where this evil tongue arises from, or when the messages started to plague his thoughts. He begins to tremble, wants it all to stop and remembers how things used to be. All the good times and talks he used to have with his best friend Beeke. Now feels responsible for his absence today. That's not what The Styx was about, they would stick together through anything. Sloo always made sure of that, now he's breaking them apart. He lies down and begins to wonder whether he should throw the commandments away. Start afresh, ignore the voices. He spends some time crying, before the lack of sleep over the weekend forces him to drift... ....

....

..........Drifting away, over the fields into the sky. Past the manor, into the trees. The air is thick and consuming. Soon he will arrive at the place where that thing always lies...

Sloo wakes an hour later.

Once again he experiences the slimy mess spreading over his stomach and dampening his boxer shorts.

'That's it. I'm gonna kill that queer faggot cunt.'

No. 5 No. 5 NO. 5 NO. 5 NUMBER FIVE.

The deal is done.

CHAPTER 8
THE APPOINTMENT

The Easter weekend is over.

The Tuesday they were dreading had arrived. Littl' Leg, Moon and Brooke all returned to work ill-rested from their four day break. Faded chances to repair four day sleep deprivation. So *time* will drag endlessly, other people will grow increasingly frustrating. Their jobs will seem pointless as midweek comedown kicks into gear.

Far better for the students of the group as each can lie in to recharge batteries. But their A levels still loom, like the dark clouds constantly filling their skies.

Tin Lid and Crane had been at Sloo's house for a matter of minutes when their History A level revision had turned into a conversation regarding the coming Thursday. The pair were feeling down after four days of drugs and debauchery, making trying to memorise the life of Charles the 1st extremely difficult. The determination they cling to in fulfilling their task is by knowing there's just seventy-two hours 'til the festivities restart. Three days back in reality however, when that last escape has been so magical, can seem arduous, somewhat painstaking.

Crane has been especially low, wanting away from the boring existence he feels his sober days have become. Whilst Tin Lid, despite waking this morning with a tremendous hangover, was using valuable revision time daydreaming about a chilled pint of Stella. Feelings of drowsiness and headaches and sickness and forgetfulness had worn off, he feels uncomfortably normal again.

Sloo is only experiencing the effects of a restless night. Woke several times through the disturbing nightmares that interrupted any replenishment sleep could have given. Wishing he'd drunk sufficiently to knock him out cold. Yet even so, he doubted whether the bad dreams would have ceased. Was told to stay in control, but now uncertain of that possibility. How could he fulfill his tasks whilst so exhausted?

'What we gonna do then?' Asks Tin Lid.

'What else but *Time*.' Answers Crane.

'Yeah that's cool, as long as everyone turns up this week.' Tin Lid designs this remark for Sloo, who realises he has been roped into the conversation and must end his fantasy about slicing a gaping gash through Beeke's throat.

'I can assure you that everyone will be there this week.'

'What even Beeke?'

'Especially Beeke, we ain't seen him for ages, 'e should be over 'is illness by now.'

'So you alright with 'im now then?' Asks Crane a little tentatively, he has noticed the tension between the two good friends since...

'Course, I was just a bit shocked that's all. I'll give 'im a call tonight, see if 'e's any better.' Sloo smiles. This cheers the other two, they are desperate to get everyone out again. Return to the classic nights.

'So it'll be round mine again?' Crane is already considering phoning Littl' Leg tonight to make sure drugs are available for the big reunion. Always has been, but Crane dreads that one time... Doesn't even like to contemplate it.

'Yeah, and this time I'm gonna whip ya at FIFA and that.' Claims Tin Lid.

'We'll see, Liddy, we'll see...' Laughs Crane '...Fuck it I can't wait already, d'ya reckon Wendy's gonna be there eh, Liddy boy?'

'Piss off Stevo you can tell she wanted me last week.'

'Crane.' Sloo butts in.

'Yeah?'

'No I was jus' saying, he just called you Steve and I corrected him.'

'Hmmm.' Crane and Tin Lid display confused expressions to one another. Tin Lid mouths the words 'What the fuck?' to Crane thinking Sloo doesn't see. The boy was mistaken. Sloo now understands that Tin Lid must be put in line.

'Well if you didn't get so smashed every week that might be true.' Crane continues with the original conversation.

'No I've got 'er geez. She'll be mine this weekend, oh yes, and your record will be safe.'

Crane giggles at the thought of the five week running knock-back he received from Claire Delaney.

'You've equalled it now geez, your name's going down in 'istory as well you know.'

'Yeah, but at least I'm gonna pull 'er at the end of it.'

'Yeah stroll on Tin Lid, stroll on...' Crane says before turning his attention towards Sloo.

'...You got your eyes on anyone at college geez?'

'Nah mate, they're all dogs in my classes.'

'What about that Lorraine bird in our 'istory class? She's alright.'

'Fuck off, she's a whore!' Says Sloo a little aggressively.

'Crane'd know all about that wouldn't ya geez?' Tin Lid defuses a potential argument.

'Well I ain't seen 'er advertised yet, but if she was in *The Romford Recorder* I'd 'ave 'er round straight away. Give her a right dam good fucking.' Crane gets up and begins imitating intercourse, adding noises for effect.

'Nah she's not all that.' Still Sloo refuses to admit any affection for a female.

'Can't understand you Sloo, there's gotta be someone out there for ya?' Crane says sitting back down, already out of breath through his exertions.

'Nah I can't be arsed with women, look at the state you two get yourselves in, and Brooke 'e's practically married as it is...' Answers Sloo, then under his breath finishes '...and I have loyalty to the commandments.'

'What?' Asks a bemused Crane.

'Nothing.'

Crane had noticed Sloo talking to himself more and more recently, but regards him as eccentric anyway, so ignores his friend's strange behaviour.

'Come on then Crane, who you after?' Asks Tin Lid.

'I dunno, there's that Vicky bird in my Business Studies class, she seems interested.' Crane seeks to distract attention away from this moment's real desire.

'I 'eard she was a right slag.' Sloo interrupts, hoping to turn Crane off any girl he may mention.

'Yeah I know. She is...' Retorts Crane "....that's the point I ain't 'ad a free shag in ages; and never a sober one.'

'What about that Tina?' Tin Lid introduces the girl Crane does have a soft spot for. The crush hadn't been admitted to the others yet for fear of ridicule if rejection is received.

'I don't know what you mean.' Smiles Crane. Finding it difficult to disguise his feelings.

'You've been 'anging round with 'er quite a bit at college recently. Even sitting next to 'er now ain't ya?'

Tina was in Crane's Sociology class. They had met at the start of term in January as she had moved to Essex only recently. It was true Crane sat next to her when she joined. He originally sat alone at the back. Didn't really communicate with anyone else there, due to his distant nature, longing to be elsewhere. Yet she took the empty seat next to him on her first day, and they found themselves gelling instantly.

The only problem being: she didn't frequent nightclubs. So despite his promotion, Crane hadn't managed to persuade her to visit *Time* on a Thursday. This would be his main stage, here he would feel confident enough to try for a kiss. Well maybe, dependent on the amount and type of drugs he is on. The eighteen year old didn't normally find himself fantasising about her type before. Went for blondes usually, yet she had a healthy combination of blonde, brown and red hair. These variants made her look intriguingly different at each viewing. He likened her to a teddy bear. Eyes big and brown and she would occasionally fall into a stare that invoked a strong desire within Crane to cuddle her. Her body was perfect, went to the gym four times a week and obviously liked to tan too. With all this going for her, Crane couldn't comprehend her tremendously friendly personality. Most of the good looking girls at the college were arrogant. Not interested to even look at a "druggie" like himself. Yet here he'd found someone even more beautiful than them, who he could gladly settle down with.

She'd left him a chance too. Before they broke up for Easter, Tina had given Crane her phone number in case he was stuck with his revision and needed a hand. He wouldn't believe it meant any more than just that though, not with someone as gorgeous as her.

Though now slips into a fantasy whereby he phones her, takes her on a date and ends up kissing her on her sweet little mou...

'She ain't all that.' Sloo says destroying Crane's mini daydream. Crane has grown bored with his argument: "well at least I can pull" so decides on:

'Yeah, you're probably right.' His confidence is low and wants to appear nonchalant. This will hopefully counteract the knock-back he expects to receive if he does ask her out. The others won't find the jibing nearly as much fun.

'Nah I think you should go for it geez, she's well nice.'

Crane deep down completely agrees with Tin lid, but continues to portray a laddish image.

'Well I'll probably see if I can get 'er down *Time* soon, if she shows any interest I might go for it.'

Knows full well he'll desperately try to encourage her when they go back to college, then imagine how he'd make his move.

Even considering phoning her tomorrow. Already got the excuse, "I need help with me study."

Sloo grins at Crane's words, truly proud at the lack of concern his friend's words display. The boy usually the first to fall in love, even if he hasn't received any similar indication from a girl.

Well done Crane, Sloo thinks, a true Styx member. Beeke however...

* * * *

Later that evening, several hours following Tin Lid and Crane's bored exit, Sloo is trying to fix his calculator. Doesn't have the first idea how, but had successfully taken out the screws and is now studying the different bits scattered about the carpet. The frustration increases, he needed to concentrate on something else before he did any damage. Still holding the screwdriver he decides it's time to phone Beeke.

'Hello.' Beeke reluctantly answers, *Eastenders* had been interrupted. The programme had provided an escape from his depression by concentrating on "*Sonia*" and her own misery.

'Beeke, how ya feeling?' Asks Sloo stabbing the sharpened flathead into a cork wall. He twists the handle, imagining he's dislodging Beeke's brain. A wry smirk.

Beeke, his stomach churns, almost sick. The last thing he was expecting was a phone call from Sloo. Now he doesn't know what to...

'Yeah not bad thanks, I'm feeling a bit b- b - better cheers.' He stammers.

Sloo enjoys hearing the tint of fear reflected in the voice. Beeke knows who's in control of The Styx. Twinges of guilt resurface, regrets having to kill him, but a rule's a rule. You must never break them. But Beeke wasn't told. Not important, the nightly visitation has ordered action. Sloo was in the right.

A Pause in conversation concerns Beeke.

'Excellent, we was talking about you on the way 'ome.'

'Who was?' Trepidation enters, this may be a threatening phone call. Yet soon calms with Sloo's answer.

'Me, Crane and Lid, we was talking 'bout Thursday and wanted to make sure we got everyone down *Time* this week, we ain't all been out together for ages. I was making sure you was gonna get yourself fit again.' Sloo continues to sneer. The screwdriver enters Beeke's eye, then gouges it from the socket

'Err yeah...'

Beeke still suffers with shock. Utter disbelief that this conversation is even happening. For the past fortnight Sloo hadn't managed more than one word in their meetings. Beeke was starting to beam. His life, with one phone call, was reverting into place. Revision now viable, he could still pass his A levels yet. At one point today he even considered never returning to college, just get a job and never have to see his friends again. Count his losses, get away from his life with The Styx. Not anymore though. Although he'd told his mother, maybe now he won't have to bother making his planned trip at the weekend. It seemed he wouldn't have to do this at all. '...I'll reckon I'll be able to make it.'

'That's cool, so you definitely in for Crane's before 'and, we agreed earlier we'd start there.'

'Yeah definitely, we'll 'ave a big night out.' Beeke's expression showed returning confidence.

'Oh yes, it's gonna be huge.' Sloo's smile grows more mischievous with every sentence.

Everything is going according to plan.

The conversation continued with the discussion of revision and the events of last weekend. It was like old times, the two of them talking like best friends, only this time Beeke didn't really know who he was talking to. The topics were the same, but Sloo totally different. His intentions have changed.

'See ya.'

'Bye.' Beeke hangs up with a yelp and punches the air.

Meanwhile Sloo falls to his knees and bursts out with laughter.

A darkness hanging over his world. He feels power over the obscurity, believes he has control over the situation. Yet the shadows are streaming in now. They start to take over his surroundings. They are all around. The storms are getting worse...

Rattling winds. The figure strolls through the trees. Beginning to pace. Waiting to take over. Then the blood will flow.

Take a fucking bow Sloo. The show is about to begin.

Take that dirty traitor's head off. Push your fist into the severed neck. Rip out his heart. Devour, taste. Feels good doesn't it. Addiction, more blood. Need the flesh. Remove the brain. Eat it. Dark red rivers. Black skies. No stars tonight, just the eyes of the dead. Coming back across the river. No longer innocent souls. Here for chaos amongst the storms. You will not see them, but they are there. Behind every corner. Waiting for revenge. Time to pay. Slice the pupils. Watch the nerves jolt. Splutter blood. Choking, severed windpipes. The real rain is coming. Wash away the earth.

Then we can start again...

* * * *

'Leg?'

'Alright geez?'

'Yeah not bad man, just wanted to make sure you don't forget to call The Geez about the drugs for Thursday.'

'Jesus Crane, every fucking Tuesday, 'ow many times 'ave I forgot?'

'Never and that's exactly why I do it.'

'Good point. Shall I get the usual then?'

'You know it.'

'Cool I'll give 'im a call now then and I'll give you a buzz tomorrow.'

'Nice one Leg.'

'Later on man.'

* * * *

The early hours of Wednesday morning throws up another treacherous storm.

Sloo is tossing and turning in his bed.

Once again a man steps forward. Appearing before Sloo in a dense forest. Gale force wind and heavy rain tries to batter through the trees. Yet the branches and leaves only allow droplets of red to enter. They run thick down Sloo's cheek. He stares at the apparition with intense interest.

'They didn't listen to me either Sloo, any of them. I had to kill them one by one. After all I done for them. I would have protected them for eternity...' The man stands tall, draped in a long black cloak. A first for Sloo to ever see his face. Warm, comforting look of a clean shaven man. Smooth untarnished skin. A texture revealing innocence, yet there is far more wisdom within his eyes than the youthful appearance suggests. He sports a laurel of twigs and leaves securing his long brown hair from the strong gale.

Although he had never seen his visitor's features through the cloak before, this was the image Sloo's mind had created. Friendly, sincere, yet a hint of menace. A person demanding respect. Sloo has always gained solace from his words. The dreams had never been forgotten. Waking after each one feeling strong, rejuvenated for his task of leading The Styx. They began when he was eight. Would always remember the man's verbal pride. Praise never experienced by the child. To the young boy, the figure replaced the father that left him and his mother the previous year. Sloo hung on every word he uttered.

Before, the apparition would only appear a few times each year. Yet the last couple of weeks had seen frequent visits. There is a crisis. The man is here to advise the approaching necessity for Sloo to destroy the outcast. Only then can he return The Styx to the Camp for salvation from the storms.

Beeke is the crisis.

'*...It was the same as a man in my charge. His actions threatened to destroy all I had built. He lost sight of who I was. Didn't recognise the saviour. Ignored the second coming. Yes I was a friend and a mentor. My task was their comfort and safety. I am here to save humankind. To begin I must take the pure to the forest. There we shall build a new home with protection against the Lord's destruction through nature. Your camp is one base. From forest to forest I've set up similar communes. There will be the purest of survivors throughout the land, then we can return back to my day. Back to basics. Extinguishing suffering on earth. The eradication of the unjustness of society. We will roam free and eternal. All the choices will be ours. We will gain the power of history. All events of the last thousand years will become our intelligence. A vast superiority unable to be surpassed.*

There are plans of Armageddon. I will save us, we can start again. You and I Sloo can be Gods of this abandoned earth.

Beech took it from me before. If he had not stepped out of line I would not have made an example of him. They have to follow the rules Sloo. To live for eternity is to remain pure. I slaughtered him in the camp at the witness of the rest. Show them what happens to the undisciplined. The new world cannot be built without morals.

One other rebelled though and woke my people from their bliss. I would not have harmed them, but my secrets need to be kept safe. Otherwise outsiders would flee to the forest for salvation against the storms. The very people we needed to wash the earth clean of.

We had to delay the apocalypse. My disciples didn't pass the test of integrity. They tried to run from me. Ha. Someone who could have rewarded them immortality. But no, they had to attempt escape from The Styx.

Murder was the only solution Sloo. Start again. But one got away, must have spread the word. Then they came for me. A lowly king leading an army ready to burn down my forests. Rightfully fearful of my power. Claiming I stole their workers, even though they were my protected disciples. It was their choice to stay with me in the forest.

They'd found Brooks and Mooning dead already. Little did they care about the men's lives, their problem was that they had lost slaves. Who would do their labour now? That was all they were to them Sloo, slaves. Yet they were still ready to burn down my home. There I slit my wrists in front of them and disappeared into the storms.

They don't understand they are only delaying the inevitable. Once they leave us to do this job we can stop this farce.

The cycle must end.

I cannot be destroyed, Gods are not susceptible to that. Now I'm here to resurrect my plans, and it's through you Sloo that it will happen.

It's almost time when you should lead your friends to the camp, this time it will work. I made the mistake of performing Beech's sacrifice before them, you must keep it discreet. Soon they'll understand the sacredness of the commandments, they will follow their leader. Once you have murdered Beeke I will take care of the rest. Remember they agreed to the rules. All for their benefit. The Styx will return to the camp. There you must obtain their vow to obey you. This will not be difficult once I have spoken to them. They will see sense. The commandments have been agreed. Now their agreement to honour you as their leader is all we need. Show them Sloo and we can rule again."

...A cold shiver. Leaves picked up into a twist. Shield your eyes Sloo. The man holds his hands to the sky. Lightning streams from his fingers. Then darkness. Gone. Alone. The blood flowing rapidly down Sloo's cheeks. Into a shower. Spread throughout the forest. Then the flow begins. Dams bursting. Crashing through the trees a river of blood. It flows once more. Sloo cannot feel it, he still protects his eyes. Doesn't see Brooks' body float past, face down. A deep slice at the back of his head. Mooning's dismembered arms wrapped around Little's lifeless legs.

He can hear the laughter though and the voices

'Listen to him. Soon they will understand and we can take over.'

Sloo promises to obey. He always did to his new surrogate father.

'I knew he couldn't be my real Dad. You I look up to, you I will obey. I'll help you Dad, together we'll be saved.'

The weakest follows...

Sloo wakes in the park, sat on a bench. He is fully clothed and drenched through. Rain has poured upon him for almost an hour.

Cannot remember falling asleep. Wonders if anyone has seen him as he sets off for the warmth of his home.

* * * *

Crane's heart pounds. The dream involved a forest. He was there eating human flesh, blood dripping from his chin. Shoots out of bed. The lights go on. Doesn't stop the terror.

* * * *

Beak likes his birds. Pretty creatures they can fly. He wanted to be like the bird and flee from the forest, away from The Styx. Maybe one day he'll be able to.

Not with a Stanley knife severing your head from your neck though Beeke, or Beech whatever your faggot fucking name is.

Sloo mumbles, gibbering as he walks through the dark dark red rain. He looks to the lightning filled skies and screams.

'WORSHIP THE KING.'

CHAPTER 9
T.I.N.A

Come on Crane just call her.

Sociology, the Wednesday before we broke up for Easter. That's when it really hit me. John Whiting was rambling his usual shite. But instead of staring into space, thinking drugs… drugs… drugs, I actually found myself listening. It was something to do with challenging Karl Marx's theories of religion. Marxism says it's the "opium of the masses" and keeps the working class in their place. With a belief there's a better place to go when we die, we'll all be content with our position on earth and don't know we're being exploited or nothing. So the upper classes won't suffer no revolt. That's all Marxism's ever seemed to say to me: We've no free will in society because we're controlled by a ruling class ideology or some bollocks.

Anyway, I got pretty fucking lost in the first year what with all the acid. Me brain don't hold up to much no more. As soon as I'm bored it cuts out and I'm dozing away in lectures. Learning about posh people's different views on stuff seems mindless compared with the work it goes through when I'm tripping off me nut. I suppose it needs drug stimulation all the time now, just to keep me fucking with it.

So John was talking about this geezer called... fuck... err... I should know this... Turner I think...

...Well it don't matter, apart from to my A level results that is.

He said this Turner bloke said, we do know we're being exploited, but there's fuck all we can do about it. Religion is not an opium, but an optional extra. In a nutshell he's basically saying something like: I hate capitalism, but I still work in it 'cause I need money. There Is No Alternative.

And that was it.

There **I**s **N**o **A**lternative.

T.I.N.A.

John wrote it up there on the board. I found it fucking weird cause at the same time I was sat next to a girl called Tina, but the real mental bit was I was actually listening. Before this moment I knew she was fit and had knocked one out about her a few times. But the day John wrote her name up, I looked at her and she looked back at me with a smile that blew me away. The sun was shining through the window next to her, making her highlights light right up. She looked blonde now, but with a glow, like some kind of fucking angel. I knew that second I'd fallen arse over tit in love and my nerves were suddenly shot to shit. I badly wanted to say something funny and make her laugh, but all I managed was "Tina… That's you."

Fucking prick.

It was our last Sociology lesson of the term and something definitely had to be said. So at the end I asked if she was gonna go *Time* to celebrate. She told me she didn't really like nightclubs, so I thought to myself that's it. A fairly easy, subtle brush off. It didn't make me look too stupid either, it's not like I was asking her out on a date or nothing. But I thought if she was interested then she would have gone down there.

Yet hope returned seconds later. She said to give her a call over Easter if I was stuck with my revision, then wrote down her number on my folder.

I'm so chuffed with this that I've looked at it every day since. Nothing to do with the fact I find it difficult to open me revision notes. Not had the guts to call her though.

Until maybe now.

It was yesterday talking to Sloo and Lid that made me want to show Sloo how 'alright' she really is. I would make another attempt to get her down *Time.* Ask her a few questions about Sociology, then just drop it in the conversation as if I'm not that bothered.

So fucking do it then Crane.

I sit here, have been for over two hours. Meant to be revising, but instead holding the phone and staring at her number. I shouldn't be this nervous. I'm only gonna make it seem like I phoned her for help, but I'm panicking like a mother fucker. I'm like *Withnail and I,* I've got the fear.

Gonna make a fool of yourself son! I know.

Really do like her now, might stand a chance; before she was a friend out my league. I've moved on in me head. The all important shift from friendship to wanting marriage. From first gear to fourth in one swift movement, that's me, no fucking middle road. I'll never learn.

This phone call's the beginning. So far I've worked out why I'm nervous, but it ain't got me any nearer to dialling.

Come on Crane.

I turn the phone on and listen to the tone for a bit. It's half six. The original plan was to call at four. The old folks have been at work all day and I wanna speak to Tina before they get back about seven. Never been confident on phones, I always feel like the old girl's listening. So now the house's silence is perfect. But my mind's still racing with all this paranoia bollocks.

Wasting valuable revision time. Sitting around all day, plucking up courage to make one fucking phone call. Been acting like a lovesick teenager. I suppose I am a lovesick teenager, but I'm eighteen now and should be above this slushy shite. You know, watching feel-good films like *Loser* and *Empire Records.* Working out mine and Tina's percentage of love for each other by that stupid name calculation. The one where the number of times the letters L, O, V, E and S in our names actually matters:

Tina Seraph LOVES Steven Andrews
00143
0157

1612
773
1410
551
106
16%. Bag of shite. Another test using the word Flames, proved that a relationship would result in her just fancying me and not marriage.

I mean what the fuck? After the results, I chose to ignore any scientific bullshit kid's tests and grow up. Because she'd definitely fall hundred percent head over heels in love with me. Only if she just gives me the chance.

Now phone her Crane. **6.35**.

This is it.

I put me ear to the phone. Some bird on a recorded message is telling me to hang up.

Fuck off.

But I do.

I switch it on once more.

Take a last look at the folder and 7 have pressed the first number. My guts are going. 5.... 3.... 2.... 3.... I'm at the last number.

I place me finger over the number 5 and close my eyes.....

5. The ringing begins.

The din spreads through the forest. On a clear evening you could hear it, but the rain drowns it silent. Shut it down but not end it. It's there now. It knows what you're doing Crane.

'Hello.'

''ello is Tina there please?'

'Yes speaking.' Fuck, Fuck, Fuck.

'All right, it's Steve... from Sociology.'

'Oh hiya.' She sounds quite pleased to hear from me. Well she wouldn't've give me her number if she didn't want me to call her. Twat.

''ow's it going?'

'Not too bad, getting a bit snowed under with this revision though, what about you?'

'Yeah nightmare, murder innit?' I'm a lying bastard. A good one though, I could lie for Britain I reckon.

'How's the Sociology been going?' She asks.

'Pretty well really, think I've got the religion bit sorted. I'm working on education now.' See.

'Oh god, the education bit's so boring isn't it?'

'You're telling me...' Shit that puts me on a downer. Ain't even looked at education yet, got all that boredom to come. Do know about Turner and his T.I.NA. though. I think about saying this, but over-talking college work might be dull.

'...So what else you been up to?' I ask after a brief pause. Almost unnoticeable.

'Nothing really, I've hardly been out. There's not much to do around here. I did pop down to Lloyds in Hornchurch last weekend, but it was pretty uneventful. What about you?'

'Err... I 'ad a big weekend. We went *Time* Thursday... oh and went down the Bridge 'ouse on Saturday to watch the footy.'

'Oh yeah, what was *Time* like?'

'It was alright, there weren't many of us out though.'

'Can't believe you go down there.' She laughs.

I dunno what she means, I absolutely love it, but if she thinks it's sad then I'd better agree.

'Nah neither can I really. Gives us some'ing to do though and it's dirt cheap.' She gives a slight breathy laugh that makes my heart jump. I've got it bad here.

'You should pop down there and see us tomorrow. Last chance for a laugh before we 'ave to start college again.' Not that college ever stopped me going down there.

'I dunno about that...' Me heart sinks. You stupid cunt Crane, as if she'd be interested in you.

'...but I tell you what, I'm sick of studying and do fancy a drink, so do you want to pop out for a bit tonight?' My heart rises. Go on Crane. This is like the fucking *Nemesis* here. I have to steady meself. This is exactly what it's like at Alton Towers, I feel sick, but real hard-core joy too. She wants a drink with me. I can't wait for this phone call to finish so I can bang on a tune and jump around my room.

'yeah, yeah definitely...' Calm down Crane, don't sound too eager '...where d'ya fancy going?"

'We could pop down the Crumpled Horn, its normally pretty quiet down there on a Wednesday.'

'Yeah cool, what time?'

'Well I've gotta have dinner and get ready...' She's going to get ready for me - YEESSSSS.

'...So about half eight, does that sound ok?'

'Yeah excellent, shall I meet you there or come and get ya first?'

'Where is it you live again?' She asks.

'Just off St. Mary's Lane.'

'Well I live down Park Drive…' I knew that. Fucking stalker. '…so it's a little way out, but if you cut across the park, then yeah, that'll be nice.' Thank God she knows I don't drive. That's fucked me chances a few times before.

'What number?'

'Seventeen.'

'Right, I'll be round at 'alf eight then.'

'I'll look forward to it, we deserve a break.'

'Too right.'

'Ok, I'd better be off because my dinner's nearly ready, so I'll see you tonight then?'

'Yeah ok. See ya later.'

'See Ya.'

'Bye.'

I chuck me mobile on me bed and go to me cd's. It's gotta be *Wu Tang Clan 'Gravel Pit'*. That still gives me a right fucking buzz.

Fucking yesssssssss.

The dance begins.

'Holocaust from the land of the lost'

7.30

I finish me microwave meal. Mum's "too busy to cook anything" and giving it the "You've been 'ome all day, why couldn't you 'ave made some'ing?" bollocks. Mental note: Old dear needs sitting down and given a good talking to.

Time for the mission of getting ready for my… date? Beginning to feel real nervous again. I've got about three hours of entertaining to do later and I don't know whether it's a date or just two friends having a break from their studies. What about an end of night kiss? Should I go for it or not? Man what a panic.

Suppose I'll have to see how the night goes, how her body language is. She might even go to kiss me. She did ask me out. Or am I getting carried away again? I know what I'm like. Oh fuck it.

I'm gonna crack open a lager, might settle me a bit. Two jars before I go out I reckon. I'll grab two Stellas from me Dad's garage. Pop one in the fridge, open the other.

Despite having serious fucking butterflies here, I'm enjoying the anxiousness. Finally a bit of excitement in me life, I'm gonna try and enjoy this one…

8.00

In my room. The all important decision of what I'm gonna wear has arrived. I crack open me second beer and open the cupboard door. Already got an idea of me best choice. From left to right, scanning the clothes... come across my white Fred Perry cardie. A Christmas present I've worn on a couple of occasions down the club; and pulled both times in.

I normally save it's power, but now it's time to unleash it again.

Top half's sorted, reckon the best partner is me Red Herring faded blue boot cut jeans. Another Xmas prezzy. These are another "best occasions only" wear.

Tonight Cat I'll be discarding me hoodie and trackies and becoming a right trendy cunt.

Dig through the old underwear drawer for me Calvin's, as you never fucking know. Now some socks without a cartoon character on 'em. Sorted.

Music choice. It's gonna have to be the awe inspiring *Wu tang: 'Iron Flag'* album. This barrage of tunes helps me confidence, big time. The message I get is to not give a fuck, be cool and just take this fucking bird.

Song number two 'Rules' is so banging I still go cold a few years after I first heard it. *Ghostface Killah* opens by offering out the "*World Trade massacre cunts*" and with the beer kicking in I'm willing him on....

... By the time *Method Man* closes with '*Wu Tang crushing yo' game*', I'm fucking bouncing.

8.15

Can't get my fucking hair to go right. It's got to a dodgy length now. What was I thinking trying to pull off a Brad Pitt toned down eighties fringe and mullet? I'm wanting to wear me cap, but know I can't. There's nothing else for it. Not that I'd tell The Styx but with his growing female popularity and my being blonde, I'm gonna have a shot at this Orlando Bloom look...

Balls. This crossover stage's doing my head in. It's not long enough to carry out his style, but too long to have a fashionable spiky look...

Trying to comb it back now, but I've used far too much wax and now I look like one of those geezers in that Michael Douglas film. What was that called again?... *Wall Street*, that was it!

Gonna have to brush it forward once more, make It look like I mean to have a weird studenty type hairstyle. Like those *Mcfly* pricks...

I finish me second lager. With lateness looking a certainty, my panic's escalating. I'm gonna have another lager for the stroll to hers. It's only ten minutes and the rain seems to have finally ceased. Might chill me out a bit. God, I'm getting like Tin lid, dependent on alcohol.

Fuck it eight twenty-eight.

I take a swig of me third lager '*Biere d'ors*', beautiful. Back to the mirror. *Time* is moving like an absolute bitch. Wish it moved this fast when I'm at college. Still I suppose it's fashionable to be slightly late, but not an hour like I'm gonna be if this shafting hair alteration don't come off. It's still greasy wet with wax and water, causing it to flop over at the front. Now it looks pathetic. I'm gonna have to fucking start over. I should seriously re-consider this Moon and Leg shaved head look. Even if it does make me look like one of the special need kids.

8.47

Finally leaving me house, fourth beer in hand. I got me hair half decent, but I'm not happy with it. It'd suit an Italian, but not pale old

Crane from Essex. It's up to the clothes to pull this one off. I haven't bothered to phone her and say I'm gonna be late, now I'm praying she ain't given up on me. Should make it in about seven minutes if I shift, but the beers are knocking me and I can't work out if this is faster than me normal pace.

Oh fuck what am I doing? I'm gonna be in the pub drinking for another two and half hours yet. With my nerves fluttering like a moth's cunt, it's gonna mean another 5 pints. I'll be fucking wrecked after nine beers. What a stupid prick! There's nothing I can do about it though, either way I'm gonna make a total wanker of meself. I just know it.

I'm wondering if I should buy all the drinks. Am I going overboard here? It's only two friends going out for a quick drink after all. I should just enjoy myself. Calm down and have a laugh.

Fuck it. With another swig of me beer it becomes apparent that I'm fucking cold here. It's only early April and I'm acting like it's summer or something. The wind's kicking up a stink too, causing havoc with the old hair.

Despite Tina having seen me nearly every day at college this year, this is me proper first impression night as she ain't seen me dressed up to go out yet. Fuck my hair.

I can tell it's gonna piss down again soon, it's hardly fucking stopped. This weather's arse. I'll stick to the path over the park, not the moors. It's turning into a swamp over here.

PARK DRIVE

The top of her road is in sight. I feel like turning round and fucking this off. Come on Crane. You're nervous because you like her. You've gotta persevere, otherwise you're gonna end up with those fat troglodytes all your life. I'm gonna get pissed, Fuck it. My aim: get totally plastered and me confidence will rise. All I've gotta do is get her steaming as well, then she won't notice me own state. I can't remember the last time I pulled when I was sober. Certainly ain't happened since I discovered the amazing effects of alcohol.

This is it. I turn down her road. House number one. Me watch says eight fifty-six. Twenty-six minutes late, not bad considering. Just hope she's not too angry and goes off me. She don't fancy me anyway, so who am I kidding?

Number seven. Bollocks, I wonder if she's looking at me from her bedroom window. I try and walk in a cool manner, but I'm too self conscious and start to wobble. Probably look like a fucking flid.

Number fifteen. Oh well Crane good luck me old son. Here we go

I turn up the driveway to a very nice house. From the front it seems about one and a half times larger than ours, and that's a fair size. Don't get time to inspect it thoroughly, I'm at the front door.

The door bell goes. I think it's one of those old style ding-dong ones like on some game show or something. But me head's ringing so much I'm not sure now whether I even pressed it. A shadow approaches the door's blurry window answering my doubts.

I don't think it's her. It's not. It's her fucking Dad.

'Hi is Tina there please?' I put on a slightly posher accent than my usual half cockney rant. I've always been majorly polite to people's parents. How's the advert go? "A suck butt!" It's normally 'cause I'm shit scared or paranoid as fuck. This time is no exception.

'Yes, come in.' He beckons, seeming friendly enough. I walk in wiping me feet thoroughly on the entrance mat. The serious arse-licking begins I think, but there's little chance before he calls out to Tina.

'She should be down in a sec.' He goes, then looks at me right strangely.

Oh my fucking life. I'm still carrying the fucking beer bottle. He must be thinking why's me daughter going out with this immature little alky?

Gotta act very quickly.

'I'm sorry, I wondered if I could use your beer, I mean bin. I didn't see one on the way 'ere...' My accent and voice volume has gone up the creek. I must sound like a fucking school kid. These sort of nights can't be good for your heart. Worse than drug nights. Must be.

'... I just had a beer while I was getting ready and thought I'd finish it on the way.' I'm lucky it was one of those shitty little French beers and not a fucking Super Tennants or something.

'Yeah sure.'

He takes the bottle off me and goes to what I presume must be the kitchen. I hear movement upstairs and hope it's Tina on her way. Need to get out of this oven.

There's stairs in front of me. The ceiling of the lower floor covers the top, so at first all I see descend is the shoes. Then legs in black tights. Yes she's wearing a skirt. Good sign. The skirt stops at the top of her knees. It's black and one that hugs the thighs. Moving on to a red polo neck. This is clingy as well and... fuck me, I can't believe the thruppeny's on this bird. They're leading her right down the stairs, I'm surprised she ain't toppled over.

Then the face. Oh man me heart sinks. She looks gorgeous, far too good for me. Man you're out of your league here Craney. Fuck it. Give up.

Her fantastic copper/blonde hair is down. There's a clip in one side giving it a fuller look. Straight away I see it, she looks like Francesca out the new Men Only. One of me current favourites.

I am in love, lust, adoration, whatever you wanna call it, but I don't stand a Morris here. Come on Crane, don't let that show. You'll get nowhere with that attitude. Spirit.

'Hiya.' Her voice is chirpy enough.

'Alright, sorry I'm late, I wanted to finish off this last minute bit of studying.' I hope that didn't sound too fucking gay.

'That's alright, I was struggling with some myself. I wouldn't have been ready anyway.' YES.

'Cool.' It is, I'm calming here. It could be the four beers or her, I don't know, but I'm actually beginning to chill out.

'There was something I wanted to ask you before we go...' Oh no what the f…

'...You know in Society and Religion? Who was it that said they think England is becoming more secular because of the diminishing attendance of churches? I don't seem to have it in my notes.' I'm fucked if I have either, I don't even know what seculo means.

'Err oh god, I can't remember that one myself, oh what was his name?' I pretend to have the answer on the tip of me tongue.

'Oh it don't really matter, I'll ask John when we get back to college.' Thank God

'Or I'll give you a call tomorrow or something? When I can check my own notes and let you know?' What are you saying Crane? Your notes from Sociology are doodled West Ham badges and random half asleep drivel about Ned Flanders.

‘Do you mind?’ Not for you, my beautiful...

‘No course not.’ Haven’t got a clue how I’m gonna find this one out, but I suppose I’ve got an excuse to phone her tomorrow. As long as I don’t make too much of a dick of meself tonight that is.

‘Dad I’m off now...’ She calls ‘...I’ll be back about half eleven.’ Wa- hey.

‘Have a good night.’ He calls back

‘See ya.’ She says

‘Thanks, see ya.’ I try to say all coolly, only for my balls to drop again and my voice to sound like Aled Jones after a few reefers.

Tina laughs.

I wanna beer.

10.00

Been moving along quite nicely. We must have got here about nine. Tina’s been on the Orange Bacardi Breezers, while I’m sinking me third pint of Stella. *Heaven and Hell* by *The Spin Merchants* has come on and I can’t help but nod me head.

‘I love this song.’ She goes.

‘Yeah, I love it when it comes on down *Time*, all the boys are up straight away.’ Not so good.

‘So what do you lot get up to when you’re down there?’ She moves in a little closer as she asks me this. We’re sat at one of those round two seater tables in the corner. It’s pretty romantic. And as she leans in, I swear I notice a glimmer in her eye, she’s really interested in what I’ve got to say. Or am I pissed here? Well I’m definitely knocked.

Don’t reckon mentioning *Time*’s excessive drug sessions is appropriate for a first date, so I skate round it.

‘We normally ‘ave a couple a’ beers before we get there ‘bout eleven. We’re all up dancing for party hour...’ Probably shouldn’t have said that. ‘...Then me mate Tin Lid’ll disappear ‘ome pissed off his nut. Oh and me other mate Moon got done on the way home a couple of weeks ago for mooning a police car.’ It’s random, but snappy.

‘What?’

‘We was walking back ‘bout three, and Littl’ Leg, you’ve met ‘im, decided it’d be funny to start mooning cars. Me and Moon was pissing ourselves. Moon thought 'e'd join in, but the first car 'e did it to was the police and it only pulled over.'

'Oh my God, what did they say?'

'They warned 'im, said they might've been thugs with knives or something, that would've taken right offence to him getting his arse out. Me and Leg were pissing ourselves behind 'im.'

She's laughing too, not for the first time tonight. Me story about Tin Lid falling onto the stage at a strip club, taking eight blokes down with him and stopping the whole show had her going as well.

Obviously I said I weren't there.

'You haven't told me why you've got all these nick-names yet, is that why Moon's Moon?'

'It's a long story...' I tell her '...another Bacardi?'

10.42

At a sensible pub volume '*Totally addicted to bass*' by, someone or other's playing. It's pretty fucking right. I could do with a bit of base now, the amphetamine kind. Straighten meself up a bit. I'm swaying at the table here.

Tina's controlling the conversation now. Had to remember, birds like talking about 'emselves. So instead of me rambling shit all night, I started asking her stuff about her life before she moved to Essex.

'When I was back home in Oxford, I shouldn't tell you this really, but I suppose you'll never meet her...' Her face lights up when she's excited. I'm hanging on every word, encouraging her forward.

'...My mate Karen went round her boyfriend's for the first time to meet his family, they were having a barbecue. Anyway she was nervous and got really sloshed, but once she'd eaten she wanted to use the loo. So she goes upstairs and has to do... you know...' She giggles, I nod smiling the whole time. Sloshed! Great word.

'...But, once she'd finished she couldn't flush it. She said it weren't a lot, but she was too embarrassed to leave it. She thought the bathroom window led out to the side alley and if she threw it out there, the family would think a cat had done it...' I'm already cracking up in disbelief, I know where it's headed.

'... So she picked it up using loo roll as a kind of glove and flung it out the window...' She breaks as we giggle more.

'...Apparently she heard some screams and looked out the window. The Dad was standing over the barbecue...' 'cause she's in bits Tina has to pause once again.

'... he had it on his head, down his shirt...' She's cracking up, I don't think she's bullshitting here. '...You can just picture him, standing there with his tongs, ready to take an extra sausage off the griddle. A ha ha...'

Normally if a girl talks about shits, I wouldn't know whether to cringe or dismiss it. But I'm pissing meself here.

Maybe I should follow it up with me story of Littl' Leg's Barbie?...

No maybe not.

It's going amazingly as it is. Let's just hope I can hold it together for the home run.

10.55

Luckily I took me time over the last Stella, 'cause I'm banging here. But when the last bell goes I suddenly sober a bit. This is it. Soon I've gotta decide whether I'm gonna try and snog her or not. Although I'm pretty smashed, I haven't felt that click yet. The click of confidence that will help me go for it. I call it the click since I read *'Cat on a hot tin roof'* in English Literature. The only bit I remember about the book, because I so related with it, is this geezer Brick's alcoholism and how he drunk till he got the 'click'.

So I persuade her into a final drink.

She gets a Malibu and Coke this time, her fourth alcoholic beverage of the evening. I decide on a bottle of Bud. I wanna click, not collapse.

I pop up to the bar. Well stumble, try to add a little composure and balance but fail miserably.

11.20

The barmaid's rushing us. Can't really remember what's just happened. Had the click after a couple of swigs of Bud. Fuck me. Hope I can walk. Come on Crane this has been smooth. Stick with the plan. Wanna listen to cd's now, have a reefer or something. Celebrate having kept her interested tonight, but still the hard bit to come. Tina's laughing at something. I don't think it's me. Probably she's battered.

You know how girls get! What the fuck am I talking about? I'm laughing and pissed.

My God. None of the boys even know I'm out with this bird. Can't wait to tell Moon and Leg. This is the nuts. Just need to balance. Whooaaa. That's it Crane you can pull this off...

Fuck knows

I'm kissing her, outside her house. Kissing Tina. So soft. So sexy. Me nob's pressing hard up against her. I can't stop it. She must know it's there, but she ain't budging. I'm grabbing her arse. So soft. Fuck knows what happened on the way home. That bud... My god can she kiss...

This is fucking brilliant. I'm sloshed and don't err rememb-ber much, anything, about how we got like this.

Who cares. I'm in. YEEEEEEEESSSSSS...

noww.

I STAGGER ABND SING OVER THE PARK
'Hiiiiiiiggggghhhhhhhhh' AT HE TOP OF MY VOICE. imm not with Tina now, but it ended great Ithink.
'Running wiiiiiiilllllllld among all the sttttaaaaaaaarrrrrrrs above.'
fuckimBOlloCKSSD.

CHAPTER 10
SO THE STORY GOES

Robert Cranley struggles to adapt the lights to his focus. Blurred visions plague him for minutes, spread across his sight before eventually coming as one. Candles scattered amongst the branches above. Everything, so far, bright and warming. Aiding to make visible the cloaks and cloths draped around him. A makeshift room with no ceiling. Can see the stars shining overhead. Relaxation stays…

Until… creeping… come creeping in…

He bolts upright and looks across the floor. Several scattered bodies surrounding. His friends. Sees Little, Mooning, Beech, Tilnid. First thoughts are for their lives. Yet he soon notices they are breathing deeply.

Where are we? What happened? His thoughts are clouded. Backtracking. The search. The forest. Smoke odour halting them. Then…

Starts to panic and scrambles to his feet. He doesn't want to shout or get the attention from… That thing. Has to wake his friends. Quickly! He nudges Hevey Little.

Coming-to, confused, the friend tries to distinguish he that woke him.

'Are you well?' Cranley asks. Receives a faint murmur in reply, seemingly satisfactory.

'We must be silent, but to your feet quickly.'

Little nods and pulls himself from the ground. His sleep had been deep and soothing. Never had he slept so well and undisturbed.

Cranley turns his attention to Wadard Mooning, but before he can alert the serf, a sound outside disturbs. The cracking of twigs. Leaves rustle underfoot. It has returned. Cranley looks back at Little, frozen to the spot.

Back to reality, a second person now recalls the events. Trembles.

Cranley too petrified to move. He sees a shadow through the hanging cloths. Approaching, nearer, nearer... It's coming. Tries to steady himself. Maybe attack now? Yet knows no chance is stood against what had caused their unconsciousness. Even if he could escape, then what of his friends? He could not leave them.

Little cowers. Cranley wants to imitate, but remains dormant. Now it's too late. The shadow is at the walls. A cloak pushes to the side. The pair stare, motionless. Hearts racing, minds clear of nothing but fear...

In through the curtains. It appears.

'Roger.' Terror turns to relief. Their lost friend. Roger Brooks. Safe. Here now. Maybe a chance for escape?

'Calm Robert, everything is fine. Awake the others and I will reassure you of the situation...'

Moments later. Roger Brooks has an audience of five men sat cross-legged on the floor. Although shaken by their situation each person had been re-energised by a deep slumber, they were now feeling fresh and less perturbed. This was aided by their first sighting in almost a week of their old friend. Here, standing before them. Dressed in a new clean cloak, looking better than any day he did in the village. Looked larger too. As if he'd eaten a months food supply in the few days he had been missing.

His face now fuller, also more rugged. He looks strong. Brimming with life. Taller even.

'Welcome to The Styx my friends. We apologise for any dismay that may have been caused. But I assure your safety now.

I would like to thank you all for coming to my rescue after my disappearance, you truly are good companions. We didn't expect to have you here so soon, under these circumstances. If you had not come looking, I would have reached you all anyway. The plan was for a night time a couple of days from now. I was coming to offer you a way out of your poor lives in the village. Our harsh existence means little to anyone there, here you can live free, like the King himself. The choice is yours my friends, but I ask you to consider thoroughly.

I will tell you my story, but you must first take a drink...'

Brooks collects five wooden cups from the hollow of a tree that makes up part of their boundary. Cranley had wondered of the contents of a beautifully carved wooden jug that his lost friend had entered the room with. Now he watches in fascination as Brooks pours faint red liquid into each of the cups, before handing them out to the serfs.

'...Here this will restore your energy further. It must have been quite some night. I remember my own first encounter with Sloo..."

Cranley looks at his other friends. They look confused at Roger Brooks' calm attitude regarding the presence which so petrified them earlier.

'... As you know, I had suffered an argument with my good wife. I miss her dearly I assure you, but you must understand she is not allowed here. One of the few rules I'm afraid. But my life is far better than I ever could have imagined at the village. I would never give this up. Hopefully you will see this for yourselves, if you desire to stay that is.

I walked away from my wife to calm my aggression and took a stroll towards the forest. There I was disturbed by some noises occurring near the manor hall. My nature told me to take place behind a tree. There I watched a shadow move as fast as the wind across the fields. It stopped at the parish and deposited something on the steps. Then as quick as it came... Gone.

I went to inspect the site. There I found the head of a wolf. My trepidation was suddenly realised. What was I doing here? I made to run, but as soon as I turned, there he was. Like you I knew nothing of what followed until I woke where you sit now. My first thought was of escape. Yet I was tied to the ground by twine branches. Not one inch could I budge. It was as though the weight of the sky was upon me. I managed to lift my head however. Looking around I noted the eloquence of my surrounding that you see now. In the corner sat a man fashioning the jug from which I poured your drink. He noticed my movement and instantly began to calm me.

His appearance and words immediately soothed my soul. He explained my restrictions, always apologising for the circumstances in which we met. Saying he would have appeared to me in this less intimidating form a few days on, if it weren't for our chance meeting. The terrifying form I saw at the parish was for his own safety. Exactly as your hunt scared him, my intrusion into his plans did too. He heard people entering the forest and chose the horrific appearance you saw, believing it to be landowners coming to jeopardise all he has built. When you see him soon, you will all appreciate the beauty he actually beholds. He is a God my friends. His forms are many, but his true form... Well, you will discover this shortly.

My Lord has been overseeing our lives for some time. He has witnessed our pain, our misery. The hard labour we undertake for the benefit of our owners has not been missed. He is greatly displeased with our land as it lay. This was why he left the animal parts in our village. They were designed as warnings to those who exploit us. He was coming for our salvation soon, but we seem to have discovered him first...'

Cranley takes sips from his drink. Had not tasted anything like it before. A world of berries and fruits mixed perfectly to form a thirst quenching liquid that appeased each and every part of him. He felt light headed, but totally relaxed. Was still unsure about meeting this 'God' which struck fear into their hearts not so long ago, but with each taste his confidence rose.

'... Here I have lived for the last few days helping the Lord to gather the ingredients for your drinks. Also gathering food for your arrival, but mainly enjoying the company of our saviour. He has tales for the future that will scare your very soul. His intentions are solely to deliver us from this evil shadowing what will be. He will explain this to you now.

Be prepared, but always remember, you can walk away if you so wish, yet I wager that you will stay. If you are all well, then I will bring him in...'

THE BIBLICAL DIRECTORY
(ii)

Time drifts by, there's no clock in this room and Tina made me switch me mobile off earlier. So I ain't got a Danny what it is.

There's talk of the serpent actually being given arms instead of having his pegs chopped. Then he was given this shitty job taking dead people across the River Styx for eternity. All worthwhile stuff, I don't think.

What sort of dilemmas do I create for meself. Even Tina's left the room to grab more teas. Wish I was a bit more like Moon. He'd have told this geezer to stick his tree of knowledge up his bony white arse.

Could do with a fry up. Two days without hardly fuck all to sleep and no eat and now he's going on about serpents and shit. Fuck all to sleep, no fuck all to eat and no sleep. That makes more sense. I think? I've had fuck all to eat and I ain't had any sleep. So I'd say fuck all to sleep. No wait… fuck all to

'CRANE.' Mother fucker! Cunt's scared the crap outta me.

'Yeah?'

'Are you with me here? This may be of slight importance to you.'

Yeah.' I am now anyway, seeing as you keep shouting every five minutes.

'So you'll give me a quick recap on Hades then please?'

'Listen I'm sorry mate, I'm tired. I really don't understand all this. I'm not gonna say I don't care because, I know it's important to ya, but I've got A-levels coming up and one of em ain't Religion.' Don't wanna be rude to the old geezer, but sometimes needs must and all that malarkey.

'This is difficult for me too Crane. I'd love to just jump in with the real reason why you're here, but if I did, you would think that I'm crazy.'

'No offence mate but…'

'Look. I know all about you Crane. You live with your mother and father. You're doing Sociology and History A-levels plus Maths GCSE re-sit. You have six friends: Tin Lid, Brooke with an e, Beeke, Moon, Little Leg without the e and Sloo. Last year you went to Ibiza and you frequently take drugs.'

'Mate if you're old bill. I can safely say I don't touch…'

'No Crane I'm not…' Tina comes back in the room with some Rosie. Lovely.

'Still struggling…' The geezer's clutching at the fringe bit of his hair as he nods. '…I'll take over.' She says. Much as I love her, this is all a tad on the weird side for me.

She puts the tray down, grabs me face and kisses me square on the lips

…I'm flying high…

and… *…Right through the clouds* *upwards*

…as we glide above the ocean *turn*

Tina's beside me, holding my hand… *Sharp*

I can hear this music.

Not the sort of stuff I'd normally like. All orchestral and shit, but this is beautiful…

…higher and higher *into the stars*

…go… *I can see*

We … *three blokes and a boy*

We draw closer and I can see it's Brooke, Tin Lid, Beeke and…it's…it's…young Sloo too, when he was about eight and shit.

They're all waving at me. Smiling, holding up beers. Except the youngster obviously. Tina leads me to 'em…

'Alright lads?'

'Hi Crane…' Beeke's saying '…Please follow Tina, she's 'ere to save ya; and all of us from an 'orrible existence.'

'But this is madness.'

'What this? You can see for yourself. Look around you...'

The hone view

Stars into. All much bigger now.

Upon each one:

Sit

a host of angels

all dancing, playing harps,

...just like you'd expect and stuff. up ahead

Even looks like a big golden gate

shining lights on

it. and everything

out like

bellow me

Choirs Dad's

.music day Christmas

"ave I done one too many d'ya think lads?'

'I wish that were the case and that.' Goes Tin Lid.

'It's Sloo mate. Not our Sloo, but this other geezer. 'e's done something horrible with our Sloo. This is Kev as 'e was before...well let's not speak too loud in front of 'im.' Brooke adds. Young Sloo's smiling at me. Makes you miss him, he was a good lad.

'That's the thing see, you're not supposed to be here. I was out with you all last night; or the night before; or... I'm not too sure when it was now, what with all this 'appening.' I'm almost pleading.

'That was when it began...' Says Lid '...and we can't get in anyway. It's up to you for that and that.'

'What am I supposed to do?'

'We can't say a great deal, just give this experience the benefit of the doubt.' Beeke joins in.

'Listen to the man mate, trust us on this one. Remember what you always said? Explore, but never get lost.' Goes Brooke

'Ok...' I go to ask if they'll be out Thursday...

but

I'm

falling
rapidly
away,
Back down
through
the clouds.
Stars
Crumble
into *the distance*
Across the ocean once more.
Then…

'Woah!'

Tina pulls away from the kiss. I'm back in the room. With your man and me girlfriend.

'Sweetheart, this is going to be difficult to accept, but we're really trying to ease you into this. We know it's hard.' She goes.

I'm sat rigid. Except me eyes. They're darting about the room like maniacs. Searching for something that might help me to get to grips with all this.

'But me mates… Then… they're alright aren't they?'

'They will be, but only with your help.' The librarian's saying. You must listen.

" Alright, alright but I gotta tell you this is freaking me out.' I ain't kidding neither.

Tina sits beside me and takes my hand again. Unbelievably calming me.

'So where were we? I need to dumb this down more, I can see that.' The geezer says.

I feel offended and set to say something, then reason that; nah he's hundred percent right.

"Inside a bathroom he could give in to the obsession with his own physical and mental state which was so often compromised by the presence of other people or the absence of a well-lit mirror. Most of the 'quality time in his life had been spent in a bathroom. Injecting, snorting, swallowing, stealing, overdosing; examining his pupils, his arms, his tongue, his stash. 'Oh, bathrooms! He intoned, spreading out his arms in front of the mirror. 'Thy medicine cabinets pleaseth me mightily! Thy towels moppeth up the rivers of my blood"

Extract taken from the novel: '*Bad News*' by *Edward St Aubyn* (1992)

PART TWO

CHAPTER 11
...AND ALL IS WELL?

Tap, tap, tap. Patiently at the window. No answer. Tap, tap, tap. Crane doesn't budge. A good night? The drink pushes him deep, deep, deeper. Nothing.

Tap, tap, tap. Insomnia laid to rest. Finally mind at ease. Smile on Beeke. Life is back? *Time* to catch up. Too deep to reach.

Tap, tap, tap. Weekend so fatiguing. Work exhausting. Desperate to recharge. Five hours not enough. Head hits pillow. Gone. Moon wake up. Nothing. Tap. Littl' Leg. Tap. TAP. LITTL' LEG. Undisturbed. Midweek come down a very tiresome drain. Gone. Hollow slumber. Sleep well now. Tomorrow I knock louder.

Tap. TAP. TAP. Tin Lid, drinking on your own now? Revision too hard? Pressure Tin Lid? No confidence? TAP. TAP. **TAP.** Not yet. That's ok. Go deep tonight. Recuperate. A busy night ahead.

A change of plan.

KNOCK. KNOCK. KNOCK.

At least someone is awake...

2.30 a.m.

...Brooke paces Gemma's bedroom. His girlfriend doing her utmost to calm his rage. Trying to comfort the man she loves. An anger arisen from a ferocious argument he'd suffered with his parents.

It wasn't even anything to do with him. Why was he being held responsible?

Ok he knew something, but what could he do? He didn't control his sister's life.

Six days ago Brooke's thirteen year old sibling, Alison, came to him for advice regarding sex. She was considering intercourse with her twelve year old boyfriend, despite the couple only sharing their first kiss weeks before.

She "really cares for him" and she "couldn't bear to lose him." Sex would "keep them together, surely?"

Brooke felt awkward. Irritated that his sister even knew about sex at her age. Yet he understood what it was like as a pubescent. Surrendered his own virginity at fourteen. But, no not her, little Ali. That he couldn't comprehend. Struggled to deal with a corrupting image of someone so close.

Brooke's advice was ignorant, he knows now it's too late. "Stop being such a kid," "wait till you're older", "girls can't be in love at thirteen." Wouldn't that be the comments of parents only encouraging their children to rebel? Brooke should have been the older brother. Talked to her, not sent her away.

Yet what right had his parents to turn on him? They were so involved with their jobs, Alison had no opportunity to confide in them. She didn't want to be an intrusion in their hectic lifestyle...

'They walked into 'er room and they were shagging on 'er bed.'

'Oh Andy, no. Didn't she hear them coming in?'

'They weren't meant to be back till twelve, she 'ad 'er music on.' Brooke finally rests, placing himself on Gemma's bed. Head in his hands, clenching his teeth. Disbelief.

'What time was they back then?' Gemma sits beside him. Puts her arm round an upset and irate boyfriend. Not seen him like this before. His attitude normally so confident, calm, as if nothing could faze him. Though instead of shying from this new side, she wants to be there for Brooke, now more than ever.

'About ten, apparently they were 'aving a shit night.'

'What did they do?' She was endearing to this new Brooke. The anger and compassion. Gemma would look after him tonight.

'Went fucking berserk. Ali was in tears when I got back. Apparently me Dad grabbed 'old of 'er boyfriend and threw 'im out naked. Me Mum chucked 'is clothes out after 'im. Then they turned on 'er. She 'ad to get dressed real quick in front of Dad. We've never known 'im that angry. She was scared shitless...' Gemma welcomingly accepts Brookes' head to rest on her chest. She has never felt this close to anyone before, not even her own family. Understood now that she wanted to spend the rest of her life with this man.

'...She tried to explain about 'er feelings, telling 'em what she told me about it. Then said I called 'er a little girl and she wanted to prove she weren't. That's when I chose the right perfect fucking time to get back. Couldn't believe it when they told me. I stuck up for 'em. Said I was sorry. Then they blamed me. Saying I should've told 'em...' There is a slight pause. Gemma decides to remain quiet. Brooke looks up at her, tears forming at the corner of his eyes.

'D'you think I should 'ave told 'em?' He asks.

'Andy there was nothing to tell. She was being immature, you thought she'd get over it. Most thirteen year-olds do get over crushes without resorting to sex. It's just the world today, it's messed up.'

Brooke flings his arms around Gemma, she responds. They hold each other tight. This girl means so much to him. She is always there for him. The most important thing in his life now.

His father had evicted him, told him never to come back. So Brooke grabbed a sports bag, filled it with as many clothes and essentials it could carry, collected some money and stormed out. He understood the impact of catching their thirteen year-old daughter during intercourse would leave a father incensed. He knew the sight would be shattering. But to upset the man enough to eradicate his son from his life? That was hard to digest. Brooke respected his father, loved him.

He doesn't need him anymore though. Would manage on his own. For now he'd stay with Gemma. Usually there every week night anyway. Her parents liked him. They wouldn't mind his staying. He'd finish his GNVQ. A job as a plumber's apprentice to his uncle an option too. Brooke reasoned he could even stay with him for a while. He could cope, so long as he had Gemma.

'I love you Gemma.'

'And I love you too.'

They begin to kiss softly. He would happily stay in the clinch forever. To shut out the world and all of its complications. Surprised at his emotions, never thought he'd find such happiness with one woman, especially whilst he had the pick out of hundreds. From one to the next he went, without showing weakness. But now Brooke was ready to settle. Stay with Gemma for good. Even if it meant eloping with her and forgetting this entire area.

FORGET.

NO NEVER FORGET BROOKE. YOU MADE A PROMISE. YOU'RE HERE FOR GOOD NOW. I WILL MAKE SURE OF THAT.

SLOO

SLOO

SLOO

OOOOOOO,

SLOoooo.

Falling deep into the land. Wanting to dance with the others. Such merriment on their faces as they dodge in and out of the trees. Laughter and songs. Nothing like this out there. Here life is to be savoured. Every precious moment a joy to experience. Outside wishing away the days. Living for weekends only. Depression, anger, hurt, disasters broadcast on the daily news. Death, War, Famine...

They're calling to Sloo. Join us here in the forest.

We know eternity. You will too.

'You see Sloo, ecstasy. Their life was freedom. Nothing could touch us here. Not even the weather. Still they couldn't appreciate this. I had to send Beeke down the River. The bloodshed could have been prevented, but I had to slaughter them. Send them into the water and start again. This time it will work for us Sloo. Soon we'll all live happily ever after.'

'My father, my Lord. Can you entrust me with such high responsibilities?'

Once more located in the forest, Sloo bows to the figure.

'You can call me Sloo.'

'But I am Sloo.'

'You are my son. With my help you will have the strength to finish the work I commenced. You above anyone else can bring these people into the forest.'

'Sloo wake up.'

'My father. They are my friends, I will only carry out the sacrifice of Beeke unto you.'

'That's all I require, the rest will see the error of their ways and then can be saved. The Styx will then be eternity and can grow and grow.'

"SLOO GET UP"

'It will take time Sloo, but we have it on our side. Yet Beeke must die on the second night from this. Ten years to the day that the deals were made. Then you must lead the others to the camp. Remember they will see you as their master, the leader. Nature has seen to that. It witnessed them make the pact.'

" SLOOOOOOOOO"

River runs red. Forest awash with blood.

The boat sets sail.

Back to time. *Lost souls needing a home. Wind for fuel. Sloo seeks revenge . The take over will be assured. Alight this time. The earth will be empty. Evil commences. Possession. Distorted minds. Enter. Destroy hope. The Styx. The horizon, through the mist. Deep. The boat is coming. Fleeting shadows on board. They had no home. Stuck for now.*

Spirits of the past. Witness the agreement. They have crossed over into death. Now cross back again. Cut their tongues off...

Thursday Morning

It takes me a few seconds to register the turning point of my life. I snogged Tina. I definitely did, didn't I? Yeah, I'm sure of it. Then what? Shit, I ain't got a Danny. My fucking head hurts. I do know that. Man a Stella hangover. Probably the worst hangovers in the world.

Yeah I kissed Tina. I fucking did it. Beautiful. Come on. Craney is the man. What a fucking night, she's the best. Never found it so easy to get on with a bird. Man this is the greatest feeling in the world.

Except for the fact I'm finding it hard to move me head without it falling off.

I realise I'm not even in bed. I've crashed out on the sofa in me other room. A remote control in hand. For the Hi-Fi.

Let's see what slush I put on when I got in. I press play. From the opening it's obvious, *James Blunt: 'High'*. I feel like singing.

'BEAUTIFUL DAWN, LIGHTS UP THE SHORE FOR ME.' Maybe singing ain't the one. I feel too sick. I'll just appreciate the *Blunt.*

'There is nothing else in the world,
I'd rather wake up and see with you
Beautiful dawn,
I'm just chasing time again,
Thought I would die a lonely man,
In endless night...
But now I'm HIGH...' Whoaaah! Flashback. The park. Singing this. Wasn't there someone with me? Nah, couldn't have been. I must have walked Tina home. Yeah I did. Snogged her on her doorstep. So who was there? Nah, couldn't be...

What do I do now anyway? Ring her today? Or is that too desperate? I'd do it this minute if it weren't considered sad. I'm still pissed and me ego has landed.

Later though, I'll know what'll happen. No don't let the doubt in. Not yet... creeping... in....

What if she only snogged me 'cause she was pissed?

Oh bollocks. You could have enjoyed the moment a bit longer Crane you annoying fucking pessimist. Will you never be happy?

Time tonight. Yes. Back up there. Drugs for me. Lots and lots of drugs. Speed and E and Acid and anything else I get me hands on. Always a silver lining...

Who was over the park?

Still, Tina is the one. I'd pack up the drugs forever if she asked me to. What am I saying? No it's true, if I play this one right, I'll settle down with her. Probably will have to give 'em up for good.

Easy tiger. Big step Crane, big step. Just hope I don't get hurt this time... Don't get hurt...

* * * *

He wants to cut somebody's tongue in half with a carving knife. NO NOT THE STYX. Just Beeke. Cut his tongue out and make him watch as he licks his own cock. Calm Sloo. Calm. You must be prepared. Practice tonight. Now Wake up.

Sloo sits for a while. Collecting his thoughts. Once again he has woken on a park bench with little recollection. He is content though. Here he can watch the sun rise over the park. A voyeur to the people that walk their dogs. The kids out early to play football. Enjoying the nice weather.

For the last time...

CHAPTER 12
MAN IN THE MOON

Thursday Lunch time

'Leg, we need a beer.'

'You're telling me mate. I'll see ya down the Peacock in fifteen.'

'Sorted, see ya then.'

'Later on Moon.'

Fucking week this has been. All I didn't want after a hefty four day Easter session was fucking Israelis in me ear. Pushy bastards. Want everything on a fucking platter and then some. They'll do anything to sort insurance. Oh don't doubt it. But I'm the mug punter having to stretch the fucking truth.

"We need to prove we can get cover for this useless piece of cement we call a football stadium tomorrow, just to keep these other cunts sweet. Oh it's falling into a nearby river, but you don't need to say that. Tell them it's been loss free for eight years against subsidence and get them to cover it for nothing. There's a good chappy." Fucking cunts.

"But are the offices sprinklered?"

"We don't know that yet, get them to insure it anyway."

"But I'll never get cover for it in a day without more information."

"Well I'll send some bollocks through in Hebrew that no cunt'll understand, tell them it's all pukka and they should cover it, then we'll send the real information through soon. You can do it."

"But..." Dialling tone...

It don't go exactly like that, but that's how it fucking feels sometimes. Do this, Do that, earn everyone else the money, then you can go home with your piddly fifteen k. While all us top rich cunts'll go yachting for the weekend. Our jobs are the most important, honest. Bullshit!

Spent Tuesday and Wednesday looking like a zombie from one of Crane's shit films. Eyes hardly opening in the morning. Braving pissing rain. Gale force winds. Just for me bit of drug money. I'll piss and wank it all up the wall this week. Then start again next week with Phillipinos, Indonesians, Europeans, Israelis and any other cunt that can find our phone number. All be talking bilge I don't really understand, just so I can go out to the market, lie me head off, then go home panicking that these fucking toilet countries might have a hurricane overnight.

Come to think of it I'm glad we ain't covering English companies at the moment. Fucking weather. Sometimes walking down Fenchurch Street's like trying to push past five rugby players at a busy bar. Fucking public school poofters.

Still I'm getting out the office now, go and have a sharp beer with Leg. He's probably going through the same shit as me. There's talk in his office that he might be broking Israeli business soon too. Moon versus Leg in the Kibbutz cover contest. No contest. I'll fucking smear the cunt's arse all over Lloyds of London's windows. Fucking muppet. Love him though.

Just file this fax, that fax. File my juicy fat bollocks you cunts 'cause the big boss man ain't around. I'm fucking off NOW.

All the other smart cunts go straight down the pub at lunch. But me, no! I've gotta go back to the office and get abused by Arabs or whatever these cunts are. I don't fucking know.

I'm Frank Bough. Make to leave the office and sure enough me name gets called by one of the secretaries. Falls on death ears. Those heifers only want guidance in their work now. How do I type this? How do I type that?

What do they want me to do here? My job, me bosses job and now their fucking job an' all. How about you all fuck off and I'll run this fucking hell hole by meself? I'd probably do a better job.

Come on you cunting lift. I've heard me name again. Come on you cunt. Yes. Fuck you Fiona. I'm outta here. Do your own fucking job.

Standing in the lift, I face the mirror. Fuck me. Eighteen going on thirty. This life's taking its toll. Two years since I left school. All I've done is sell insurance and take drugs. Still, I could be a student grant like the others. Scraping together their pennies for nights out.

Not for me thank you. Cocaine will be sniffed my friend. Don't get me wrong. I still love me speed, but I'm gonna start cutting down on that evil shit. I need sleep. That stuff just makes me wank all night. Feel like I'm ready to grow out that shit now. But it's gonna be fucking hard to give up. I mean I've shagged a few birds, but I swear nothing compares to banging on a 3 hour hard-core porn tape and watching it twice through. All whilst feeling like the star of each scene. It's the fucking nuts. But the next day. No. That shit shouldn't be allowed. No food, not wanting to move. Joints all fucked. Heart racing. Yet having to convince underwriters to cover a Philippine shoe factory that wouldn't withstand one of my farts. It's gotta stop. I'm sorry lads, you cheap pricks. I don't care if you ain't got the money, I'm moving Thursday nights to Friday. Inception today. Moon has spoken. I ain't gonna finish this account tomorrow with paranoia and a sore nob. No fucking way.

Ground floor.

'All right Jan, I'm off for a sharp one love.'

'Ok Bradley, don't drink too much.' What's it got to do with you receptionist? Just 'cause you've been sat on that desk for thirty years, doesn't mean you can tell me what to do. And this Bradley shit. Tart.

'I won't.' Soft cunt.

Aaahhhh fresh air. Light a Benson. At least today's started off all right. Bit of sunshine, winds dying down. But I can see the dark clouds moving in. The Gods getting ready to piss over our poor fucking insignificant heads once again. Well not me. I'm the Moon and I'll take you all on. All yous fucking suits. Look at ya. Talking your shit. Getting in my fucking way. Move you cunts. Fucking rows of people, walking like I've got strings on 'em and having one momentous game of tug-o-war.

Fucking hell I've got the hump today. That's another thing with that fucking speed. It don't take one day to recover. No, all midweek I'm suffering with a case of I hate the world. Normally by now I'm coming round, but this week I'm feeling exceptionally pissed off.

Move you Elephant jisms...

The Peacock. The Essex bar of the city. You can have a game of pool and straight fucking lagers. This is where the normal blokes who work in this testosterone charged city come. A few secretaries as well, normally the nice looking but absolutely brainless birds from Kent; or some other wannabe Essex place. I do like it here.

I get a couple of Stellas and find a table. Leg ain't here yet. Probably still licking his bosses arse. "Are you sure I can pop out for a quick drink? I'll have one Coca Cola and be straight back, honest!"

'Alright Leg?'

'Corrr, you look cheery today, you miserable git. Can't take the pressure, darling? You wait 'til I come up against ya, you'll be crying all the way 'ome.'

'You ain't coming anywhere near me, you arse bandit. Anyway, leave off Leg. You stand as much chance of taking accounts off me than we 'ave of beating the Arse Wankers Saturday.'

'It's gonna 'appen. You wait, I'm sticking an Ayrton on a 1-0 win.'

'What, with our defence up against Henry? You really are a muppet sometimes Littl' Leg.'

'You've gotta 'ave belief son. We done it a couple a` years back. Anyway what's up with ya, moody cunt?'

'Got all these mad Israeli cunts on me back. I think tonight's gonna be outta the question mate.'

'I'm glad you said it. I'm fucked meself at work. Didn't wanna be the only one wanting to leave it.'

'What's your problem? Your boss got the shits? Run outta toilet paper? Now your 'ands getting all shitty?' Even he has to laugh at this one. I'm laughing too now. There's nothing like good banter with your mates to brighten the day. I love this cunt, 'cause he gives as good as he gets. That Crane's a crafty little wanker too. He ain't as loud with it. But when he gets something on ya, he's clever enough to even turn me claret.

'Yeah what about you? Bet everyone's been shagging their Misses last night and no one wants a blow job. Bet your crawling round under desks, everyone booting you away like an unwanted puppy.'

'They've not been shagging their Doris's though mate. They've all been at your 'ouse queuing up to fill your Mum's orifices; with ya Dad sat watching in the corner knocking one out. Plus I'm all knackered out after ya sister.'

'It's lucky I was up your Mum's arse last night then. Cause if I ever saw you with my sister I'd 'ave to break ya face.'

'One day Littl' Leg, you might be big enough to take me. That's a long way off yet.'

'Dream on Moon, dream on…'

Reckon we both needed this. Let it all out. No bottling it up with this cunt here. You can say what ya like and he'll keep coming back. Top man. Still back to the matter at hand.

'Anyway what we gonna tell the others? Crane's gonna be right pissed off we're pulling out tonight.'

''e's gonna 'ave to face up to it ain't 'e, the student. 'e ain't gotta get up like us. Bet 'e still ain't done no fucking revision either, waster. Still we're only rearranging it 'til tomorrow.'

'Give 'im a call will ya, 'e can get in touch with the others then, me battery's fucked.' I order. Ha ha ha. Watch how he obeys like the dog he is…

'Crane.'

'Alright geez?'

'I'm 'ere with Moon and we've got a bit a' bother about tonight.'

'What?'

'Me an' Moon are fucked at work. There's no way we're gonna get through it tomorrow after a *Time* night.'

'Ah geez, I'm itching for it 'ere.'

'You can wait one more day can't ya? It's not like you've got anything to do 'til then.'

'Oh man, I've got shit loads of revision to do.'

'Then you can do with an extra day then can't ya? Wish all I 'ad to do was revise, you jammy cunt. We'll do it all tomorrow. All the drugs are sorted.'

'Really, what 'ave ya got?'

'What do you think? I'll tell ya what though, The Geez told me these acids we got are properly mind fucking. One of these bad boys and we're all gonna be insane.'

'Really? Oh go on, let's do it tonight.'

'No can do, one more day geez it'll all be worthwhile. You've gotta give the others a call as well.'

'Yeah, they're gonna be pissed. Especially Tin Lid.'

'He's always pissed anyway. So what's the problem?'

'Not like that.'

'I know not like that you thick cunt. It's called Irony. Don't you learn that in college?'

'Yeah, yeah.'

''ow ya getting on though geez.'

'Fucking brilliant. You'll never believe who I went out with last night.'

'Who?'

'That Tina bird I told you about, in me Sociology class.'

'Really? 'ow d'it go?'

'Pretty mint, I think. Remember snogging 'er. But the end of the night's a total blur.'

'Did ya shag it?'

'Nah, she ain't like that.'

'That's what you think mate. She was going ten to the dozen with me last week.'

'You cunt.'

'Nah, well done geez. I'll give you a bell later and you can tell me all about it. Just make sure you phone the others, yeah?'

'Yeah, I will.'

'Nice one, I'll speak to ya later.'

'Yeah laters.'

'What's that cunt been up to?'

''e took some student bird out last night.'

'Did 'e? Is 'e sure it ain't one of those lady boys?'

'Probably. That's why she wouldn't let the slow cunt get in 'is knickers.'

Beautiful Leg. Couldn't put it better meself. Tonight's sorted then. That's cheered me up no end. I can get a good night's kip then get properly back on it tomorrow.

'What about these acids then? What are they called?' I ask.

'Don't know, they've just got a picture of a tree on em. The Geez said 'e did 'alf last night and thought 'e was on another planet.' The Geez. The unofficial eighth member of The Styx because of his prolific supply of quality drugs.

'Nice, well that settles it. Imagine doing one of those tonight and coming back 'ere tomorrow. We'd be 'iding under our desks.' I goes.

'You'll be doing that anyway though won't ya Moon?' He's making blowjob actions. Cunt. Got me there...

Wait a minute. There's that cunt.

'There's that Cunt from the Norwich Union I was telling ya about Leg.' Terry Collins, the insurance underwriter from hell. I swear one day I'll kill that wanker. Went and saw him the other day with some of me accounts. He told me not to waste his time; and to fuck off out of his office and not come back 'til I've got some proper business to show him. Granted I did try and sell him a big pile of shite, but that's not the point. That cunt'll get his. If it's not from me, then some other poor sap will fold and knock his fucking head off.

'Why don't you go over there and knock 'im out then?'

'Yeah, that'll really 'elp me climb the ladder. Nah one day Leg, one day 'e'll get it.'

'I bet 'e will, you queer cunt.'

Fuck sake, I'm slipping, Leg's about three-two up here. Come on Moon, concentrate. Chin up. Second half, still plenty of time to bury this cheeky wanker.

'So what's the koo with Sloo? 'as 'e sorted it with Beeke yet?' I'll change the subject and look for an equaliser there.

'I'll never know what the koo is with Sloo. But Yeah, 'e called Beeke on Tuesday apparently and invited 'im out for tonight.'

'That's sorted then. 'e ain't been too bad about it. It's been 'ard for all of us to take. So at least everyone's ok with it now.'

'It is good.'

'Must be for you Leg, you can come out the closet ya'self now you know we'll all get over it.' That's it Moon three all. We'll have this cunt.

'I'll tell ya what though, Sloo's been getting stranger by the day ain't 'e?'

''e's always been fucking out of it. Nothing 'e does surprises me any more.'

'Nah, suppose you're right. It'll be the nuts to get all the lads out tomorrow though. I'm gonna get fucked.' Wait for it Moon, too easy, there'll be a better opportunity.

'Me too. Bet everyone's gonna be banging drugs like nobody's business. You got some of the bugle in as well?'

'Colombia's finest. Gram and half each I thought. That way we can sort the others out a line or two.'

'Yeah the fucking ponces! Can't wait 'til they're done with this student lark.'

'Well that ain't gonna get 'em anywhere anyway. They'll all fail and be back next year doing retakes.'

'Fucking losers. So what ya gotta do this afternoon?' I ask him, searching.

'I've got shitloads of South America stuff to sort out.'

'Thought you'd sorted out the Coke?'

'Yeah, nice one. Hilarious Moon! Funny you should say it though, coz I'm trying to place the Argentina Coca Cola factory.'

'Do they drink it over there? Didn't think they could afford it.'

'Yeah, it's dirt cheap.'

'Just like ya mama...' That's it. It's there. Moon seals the game with an easy goal. But what a cool calm finish. I stand up and slam me empty glass on the table.

'...Come on Leg that's 4-3...' I shout '...Get ya losing arse to the bar and get the beers in ya cunt.' I say proudly.

Leg gets up, shakes his head and goes to the bar.

Moon wins. Fact.

Thursday evening

SLOO

I feel great tonight. A resurgence of energy from within. All those sleepless nights forgotten. No speed, coke or E could compare to this, who needs that shit anyway? I am the person entrusted to save mankind. This is something else. He believes in me, I won't let him down.

Just got off the phone with Crane. Tonight's off. Good. Time for me to get in the swing of things.

I've never killed anyone before.

My real father is here. Knew that faggot before was nothing to do with me. Left when I was seven. Mother tried to stick up for him. "It never worked out for me and your father, some things are like that in life. You think you've found the perfect partner, yet time draws you apart. He was a good man." Fuck that. I'd love to murder the arsehole.

A few years ago, I went to a family party at an Aunt's in Walthamstow. Was fifteen and mother said it'd be ok if I had a beer or two. So there I was sinking Fosters like nobody's business, pissed out me nut. Got talking to a cousin. Tony. Same age as me, but only a raggedy little cunt. We'd been getting along, bit bemused, but proud of the mental family we were a part of. Trying to prove we could handle the booze as well. Neither of us could.

Then he started babbling, "I was sworn to secrecy" he was giving it. You could tell the sauce had him talking. Pissed talk, I thought. I just wanted to shut his fucking mouth with my fist.

Looking back on it, see I was a bit harsh. He was only telling me what his old man had told him. Apparently "Dad" left my mother for another man, one of his supposed friends. All the proceeding years he told me Mum, he was "popping down the boozer with Mark. Few beers, wont be late." That sort of shit. Instead he was going round this queer's for a bunk up.

Me mother let it all out to me Uncle soon after he left her. One of those moments. She'd taken a lot on fucking board, needed someone to turn to. You've just been told by your husband of nine years and childhood boyfriend, that they're leaving you to go off with some fucking poof. Who do you turn to? Gotta be the family. They'd be sympathetic, give you a shoulder to cry on.

No not my fucking cunt of an Uncle. Straight away he's telling his kids. Probably round the dinner table having a right good fucking laugh at our expense. Our shame. "You'll never guess what family, me sisters husband's only a chutney ferret ain't he. Ha Ha..." Fucking ha.

Needless to say I weren't fucking amused. First I smacked Tony right in the fucking hooter. Broke it good. Then stormed over to me Uncle and offered the fat cunt out. He weren't having none of it. Thought "look at this pissed up little cunt getting fucking aggro." It took two of me second cousins, big geezers, to hold me fucking back. Me Mother grabbed me and led me out. I didn't get aggro with her. Not me mother. Once she was involved in the situation I cooled it a bit. All I remember is her having a go all the way home. "I trusted you to have a few drinks and this is how you repay me. You've made an embarrassment of me. I'll never be able to show my face to my own family again. My own family."

I was keeping quiet at first, but something had to be said. At the end of the day she was the one that stitched me up. I was the one they all must have been laughing at. The one they was probably saying "do you think he's the same?" about. Fuck that. "Me neither." I told her.

That's when she really started having a go. All the crap that was coming out her mouth is a bit vague now. Yet I waited. Waited for a fucking pause of breath. Well you know with women that took a while. When she stopped for a second, I turned to her and said "Mum was Dad gay?" She just broke down there and then. Sobbing her eyes out, had to pull over.

There was me answer. That would do. I comforted her as best I could. Felt for her. It must have been one fucking harsh experience, turning someone bent. Fuck that shit. Still it ain't all her fault. I didn't like seeing her like that. She was, is a good woman. It's that cunt I'm fucked at. My supposed father. Bollocks to that. I never told any of the boys the truth, I didn't need to. My real father's arrived now. The one that will save me. Take me away from all this bullshit.

Fucking faggots everywhere, their bullshit diseases fucking this Earth up. Pakis, Niggas, Bosnians taking over our fucking country, making up their own rules. Changing our ways, taking our money for doing nothing. No wipe all the cunts out I say. Can't fucking wait. Just me and the boys. Moon, Littl' leg, Crane, Tin Lid, Brooke, all safe forever. The six of us. Ruling the fucking world. That's the way.

It's gonna be a shame about me mother. I do love her, but she supported that cunt. Let me look like a fucking fool. She'll have to die with the outsiders.

Simple as that.

I've taken to buying tools recently. A bit of a hobby you could say. With the money I get from the garage. I stash away a little for beers with the lads. The rest, the rest I take down to Homebase and get a different weapon every week. Absolutely fucking love it. At first I thought it'd be for a future as a mechanic. You know do me own little jobs. Put an advert in the locals, go round sorting a few people's motors, build from there.

There's no way this college shit is getting me anywhere. You can fucking stick your revision up your arses. Especially now. It ain't gonna be worth shit for no-one.

So now every time I go and pick up the tools, I stand in the store inspecting 'em. Thinking about what damage it will inflict on that queer cunt Beeke. Kill him in the woods and keep the tools with me. While I'm waiting for my master to do his damage to the earth, I'll do up the camp. Give The Styx somewhere nice to shelter while the storms fuck up the world. I'm the new Noah. No animals though. Just my five best friends to save. To start the world with again. Along with the worthy people in all the other forests. They'll probably be setting up already. My turn now.

Now I will rule.

First though there's a little matter about going down the pub with Lid and Brooke. Brooke's down about something. Hope it's that Gemma. Maybe she's dumped him. There's no room for her in the camp. Looks like my father's doing the business already.

It begins tomorrow. But am I ready? I inspect my tools, tonight I'm gonna find out. I know I can do it. Can't wait to show the Lord.

They've got to be well concealed in me pocket. Let's see, tonight I'm gonna take the screwdriver, the Stanley knife and ...the hacksaw.

That should do...

CHAPTER 13
FLASHBACKS, I WAS LAUGHING ALL THE TIME

This week's been the hardest yet. I'm fucking mullered. There weren't a recovery period after that banging weekend. Normally I'll have a few beers on a Saturday, then veg out on the Sunday. Back on form for Monday. With the two drugs nights and three piss ups over Easter, I'm ruined. Pushed to me fucking limits here. Fucking glad Moon's in the same boat. I wouldn't fancy the ribbing if he was still up for *Time*. "Can't take it can you Littl' leg. You're not playing with the little boys no more. This is real men's stuff." I can just see it now, the cunt.

No way. I wouldn't be having that. I'm top of the fucking Premiership when it comes to drug consumption. The Chelsea... No not them cunts... The West Ham 85/86 of narcotics handling. I'd have proved it as well. I'd have fucking gone out, just to make a stand. Then phone up Moon at his office tomorrow morning. Let him know I was feeling top of the world, and how was he? That would wind that miserable cunt up. It's all irrelevant though. Thursday night off. Match postponed- waterlogged pitch. *Time* to heal the injuries so we can send a full team out tomorrow night.

Sloo tried to get me out for a few beers with Brooke and Lid, but I can't be fucking arsed. Early night, save meself. I'll watch a bit on the box too. Vegetable time. Need to restore the energy draining fast.

I'll have a sit down on my bed right now in fact. Won't take me suit off yet. Have to get me mind together.

Head's started buzzing. Like a bee got in me ear. Louder. I'm going all fucking dizzy here. I don't do this, I'm above this. My body can withstand all the pressures. Drugs, tiredness, drink, whatever you throw at me. Struggling here though. Really struggling. Man this fucking room is spinning like a... Fucking something. Gotta get me head together. Fucking Hell, this ain't good. Me *Daft Punk* album's making weird noises. This ain't a song. Someone's babbling. Mumbling shite. Room stops spinning. A man comes out my wall. A cowboy. A shadow of a cowboy. It points a gun at me. Bang. Back in the wall.

Lie down Littl' Leg shut your eyes.

This is just one mental flashback.

FLASHBACK.

Acid night.

Easter weekend, Two years ago.

'What ya talking about Crane?' I'm asking the boy. Fucked.

'Didn't you just say you're going to a horror convention?' He looks at me bemused. This lad's out there, really struggling. It's piss funny though.

'Crane you fuck'ead. 'ow's it whenever we're on acid we still 'old it together, while you 'ave these imaginary conversations with people?' Moon's helping us out, but I'm gonna have to pull the cunt up about this one.

'Moon, you 'old it together? I found you fucking babbling about the Boston Red Sox in *Time*. When 'ave you ever liked Baseball?'

'That's bullshit Leg.' Never.

'Lads what 'as all this gotta do with a horror convention?' Crane's off again.

'No one's been talking about no fucking 'orror convention Crane.' Moon confirms. Crane looks at the floor and shakes his head. You can tell he's really trying though.

'Where the fuck 'as Sloo gone?' *Time* seems to be jumping. I could have sworn he was sat next to me a minute ago.

Six of us.

Tin Lid asleep in armchair. Check. Beeke rolling round the floor in uncontrollable fits of laughter. Check. Crane talking shit in other armchair. Check. Moon sat on stool over in corner. Check. Me. Check, I think. Sloo sat next to me on sofa. Gone.

'I think e must 'ave gone to the bog.'

'When? I didn't see 'im leave.'

'Me neither.'

I look at Moon as he says this. He's grinning away, tripping out his nut too. We both start laughing. Can't remember when I stopped now. Crane looks up and begins giggling. You can tell by the cunt's boat he ain't gotta Danny what he's laughing at. But there's five people in a room with no other sound except laughter. You're on acid. What the fuck else can you do?

In amongst these fits I realise...

'Didn't we 'ave music on a minute ago?'

'Yeah, it was *The Streets* weren'it?' Oh hello Beeke's back.

'Crane this is your gaf, can't you sort out the music?' I can make out from Moon.

'Can't Beeke play 'is harp for a bit?' Crane's being deadly serious here. He looks in anguish, but you can see he's having a whale of a time. He won't remember fuck all of this tomorrow though.

''arp. When did I ever play an 'arp?' Beeke sits up as if he's forgotten he used to be a harp player or something. Dog hairs covering his clothes.

'You was telling me you were taking lessons a minute ago.'

It's like Crane's right eyebrow is on a piece of string, that some puppeteer's got hold of. His confusion is unbelievable. Second to none on acid. He really believes he's hearing these things, but as soon as he repeats it, there's a realisation of its fucking stupidity written all over his boat. A battle in his mind. Suddenly it's what the fuck are you talking about Crane? Have you ever known anyone who plays the fucking harp? It's got Beeke off in bits again though, proving the boy Crane's a first class acid partner.

'We're gonna need another reefer 'ere Moon...' I say '...Something's gotta be done.' Did I just say that last bit?

'Yeah that's gonna really 'elp the confusion. i'M FUCKED IF...' He starts to shout '...Sorry was I just shouting then?' I nod in laughter.

'I dunno why I did that. What was I fucking talking about anyway?'

I can only shake me head.

'It won't work though. None of the mirrors work 'ere.' Crane joins in.

'Crane...' I can't think of anything to say '...What?' That'll do.

'Tin Lid was asking me if 'e could do 'is 'air.'

'Tin Lid's been asleep about 'alf hour, ya prick.' Moon looks at me and shrugs. I'm loving this cunt at the moment. He's still with me. It's a conversation partner. Not much of one at the minute, granted, but it's definitely one. Crane's lost it. Beeke? Fucking hell.

'Fucking 'ell, Beeke ain't you 'urting?' He's still pissing himself. This is unbelievable.

'Sloo?'

'Yeah.'

'What the fucking 'ell are you doing 'ere?' He's sat next to me again.

'I was invited ya cunt.'

'No, you weren't 'ere a second ago... Here I mean.' I point at him.

'I just been trying to piss. I'm about to piss meself, but I keep going to the bog and end up staring at the mirror. Then I forget what I'm doing there so I end up back 'ere again.' He moves uncomfortably on the couch.

'Did you see Sloo come in, Moon?'

'Nah I'm skinning up.'

'I thought you just said you weren't gonna.'

'Now do you think I'd ever say something like that?' I do very much doubt it, but I'm sure. Fucking sure of it. Sure of what?

'What the fuck'shup wi' Crane?' Sloo slurs. Sloo can talk, his head's swaying like a cunt. Or can't talk properly.

Crane is worse off though, sitting there, head in hands, wounded. Oooop, here he comes. He smiles. He's alright, but can't talk. We'll have to wait for the next pearl of wisdom.

'Do you wanna bang some music on Sloo?' I ask hopefully. Fucked if I'm gonna get up. I wouldn't make it through the bodies. Sorry body of Beeke. The way he's rolling around though. It'd be like fucking '*It's a knockout'* or something, trying to get past him. Except I ain't got a big rubbery King's costume on.

'I'll give it a go. I ain't going up to Crane's room though. I'd never make it... and 'is music's shit.' Sloo adds to our delight.

'Eh?' Crane musters.

'Fair play, bang on the radio then.'

'Yeah will do.' Sloo doesn't move. Looks like that one's already forgotten. Done and dusted. Everything that goes on here seems to disappear into a distant past.

'Leg, you got any Bensons? I'm out.' Bollocks now I'm gonna have to move. It'll be worth it though. Reefer! I reach in me pocket. Pull out a flyer. *Time's Out* party night.

'You're telling me.' I tell it. I look up.

Sloo looks at me all strangely. What have I done?

'Come on Leg, ya dopey cunt. Give us a Benson.'

'Alright keep your 'air on.'

'You've been looking at that flyer for ages. Now ya fucking speaking to it ya cunt. This reefer's waiting for you.' It's probably true. I am still staring at it. Look back at Sloo. He's not looking at me at all.

Sloo's concentrating on his hand.

'Fuck me, geez.'

'Leg, BENSON.'

'Yeah, sorry.' Back to the job at hand. I rummage round and finally find the fags. Chuck one to Moon.

'Is that Brooke on the phone?' Crane asks. Through squinted eyes he tries to search the room for some imaginary mobile.

'No Crane.' Moon says. Crane returns to his other world.

'Where is Brooke?' Sloo asks.

'Think 'e pulled.'

'Didn't 'e take no acid?'

'Nah, 'e ain't done for a couple of weeks.' I answer.

'Fucking loser.' Sloo says.

Blackout.

Reefer's on the move. My turn. Beautiful. Don't know how much time's lapsed since... since... something. Same positions. No-one's speaking. Beeke's still laughing.

'I'm fucked.'

'We need to get some'ing on the box.' Moon goes.

Oh Oh. Crane's suddenly fucking with it.

'Let me put on some'ing.'

'Oh for fuck sake. Moon that's your fault.' I know exactly what Crane's thinking.

'Look even if it's Revenge of the killing Vampire Zombies from Hell on Mars Part five: Jason's grandson returns and 'e's pissed, I don't care. We need to fill this silence with something.' Explains the dickhead.

'Yeah, I don't mind neither.' Agrees Sloo.

No chance of Beeke backing me up. Look at that cunt. I don't wanna be harsh, but he's rolling around like a spastic. Tin Lid ain't even moved. Crane jumps to his dvd cabinet. I'm fucked anyway. I'll probably drift away with this reefer.

'Didn't Lid take an acid?' Asks Sloo.

'Yeah, but 'e drunk about ten pints too.'

''ow the fuck 'does 'e manage it? Once acid kicks in for me, drink's the last thing I'm interested in.'

'You know Tin Lid.' I say.

Crane's eagerly fucking around with dvd cassettes. I can't wait to see this choice, I don't think. This boy's one fucked up character. He holds one up. Not '*The Evil Dead*' again. Just fucking mint...

Oh well sit back Littl' Leg, take this reefer in. Lovely bit of skunk. Real smooth shit. The voices around me rambling. I'm not joining in with this one. Too wankered. Sloo says something about the forest setting. Crane is asking if the ants would survive the evil there. Moon is trying to shut him up. Leave this one well alone. Bring the skunk on...

...The voices become one. Strange monotone. Sloo, Moon, Crane bickering. No ants could live in that evil. Crane organising. Screen is on. Fuzzy. Another toke. Let the fuzz stay in me lungs a moment longer... Exhale....

... Smoke clouds my vision. Clear now... Then Mist, the film begins? *A branch. Dusk. Over a lake. Crooked branch. Like a severed limb... We're swaying from side to side. Picking up speed. A car. Woman singing. Over the thick floor of leaves. Deep humming. Industrial noise.*

Through the thin trees. Swaying in and out. People talking. Closer. Leaves. Closer... Jump. Almost smash into lorry.

I'm back.

This film's doing me the world of good. Try to settle. Pass reefer on to Sloo. Following the car. *Through the forest. Sunshine now. A hut in the middle. Nothing for miles around. Autumn trees. The leaves covering the ground.*

Trees all around me...

....

.......All around...........

....

....

....

These drinks are so good Roger. Something else. So happy. What are the ingredients? ... It smells and tastes so nice. Where does the energy come from? ... I want to laugh and dance and sing. I like it here. Never felt so happy. Better than the outside. We're so safe. Summer in the forest. With Sloo. You're right he does seem friendly. Sincere. He will keep us here? ... Why us? ... Where did he come from? ...

You're right the questions are pointless. Be happy. Stay happy. Enjoy the surroundings. The laughter. Look at my friends... So used to them in fields. Working, always working. Always so tired. End of day. Not enough food. Straight to bed. Repair for more work the next day.

Not here though. Here my energy so high. Where is the cold in here? ... Nowhere... No ceiling, yet no rain touches us. The cloaks, our walls, are thin yet they do not blow. Is life always going to be this good from now on? ... Well I feel safe. Yes I want to stay. Drink these drinks. Help make these drinks. Look at my friends. Some have removed their clothes. Naked, dancing, singing. At one again with nature. Robert dances. Adam laughing, Wadard singing. I Hevey Little will do the same. Yes shed these clothes. Enjoy nature. Sloo watching over us. Our saviour. Taking care of our lives. His smile so comforting. Urging us to drink more and be merry. Not much work here. A little every day. Little, Ha, Littl'. The rest is merriment. Can't believe this feeling. In the woods. Like a cottage, yet no shelter. This is so good. I feel so well. Stay like this forever...

SHHH. *listen to this, this is the tape I found* **downstairs**. *...Dancing amongst the leaves. Brown and wild. Dance William...* **Roughly translated** *the book of the dead. Inked in human blood.Possess* **the living**... *I could live like this forever. Always drifting...*

Strange languages. Thunder... Not here... **Condor**. *Smashing ...*

Leg...

Heart beating, not wanting out of this scene yet... hE'S GONE... Was that Moon? ... Alfred where are you? ... Hiding amongst the trees? Playing? Where has everyone gone? Why have the skies turned so grey? Images of glorious summer drift to deadly winter.

We stand before the table. Alfred Beech lays flat. I'm sure this is not how it's meant to be ... Darkness round the cabin. Deep sounds from hell. Beating into our world. Looking at us through the window... Behind the trees.

ACROSS THE RIVER A BOAT COMES TOWARDS US. Seemingly empty. Slowly. Watching Sloo raise the dagger. My joy and energy overcome my confusion. Yet this is not how it's meant to be. Protection, now black clouds. Alfred Beech had done something wrong. For our own safe-keeping this happens. I look around. Everyone seems happy. Smiling, giving into the fact. He must die. Sloo is saying something. Strange languages, can't understand... jugs and buckets. To catch the blood. We will have to drink the blood to save James' soul. Appease the God. Appeasing Sloo. I take a drink. I feel safe again.

Clearer skies. Witness the sacrifice. Beech must have done wrong. Sloo would not do it otherwise... The trees are alive. I hear the screaming of a young woman. The wind breathes hard. Raping. Branches, twigs entering the vagina. The cunt... Blood running fast. I can hear the rain. Yet still it does not affect me. The boat waits on the horizon. Everybody happy? Not Robert Cranley. I see the fear in his eyes. Why? His confusion shows. Why? I raise my glass. Drink Robert. He looks at me. As if I were not who I am. I am Hevey Little. I have not changed. My life is better. Here... In the woods... They're alive... Trees do not attack people... Floating light headed...

Watch the dagger come down. Alfred does not squirm or squeal AS IT PIERCES. THRUSTS INTO HIM. Seems dead already. Punishment. Robert shifting uneasily. I raise my glass once more to him. Drink, Robert. This potion will ease all your fears. Safe. HerE. It will not change.

Blood squirts. Showering us. Covering Sloo's cloak. He catches the blood. Keeps piercing the body. Thrusting. More blood. Thick and Red. Juicy. Thick and red. Blood. Drink. Our sweet beautiful drinks. I will keep drinking the potion. Sloo removes the head. Slicing. Cutting. Gripping Alfred's head by the hair. Pushes his other fist in through the neck. Pulling at something. Something inside. The lifeless head of Alfred Beech. The eyes. Horrible eyes. Staring. Pulling inside. A large lump. Whiteish. Clumps of clouds. Smeared with red. RED. Robert be still. Jumping in his seat... Woman screams...

Can't enjoy the show. Sickened. Don't want to drink. Don't make me. NO............. **act** *of bodily dismemberment. For myself I have seen the* **dark shadows moving in the woods and I have no doubt what I have resurrected in** *this book has Come calling for* **me**. ...... *Robert jumps. Runs. Where are you going? ... Sloo's anger, he looks upon us all. Frightening me. Coming towards me. Can't move..................................* .... **I guessed the** *cards right. You know like* **E.S.P**................ .... *NO LONGER SAFE. THE BOAT IS COMING. THE RAIN GETTING IN*..**It's** *a seven.Ace of Spades.* **Queen** *OF SPADES FOUR OF HEARTS*

EIGHT OF SPADES TWO OF SPADES JACK OF DIAMONDS JACK OF CLUBS.AAAAHHHHH.

I jolt like a fucker. They look at me and laugh, all giggling away. Awake to see some devil zombie floating round the screen, talking about being disturbed. You can talk. Her fucking evil eyes... *'You will die, one by one we will take you.'* Still the boys are pissing 'emselves. Shit I was feeling good there, then fucking scared. That's Crane's fault. One of his stupid horrors getting in me head. Normally so relaxed on reefer and acid. Now I'm feeling the worst side of it all.

Bad trip.

'Crane turn this shit off.'

'Nah this is good this one...' I don't believe Sloo at times.

I'm gonna have to leave the room...

...Soon as I figure a way to work these legs.

BACK

That little sleep was so needed it was unbelievable. So tired I start seeing cowboys coming out me wall. Tired or flashbacks. Flashbacks absolutely love 'em. If this is the sort of trip I'm gonna get two weeks after some mediocre acid. Imagine the fucking flashbacks from one of these insane tabs I've got hold of. Corrr... I daren't think about it.

Time for a bit of dinner and T.V. Come on Leg.

* * * *

'and I don't feel like dancing, no sir no dancing today.'

Cheesy Scissor Sisters songs for me now. Something to sing along to. Gotta replace the lost party hour somehow. I absolutely love it.

Tina's agreed to go out with me again Saturday. This could be the best moment of my life. Undoubtedly.

The only downer was Moon and Leg moving *Time* to Friday. I'm so bang up for the drugs. The last couple of days have been right fucking nerve racking. I want to get out with the boys and fuck me mind up.

Oh well, I've got another date with Tina. Beautiful.

Oh shit.

Time on Friday. I didn't think it through. Taking shitloads of drugs tomorrow, then seeing Tina the next day. Bollocks. Have to go easy on the drugs... HA HA HA. When have I ever managed that?

Money's low too. Still, good thing that Mum and Dad are off to some wedding in Hereford this weekend. I could get Tina round here Saturday. Save some money. I won't go out tonight either. I'll do some revision. Gotta start sometime.

'Don't feel like dancing, dancing, dab a da bad a bad a dab ba dooooo.'

THE BIBLICAL DIRECTORY
(iii)

'Right look.'

The geezer takes out a sheet of paper. There's a list of numbers and names on it. Three columns, quite small writing, but done on the computer so you can see it clearly.

'Right, you have a telephone directory yes?'

'Err the Yellow pages? Yeah.'

'Ok good. Now these yellow pages here are if you need to call anyone important on the other side, i.e. Heaven, Hell, the Underworld… whatever. You know the number of the devil yes?'

'Geez, I've seen the original *Omen* three times. 666.' My earlier experience seems like a distant memory already. Fucking crazy man.

'Correct, and here is the list of the other most important. From 1-999. That's all we need right now.' He shoves it in front of me and I take note of the first few:

#001 The Lord Almighty

#002 Jesus Christ

#003 Zeus

#004 Noah

'That's wicked man.' The first ever phone numbers.

'Right…' He goes '…The number you need to take note of at first is here.'

He runs his figure down the third column of the list 'til it stops at #768

 # 768 Charon –The Riverman.

'Cool.'

'Now, and you're the only person alive who knows this remember, Charon is the serpent, banished from Eden for his betrayal of God. Assigned the down-hearting task of ferrying dead souls across the River Styx; to heaven or the underworld.'

I'm the only person alive? So what about this geezer; and me bird and such. I leave it

'Are you with me now?'

'Yeah. I've woken right up.' Not sure what on earth is happening to me here, but it's fucking exciting. Life for me revolves around me drug night down *Time.* Two dates with this girl, now look what I'm involved in.

'So Charon has suffered for eras upon eras with this arduous ungratifying responsibility. He doesn't like it, but there was nothing he could do about it. Until one thousand years ago that is, when someone uncovered something very unique. Still I run ahead of myself. This is the moment where you must brace yourself...'

I don't know how to brace, but if it means sit rigid and uncomfortable and totally head-fucked, then I'm there.

'...Charon hates this name he was given. He was a serpent remember and whistling was something he could never master. As he travelled about the garden, before his moment of madness, he would desperately try. Yet his forked tongue left him making a noise like this.'

The geezer puts his hand over his mouth, then makes this weird noise.

'SSSSHHHLLLLLLLLLOOOOOOOOOOOO.' High pitched, horrible. How the fuck he does it I do not know.

'SSSSHHLLLLLLLOOOOOOO.' It's like the old nails down a blackboard jobbie.

It's not doing me old nerves any good whatsoever. I think I'm wrapped up in some cult here. Oh not again.

'SShhlllllooo...' Bit shorter and sharper this time. Thank God.

'...Is this ringing any bells?' He asks. I shake me head.

'Shloo, shloo, shloo.' Now he's doing it much quicker, as if he's sneezing or something. He looks at me. I'm just sat looking puzzled. He takes his mouth cover away and says.

'Sloo. Sloo. Sloo?'

'Sloo. What my mate?'

'Yes; or what used to be your friend. Because of this noise, creatures of Eden knew the serpent as Sloo. He liked that moniker, but God had different plans. Well once he stepped out of line that is.'

'So what's this gotta do with me mate?'

'Have you noticed your friend acting strange recently?'

'Recently? Sloo's been mental for years.' I laugh

'Exactly. Sloo, or Charon, began the possession of your friend Kevin a decade ago.'

'Fuck me...' They both look at me as if I've shot someone '... Sorry.'

'He managed this with the dealings of a friend. This number here...'

He points to near the bottom of the first column

 # 327 Hades.

'...Hades. The God of the underworld. An evil warrior who granted Charon with a portal to Earth, all in accordance with the time of his number: Three, two, seven. At this hour Charon could then enter people's dreams to influence his task...'

This is madness man. I'm glad I'm used to horror films. Don't think I'd cope otherwise.

'...Now if Charon would be victorious in this quest, then Hades could become his number two. He'd basically be in charge of the Earth alongside Charon.

So how could Charon achieve this? You may ask...'

I got a few questions, but I'm not sure that was high on me list. I can't think straight at the moment. Sloo possessed by the Serpent that fucked it for Adam and Eve. There's me brains main stumbling block.

'Well I'll tell you...' Please do. '...I'm sorry to throw all this at you in one go, but here's the next important name for you to know...'

He moves his finger up the first row. Stops at:

#230 Hermes

'...Now Hermes was a very good companion to the Lord. Someone that the Lord mistakenly...' He stops and looks up to the ceiling and mouths '...Sorry Father...' Another first for me today.

'...trusted with the secret of the Universe. I cannot divulge the details, but it may help if I translate a quote from Hermes himself: "If then you do not make yourself equal to God, you cannot apprehend God... Think that for you too nothing is impossible."'

'I don't get it.' This is interesting though. Like real life *Omen* or something.

'Unfortunately this is all I'm allowed to say on this subject. This probably doesn't make full sense to you...' No shit Sherlock. I shake me head.

'... But these are only finer details. It's best you have some background knowledge. It could become important to your quest.'

'Now 'ang on a minute. Quest? I ain't signed up to no quest.'

'I do apologise. I'm not trying to scare you, but please let me continue...' I suck through me teeth. Show some displeasure in this quest talk.

'...Anyway, Hermes became obsessed with Our Lord's tempting secret. Soon he was plotting against our father with ambition to rule the Earth himself. Greed is a powerful tool young Crane; and with the loss of his friend to its lure, became The Lord's most despised sin.

Yet no-one suspected this of Hermes. At first, at any rate. He was very surreptitious in his scheming. Willing even to stab our very Lord in the back. He was also a cracking mathematician, understood the importance of numbers. Created formula upon formula to crack the code. Eventually he found some success. Using his numbers he found a way to enter the dreams of humans. He believed possession of mind to be the answer he sought.

Following this Hermes made nightly visits to an Emperor called Decius. Decius however, misinterpreted the messages he was receiving. The subsequent persecution of many Christians left a very sour taste upstairs, let me tell you.

Hermes' lack of insight and insufficient thought was apparent. When our Lord discovered he was to blame for this; another was banished to the underworld and the charge of Hades...'

Man I wanna go to bed. The long words remind me of college. I'm still nodding away in pretence that I have a clue.

'...Though very wise, Hermes now knew he couldn't achieve supremacy alone. His only hope would be to introduce another to the potentially dangerous insight. As you say here: two heads are better than one…'

Where's this geezer from anyway?

'…That way he could share leadership. From then on…who knows? Hermes is not a man to be trusted, his greed clouds thought. We know he would soon do a Brutus, but there's too much excitement in the Underworld for anyone to see this. Anyway he was the instigator of this plan. Held vital information. That the directory numbers here were the co-ordinates for success, but how?'

How indeed? What?

'…To know this they required the greatest philosophers and magicians Earth has ever produced. So Hades gave Hermes charge to lead souls over a crossover section of The Styx:-The River Acheron, to find them. Hermes had to take the dead to three judges, whom I won't name. Too many people may confuse you…'

Yeah too many people. Now that'd be confusing!

'…These judges decided on where the souls should go. Heaven or the Underworld? Do you know of judgement day?'

'Yeah I've seen films on it, but...'

'Good. So you understand that evil souls will go to the Underworld…' I dunno if that was a question or what, but he ain't stopping for an answer. '…Hermes witnessed the judging process and saw the potential capabilities of the wicked souls he was transporting. Once they reached the Underworld, Hermes gave Thanatos the responsibility of minding the select few, until they found the answers to the Universe. Here's Thanatos, the God of Death:'

He points to near bottom of the second column.

#635 Thanatos

Too many names man. I hope this ain't all in me test.

'Should I 'ave a pen and paper 'ere?' I ask

'Unfortunately there is little time. You will get it Crane. I believe in you.' Tina states.

Still holding on to me hand. Love her, but what a mug! Me get this?

I have a sip of me tea…

CHAPTER 14
PRACTICE MAKES PERFECT

'I'm gonna j-hic-jump on thish Shloo.'

'Alright Tin Lid. Thanks for coming out.'

'No problem. You-hic-you know me, few beersh and all that.' Love it.

'You're a good friend Lid. I'll see you tomorrow, because I fancy a walk.'

Fuck that. It's piss down soon. **248** it home to bed. My fucking glorious bed. Legs won't carry me no way anyway. Leathered man.

'Yeah. Huge.' Aaahh Bisto. Bus busting Dry…

'Fucking what is it? Pound or some'ing?'

'It's one pound-fifty please mate.'

'Fuck me-hic-xtortion.' Now where's me change? Fucking zip pockets, fucking joke. Got some, pull it out, all over the fucking floor.

'Oh bollocksh, shorry-hic-ate.'

'Listen don't worry about it. Pick up your money and go and get a seat. Just don't throw up ok!'

'Oh fucking-hic-nice nishe one…' Get grip on pole. Eyes ain't focusing on no shit.

'…fuck me ch-hic-change. Better sHit...' Cunt pulls away. Grip slips. Next thing I'm on me arse. Some prick's laughing. But I ain't I any state 'ere. Could just fucking sit here. Nah bollocks don't wanna definitely no get chucked off. Ain't strolling it, no way strolling. Use some strength, swaying. Grab pole. I can fucking do this. Someone's pissing 'emselves. 'Bollocksh.' Cunting bus, sharp corner. Over vertical poles, heaped in baggage compartment. This is gonna fucking hurt come sunrise. For real like. Pocsy laughter ringing round me ears. Ringing round effing bus. Even the driver's having a bubble at me. Wanker's probably all on purpose and shit. Gotta even get up, sort these wankers out or… some shit. Grab poles even side. Jimmy nast Tin. Think jimmy nast… Face squashed against plastic glass against staircase. Big breath. Straight again. If only me head weren't fucking lead, could get me legs syncked up or some'ing.

'Man get me off th-hic-this fucking thing.'

'No probs mate.'

Slam on brakes. 'Eeeurgh.' Flying down bus. Flat out, middle of everyone. See group of cartoon birds in sky. Fucking swear it. Or is it the fact all cunts are pissing it?

'fucking cunts.' bastardss. Someones' lifting me underneath me armpits. Pushed down steps, crash onto street. Doors shut. Screech……. bus pisses off. Where fuck am I? Who cares? I need to puke

'ere'll do…

* * * *

Having left the pub slightly earlier than Tin Lid and Sloo, Brooke arrives at Gemma's house. Returning to his girlfriend's open arms.

'Feeling a bit better?' She asks. Brooke accepts the loving hug and kisses her.

'Yeah, it was good. Took me mind off things a bit.'

'How's the boys?'

'It was only Kev and Ad out, but they were good. Think Ad's pretty 'ammered.'

'What about you?'

'Nah, I've only 'ad a couple. Didn't want to bring meself down. I Didn't really need the drink either cause Kev was right chatty. Couldn't believe it.'

'What 'elping you out?'

'Yeah, mostly. 'e seems right excited about some'ing.'

'What?' Gemma laughs.

'Fuck knows, but 'e really 'elped me out tonight.' Sloo helpful.

SLOO HELPFUL?

Helpful SLOO

HELP Sloo

SlOo Help

HELP FOR SLOO

SLOO HELP? ...

...Won't need help tonight. I've got the approval of my Lord. If he believes in me I cannot fail.

Approaching the park. Quicker. Can't wait to do this. Past shops... The Essex Yeoman... Upminster station.

A few late night drinkers making their way home. Loud. I'd shut their fucking mouths. Yet their time will come...

Lights diminish, darker here. Large houses, sleeping. I can hear music. Low organ sounds. The notes dragged out. Like some horror film. Can't work out if it's in my head or from a house I pass. My walk orchestrates the song. Violins, cellos. Deep bass. Feel the build within my thoughts. Angelic children hum. Pace quickens. I'm Ready now.

Three pints to boost my courage, I see I did not need. My lord's words ringing round my ears, inspiration enough.

"You are my son Sloo. With my help you will have the strength to finish the work I commenced. You above anyone else can bring these people into the forest... You above anyone else." I will, but first my father I must clear the unwanted rubbish.

Set up our home, ready for The Styx return. Something there polluting our camp. Obstructing the coming. Must be destroyed.

Yes, I've seen you there, tramp. It may keep you safe from the storms for now. Dry against the rain, but it's not your home. It's not there for your protection. Only the chosen ones. Those prepared to rebuild the earth.

The rain grows heavier. I see the park draw nearer. Darkness covering green, where we used to have such fun. We will play there again. This *time* undisturbed.

Upminster court. Legal system futile now; soon.

Reaching **RIVER DRIVE** Where salvation lies. To think the small wood where The Styx would come each summer will soon be our home, 'til the storm clears. Thunder. The rumbling a threat of a further downpour. Cleaning the earth. A warning to him that sleeps.

RIVER DRIVE

I've witnessed you tramp. Been hiding amongst the trees, watching you at night. This is our home. This is where the River returns. You make it stink with your filthy clothes. Dirt covering your body. You're not worthy to be our slave. Sacrilege of our site.

Reach into my pocket. Pull out the knife. The last remaining light. The row of houses heated. Comfort. People inside now, retiring to their warm beds. Safe from the rain. Soon it will wash you all away. Not us.

The orchestra builds.

Hollow church sounds. Picturing a funeral. People dressed in black, walking solemnly, heads hang low. You know who you are. Ever closer.

The footbridge. Trees expanding. The forest becoming vast. Swamping the surrounding lands. Like the old days. Before you wrecked it with buildings. Destructing creation. You can't fight against nature. Now it will destroy you. You can hide for now. Houses protecting against the storms. Not for long. You damage our sanctuary, I will obliterate yours. The forest my home. I've returned and those that spoil my residence will see my vengeance. Vagrant. You should have stayed clear, you'll soon realise. Then it will be too late.

Leaves crisp underground. Love the crunching sound. Thick and brown. The darkness cuts the distance for those who do not own these forests. Huge trees. Reaching to the sky. Guiding me. I can see the route. Deep, deep into the forest. Searching for the runaways. Trees coming to life. Show me the way. Point your branches at those willing to defy your God. The rain heavier outside. I feel it only slightly here. Yet glory in its thick texture. Washing me clean. The blood of the past.

Screaming twigs. Leaves scratching. No sound to the outside world. This is our own hideout. The Styx Only. Visions grow stronger. I remember the times. Take me back…

The flashbacks. Adrenalin rushes. Making me laugh. The potion still lies within me. I'm fed for now. We need more food Sloo. Give us the power to rule again. More blood. More flesh to feast upon. Ever nearer.

Brown arms twisting. Outstretched fingers pointing.

This knife will carve you apart tramp. It's time for you to vacate the camp. Keep sleeping. Soon your slumber will be everlasting. You thought your existence worthwhile. Never suffer the slavery of work. Live your life from dustbins and skips. Never begging for money, but receiving charity. Who needs a home eh? We do tramp and you're trespassing. You're stealing our abode.

Flashbacks. The route for the forest is quicker for me. I know the way. Dense. You may run, but you don't understand it's complexities like I. I've been here for eternity. Searching. Now I've found them. No one can hide from me. This is my territory. Our domain Sloo. Do you recall? Remember how we showed them as we stabbed and stabbed at Beech. Remember the drink covering our face. Our liquid for vitality. Cranley ran. We'll find him. I'll find him Sloo. Soon your work will be done. Just need your committal. I am pledged to you father. I walk with you. Thy deed will be done. I will save myself and my friends unto your power.

Yes Sloo. Your safety is guaranteed.

The trees thicken. Black enveloping the site. Yet I see. See things going on here.

You must ignore the visions of the past Sloo, that is all they are. When the plan didn't work. The killings were for their own good. So they could return and be saved this time. They lost belief then. They will trust in you. I will ensure it. Loud clashing. Thunder or cymbals? Reverberating around the forest.

I see things.

Ignore the dismemberment for now.

I see the branch move. Smashing into Brooks' head. Breaking his skull. Denting the membrane. Twitching around in fits and spasms.

Ignore this Sloo. It was the Brooks of old. Your friends will not be affected. Do not turn away from the task. Murder the person that litters our home. Take him apart. I will father. Tears running down my cheek. Mingling with the rain and blood.

Ramming the stick into Brooks writhing face. Red and black marks thicken, multiply. Keep pushing the stick into his eyes. He will not see his own death. He didn't feel it Sloo, the most painless way. Severe the nerve in the brain.

Ignore the visions. That is the past.

Pushing him into the river. Floating away face down. Is that one of the others. Coming to save his friend. No, big mistake. Branches move out of view. The tunnel to the Camp. Brooks is finished. Gone to The Styx.

The boat sails, approaching. Hear the souls whispering around you.

Time to transform. Tilnid sees what he's up against. The tree comes alive within me. Growing higher. Swamping the weak slave. Fangs hungry for his blood. Limbs of trunks. Twisting fingers reaching further. Grab the ankles. Pick him up. Stranded in the sky. Hanging upside down. Clasp tighter, cut into the ankles. The blood drips over my leaves, my twigs. Underneath the skin. Slicing through the bones. Drops to the floor. Try to run without your feet, disciple. Lick my fingers clean. Even more energy. I grow further.

Ignore these. This was all for us now Sloo. This *time* we will do it right. Ignore the visions. They will only harm.

See the fear in Tilnid's eyes. Can't even hobble. Balance diminished, can only claw an escape. Not fast enough. More food. Come crashing down on him. Crushing the life through his mouth. Up and down shoot his insides. Secrete from the orifices. Watch the organs ooze out in a red sea. Scattered around his crushed skin and bones. This way our food's untarnished.

Ignore. Concentration Sloo, this is your *time.* We will feast on the tramp for now. Then Beeke. Your work will be done and you and your friends will shelter here from the storms. The earth gets washed away in a tide. We will be safe from the waves. Then gorge for eternity on the outsiders. Our food is plentiful.

The camp is in sight. Cloaks hang from the trees. New material shielding the inside from the winds.

I can hear the snoring. The breath an impurity to my home. Polluting the air. Feel the energy from nature. Forcing you toward him. Clean the atmosphere with the smell of death.

Revenge…

Sloo stalks further, arriving at the cloaks. He pushes one aside and peers through. The tramp's head protrudes from a filthy mattress. Not the bedding Sloo would choose for his home. An unaware peaceful skull, the White hair overgrown, mingling with a wiry beard. An obscured face grimy and unwashed.

The tramp dreamt of his earlier days. At dinner with his wife. Her death had destroyed Bill's enthusiasm for life. He'd given up his job, his home, considering assets immaterial without his loved one to share them. She was killed in a car crash. Strong winds, rain clouded her vision through the windscreen. The oncoming lorry having the same difficulty. Bill's wife killed instantly, glass slicing her throat. Life would not be the same for Bill. On hearing the news he took to the street. Walked away from everything he had built. Now he lies in moderate comfort, fantasies infiltrating his mind. Chews on a chicken leg, shares an anecdote with his partner over a candlelit table.

Sleeps with mouth wide open.

Sloo raises the Stanley knife high.

Directly above the weary mans head...

An almighty force from the wind pushes his arm down. Sloo lacks control. Taken away like his lost innocence. His image flashes into his dreams. Here is his father reigning down above him, taking control of his limbs.

Sloo watches the knife swiftly pierce the cheek. Straight through, the blade avoiding teeth and tongue. Pushes straight through the other side and holds fast in the ground. Bill's pain is sudden. He wakes with a jolt, tries to get up. Understand the cause of agony, but only succeeds in ripping his face open. His lips are increased to twice their length.

The tramp wobbles on his feet. In shock he can't comprehend the attack. Why? Who? He sees the shadows before him. Trying to lash at one, his hand disappears into darkness. Nothing there. The attempted force in his own punch and the ache in his face sends Bill crashing to the floor. Collapsing into the leaves. He twists round to face skywards. See where the next attack will come. Only black surrounding.

Once more he tries to climb to his feet. Yet a weight is upon him. Or pulling from beneath. Under the leaves. Sinking. Unexplainable gravity from below. A deep bed slowly beginning to engulf him. Drowning, while the shadows splice, then loom over. Sloo pulls the hacksaw from his pocket. Bill trying to rise. Trapped, arms no longer willing to work. Blood dripping from his cuts.

Sloo takes the tramp's head in one hand. Getting a grip with clumps of hair. Sloo brings the dome up.

Face to face.

Bill can now make out the young adult attacker. Yet as he looks, the image seems to increase with age. The jaw line strengthens. Stubble becoming apparent. The hair increases its length. For an ecstatic second, Bill figures it must be a dream. But the pain. Crippling. Surely he would wake now. Staring into the eyes of the captor. Finished, dream over...

Yet still he stares, witnessing the assailant's face contort. Reverberating, shuddering into something else. Horrifying images of suffering. People strapped to trees. Stomachs cut open. They're still alive. Screaming as a tall reptilian creature laps at their wounds with a four forked tongue. Long sharp teeth point outward, circling the protrusion.

Bill tries to shut his eyes to the visions, but they only appear more vivid in total darkness. Four spikes crown its head, more line its back and tail. It's Brown cloak tattered with the sharp spine. Continuing to lick dripping blood from the sores, it knows something is watching. Bill doesn't want to see the eyes. He opens his own, but baring down on him for one second, there it is. Pupils almost disappearing up into the forehead, leaving bloodshot white filling the sockets.

Bill rejects his stomach, excretes himself. Still he can't struggle free from the leaves. Again he closes his eyes. A demonic tiger runs at him. Opens them, once again just a young adult. The tramp prays for the insanity to end. To be killed and rejoin his wife.

Sloo has other ideas.

Lightning and thunder ring above. Shrill laughter throughout the forest. All shadowing the tramp's screams. The rivers' flow reverses. It's coming.

Sloo puts the hacksaw to Bill's nose. Ripping and tearing through the bridge. Working its way down. The bone breaks. Chips of brittle fly away. Speed and force, the flesh cuts easily. The nose comes away.

A face now unrecognisable through deformities. Behind the blood a hole opens, while his mouth hangs open baring clenched teeth.

Bill fears to shut his eyes. Terrified of darkness, the visions. Preferring eyes of a maniac removing his features. Staring into them.

Hypnotised by the age of nature. Watches as the screwdriver appears. Can't close his eyes anymore, transfixed. The point draws nearer. Filling his sight. Now only the point. The only thing to see, to feel, as it pierces into his pupil. Blood splutters up. Blurred vision. Bill screams. Lost in the wind.

Sloo's face bears down upon him. Drinking from his eyes. Loss of liquid drains the energy.

Can't move. Wishing the pain to end. Through his remaining eye sees three arms thrash wildly above. Once again the hacksaw hones into distorted focus. Doesn't even see the screwdriver crash into his front teeth. Shattering pieces. He screams again. A hand clasps his tongue, pulls on it. The hacksaw. Lined by the side of the fleshy muscle. Sawing. Bill tries to pull his tongue back into his mouth. No use, the grip far too tight. The slicing continues. The tramp's throat fills with blood. Choking, gagging. Finally this torture causing him to pass out.

Sloo takes the severed tongue and places it in his own mouth. Chewing on the gristle like gum. Drinking the juice flowing from it. Slithering down his throat. Refreshed. Sloo looks down at his work. At the unconscious disfigured tramp. Have to wake him for the finale. Let him experience torment for spoiling the haven.

Sloo bends over the dismantled face and takes hold of the left ear. The hacksaw rips through lobe sweetly.

Bill wakes into the nightmare once more. He feels a release from beneath. Can finally pull himself to his feet.

Sloo still appreciating his new found power. Experiences a joy at the ease of cutting this man's face apart. The tramp wants to fight. Catch attacker off guard, reflect his own agony on this psycho.

Sloo feels a blow to the side of his head. There is no pain. He laughs. Lifts his head to the sky. His bellows echo with thunder.

The tramp senses an audience surrounding. Witnessing the attack, humoured at its severity, accentuating the level of cackle. Bill tries to lash out again. Only for his fist to be halted. Twigs wrap around his wrists. Once more trapped. His other arm. One last try. Punches towards the maniac. Again he cannot reach before his hand is locked by a hidden force. Thorns rip into his forearms.

Sloo stands before him, continuing to laugh at the vagrant's audacity.

With pressure greater than a hurricane, Bill is pushed back. Slamming into a tree. Falling to the floor, knows instantly that his hands have been ripped from arms. The tramp remains grounded. Rolling around, holding chest with the stubs he has left. Bill can't fight anymore. He lies motionless as the man moves toward him.

Sloo drops his weapons. Clenches his hand into a claw and thrusts it into the victim's chest. One last stunned moment before Bill feels his heart being ripped out. Beats a few last times. The tramp excretes again, urinates in his trousers. His body piled into a mix of disfigurement and fluids.

For Sloo this comprises another feast. This human's life force giving him the strength to come ever closer to the return.

As he bites once into the heart, he experiences an increased power over his new body. The possession nearly complete. Once Beeke is slaughtered, Sloo will arrive to finish his work. So impressed with his choice. Easy to persuade. The boy with such little will power doing him proud.

Soon he will be that boy.

Then he can come for the rest of them.

For now he stands beside the eighteen year old. A shadow whispering in the dark.

'Now go to where the leaves are thick.'

Sloo goes to the area that encased the tramp in his battle for life. He instantly knows to pull the leaves away. Once removed a large hole gapes before him.

'Reach down, there is something for you.'

Sloo follows orders. Takes hold a sheet of paper. Removes it from the hole, folds it and places it in pocket.

The hollow proves a satisfactory place to bundle the tramp's remains. A wind kicks up within the camp and leaves push back to their original setting. Covering the signs of Sloo's victim.

'You can return home now Sloo, do not fear, the rain will wash away the blood.'

Sloo walks blankly from the camp, eagerly anticipating the contents of the paper…

* * * *

Can't believe old Sloo, always walks it... Well glad I got the bus. Would 'ave been soaked if I ain't…

"ang on a minute I'm fucking drenched 'ere. I get me mobile out. 'alf one, you must be 'aving a right bubble bath. I've lost two hours. Again. What on earth, this time?

Didn't think I was that pissed and that. Was gonna save meself for the biggie tomorrow.

Get Wendy tomorrow...

Man, what 'ave I been doing? Me hoody's stuck to me. At least I'm on the right road home…

Few beers, good night down Bridge House and that...

Shame about Brooke. Fucking bad his Dad chucking him out. Sloo was mint tonight. Really took his mind off it. Ain't a bad bloke when it comes down to it!

Bit weird about the whole Styx thing though. Asking me if I've told anyone about the commandments. No. I'm eighteen. If I told anyone, they'd think I was well out of it. Normally am though. The way he said 'Good', smiling. Strange fucker, means well...

Getting nowhere with this boring college work shit. Really fucking me off and that. I just ain't got a Scooby about it. I just wanna drink all the time and that…

* * * *

Crane and Tina are on holiday in Neath, Scotland. Crane had never been to the place before, never really heard of it. This added to his surprise at the town's beauty. An historic cathedral stands proud in the city centre. Its construction magnificent. He wants to stand and admire it, but Tina wants to soak up the sun... They sit in a huge park, similar to where Crane played football as a child. As he sits with his love he watches tens of children dancing in a circle. A Scottish pastime? He wonders... A group of picnickers enjoy the rare sunshine in their country... He sits with Tina on the beautiful sweet summery smelling grass... A group of young boys excitedly fly a kite. A beautifully coloured diamond. The sun reflects upon it causing a strobe light effect around them. Flashes of blue, red, gold. Dazzled... Crane cuddles Tina, wants her to fully appreciate what he sees. She wraps her arms lovingly around him. He feels so comfortable. The couple kiss for a while before Tina stands.

'I want an ice cream!' She states in a childlike manner that he finds so sweet.

He also feels a dryness in his throat. He'd love one too... Despite considerable protestations, Tina insists she will go to the ice cream van to purchase them. Crane watches her stroll confidently away, then once again focuses on the colourful kite...

Someone sits beside him. Tina was quick he thinks, turning to face her.

There sits Sloo. He looks upon Crane with disgust.

'What are you doing 'ere Sloo?'

'I was about to ask you the same thing.' Sloo answers petulantly.

'I'm 'ere with Tina. She's gone to get some ice creams.'

'Good.' Sloo's face distorts. Crane knows it's him, but he looks different, somewhat older. A dark cloud passes over the sun, giving an impression of night. Shadows fill the landscape.

'I'm here to see Freddy Flintoff play a bit of cricket. You fancy a bite to eat before he comes in to bat?' Sloo asks.

The thought of Tina evaporates from Crane's mind.

'Sure.'

The background changes. A dismembered body. Fresh smelling, raw meat. Torn limb from limb. Cooking slowly now. Strong aroma of Indian cuisine possesses Crane's rationality. Tempted by the flesh. Sloo hands him a sizzling arm. It looks so tender. Crane takes a bite. Succulent meat, can't get enough of this. Sloo also takes a chomp, then like rabid dogs they ferociously chew and savage their way to the bone. Crane's hunger rises. Blood drips from his chin. He spits out a bone, then chooses a thigh.

Before he starts the next course he takes a look at the holiday chalet in which he feasts. ***DANK****. Ragged dark clothes hang from the ceiling. All are smeared with dirt and blood. A smell of spunk and rotting flesh fills the room. Crane has to hold his nose, yet he keeps on eating...*

Sloo **SHAKES**.

The image of his friend stuffing a penis into his mouth shocks Crane.

(Awake).

Police looking for the murderers. The body had been found in the chalet. Crane would have to go on the run. His Mother suspects it was him. Coming up to his room to confront. He has to climb from the window... Get Tina. But wherever he searches he cannot find his girlfriend... The front cover of a newspaper floats across his path. Headlines report a cannibal attack in the park. Suddenly comprehends the signs of danger. Dashes to Sloo's, see if he's been caught. There his friend's parent tells him her son has gone to Neath. Crane instinctively knows Tina's in trouble...

He makes the road trip to Scotland. This time the park is empty. Black clouds hang threateningly. Crane has to battle against strong winds across the park to reach a caravan situated in the middle. He walks to the window and peers through. Sloo looks up at him, eyes white as snow. There with Tina tied to a chair. Crane tries to break the glass, causing his deranged friend to shriek with patronising laughter. Then Sloo takes a deep bite into Tina's shoulder. The love of Crane's life screams... ***Screams****......*

'*WUURGGRRHH*'

Wakes. *Time* to put the light on, make sure. You don't want to return to that dream. To see how it ends!

'Jesus Christ I gotta lay off the drugs.'

* * * *

Sloo feels refreshed. The rain has cleansed him. To others he looked the stereotypical unfortunate. Like someone caught in the storm on their walk home. They would not have envisaged the horrific act this young man had just carried out.

His Mother sleeps soundly in her room as he creeps past. Into his own. Places his tools into a box he keeps at the back of the wardrobe. Salutes gratefully at the success of their first outing. Now the moment he has waited for...

The piece of paper is tatty, but its scrawls clear.

THE SIX COMMANDMENTS OF THE STYX.

1. Once thy has pledged thy future to The Styx then thou shalt not leave the forest.
2. Thou shalt not commit any sexual act towards another member of The Styx.

3. Thou must obey Sloo.
4. Thou must not fight another member of The Styx.
5. Thou must not steal from another member of The Styx.
6. Thou shalt carry out the respective given tasks for the good of The Styx.

Cranley:	*To gather food by hunting in the woods.*
Mooning:	*To gather nuts and berries.*
Little:	*To prepare food.*
Tilnid:	*To protect North and East side of Woods from visitors.*
Beech:	*To protect South and West side of woods from visitors.*
Brooks:	*To collect water and fish from the river.*
Sloo:	*To protect The Styx from illness and harshness of weather.*

Behind, Sloo can feel a presence. Yet he does not turn.

'I could have given them a life free from worry. Free from the constraints of the outer world. The return to primitive. A community to take care of each other for eternity. I would have given them immortality. I can do the same for you and your friends. You did well tonight. Now all that is required is the slaughter of Beeke. As you can see from the commandments he will not comply in our land. Beech of old was the same. You can see why it will not work in The Styx. It is not the way of life I want to provide. Kill him at this time tomorrow. After he pledges himself to you. I will be with you.'

'Yes father.'

Hailstones battering at windows. Shaking the streets. Car alarms sound. Waking people from their slumber. Thunder crashes. People struggling to sleep. Except some.

But their visitor is coming…

The boat is near....

CHAPTER 15
DREAMS

'I am here to save you Moon. All that was good in this world has returned to deliver you to serenity. A habitat where everyone will help each other. Not like your work place. Selfishness, the greed. A battle to become richer than the next. No community, there is no sharing on this earth. My locality is most different. Let me show you.'

FLASH

Spiralling. Feel so small, so young. An autumn atmosphere. Fresh smelling clean air, leaves and twigs scattered about my feet. These forests so familiar, can't be our woods, surely? Expanse far too vast. Trees that must have stood for over a thousand years. Tall, never ending, reaching to the heavens. I look up at their splendour. Full of life, untouched. Proud they stand, alive.

I can experience their vitality. Head to toe, I'm filled with wonder. Magnificent buzzing reaching my fingertips. What drug is this?

'No drug Moon, reality. Listen to Sloo and receive this everlasting divinity. Now look, watch your friends.'

The Styx come running past. I turn quickly to see them dart away, leaving a trail of laughter. Chasing in amongst the trees, they look like boys again. How I remember them from childhood. Their singing, never heard such jubilance. I want to join in, have to join in. I make to run, to be with them, yet I'm stuck. A force pulling me back.

'Wait, you can partake soon. If you make the right choices. There is an alternative however, if you make a serious error of judgment.'

FLASH

I'm sat behind a desk. The whole scenario seems familiar. Recognition of my schooldays. This is my old classroom, yet it's bare. My friends are nowhere to be seen. No teacher or blackboard. Though I see a projector screen's been set up. A man appears beside it. Must be thirty or so. Clean image, the structure of his jaw matches perfection. It's not just his mouth that smiles, every feature beams with delight. Long brown hair resting on his shoulders. A laurel of twigs and leaves. Tan skin, an epitome of mankind. Friendly glinting eyes. Warming. His long brown robes put me in mind of a monks. I feel as though I know him from somewhere, but I can't figure why. He stands next to the screen . It begins to flicker, I've an enthusiasm to see what it shows.

FLASH

History class, 13 years old. Mr. Smith makes us watch War documentaries. Horrible footage. Death, lifeless bodies everywhere. The Jews ordered to concentration camps. Terror in their eyes. A time *for real fear. I couldn't go through it. Never in a million years. Another World War and Moon wouldn't be there. No way. A call up letter and I'd be missing. It scares me to my very soul.*

FLASH

Suddenly I don't want to see the screen. Petrified of the horrific visions of War. Want out of this room. But he is here calming me. Telling me to relax. Everything will work out for the best, if I trust him. I do. His voice so soothing. Like my Mother's reassuring tone when my Dog died. Similar to my Dad when he put an arm around me as a kid. His comfort when I missed a penalty in the final. Everything that makes sad occasions better portrayed in one tongue. Confident body language. Stern honesty, with an understanding. I remain in my seat, happier now to listen.

'2009...' The screen rolls more images. '...The World after the first Nuclear war." Ruins, dust. Buildings collapsed . Nature disintegrated. Deserted wastelands. No sign of anyone. Then three people emerge from a bunker.

'In hiding for over two years Moon, these are sole survivors in one County. No one you know. They emerge to see...' Then the bodies. Visions of History. Burnt black crumples. Tatters. Skulls. Limbs. The blood. The

screen goes red. The sky is red. Glowing. Burning. It's sweltering here, like an oven. I loosen my tie. Have to take off my shirt. Can't bear the heat. A dead baby, in the arms of the skeleton mother. Burning up. Sweating. Please cool me down.

'...Calm Moon, just a slight experience of the pain you will suffer when the world comes to a halt...'

' ...The warnings are being ignored. The Middle East, Afghanistan, Pakistan and India, Lebanon, Iran, Iraq. It's all coming to a head. Yet people continue with their lives. Not preparing. Believing like all the other times, the concern will pass. Still they work and for what reason? To be ejected from bunkers when provisions run to a minimum. Enough food for the powerful, the rich, the people who supposedly matter. Sufficient supplies for a year, then starvation threatens. Your family Moon: ...'

I see my Mum and Dad on the screen. A future me. Looking worn. Unkempt. Being ousted. Told we have to go outside. We are not worthy to be kept alive. They push us out into a tunnel. We sit for a while. Our bodies scorching. I'm crying, having to say good-bye to Mum and Dad together. Their last embrace. All hope is forgotten. Crawling up the tunnel, time to face our fate. Showdown with death.

'...Like everything on this earth, it was each for their own. Little did they know their world was over anyway. Nothing to return to. Total destruction. They were only prolonging the inevitable. Starvation, malnutrition. The Fourth World. Know how they suffer. This is your future Moon, but you can be saved. Listen to Sloo. You have to listen to Sloo or....

Skin flaking. Peeling. Watching my Mother burn as if she were on fire. Yet there are no flames. Just intense heat. My Dad's face, sores. His hair disintegrating. Eyes burning red. Melting. His skin drips to the floor. I can't even cry. Too hot. Can only watch my Mum and Dad scream. Fall down, laid out. Blood boiling spilling out over the ground. My mothers skull, her eyeballs pop out. Roll like marbles. Everything bubbling around me. The sky Red. A different world. Another planet.

'Listen to Sloo. Listen to Sloo. Listen to Sloo. Our world is in the forest. The trees will save you. There you can help each other. The Styx together... Listen to Sloo.'

Fucking hell. My heart's gonna explode here. I put my hand to my forehead. Feel the sweat. Like I've been in a fucking shower. I'm ringing wet. Need a drink of water. Was that some sort of fucking message or something? I don't normally remember dreams. That was too fucked up. I visualise the images, my parents in pain. Get it out of your mind Moon. Something I never ever want to see. If that was a fucking prophecy then what's all this "listen to Sloo" about? What can he do to stop a Nuclear War? Gotta stop thinking about it Moon. That charcoal baby. Oh fuck, I feel sick. Who was that fucking bloke? Get a drink. Get it out your mind man. I can't, I just can't.

* * * *

Gemma, woken by Brooke's murmurs. He can't lie still. She puts an arm around her boyfriend in an attempt to comfort.

I've had a major row with Gemma. I must be so pissed, I can't even work out what it was about. She'd stormed out the club half hour before I left. At first I was so annoyed I just let her go. Now I'm worried about her, hoping she made it home safely. My fear is rising. I can't go home to my parents. Haven't even spoken to them since the row. Going back to Gemma's. She'll probably still be up, if she's upset. She'll know that I'll come back. We'll sort this one out. Even if I have to wake her parents, I've got to go back. Need to know she's safe.

I'm panicking as I arrive. A red glow around the house. Danger approaches.

The door is slightly ajar. I figure she left it open for me. Worked out that I'd follow her. Should have left earlier I know it. She must be well angry now. For the life of me, I can't remember why we were arguing. Won't lose this girl. No way. We'll get over this one.

The house is silent. Left in darkness. I shut the door behind me.

The Hallway. Stairway, noiseless. She might be drunk too, could be passed out in bed. Maybe she's forgotten. We'll wake in the morning as if nothing has happened. Stupid for us to fight.

Climb the stairs, careful not to wake her Mum and Dad. Each step I miss the squeaky boards. This has to be a first. Reaching the top, the darkness still daunting.

The landing. There are rays of light seeping through her door at the end. I hear slight groans. Hoping she's ok. My mind is racing, for some reason I feel terrified. Heart beating rapidly. Slowly approaching her room.

Hand reaches out to open the door. Like a horror film. Flashes of Crane showing us more of his disturbing movies. Half expecting a disfigured man to grab me from... anywhere. I look around, waiting for the jump moment. Cringing within. My skin crawling. Closer to the door. Still the groaning, louder and louder. Praying it's not the sound of her crying. Has she been hurt? Attacked on the way home? Or a man in a Hockey mask waiting to scythe my head clean off. The door is hot to touch. Use fingertips to push it open, exposing more light. Revealing the noises. Vision blurs...

...begins to steady. There she is. Naked. On all fours, thrusting forward and back wildly. Screaming with delight. Push the door a little wider. Paint the whole picture. That man. Paul from her work-place. Kneeling behind her. His cock entering my girlfriend. Pushing into her vagina and out. I stand mesmerised, then the fury rises within me. I knew it. It comes flooding back to me. Her on the dance floor wiggling her hips against him. The argument: "You're acting like a slag Gemma. What's going on?" "Nothing!" She told me.

Don't look like nothing to me. I'm gonna rip that cunt's head off. I make a dart toward the bed, but one firm hand on my shoulder holds me still. I spin round ready to punch my restrainer, but as soon as I see the eyes, I halt. Lost.

Out at sea I float, looking deep into the water, pale green surrounding. Holding my breath for what seems like ever. No problem at all. As if I was already d....

A hand grabs at my hair and pulls my face from the river. Take a step back. Visions that were so real, all captured within his stare. I know this man, I'm sure of it. The long hair, the laurel. Young features filled with the knowledge of time. Before he can tell me to I settle, ready to obey this man.

'Calm Brooke, my son. Violence will achieve nothing. You've lost her now. It's been happening for a long while. You could kill them both, yet that will only end in prison. Leave it Brooke. This is how the world works now. Trust in anyone and this is how you get repaid. How many relationships stay together now? Divorce is rife. It's over with her, there's only a few you can trust. Turn to your friends in the hour of need. Especially Sloo. He will guide you away from the pain. Trust him Brooke. If there's one person, trust in Sloo. Not her...

I'm back facing Gemma. Her mouth around this prick's cock. Him smiling at me. Spunk shooting over her face. In her hair. She licks it off the end of his helmet. Looking at me. Drinking his sperm. The cunt I'll kill the fucking cu...

Brooke breathing heavily. Struggling for air, reaching for calm. His bearings become apparent. Gemma is there stroking his hair.

'It's ok.' She muses 'Just a dream.'

'Yeah sorry...' Brooke replies breathlessly. He turns to the side, facing away from her. Now staring intently at the wall. '...Just a dream.'

* * * *

Littl' Leg had scored the drugs for the weekend. Ten grams of speed for Moon, Crane, Lid and himself. 6 tabs of acid, everyone except Sloo. Five pills for Beeke, a gram of coke for Brooke and a quarter of quality skunk. The Geez had come up trumps once again. With promises of its quality ringing in his ears, he smiles on the walk home. Early evening, a red sky. He murmurs the rhyme:

'Red sky at night, shepherds delight.'

Anticipating a hot, fun weekend. Looking forward to a day off work tomorrow, relaxing in the sun. A couple of warm-up reefers for the night out. Moon and Crane would be round. It's gonna be a classic. Life is beautiful. Leg in the clouds. Doesn't see the police car pull up alongside. Only hears the voice.

'Excuse me sir.' Reality. A policeman leans out the Panda Car window. Littl' Leg begins to flush. Heart pounding, sweat mounting on his brow.

'Yeah?' He half squeaks.

'Could you get in the back of the car please?' Two options. Run or certain incarceration. Littl' Leg commences the sprint. The car starts, sirens sounding, follows. Leg recognises his surroundings...RIVER DRIVE.

He could beat them to the woods. Faster he goes. Fitness not even a factor. Legs bounding forward. The police car stops. He hears the door slam, footsteps chasing close behind.

The footpath.

Hurdles the small wooden fence easily. Right. Into the trees. Adrenalin pumping, knows they can still see him. Needs to disappear. Seems more dense here than usual. Trees higher. The forest bigger than he recalls. Leg begins tiring. Excessive drug abuse and lack of exercise now telling . His breathing heavy. Chest tight, lungs burning. Must persevere. Can't face prison. Fear pushing him on. The policemen fitter. Trained for the chase. But Littl' Leg has the trees. Zig-zags. Tries to throw confusion at his direction. Deeper he goes. Darker.

The Camp Styx appears in his thoughts. Protection there. Hidden. Terror, thoughts of cells and arse raping convicts, driving him forward. Ducking in and out of trees. Avoiding the branches as if they move for him. Camp in sight. He can still hear them following, but not so close. Praying that he's lost to the authority.

Trees warming to Littl' Leg, welcome his presence. Clearing the path, a tunnel to safety. Protection of the arch above. Trees intertwining, locking together. Holding for the makeshift roof. The rug. Hide beneath the rug. Swamps him, pushing him deep in the ground. No clues for the pursuers. Littl' Leg sensing them run past. Dispersing within imagination. The forest expands.

'Hello Littl' Leg.'

The voice an intrusion to his safety. Yet no fear. Confident this was no policeman, he lifts the cover. Confronted by a cloaked man. So familiar. Consoling.

Drinking from the purest fountain. A stream of vitality flowing within his soul. Vigour cancelling weariness. Can feel his very veins tingle. Senses alive.

Steadies vision with a blink and shake of the head. Looking within this man's eyes stronger than any pill.

'Let me tell you something about survival Littl'. Make no mistake, what you have just experienced is your future. Yet in reality the camp will be out of reach, there will be no escape. Imagine prison Littl', ten years incarceration. Criminals making you suffer for your every move. Envisage the fear...'

Littl' Leg shuts his eyes. Lightning flickers, reveals a blurred picture. Concentrate on the image. Flashes that prolong each time. He sees himself. Eyes bruised, mouth swollen. A scar lines his cheek. Littl' Leg plodding towards himself. Sees the lost hope in his own eyes. Experiences the throbbing pain in his face. Watches the tall convict appearing behind. The scene becoming clearer. Illuminations holding as one. Showers. Water, the only soothing factor. Tenderising the agony for now. Rejecting the struggle. Willing himself to get out. No, already given up hiding, abandoned running. Deserted all aspiration. The skinhead towers above a now frail boy.

'I'm not finished with you yet sonny.' Can only close his eyes and wait for his arse cheeks to be spread without consideration. Intrusion, the skinhead's erection raping the boy's essence.

Leg opens his eyes, sickened by the prophecy. Tears streaming down his cheeks. From the youthful reflection he knew that scene was not far in the future. He hadn't changed, except thinner… and that look in his eyes. Desperation, no hope, courage extinct. His life would end there.

The figure still stood in the camp. A soothing voice.

'It's hard to take, I know. It will be too much for you then too. You are found hanging in your cell the following day…'

Littl' Leg shakes his head. A reaction of disbelief, yet enlightenment of recent paranoia.

'…I'm afraid so. Shortly after news of your friend Beeke's death, you struggle with the rest to continue reality in the normal way. The Styx give in to drugs entirely as addiction takes hold. Constantly on cocaine, speed, ecstasy, all to take the hurt away. Purchase of the substances become frequent, daily. Suspicious neighbours call the police to check on you. They arrive to find you high. A search of the house and the quantity of stored drugs warrants charging with intent to supply. The court gives a ten year sentence to set an example."

'How do you know this sir?' The young man now blubbing.

'I once ruled these woods and your predecessors. When their existence was solely for the benefit of others, I arrived as their salvation. Provided for their every need. Here we lived in comfort.

Again I've been witnessing the same exploitation of people near my forest. How you suffer long working hours, slave to make others rich. I detest this hardship. My presence remains to decipher who should be helped. Intuitively the time is right for a full return. You must let me in your heart Littl'. Let me save you. Open up to me and I'll provide sanctuary within the forest. All is not lost to the future. Together we can change it. Obey Sloo and witness your future now.'

Tight. Water saturating. It becomes refreshing. Looks to the air. Birds fly in amongst the branches. Distant singing. Moon and Crane return with the food. They will eat and drink well tonight, then sing and dance around the camp. Ecstasy overwhelming Leg...

Back

'Just a brief glimpse of what could be. Imagine feeling that way for eternity. Sloo will deliver this.'

'So what must I do now?'

'Listen to Sloo, follow him. He will guide you away from evil when the trouble begins. Once you lose hope in your world, give in to mine. Instantly the change will take effect. Total elation taking over your heart and your very soul.'

Littl' Leg disappears, but the scene continues. As if it were happening. Leg seeing through futuristic vision. Momentarily transported to this man's world.

Drifting away, picked up by the sky.

Floating.

The landscape becoming distant.

The man waves him good-bye.

Littl' Leg waking from the dream.

Though it never ends.
No longer his
subconscious
playing
the
film
in
his
mind,
but
another
world
infiltrating
his
psyche.

Littl' Leg is out of sight.

Sloo remains.

"Soon, my revenge on these traitors.
Then show the god forsaken outsiders they can
never stop me. This is my domain."

Starting reality. Dream versus reality, the moment of insanity, irrationality. Is it true? Where am I?

To come round, realise the realistic scenario was a far out dream.

Heart slowing to a comfortable beat, my consciousness remains. This was all too real. Something to treat with caution.

My worst fear actualised. Seen it clearly with my own eyes. I refuse prison. A sign to stop current lifestyle? Not just for myself, but Beeke. Beeke's death? How?

Come on Leg it was a dream.

Visions and a warning I will remember always.

* * * *

Tin Lid staggers into the depths of the car park behind Time's Out nightclub. Unsure of why he's here and why he left so early. Yet nothing tends to make sense after twelve lagers and acid. The cars are sparse. He reasons that drinkers must be starting to see sagacity. Drink/driving a perilous hobby.

Then none at all. Darkness. Can hear the bass from the club. Like a deep thudding heartbeat. Tin Lid's heartbeat. He turns around, there is no nightspot. He stands alone in the gloomy wasteland. Cannot see far. No surroundings. Nowhere to run to. The drink or the acid? What was in control? Trepidation climbing...

Something grabs his leg from the shadows.

'Hi ya lover.'

A tramp flits eyelids at the drunken man. Sitting cross-legged. The smell wafting up, stench of urine and dilapidation. A sickness swarms over Tin Lid. Giddiness. His fright within, doesn't match his actions. Discipline vanished. Go home to bed. That's what he normally does after Time. Why is he at this locale? Why does he lower his posture and fling loving arms round this stinking bearded vagrant?

Face to face. Their lips drawing near. Tin Lid feels the crumbs of stale food that swamp this man's white facial hair. A breath.

Remembering the sewers. The Styx on their bikes. River Rom. In further, down into the tunnel. Along the raised ledge. It ends. Tin Lid's bike falls head first into the rank water. He goes deep too. Covered in waste. The Laughter. That smell... Tramp's breath.

Still Tin Lid widens his mouth. Wants to taste it again. Can't suppress the intrigue. No, this was not right. Tongue extended. Touching lightly with the vagabond's. Instant alcohol mixture. Dirt tobacco. Foul sewerage. Unable to pull away, petting heavily. If Wendy won't kiss him then this will suffice. Feels the tramp's hand moving down his back. Grabbing his behind.

Tin Lid ends the lip caress and straightens. Can now feel his bulging erection pressing hard against his fly. What was going on here? Why can't he stop himself doing this? The drink or the acid? Senses exploding.

'Are you ready?' The derelict asks.

Lid tries to shake his head. Attempts to ask "What the hell is happening here?" All he can do is nod. His body defying brain. Yet his mind still works. Alcohol normally disconnecting his memory. Now he sees and feels all. Not wanting it to happen, but wanting it to happen. Something incomprehensible.

Two dustbins appear. Tin lid dreads the unexpected. Still does not run. Black all around. Safer here than out there. He watches the tramp reach between the bins. Pulling on a lead.

Out from the hidden, step forward a dog. The whole scenario equating a magic act. Like a rabbit from a hat appears Spanner. Tin Lid's deceased Dalmatian. He wants to cry as his pet appears in the obscurity. The hobo strokes the dog's head.

'That's right boy, our friend is here.'

The dog livens. Starts to yelp and jumps up at Tin Lid. He doesn't want his dog here. Remembers the pain at the death. An accident. Let out in the garden. Harsh winds. Spanner needing to wet. Tin Lid had to let him out. Watched as the metal washing pole came crashing down. Flat on the dog's back. Goes rushing out to his friend. Discovers its whimpers, breathlessness. A collapsed lung, his pet put down. Post death suffering. Wishing he never let it out.

Now Spanner was here. Tin Lid despising his appearance in this scene. Not with this tramp. Not with what's about to happen. Wants to boot it. Run and end all this now. Instead he bends and tickles under the excited dog's chin.

'Who's going down tonight, my friend?' The vagrant looks up at him, a leering glare. Tin Lid wants to say "fuck off, I'm out of here." Tries to.

'I will, we'll swap places.' Drops to his knees in despair. Gazing as the tramp rises.

'Just the way you like it eh lover?'

Too much for the teenager. The lagers and hallucinogens should close his mind to this. Shouldn't even know it's happening. Shouldn't even be happening.

He feels sick, yet the more disturbed, the more his penis lifts. Unwittingly releases it from its hold. The tramp copies the action.

Tin Lid turns his deceased pet around to face away from him. Good. At least Spanner can't see this, he reasons. The dog lifts its tail and stands expectant. Comprehending what's about to happen, the terror streams. Why couldn't he stop this?

The derelict now pulled at his own cock. Blistered, sores. Pressing it at Tin Lid's face. The boy desperately trying to restrain his hand moving toward the dog's back end. Unsuccessfully. Tin Lid begins to rub at the slimy area. Spanner yelps with excitement. The boy brings his throbbing penis near to its wet entrance. The vagrant thrusts his own organ forward. Into Tin Lid's mouth. Lid, without triumph fights against his own every movement.

Struggling to fit in the dogs arse-hole. Tight, but eventually gives way. Soon Tin Lid was plunging into his pet, whilst sucking the dirty foul tramp.

Wants to die. His body rejects his brain. Can't even force himself to vomit.

"NOOOOOOHHHHHHH"

Tin Lid lashes out, punches the wall beside him. He struggles against the surrounding blanket entrapping itself around his body. Managing to free himself, sickened. Sits up. Faced with a dark figure at the edge of his bed. Instantly Lid experiences halcyon. The figure becoming clear in the dark. A glowing light encompassing. Stares deep into the man's pale green eyes.

Rushing nearer the waterfall. Filled to the brim with potion. No sounds, no senses. Doesn't understand much of this new life. Yet wants to remain forever. No insecurities. Confident, wants more. About to dive in under the waterfall. Swim forever more...

Caught in the process. Dragged back to the here and now. Tin Lid suddenly content, forgets the dream. Only for a second. Like a sudden glimpse of the past, the vision re-emerges.

'Why?'

'Calm down young Tin Lid, it was only a dream.'

Preferring to be here than the car park. The young man now ready to converse with an uninvited recognizable stranger suddenly visible in his bedroom.

'But it was too real. Why didn't I wake up before I 'ad to experience that disgusting...' He can't finish the question. His dick in Spanner's hole, a vision that couldn't be dealt with.

'Scary what you don't know isn't it?' The apparition states.

'I couldn't fucking stop it, I just couldn't control meself.' Tin Lid weeps.

'Like when you are drunk, am I right?'

'Well yeah, but I don't remember things when I'm drunk.'

'Exactly, you blot the bad memories of your drunken actions from your mind.'

Tin Lid sits sharply up in bed.

'But there's no way I could ever 'ave fucking...' Once again he halts at the image.

'Don't worry, it's nothing that disastrous, but what you don't know doesn't hurt you, right?'

'I'd never do that though.' The eighteen-year old pleads in fear, trying desperately not to conjure any inebriated images that could make this dream a reality.

'No you wouldn't, but it proves that you don't even know, or sorry, can't be confident that you haven't'

The figure speaks to the confused Styx member in a calm unpatronizing way, reassuring the teenager he's nothing to fear in him. Tin Lid strongly believes he knows this person. This man enlightening the boy with words of sense. No matter how distressingly sick the dream was, it's a fact he loses hours of memory each week at Time. Was never entirely sure what could have occurred.

'I can show you a vision. A stored memory of a journey home from your precious club. Locked deep in your subconscious. If you would like to see it that is?'

Tin Lid's mind races. How did he get home from Time? What events took place when he left earlier than the rest? He nods.

'Lay back down then young Tin Lid, close your eyes, then you will see, but don't fear the memories. You can alter your future. Stop them from happening again. IF you are willing to heed my advice.'

Tin Lid follows the instructions. Sleep immediately engulfs him. Falling...

...Falling

down

steps

from

the

bus.

...He appears on a main road, picks himself up and staggers forward toward home. Experiencing extreme anger. Can't understand why Wendy would not kiss him tonight, after she showed considerable interest last week. Realisation. Who's fault is it really? His and he knows it. Too drunk again. Left early, she was still there. There for the taking, and where was he? Nearly home.

Starts to curse, clenches his fists. The final part of his journey becomes a slow stumbling waddle. He crosses the road and reaches a sheltered bus stop. It seems like seconds ago that he was stood patiently waiting there. Off to Crane's for the pre-Time drink. Now he turns his aggression towards it.

The street is quiet. A chance to vent his frustration. He throws a crashing fist forward. A strong punch connecting with the timetable's glass protection. Yet the cover's far too strong. Not even a crack appears.

Tin Lid holds his fist, although it smarts the alcohol eases the pain. But his anger rising. Thinks about kicking it, but doesn't trust his balance. Looking around, trying to find something to smash it with. Occasionally a car goes past, but no driver concerned with this drunken man's actions. He discovers a large sharp edge stone. It fits perfectly into his grip. With force this should give the desired effect.

Checks the road, no more vehicles. A surprisingly quiet night for Tin Lid to resume his mission. Fortunate because his inebriation overrides his cautiousness.

He moves round to the back of the shelter, now deciding to smash the three panels of glass. Then run. Listens intently, still no sign of any distant motors. Tin Lid pictures himself with Wendy. Trying to imagine the state he must have looked before he left the club. His humiliation takes control. So stupid to have to get like that. What does it achieve? Tin Lid's face glows red as he grinds his teeth. Ready now.

The vandal makes a sharp turn and smashes the jagged edge on the pane of glass. It shatters immediately. Small fragments sprinkle over the pavement. The ruckus instigating a chorus of dogs.

One more will do it, he decides. His drunken state would hinder his getaway and already a light has appeared in a house opposite. Pulling his hand back one more time...

The stone comes crashing through a second panel. More lights go on.

Tin Lid off on his toes. Toward home and bed. Looking forward to sleep...

Tin Lid wakes. Still the visitor with him.

'That was me?'

'Yes, I'm afraid so.'

'I was cursing whoever done that. I was waiting for a bus to college the next day and rain pissed through those panels.'

'Aggression and alcohol are quite clearly linked Tin Lid. Especially when the drinker has continuous memory lapses. This is also not your only moment of destruction...'

Tin Lid fears to see more damage he may have caused. His face suggesting distress. Yet the man continues.

'...The smashed window in Woolworths, did you hear about it?'

Tin Lid raises his eyebrows. He had read the story in the local paper.

'It couldn't have been...'

'Once again I am afraid so. Not only this; three weeks ago when you woke with that bump on your forehead...' The apparition waits for recognition from Tin Lid before he continues '... That was gained from head-butting an innocent passer by. It seems your frustration was caused by the girl yet again.'

Tin Lid, shaking his head with scepticism at this unbeknownst destructive side.

'Why must you punish yourself for this girl young Tin Lid?'

'I really do like 'er, she's beautiful.'

'Yet not once have you kissed her, or ever got to know what she's really like. She is no good for you. Very dangerous, any girl that brings out this evil side within you. Such a person cannot be trusted.'

'But she's really nice. She always talks to me at Time. It's my fault we ain't kissed yet, I always get too pissed and blow it by acting stupid.'

'Or is it because she flirts with you to gain confidence? She knows you like her, you're always haunting her in the club. She can have you any time she feels and unsurprisingly wants to keep that. Wouldn't you?' The words of Tin Lid's visitor hit hard, but also showed perfect wisdom. He tries to deny it one last time.

'No I don't think she's like that.'

'They are all like it. Man and woman. Humankind wastes its energy on emotions. At some point in each person's life, lost love has come close to destroying them. Your time will come soon too, if you carry on this pretence that Wendy wants to spend her life with you.'

'Please no.' The youngster folds under the words of perception.

'Lie back you will see.'

Once more Tin Lid lay back in his bed. Constantly unaware of this hypnotic spell. If it were The Styx saying these things? He would dismiss it as ridicule, pessimism or jealousy. Now he believes everything he hears, brainwashed like some cult follower.

'This is what will be.'

The last thing Tin Lid hears. Dropping rapidly into his own body.

Time. Loud music. Lights. Laughter. All oblivious around him. Here he is in the middle of an embrace with Wendy. Tin Lid no longer feels he is there watching. He knows this is a prophecy and half expects to experience more discouragement. This scenario surprises him immensely. Drunk though, he can feel that. But also believing the barrier is broken. This has been his desire for so long. Now evident confidence. Can stop drinking, he's got her now. The rest of the night can be spent in her arms. No leaving early tonight. Success.

Just as Tin Lid fully appreciates the moment, Wendy pulls away claiming she needs the toilet. Bad thoughts infiltrate.

What if she doesn't come back? Is she pissed? Has she made a big mistake?

Why must he be so defeated like this? One more drink, that'll calm these thoughts. A celebratory one, surely that won't send him over the edge...

He goes to the nearest bar, keeping an eye out for Wendy. Served quickly, his attention dislodged. Orders a J.D. and Coke. Doesn't notice the girl leaving the ladies toilet, sneaking away from where she'd left him.

Tin Lid returns from the bar, swigs his drink. Hoping he can finish it before she gets back.

Sits waiting. No sign. Worry increasing, the alcohol flows more freely...

Still no Wendy. His drink finished. The one to take him to that place. No, Tin Lid writhes. A suspicion of being watched. Knew the warnings, but didn't listen. He tries to keep thinking about the kiss. Tells himself he's not that drunk. Mind lapses disagree.

Can't wait here all night, maybe she got lost? Take a walk, disguise the inebriation. Circling the club, now in search. He figures he may have missed her at the bar. No Wendy, but here's Crane. Sweat covers his friend's face. Pupils wide, huge smile. Tin Lid knows this must be a dance floor break. A chance for his friend to chat nonsense to an unfortunate.

'Alright there Liddy, what you still doing 'ere?'

'I just got 'old of Wendy.' Lid answers looking very pleased with himself

'Waaaaiiiiihhhhh, go on my son. Don't let anyone say she's not right for you. You hear me Tin Lid? Anyone.' Crane gives him a hug and offers him his beer.

Surprised at the forthrightness of the reply accepts a couple of big swigs, before making his excuses. He must find her now. Now their future relationship was underway.

Continues his mission, fuelled with more beer, eager for Wendy's kisses. Too many people. Like a dodgem car bumps them from his path. Their fault, his? He doesn't care anymore, the J.D.'s kicking in...

Eventually he spots the girl standing by a Fire Exit. She is talking to a man. Close. Their faces nearly touching. Tin Lid's heart sinks. Feels it then . Feels it now. No longer the message he first perceived. Now it's all so real. The drunkenness, the anger. Wasted weeks on this girl, this is her expiation? Tin Lid stands back for now, watches the scenario unfold. Prays that the man is just a friend to her.

A light seems to diminish above them.

Darkened realisation washes over him. A voyeur as Wendy leans in. The pair begin to kiss. Soft, her hand reaches down to his crotch. Rubbing the area.

Alcoholic fuelled fire burning inside. Tin Lid finds himself barging people to get this betrayer, this slag. Arrives unscathed, taps the man's shoulder. Their osculation ceases. The aggravated man, looks upon him with scorn.

Through the dance sounds of Stretch and Vern, Tin Lid registers the words:

'What the fuck you doing mate?'

Before thought, prior logic. How did the man know this was Tin Lid's girl?

A swift hard punch. Lid sends the man crashing through the Fire Exit doors. Onto his back.

Wendy looks at the crazed attacker in shock, never seen this side. That bloke who bothers her every week, the one she snogged to get him off her back. The always drunk Tin Lid. She tries to calm him, taking a step forward. Once more he strikes. A fist lands cleanly on her nose. Lid feels the satisfying crunch. Blood splattering. The red liquid… Visions. Drink, Tilnid. No aggression with our potion. Just serenity…

Lost for a second in his actions. Standing still.

Two bouncers steam through the onlooking crowd. Tin Lid ready to take on the world. Too drunk.

The first doorman's swift action is to knock the boy to the ground. A wide fist, to the temple.

Abruptly awake. The fear of his capabilities. A comforting hand upon his shoulder.

'How can I stop it?' Lid asks in desperation.

'It will become clear. For the coming few days stay in control. Forget this girl, stay away from her. Those men would not have let in, until you were a bloody mess outside the club. You can alter the person you just witnessed, you can change the future. Unless you bow under the other force. These are the pressures of society. We have the drink for you. Only joy. Follow me and you will be saved. Follow Sloo. Follow Sloo. Follow Sloo. Hang in there...'

Tin Lid opens his eyes.

Lets out a short scream. Nothing is there. Clambers from his bed. Needs reassuring light.

Time to take stock of the situation…

CHAPTER 16
OPENING THE LID ON THE PREPARATIONS

Friday

I Remember the first time I got wasted.

About the only time I do recall getting pissed. Think I was thirteen? ... Yeah thirteen, at Brooke's house. His family New Year's Eve party. It was me, Sloo and Beeke he invited. I think the others were doing their own family things and that.

There was gonna be a lot of booze at the do, but Brooke said his mum'd be watching us. We could get away with a few little schnifters there and that, but she'd probably be counting and shit. Eager to join the adults in getting smashed though, we thought we'd have a drink before hand. Wanted to experience what all the fuss was about. This'd be perfect.

Brooke pretended to be coming round mine during the day. Instead we met up with Sloo and Beeke, and the four of us went to the offie. We sent Sloo in, he was growing pretty fast in those days. He didn't look eighteen, but the paki behind the counter weren't bothered. Easy. He bought two large bottles of Thunderbird. A tasty little livener in our early days, but I wouldn't dip me dick in it now. I remember we was right chuffed, felt right old and that. Part of the big boys. Wait till Moon, Leg and Crane hear what they missed out on, all that stuff. We ended up singing as we headed off to the park.

Sitting round the back of Upminster Hall, we took it in turns downing the shit. Fucking rank when I think about it now, but it tasted pretty good then. We was all lapping it up. Needless to say half a bottle of Thunderbird each for our very first drink and we was half-cut walking to the party. Beeke and Brooke were having a sing along, while me and Sloo had a chat about West Ham and some other shit. I was holding it together pretty well, seeing as I was the smallest out of us and that. Plus bearing in mind I'm always the most pissed now, I reigned on that day.

What an excellent feeling, your first ever drink. You never turn back.

Arriving at the top of Brooke's road we pulled ourselves together a bit. Had a bit of a sit down on a wall, psyche each other up for our big entrance. It was only about eight. Four hours 'til midnight; and then some, all with free booze. The best kind of party in my book.

Brooke walked in first. We was holding it down pretty well considering. I can remember the buzz. This confidence. Never known nothing like it. I'd always been pretty shy really, but here I was walking round the party introducing meself to loads of Brooke's family.

We'd soon cracked a beer open each. Swigging the Fosters alongside adults was fucking amazing. While the others complained about the taste, straight away I was head over heels with the lager. Happier with their shitty cider stuff, or whatever you class that evil wank Thunderbird. No leave that right out, I was hooked on beer from that night on. I remember Brooke saying: "`ow can anyone drink this shit." I knew; and I think once he'd actually finished his can, he did too.

It was going perfect because Brooke's mum was getting pissed early doors and that. All she was bothered about was whether the party was good or not. She stopped caring about what we was doing. Bet she wished she'd held it together now. Brooke's Dad was well cool about the situation.

For once it seems.

He kept saying "go and help yourself to a drink." We did.

I don't think I've never drunk so much as that night. There I was on the Guinness, cheap wine, Boddingtons, Tetleys, Stellas, you name it. I don't know if it was me liver being fresh, soaking up alcohol like a well oiled machine or what, but I was well knocking 'em back. Not once embarrassing meself. Became proper suave and that. Even pulled one of Brooke's cousins and that.

It weren't cold that night, well either that or we just couldn't feel it, so the four of us took the party outside. Beeke was pretty lashed and Brooke thought we better get out the way for a bit. He had this little shed at the back of his garden what was perfect. It had an old two seated sofa and matching armchair in there. As soon as you looked at 'em you knew they were the houses eighties discards. There was a little crappy plastic seat too. The sort of one five-year olds sit on at school and that. I remember Beeke getting there last because of his staggering and stuff and having to sit on it. We was all pissing ourselves. The bonus was the old black and white TV and mini Hi-fi. A perfect little set up, apparently for when Brooke's dad wanted to get out the firing line. Bet he's using it a bit at the moment.

So there we was. Made our escape before his mum noticed the big change in us. No matter how pissed she was getting, she'd clock it at some point. Especially with Beeke out his nut. We'd all chaffed a couple of beers for the excursion too. It was probably about half ten.

Brooke put some tunes on and we had a good chat. Letting out all our secrets and that. Who we fancied at school, what we thought of each other "I love you man" and all that bullshit. It was fucking amazing. Like we'd come a real long way together and shit. We hadn't really I suppose. Yet we had got through infants and the first two years of senior school as best friends. That's an achievement of some sort. You know you're with pretty special people and that.

There we were having our first drink together.

We was saying how we wished Moon, Crane and Leg were there. I suppose the four of us bonded most since that night. I mean I love the other three, but they seem to have their own special little drug thing going on. In that they love drugs the most. That's the way it goes sometimes.

Sloo was fucking mint in those days too. I do like him now, but there's something going on in his head that I dunno. In those days for him, it was all about a laugh and sticking up for us if we had any trouble and that. I remember him that night. Up and dancing in this little shed. I don't know what song it was, just remember the smile on his face. He held up his bottle and was so... so happy. Then there was

Beeke sat there in his little plastic chair, fucking head nearly dropping off. We had to shove him every so often to wake the boy up. He'd open his eyes and straight away take a swig from his beer.

Brooke had lost sense. Was preaching, not getting aggro or nothing, but saying: "Fuck me mum and dad if they've got a problem, Thirteen now, I can do what the fuck i want." Some shit like that anyway. We all cheered.

I remember we went on about The Styx and the camp and shit. For the first time we opened up about that day over the woods, when we got our names and that. All four of us felt something a bit weird that day. None of us had mentioned it before, didn't wanna seem like no nutter or nothing! But with the drink, we was all saying how it felt like we'd made a bond for life that day. That we'd never split up. We was still young, didn't really realise the changes you go through. But we really have come a long way together. Something just tells me it won't last forever though. Eighteen now, these are the major changes in our lives. The age of consent, birds, jobs, whatever. Nothing lasts forever, but that night it felt like anything was possible.

Eventually midnight was creeping up. Brooke said we better go and show our faces. Beeke had totally gone. We tried to wake him, but he weren't having none of it. Brooke thought it'd probably be better if we left him there anyway. Us three could just about pull it off. Well me definitely, I was still thirsty for more. We figured all the party'ers would be well pissed in the house by then and not notice our state. Carrying Beeke around with us might be a giveaway. We left him a light on and closed the door.

One down. Three to go.

I was on a roll man. Had this in the bag. Smiling like a nutter, but not slurring or nothing. I still knew exactly what the fuck was happening, more than ready to socialise with anyone the party threw at me and that.

Three, two, one… Big Ben and all that shit. Brooke was hugging his little sister, then all his family members. One by one cheerily wishing them all the best. No matter how distant a relative they was, he loved them more than anyone else there. Me and Sloo had a handshake and a hug.

Then I see this fit bird. I call her a fit bird, but I suppose she was only about thirteen herself. Probably with trainee titties and shit. But she caught me eye. Big time. Sloo came over and said she was Brooke's cousin on his dad's side, he'd met her before and that. He said she was up her own arse, I ignored him.

She was with a mate and they both looked pretty pissed 'emselves. I thought I can take 'em on, no sweat, but Sloo was having none of it. No bottle. I had to move fast too. Despite there being two of 'em, this bird was by far the best and I reckon that cheeky bastard Brooke would've took on his own cousin. No doubt about it. Any bird for him at the time. He had 'em eating out his hand. I remember thinking not tonight sonny jim, this is the turn of the Tin Lid.

I left Sloo talking shit with Brooke's nan and went over there.

I don't know if it was crap or not. What am I talking about? It was shit, but because I knew it was one of Brooke's dad's family and that, I goes to her:

"I see Brooke gets his looks from his dad's side of the family." It's pretty out of order when I look at it now. Bit of a dis to his mum and all her family and that, but none of 'em heard anyway. She laughed, I remember that.

It weren't long after when Brooke saw the scenario and was over chatting up her mate. You could hear the little wind ups from his family, but that only spurred the smooth bastard on. His bird was soon putty too.

We told 'em about the shed. They said they wanted to check it out and that. Who was we to deny them the opportunity. So we walked back through the party and I remember seeing Sloo. He had one arm round Brooke's nan and the other round one of Brooke's aunt's. He was smiling like it was Angelina Jolie and Jessica Simpson and shit. I remember Brooke turning round and saying "Sloo's on form." About his own nan, sick cunt. Well funny though.

We went out to the garage, grabbed a bottle of wine and a few beers. All set. Me, Brooke, his cousin Zoe and Caroline staggered off up the garden. We looked like those posh wankers that come out their mansion parties. The ones who carry the champagne and glasses and that, always with a bird on their arm cause their so fucking rich. Lucky wankers.

When we got to the shed we found Beeke still out cold. He was in the same upright position with his head hanging down. He was pretty scrawny then, and you could see this little thin neck holding it on. I felt sorry for him the next day man.

So there we was, me and Brooke. Sorted with birds. Started to feel like his pulling partner, what with the old school disco and our first snogs the year before. Plus swapping birds there too.

It all changed a bit after this though. He got through nearly every decent bird at school, I started to falter. Drink helped me find the rotters sexy. I got a bit of a name for it. Champion minger stinger. When I got that tag it didn't go down too well with no stunners, I can tell ya.

Still this Zoe was a sort though. I was turning on the charm, making her laugh, swigging the beers, absolutely loving every fucking minute of it. Brooke was on the armchair with Caroline on his lap. She weren't hanging back 'cause the old booze was flowing down these birds Gregory's for the first time too. My situation was not much more difficult. Me and Brooke's cousin were sat on the sofa next to each other. Brooke started to snog this other bird. I thought the time was right and Zoe didn't deny me the opportunity either. No problem at all. The booze giving me the confidence to do things I was so normally shit scared of. If it weren't for the old alcohol, I reckon I'd have been sat there for about an hour and shit, awkwardly chatting to her, while Brooke was getting lucky.

I put me arm round her. Soon there we was snogging away. I remember I was facing Brooke and saw the cheeky bastard sticking his hand up this bird's jumper. I thought I'll be having some of that, thank you. I hadn't groped a bird before. Never had no bollocks and that.

Anyway first I'm rubbing one of her Bristol's over the jumper, warming her up and that. Then to try me luck with the old under jumper over bra thing. It was fucking nice man. She was squirming a bit. I bet me hand was right freezing. I'd had about fifteen different alcohol drinks and couldn't feel no cold meself.

These was the days when snogs were snogs. If you pulled a bird you expected a real hour long tongue session and that. So you know every few minutes I wanted to go a bit further. Me eyes were closed. Concentrating on me kissing. I remember a bird at school that said kissing me was like snogging a washing machine. So I'd been doing plenty of practice on the back of me hand and shit. Loser, maybe? But this was where the practice counted.

Eventually I moved onto the bare tit. I remember her shiver. The little pert titty, hard nipple. Is it bad that I'm getting fucking hard over this shit now? Even if she was thirteen and shit. At the time I had a raging stiffy though, I don't deny it. Was thinking you are the boy Tin Lid. Take that Brooke, I'm matching you all the way; And it's your cousin.

I opened me eyes to see if he could see me, but he was engrossed with this Caroline bird. So much so he only had his fucking hand down her trousers. Still, I weren't gonna let him defeat me. The booze, the party, the bird, all spurring me on. I was on a fucking roll here and was ready to make the big jump from only ever having snogged a bird, to shoving me finger in one. It was a big step and that, but fuck it.

I moved me hand down towards her belt. She was having it, sort of. Her legs pulled together, but she weren't twisting away from it or nothing. She probably didn't have a fucking clue what to do, what with all that wine she'd downed. The belt come away, then the button, next the zip.

I heard a bit of a groan from Brooke's bird. Right at the time when I slid me hand down Zoe's trousers. Then another groan. I moved further down and under her knickers. Felt her thin wiry hairs. They was pretty sparse, obviously weren't developing that quickly.

Another groan. Louder this time. Then...

"Ah, you fuckers." Beeke had woken up. What he must have last seen was Sloo dancing, and me and Brooke sat chatting. Next thing the poor bastard knew, he'd missed midnight and had woken to see me and Brooke with our hands down these bird's pants.

I was well fucked off, because me hand hadn't quite reached the hole. This outburst from Beeke, who'd stormed out the shed, stopped Zoe kissing me. I looked at her, still me hand in no man's land. Wanted to see if she was prepared to carry on and that. She looked back at me all confused, as if to say "Where the fuck am I?"

Didn't really care at the time if she was clueless or not. I was gonna still fucking go for it.

Instead what she did... Laugh at it now and that... She only went and puked all down me top.

I had to pull away with that shit going on, first finger or not.

Remember Brooke started getting all panicky. "Oh fucking hell" he was going, "me Dad's gonna kill me." We thought we better get her outside 'cause she looked like there was more on its way. Me and Brooke got either side of her and draped an arm each over our shoulders. Then we pretty much dragged her out, feet was just dragging along the floor and that. She was fucking out of it. Like dead you know. We started staggering towards the house, both struggling because of this dead weight we was lugging.

Anyway it was pretty dark in the garden and Brooke tripped over something. We all went completely arse over tit.

More fucking groans confirmed our obstacle was none other than Beeke. He'd only gone and fucking passed out again. Brooke's bird stood there absolutely pissing herself, then decided it'd be well funny to fall on us all.

Not that I minded a great deal, but her body was holding me down. So the only geezer who could have sorted the situation was trapped. This was the moment when Brooke's mum and aunt chose to come looking for their kids. Still thankfully it weren't minutes earlier, when fannies were being felt, know what I mean?

They had to haul Brooke to his feet. The boy was definitely on his last legs. They see Zoe as well, belt and trousers undone, all passed out and shit. Then me with fucking puke down me top. What a sight for 'em. I managed to clamber to me feet once Caroline had sorted herself out.

Brooke's mum had sobered up a bit with these goings off. She started giving Brooke the old disappointed talk and that. I don't think he could even hear her though. He just wandered up the garden towards the house and was next seen crashed out in his bed. I borrowed one of Brooke's tops then helped the aunt get Zoe to the toilet. Left 'em together to deal with the violent vomiting. The aunt was right grateful, "you're a nice young man", all that shit.

Little did she know that a few minutes before, I was centimetres away from breaking her poor daughter's Bill Wyman. 'Cause I just know she'd be blaming Brooke for the open trousers shit.

The black coffees started going on for the wounded. Beeke thought he could start walking by himself and crashed over once again. This time in the garage, he knocked all the tinnies flying. They left him there, out of harms reach. Sloo had disappeared. So it was me and this Caroline bird left. I wanted another beer and managed to nab one on the sly while Beeke was doing his Bambi on ice. Asked Caroline if she wanted to go and share it on the patio and that. She was well up for it.

We sat and talked, all whilst Brooke's mum took coffee to Zoe and got Beeke and a bucket to her son's room. Still no sign of the forgotten Sloo.

Left alone and fuelled with beer. It didn't take me long to slip me tongue in this bird's mouth. Not for the first time I was snogging a bird straight after Brooke had. Bit fucked up when I look at it now.

Everything was going cool. The party had dwindled slightly, at what must have been about three. Once Zoe had calmed, she got carried out to a taxi by her parents and shipped home.

I was there, arm round Caroline. Properly loving the moment. Looking up at the stars and that, nice looking bird on me arm. I'd had me first grope, felt a birds pubes and it weren't even this Caroline's pussy... The night was perfect.

Then we heard the screams…

Apparently Brooke's little sister, who must have been about eight at the time, had stayed up late for the occasion. She'd taken it upon herself to go to bed. Must have been knackered, poor thing. She didn't even turn no light on to get in her bed. Felt an arm wrap round her.

Loads of people went storming upstairs, all shitting 'emselves about the kid.

When they got there, they saw it was only that big fucking ape Sloo. He was only all tucked up in her bed, cuddling this screaming little girl. Totally fucking oblivious.

It took four of us to carry him to Brooke's room. He slept on the floor alongside Beeke. A nice shock for 'em both in the morning. I was thanked and given an Irish Coffee at about half three. They left me to sleep in the front room with this Caroline bird. She passed out after about two seconds of sitting down though.

So it was just me. Sipping at me drink and that.

Lovely.

That was a right fucking night. When alcohol became a big thing for me. I didn't have another proper drink for about a year after, but when the boys started full time I was there on the Super Tenants, Special Brew, Gold Label. All that shit that gets you leathered after a couple.

We started our drinking over the park each Friday and Saturday. I remember always pretending to me Mum and Dad that I'd been at the pictures or some shit, but used to roll into me house about midnight, obviously well out me fucking nut. Saying I was just tired and all that.

Those were the fucking days man. It was all a big grin. Big crowds of us at the park. The Styx and some of the other geezers at school, all swapping saliva with loads of birds, going as far as they'd let us.

More with the rotters in my case. I never handled booze like I did that New Year's Eve. At times I'd make a right prick of meself, but it was innocent fun.

Now it's all getting a bit fucking nasty.

When we started doing the drugs and shit, it was like I could get drunk and keep going for as long as I wanted. So I started to drink more. Then the old memory started going. Soon I was like a goldfish. Could go from one corner of *Time* to the next, without having no clue how I got there. Hours of nights disappear like I ain't even there to experience 'em.

It's shit man, I die for the *Time* Thursday all week. Live for 'em. Then don't remember nothing about it. Now I'm drinking with every chance I get, stealing from me parent's supply, all that shit. Little splashes of everything, thinking they ain't gonna notice.

All this just to get to sleep at night.

Now this dream. That was fucked man. So fucking real. Never had no dream I couldn't get over within five minutes. This one's had me going all morning. I don't know if all that shit was true, but it's certainly got me thinking. Would confide in the boys, but they'll just think it's a bunch of shit.

One thing I definitely won't tell anyone about, is me dog. That was fucking awful man.

I'm gonna have to lay off booze for a bit. Cut down. I'll take acid tonight and that's it. Have a good laugh and that. Won't need the drink. If Wendy's there then fuck it, I'd have got off with her by now if she wanted it. Knock it on the head and have a good fucking time with the lads. That's what it's all about, them lot.

Can't wait for it. What a reunion it's gonna be.

You do not stand a chance. I will witness you drink tonight. Fall into my trap. An alcoholic at eighteen, so sad. Tonight when you fail to resist its power, you will wish you listened to me young Tin Lid. Only more reason for you to believe later. Each piece moves into position.

I play this game so well.

* * * *

The credits roll. *'Zombie Flesh Eaters: Extreme version'* finishes. Another hour and half wasted, good going Crane. Only a few weeks till the A levels and still you've done no revision.

Can't be arsed to start now. It's the *Time* reunion in six hours. Wouldn't be able to concentrate. So instead of killing time usefully by getting some study done, I'm watching horror films. That was a good one though. I'd got it copied by Leg off a Blockbusters dvd a little while back. I only see it before when I was pissed and couldn't remember it that well. Surprising that, what with the scene where this bird gets a splinter of wood right in the eyeball. Clear view of it as well, fucking sick. Beautiful!

I love zombie films, although they're the most ridiculous, they scare me the most. I hate the thought of being trapped while all these relentless... dead people try and break in. All they need is one bite and you're one of 'em. They always go straight for the jugular too. Fucking oozing blood, spraying out the vein.

I dream a lot about zombies coming after me, ever since I saw *Night of the Living Dead* a few years back. Just one bite and you're fucked. That's what gets me. No doubt this film will have some serious repercussions on me mind too.

It's only half one. The boys'll start filtering round about half seven I reckon, so I'll have dinner, about six. Me Mum and Dad set off for the wedding at midday so it looks like it's gonna be another Crane microwave special. Then I'll start getting ready about half six. Can fucking whack the music up loud and have a beer while I do. Love it.

Must keep telling meself to take it easy on the drugs though; what with the big second date tomorrow night. Can't spend all tonight wanking.

Still I could spend tomorrow sleeping if needs be. Me Mum and Dad won't be here, raising suspicion at me exhaustion, so I've got fuck all to worry about. Just the next day weirdness.

There I go again, no fucking willpower at all. For fuck sake I am useless. Got to go steady Crane.

Mate, hours to kill. Could get cracking on some Sociology revision I suppose, give me something to discuss with Tina tomorrow...

Or I could watch *Land of the Dead*?

What a tough one!

* * * *

Lunch time, Fenchurch Street. Having just bought a sandwich from Benjys, Littl' Leg spies the gathered crowd on his return to the office. Like them, his curiosity aroused. Must discover what's happened. The ambulance appears within his vision. Intuition telling him it has to be a road accident. For the first time, he detects the street blockades. He looks back and sees the traffic pile up. Must have been in another world not to notice that, he thinks. More crowds.

Indecisiveness arises, not certain that he wants to witness the occurrence anymore. It has to be pretty serious if they're obstructing roads. Yet the more he tries to resist approaching the scene, the higher the temptation becomes. To Littl' leg everything seems deadly silent through the commotion. As if the only sound was taking place in his head. Along with the battle to decide whether he is prepared to witness...

A tramp, being helped by two ambulance men. Littl' Leg has to manoeuvre his angle to see the full picture. He spots the stretcher. Watches as the man is lifted onto it. Shocked by the stumps where his legs should be.

Tries to survey the area more thoroughly, but people still obstruct his sight. He can disturbingly see the steady flow of blood however, dripping from the man's lower half. The ambulance men cover the amputated area in towels and place him onto the stretcher. The tramp squirms in agony, yet he doesn't scream.

Littl' Leg panics, wonders if his hearing has deserted him. Wants to ask a member of the crowd what has happened, but fears to be deaf of his own voice.

Where's the rest of this man?

Stands on tiptoes. Knows it's the last thing he needs to be seeing now. His state of mind still disturbed from last nights dream. But he can't resist. Has to get finalisation for his inquisitive nature. Closure of the events.

Then he sees the legs. On their own in a puddle of blood, seemingly placed side by side. As if the vagrant lay on his back whilst they were sliced clean off.

What the fuck could have done it?

Littl' Leg tries to get a perspective of the sickening scene. Surely a car would flatten or simply break somebody's legs? Not cut them off so precisely that they could be sown back on right there and then.

On closer inspection however, he eyes flatness at the top of the limbs. They had been squashed. Struggles further for an improved view. Flesh, bone and skin was scraped across the concrete.

Wonders why this is taking so long to focus on. Still he can't believe it. Doesn't want to see anymore. Like a freak show. Why don't these ambulance men deal with the poor man's severed limbs first? Cover them up, anything. No one wants to see that. Except for the sick bunch here; all nosing to see what will happen next. There's not much to witness now, the accident's already happened. The tramp's gonna get carried to the van then rushed to hospital.

Go back to your offices. At lunch time as well, how could anyone go back and eat now? Littl' Leg doesn't feel like doing so. Wants to throw away his Benjys snack.

No bins to dispose of it though. London bomb scares. This deranged world.

A skip up the road though, near some construction work. Decides he'll drop it in there. Ditch this horrifying scene and get back to work.

He nears the container. Mouthing curses all the while. Disgusted at the human nature of uncontrollable curiosity of terror. Their fascination with the news. Only wars, death, murder and racist attacks get covered. Bad news. A mass craving for hospital dramas: *Casualty, ER, Holby City*. Their realistic portrayal of repulsive injuries played out on screen for entertainment.

Entertainment? Horror films, Crane and his horror films. Vampires sucking blood, zombies chewing flesh, crazed maniacs decapitating victims with garden tools. It's all sick. What is this human obsession with death? Littl' Leg utters imprecations against himself too. He was intrigued, just like the rest. Had to view all the gory details. What makes him any better? What gives him the right to judge?

These damnations flow through Little leg's mind as he reaches the skip. Prepares to trash his sandwich. Perhaps could eat later. Once the image of a dismembered tramp clears.

He peers into the skip. Curiosity. A pile of dead bodies. Lifeless figures dumped like mannequins. Men in work suits, pale faces turning blue. Eyes staring into wilderness. Attractive young women dressed neatly for; this.

A banished respect for humanity, life. What kind of funeral? Twisted interlocking limbs. A heap of corpses in a skip. Fresh people murdered. So irrespectively thought of, as to be thrown away when they die...

PUT IN THE FUCKING SKIP.

Littl' Leg wakes. Had fallen asleep in a lavatory cubicle. Stopped in the London Underwriting Centre sixth floor toilets for some shut eye. A serious lack of rest last night, added to early morning rises for work taking its toll. Thought half an hour in his regular hang out would restore energy.

The cubicles were roomy, they had a shower and space for towelling that included a fold down chair. Littl' Leg always caught up with sleep there, especially before or after a big night. Yet weird visions still plague his slumber. Depressing thoughts almost determinedly keeping him awake. Causing more tiredness. More despondency...

* * * *

This insurance lark's a right bitch. I've royally fucked this one up. What is wrong with these underwriters? Meant to be fucking Friday, the miserable wankers should be pulling a few favours for me.

With five percent to place at **4:50**, went back to the boys already covering, see if they could increase their share a bit. Not fucking having it though. "Our capacity's all taken up in Israel." Bullshit.

Cunts, wankers, fucking penises, I'm fucked now. Heading back to the office, tail between me legs. Preparing meself for a right fucking bollocking from that cunt boss Chris. Started pissing down too, I'll be soaked by the time I get back. Just fucking beautiful. Then I'll have to phone the Israeli's, "I ain't got it done!"

Haven't got it done! The first time I've actually failed. There's been a few close shaves before, but near the deadline I've asked a couple of other brokers for a bit of help. They'd always get it finished, somehow.

This time though I got all Billy Big Bollocks. Thought I don't need anyone's help no more. I'm a big boy now, I can place me own fucking insurance. Well, can I fuck!

I know what's gonna happen now too. The Israelis'll say put up the five percent anyway, their company'll cover it. Then they'll blag it to the reinsurance company that old Bradley's sorted it.

I'll have to next Monday, the day after inception. It's gonna be panic time Sunday though. If there's a fucking earthquake in Tel Aviv it'll cripple our Israel office. In turn that'll fuck us right up too. Can't tell Chris we'll do that though. Just a little secret amongst me and the Yids. That's all I can do.

Moon has blown it. What a prick. Took it too easy, took me foot of the fucking peddle, now look what's happened. I'm only eighteen though for fuck sake, I shouldn't be piled with this sort of responsibility. I could bankrupt a firm, get sent to prison even.

There's that option I suppose. Say I've fucking done it anyway. Royal/ Sun Alliance finished the order. I know I can blag that Nigel cunt on Monday to change his mind. Get a lunch sorted for him. Fucking positive.

If me direct boss Dave don't check me e-mails too thoroughly, I'll get away with it. Then I'll be covering five percent of the damages meself. I'll only lose out if there's one massive earthquake on Sunday.

There's a Possible Maximum Loss of fifteen million dollars, so five percent of that's seven hundred and fifty thousand dollars. About four hundred grand our money. Yeah, right. I'll just draw it out the bank and have to stay in for a week.

It's a bullshit idea anyway. Can't walk back say I did it, then them check me slip and find out I'm talking shit. They'll have me bollocks on the line. No, it's the Israeli's move now. I know they'll put it up for me without my fucking fax. I'll be covered, but it only means slugging me bollocks round Monday, trying to get someone to insure this fucker.

Feel like I've been everywhere, so I dunno what me next step'll be if Royal don't do it. I'm on me own now, too late for help.

Gotta keep a low profile, don't want everyone in the office knowing old Moon couldn't even get a fucking football stadium covered. Fucking "lump of concrete" as Dave puts it. It's the stingy Yids though; if they were willing to pay sufficient premium for it, I'd piss it.

That ain't the fucking point though is it Moon? Any other tin pot company and wankie broker would manage it then too. That's what separates us from them. Well that's what I thought. Now I see I'm no better than fucking endorsement runners. Soon I'll be working for a shit company where me wages'll reach a cap of twenty-two k all me life. I've proved I can't cut it.

Leg'll be more respected in the market than me soon. I'd have to fucking quit then. Throw in the towel and suicide. Leg a better broker than me, no fucking way.

Five-fifteen and still traipsing back to the office. All the secretaries and juniors leaving their shit hole places. Used to feel right good about it, proving to them I'm better. Younger and working late 'cause I've got an important job. Not like those filing and photocopying wankers.

Now I'm just jealous. Off home they go, preparing for their weekends. I won't get out till seven or some shit. Be late round Crane's and miss the start of the festivities.

No. BOLLOCKS to that.

I've fucking had enough. I don't get paid enough to worry like this. I'm gonna piss off at six. Get me most important e-mails sent, get shouted at by Israelis, then fuck off.

Work seems pointless now anyway. The world's turning into one fucked up place. That dream. Fucking charcoal babies, is that what it'll become?

Being in constant contact with Israel, I'm always hearing about suicide bombers. Mad fucking Palestinians or Lebanese fucking shit up. Israel retaliating. It's all madness. It won't surprise me if we do have a nuclear war soon. Then what's to become of old Moon. Chucked out the bunker and left to watch his Mum and Dad melt alive.

Like fucking chocolate in the sun.

So what about insurance? It's sheer bullshit that's what. I'm going out tonight to get off my fucking tits and that's all what matters to me right now. All these cunts can keep their fucking jobs. First they should get out of my fucking way.

You tossing monkey spasms.

* * * *

On his walk to Fenchurch Street station with a colleague, Littl' Leg spies the distant crowd gathering. Sirens flashing red and blue amongst the bodies. He turns sharply on his feet.

'Fuck that shit, I'm going to Liverpool Street.'

* * * *

Despite Sloo's phone call, I'm still shaking here. I've gotta make sure everything's still cool for tonight. This feeling of dread that he's changed his mind has crept up on me these last few days. Since he phoned me to see if I was coming out, I haven't heard from him. Hidden myself away to do a bit of revising too. Helped me spend the last few days a lot happier. Now *time*'s passed, have things changed? With Sloo sometimes you just don't know what he's thinking.

I get this feeling he's gonna start ignoring me again. I thought if I stayed away it'd give him no reason to hate me. By seeing me it might be a bad reminder. Yet I've got to do it. Gotta pretend like everything's normal. He knows I'm gay now, there's no need to mention it again. I'll never show myself with another bloke while he's there, or any of the others; nothing like that. I've got to prove I'm still one of the boys. They can talk to me like they always have done. No threat.

I'm looking forward to seeing 'em all tonight. Want it to be a real good one. Proper old school. Loads of drugs and a proper laugh. I'm not stupid enough to think it'll ever be the same for Christ sake. Some of 'em are gonna be treading real carefully round the whole subject. But I'm sure it'll improve. With Sloo though, well I've gotta make sure he's still cool with me. That's what matters most. I don't wanna turn up round Crane's later and have him snub me all night. If that was the case I'd prefer not to be there. Why else would I put myself through this torture?

My mind rushing with pessimistic thoughts. I've gotta stay strong here, just be cool.

Sloo's driveway… it's been a while.

The Stanley knife feels sharp. Even cut the tip of me finger just by running it real gently along the sharp edge. Also spread out in front of me is a corkscrew, cleaver, pincer and a hammer. My final selection for the crowning moment. I know me Mum won't miss the cleaver for one night. She's meant to be working late and she'll make something simple for dinner.

I'm gonna have to get over the camp soon and store my choices. Was gonna narrow it down to two, but I can't really see which of these I'm not gonna need tonight. Each weapon could do it's own little job on Beeke's face. Slicing, hitting, piercing, twisting. All of them fill me with pleasure. Last night's warm up gave me a real urge to take out some proper surgery on that queer's face...

Doorbell snaps me from my trance. Man, I was enjoying that one. I was grasping Beeke's hair while I shoved the pincer right in his ear.

I slide the weapons under the sofa, whack on the TV, then go get the door.

''ello mate.' Sloo answers the door, eyes looking all groggy. He seems happy enough to see me. That's a relief, but I'm still trembling here. As I get ready to speak I feel proper self conscious, try not to let your lips tremble Beeke.

'Alright, I w-was just on me way 'ome from... Upminster and thought I'd p-pop in and say 'ello.'

It doesn't work too well, I'm crapping myself here, with me own best mate for Christ sake. This is fucking awful.

Run my hand through my hair. Vitalisation gained from Beeke's uncertainty. Look at him trembling before me. The fucking faggot. Still I must put on the performance, can't ruin our plans.

'Yeah come in, I was just watching *Neighbours* before I get ready.'

'Cheers.'

'Nah *Neighbours*.' I laugh.

Cheers queers. Fucking poof. I lead him into my living room, feel sick knowing he's close behind me. The sick cunt probably wants to grab my arse now. That's probably what he's come round for. Well no Beeke, I'll carve you apart here if I have to. Pull the carving knife out and ram it up your arse. You'd like that wouldn't you?

No. That's not right. Must wait till the camp. This cunt wouldn't have the balls to touch me up anyway.

Luckily the TV's tuned to BBC one and Harold's rabbiting some shit to Lou. All making my lie at the door seem real. Same old, same old.

'Sit down if you want. D'ya wanna drink?' I ask all nice. Gotta keep the comfort factor up. Make him feel safe with me. Then he'll follow, I know it. Even seem fucking camp, lead him on a bit. It's the price you have to pay I suppose, when you're about to inherit the earth.

'Err, no I'll be all right, I'll only stop a minute, gotta get ready for the big night meself.'

I imagine the queer putting his dress and make up on, fucking sick cunt. I shudder, but won't let it show. I'm in control here faggot and you fucking well know it, don't ya?

'What ya been up to then?' I ask sitting down on the chair opposing him, don't wanna give him any ideas yet. I lean forward and spread my legs, clasping my hands in between them. Hoping my body language gives him confidence in the situation.

'I've been trying to do some revision, but it's well 'ard work. I don't think I've got the attention span for it.'

'Yeah or the brain.' I'm laughing as if I'm taking the piss out his intelligence. Really I know he won't have the brain soon cause I'm gonna pull it out his fucking head.

I laugh at Sloo's joke, it chills me out even further. So glad he feels comfortable enough to do a bit of piss taking, like the old days. Sort of thing Moon or Leg'd say. The way all of us would talk to each other. This is going really well. Still awkward as fuck though. He knows I'm gay and it keeps running through my mind. I'm struggling to think of anything interesting to say.

'What ya been up to today?'

'Nothing. I've been in all day trying to revise as well. It's piss poor, innit?'

'You can say that again. Looking forward to tonight?' Really conscious of my fidgeting. My leg's jumping around each time I speak. I'm doing alright though I hope.

'Yeah it's gonna be good for us all to get out again. Everyone's looking at getting 'ammered, what about you?'

'I'll get battered I reckon. Leg's got some mad acids in apparently.' Need to get off my face after this. My stomach's started making noises.

'I 'eard about that, don't think I'll bother too much with drugs. They don't really agree with me no more, they just get me down, know what I mean?' He's saying leaning back; a picture of confidence. Makes me jealous.

'I suppose you're right. It's not worth taking nothing that's gonna make you 'ave bad comedowns. If they get worse than the ups you know it's time to stop.' A little adage I've learnt in my short time as a user.

'Exactly, I'll still get a few beers down me neck though.' He says looking all happy about something, I like to think it's my arrival and our getting on again. Maybe he's missed me?

'Me too, what time we meant to be round Crane's then?'

''alf seven. Think 'e's getting the FIFA set up. Get back to the old days eh?' The night'll be a bit different though when I rip your fucking chest open with me knife. I don't think that's ever occurred in our nights out before, has it?

'What drink ya getting in?' He's asking me. I hadn't really thought about that, suppose I'll have to get a few tinnies in. Make it look like I'm actually going on this excursion to get pissed.

'A few cans of Fosters probably, don't wanna get too mashed before I get there. When I'm not on the gear I'll struggle to keep up. What about you?'

'Don't know yet, probably get 'alf bottle of vodka, some'ing like that.' I knew he'd say something faggoty. Why can't he drink a fucking lager? I'm gonna love ripping your head off you cunt.

'Are you gonna take one of Leg's acids then?'

'Yeah, Leg said they're pretty 'ardcore. Should be a giggle.' Too right I'm dying to take one, I ain't had a good laugh in ages.

'I bet you'll all be fucked, I'll probably 'ave to look after yous again.' He says this raising his eyebrows in a "I give up on you lot", jokey sort of manner. I laugh again. Sloo really does seem cool with me. This is exactly what I've been so desperate for these last couple of weeks. Things getting back to some sort of normality. Beginning to feel right at ease.

'Yeah, I reckon so. Crane, Moon and Leg'll all probably really go for it as usual.'

Knew Sloo was a good bloke. Must've been a major shock to find out your best mate's gay. His reactions were totally understandable. He's had a bit of *time* now, getting over it all.

Those three. The Magic Number, don't think I don't know. Must watch them. Make sure their safe. Be protected for eternity. If they don't stray...

Have to get back with the conversation. There's been a pause. Sometimes I can't even register when the silence occurs no more.

'Not forgetting Tin Lid, he's probably started drinking already.' I gives it. The faggot's having a chuckle.

Good, still pulling it off. To a certain extent. Mother says it's like she's talking to a ghost sometimes when she's rabbiting on at me.

I haven't got time for her fucking useless little trivialities, that's why. Soon.

'Is Brooke out?' He's asking, Brooke better be fucking out, or they'll be no room for him come the calling. Have to stay out with the rest of 'em. No Brooke's alright, he'll come. He's needed in the camp. The Styx together. Six of us. That's right faggot, six. Tonight you die.

'Yeah.' Sometimes I wonder who's answering and who's thinking with me. Mind's that occupied with all this end of the world shit. There's disarray within me, I don't doubt that.

Beeke's said something, but I've lost him. Bollocks, I'll fuck this up if I'm not careful. What do I say now?

'Yeah too right.'

That was a bit distant. Still going off in his own little worlds. It's what I like about Sloo, he's a thinker. I'll stick with him like I always used to, when all of a sudden his answer wouldn't match the question. "Yeah, too right", when I asked him if Brooke'd sorted things out with his Dad yet. Now to channel into Sloo's thinking. Make sure he don't feel uncomfortable, just like he's trying to do with me.

'Yeah I agree he should sort things out with his Dad.'

I nod. Yet realise I've given the wrong answer. No way should Brooke sort things out with his Dad. Family, like girls, can only get in the way at times like these. It's the hour to shed our worldly responsibilities. Return to the camp, our obligations will soon increase. For the sake of the future earth.

'Think they're both pretty stubborn.' I say, pulling the plot back together. If he sees any signs of me thinking about his bent-ness, he might shy away from me. I weren't quite prepared for this little show by Beeke. I'll give him that. Had everything sorted for tonight. The preparation, maybe a visit from my father? Instilling belief.

'They'll sort it out... Listen I better shoot off. Still got a bit to do before I get out...' Bit of gay porn to wank to eh? '...Just thought I'd pop in while I was passing and say alright.'

'Yeah nice one. Looks like I'm making me own dinner again, so I better get sorted too.'

Not really. I've gotta get over the camp and store the tools I'm gonna use to disfigure you, poof!

Short and sweet that's it. Still not perfect here. I'd be a mug to think any different. It'll take *time*, but he's making the effort at least. Be better tonight when we've had a couple of beers and the drugs boost my confidence. I get up.

'So I'll see ya round Crane's, 'bout 'alf seven then?"

'I'll be there.' He gets up too, with a smile and shows me out the door. What a relief to have my friend back. I didn't expect I'd be going to *Time* at all this week. Let alone be with my mates again. Thought I'd lost them forever for Christ sake.

Thought I'd be up in Yorkshire with my Dad. Had it all planned, my Mum even sorted train times out for me and phoned him.

I'll see how I feel Saturday, might still pop up there. I'll feel bad on him otherwise.

This is sorted. I'll enjoy a Benson on the way home. S'why I need to be out fast. Desperate for a burn to calm me. I lead the way out. Sloo behind me.

'See ya later then.' I leave his house with a wave. He says bye with a smile. Now to wander off home and get prepared for tonight. Won't go out all flashy. Dress sensible. Don't wanna piss any of 'em off. If their gonna make the effort to accept me, I'll make the effort to be accepted.

What a night it's gonna be.

'See ya, Beeke.' I close the door.

The last day of Beeke's life. Weird when you think about it. He seemed pretty nice then. No he seemed like a queer cunt, trying to find his way into my arse. Oh no, we can't be having that.

Still losing a good friend though. Why did he have to defy me? Defy all of us? End up like that cunt who called himself my "father" and abandoned his family? Remember Beeke deserted us. This is for the good of The Styx. His death will be the only casualty suffered. Then it's eternity for the pure.

Better get back to my tools. I'll take the lot of 'em over. That's settled. Almost *time* to slice the faggot apart...

CHAPTER 17
REUNION

Can't believe we've finally fucking made it. Buzzing.

Been dying all week for this moment. The reunion Friday: 25th April.

Been pumping out *The Mitchell Brothers'* tunes for nearly an hour now. With me Mum and Dad away I can use their huge hi-fi downstairs, a vastly superior system to mine. Means I can have the sounds reverberating round the house like a fucking drill.

The full return to *Time.*

Last night's cancellation was a major blow. Been wanting to get on the drugs for ages. Nearly whole week gone by. Dread to think if I'd actually some work to do. Suppose I've got shit loads really, but college stuff can wait. The delay of the inevitable.

Tonight's here. Friday night, the boys are going back to *Time* and we're getting obliterated. All of us. The whole Styx crew.

Never thought we'd see this day again. Especially after all the commotion recently. Thought Beeke's' coming out had destroyed that dream team. Now a fucking swift change of heart by Sloo and the boy's been recalled.

Still, something's not right. I knew that when speaking to Lid a bit earlier. Told me about last night. Him and Sloo went out to cheer Brooke up after his big argument at home. Lid said Sloo was being well cool, giving him loads of encouragement. Apparently really listening to Brooke as he bled his heart out.

That's not the Sloo I know, most of the time when a few, or all of us, are out together he's away in the fucking clouds. It's all a bit sudden his acceptance of Beeke as well, with someone like Sloo you've gotta live by his ideals to keep him happy. I mean I know none of us really do, but we all still hang out together and look out for one another. We're ya standard lads, drugs, boozing, football, women… all that stuff. That's enough for Sloo. Now one person strayed from normality. Thought it'd take years, if ever, for him to get his head round that one.

Now he's ok with it?

Just seems weird, but fuck it! Who gives a shit as long as it means we're all back together?

Lid was going on about dreams as well. He'd spoke to Brooke before and said they'd both had this fucked up dream where some geezer told 'em about the future and stuff. Did seem a bit weird, but it's only subconscious shit.

I 'ad a right fucked up one meself. I was eating human flesh for fuck sake, but you don't see me going on about it.

Really freaky bit though was Leg. He said him and Moon both had dreams with some bloke warning 'em too. I told him about Lid saying the same and that was it. He was gonna get straight on the blower to discuss it. Doubtlessly they'll be blabbing on about it later, as if some kind of major thing's happened.

Suppose I feel a bit left out really. The only geezer that visited me in my dreams was that mad cunt Sloo; and he was trying to eat me bird. Again.

I don't know, maybe we should lay off the drugs for a bit.

After tonight anyway.

Waiting for the first arrival…

7.30

Ready on *time*, this is it. Just wish it was a nice sunny evening out. Summer trips to *Time* were always the finest. Instead it's dull and drizzly. No real surprise that though, what with recent showings. Probably have to get a cab up there. The journey home? Who fucking knows? Who fucking cares?

The doorbell goes. I turn the music down a bit. Figure it must be Tin Lid, always here first for getting pissed. You can always rely on Liddy.

Here we go, let the fun begin...

I'm surprised to be faced by Sloo. He's never first. Normally invite him fifteen minutes later than the rest, 'cause I can never talk to him as easy. Must have forgot.

At least he's here and smiling. I suppose.

'Alright Crane?'

'Ello Sloo, 'ow ya doing mate?' I motion him in.

'Very well thank you, and yourself?'

Sloo sounds like a right fucking posh boy here. As if he's come to a dinner party in Surrey or something; and not the cockney drug-fest 2007.

'Good, thanks.'

'Anyone else arrived yet?' He asks walking past me. Cheeky cunt heads straight upstairs without so much as an offer.

'Nah you're the first.'

'Perfect.'

I screw me face up as I follow behind. He amazes me most days old Sloo, but he's properly freaking me already tonight. Hope the others get here soon. Maybe it's that dream I had, but I'm well uneasy with him. He walks in me lounge and plonks himself down on the sofa.

'I'm just gonna nip down and get a cd.'

The nutter nods as I leave.

Take this easy Crane, the faster you get it, the sooner you'll have to speak to this maniac. What's all this accent malarkey? The geezer's not sorted in his head about Beeke, I fucking knew it. He's gonna put on this act all night. His own childish way of sulking: "I'll only have a couple of drinks and be a moody cunt all night", I can see it now.

Still I'll let Moon or Leg take the piss out of him. They can handle him better than me. Suppose I'm still intimidated by Sloo. Like when we was at school. Meant to be me mate, but I never feel truly comfortable with him.

An image of him crunching into Tina's shoulder flashes across my vision.

I shudder as I eject me cd. Gotta go back up now. Don't want him getting all suspicious. What the fuck am I talking about here? It's Sloo; he's always been a funny git. What's he gonna do? Murder me? What would he be suspicious of? I'll shake me head and put it down to drug paranoia, always do. Best way to be. Fear don't really occur in me head no more, just paranoia; and it's all drugs.

There's nothing under your bed Crane, it's just the drugs. Then I'm a kip before I know it. Beautiful! Unless that fucking jester's in there...

No conversation's kicked off yet with me and Sloo. So I grab me Stella and take a huge gulp. Suddenly he looks at me as if I called him. I stare back wide eyed, confused. Speak then you fucker...

'Did you hear about all those strange dreams everyone had last night?' Finally.

'Yeah it was a bit fucked up innit? What did you 'ave one as well?' It's something to talk about, even if it's probably what everyone's gonna be yapping on about all night.

'Well I had a strange dream, but I found it rather enlightening. Like a friendly warning of the future tasks I have to complete, to make sure my life fulfills its correct path.'

That's it! That's why this bastard's acting like an upper class twat. I reckon this dream's told him he's gonna be some sort of world leader, Prime Minister or something. And he's only gone and fucking believed it! Now look at him. Fucking all wrapped up in it.

Start to ease as I figure out Sloo's cause of insanity once more. It always takes a minute of freakiness before I suss him out, but I get there. Crazy mother fucker.

'Moon and Leg said some'ing about warnings, as well.' I tell him as I sit beside him on the couch.

'Yes, these are strange times we live in, and I don't think the warnings should be taken too lightly.' Just listen to it, "don't think the warnings should be taken too lightly." I have to start giggling. You can't take me off this buzz Sloo I'm afraid. No matter how fucked up you are. I've got a bird and I'm off to *Time* to take drugs "*holi, holiday.*"

'What about you young Crane? I was told you had a dream yourself. What was your guidance?'

"Young Crane", "guidance?" Man this is priceless. Wish Moon was here, he'd be lapping this up. Bet Sloo takes off the act when he arrives. He knows with me he can get away with it. I don't like to cause a scene.

'It weren't really any warning, just a fucked up dream.' I tell him.

Sloo looks at me all suspicious, as if I gave the wrong answer or something. Come on Lid, anyone, please get here. Still no sign.

'And what was it about?'

'Mainly 'bout me and Tina. You was in it too.' I laugh. I'll tell him if I have to, like I say it's only a fucking dream. Don't mean shit. I know Sloo's cracked in the head, but he ain't no fucking cannibal. Neither am I.

'Aahh Tina, and this is the new girlfriend?' Stop talking to me like your some kind of lawyer. Jesus!

'Well yeah, but I wouldn't say girlfriend yet, we've only been out once.'

'No neither would I.' He goes with a hint of sarcasm.

'Eh?' Starting to get the hump a bit with this, Sloo or not. He ignores me anyway, keeps looking at the wall.

'And how did I appear in this dream?' Here we go. I'll tell you Sloo, shall I?

'You was a cannibal strangely enough and you got me in on the act as well.'

He starts to laugh, properly this time. Bit more like a mate. Let's have a giggle. Alton Towers opening *time.*

'How did it end?' He asks.

'Well you kidnapped Tina and tried to eat 'er, but I came and saved 'er.' Thought I'd make up me own ending. Don't wanna tell him that when I tried to get in the caravan, he just looked at me and laughed.

Momentary glimpse of that face. Fucker!

Gotta show him he don't win against me all the time.

'And me?'

'Sorry mate, but I killed ya.' I gives it, all nonchalant.

Then as if in response I get another flash of Sloo's dream guise. All in an instant. His eyes pure white, screaming at me through the window...

Enough to fuck me up a bit. I'm not questioning me own attitude here.

'You chose a girl over me and... killed me? ...' Looks at me all funny '... Shame on you Crane, what about the Styx?' He breathes out several times through his nose, denoting laughter I suppose. His little joke? Surely he's not offended by me dream. The rest of 'em would probably get me in headlock, call me a cunt for killing 'em over some slag and have a bit of a bubble.

Yet with Sloo I'm not so sure he realises it was just a dream. Something that I couldn't control. I don't fucking know. He continues:

'..Have you ever told anyone about the commandments Crane?'

The commandments? Surely he don't mean The Styx commandments. As if I would! People'd think I'd gone loopy bringing that shit up. Just like Sloo.

'Nah.' I shake me head and laugh. Hope he's on a wind up here.

'Good.' He goes all happy. I wonder what would've happened if I'd said yes? Wish I had now.

The doorbell rings. Thank fuck for that. Feels like I've been sat here with him for hours.

'I'll just go and get that.' I leave Sloo staring at his wall, he's smiling mischievously.

Run downstairs scratching me head. Have to laugh. You've got to. It's alright anyway the madness is over now, someone else is finally here.

Brooke...

Listen closely

Brooke joins Sloo in the room. Sloo's now looking through me cd rack. It's good that he's finally moved and doing something, but if he thinks he's gonna stop me cd when *Ruff Ryders* has just come on, he can bollocks. Sloo turns round, looks at me first. Strangely, as if he could hear what I was thinking. Drugs paranoia. Then turns to Brooke.

'Hi Brooke, how are you?'

'Not bad cheers Sloo.' He answers a bit more cheerily. They're probably best mates since last night. Doesn't feel like this is my house anymore. I feel like Sloo's fucking butler or something.

'Right... Crane and I were just discussing this dream episode we had last night.'

Sloo's continuing the posh boy voice that's really beginning to piss me off. Brooke shoots me a glance as he off loads six cans of lager onto the floor and takes a seat. At least he's noticing it too. Feel more uplifted now, plus not alone, especially as Brooke straight away cracks open a tinnie. Finally someone with the right idea. I sit cross-legged on the floor, downing me Uri. Staying out of it for a bit.

'Yeah, bit too vivid and coincidental for my liking.' Brooke tells Sloo as the nutter sits beside him.

'I heard it was something to do with Gemma.'

'Err yeah, I did tell Lid to keep it down, but that boy's got a mouth like a motor on 'im.'

'It's ok Brooke, you can tell me... Crane here had a dream that he killed me. Imagine that.' Brooke laughs at this. Like you'd expect from a mate. Started worrying that I might be the crazy one or something.

'Crane you bastard!' Brooke looks at me smiling. I snigger too.

'So what happened with you?' Sloo begins to pester him some more.

'I caught Gemma shagging this other bloke, I was trying to stop 'er, but she just looked at me and laughed. It was well fucked. Then this geezer comes along and said it's been going on a while, for real like. He was right familiar too, well convincing.'

'The same person that warned myself, dressed in a black cloak yes?'

'Yeah 'e was. Lid said 'e saw 'im too.' Brooke agrees.

'Yes I'm afraid we all had a visitor last night...' Oh my life '... or some kind of message, except for Beeke. Littl' leg said the visitor informed him that Beeke was going to die.'

'That's a bit fucking much innit?' Brooke's saying.

'Yes it is very worrying, but I'm sure it doesn't mean anything. There could be hundreds of explanations...' Here we go '...something to do with a conversation we had about the future...' I don't remember that one '... Or because we're getting to an important age now, having to think about where we're headed in life. That could be getting in our subconscious and portrayed through our dreams.'

'Probably, or Crane's subjecting us to too many horror films...' This makes me laugh; at least Brooke's making a bit more light of the situation.

'...It's still a bit weird 'ow this 'appened to us all on the same night though.'

'One of those things, but we should be careful. You never know. We'll have to keep an eye on Beeke for a bit...' A minute ago it was gospel what this 'visitor' said. A fucking prophecy from Nostradamus or something, now he's playing it down like it was nothing. I still keep me mouth shut.

'...And for you Brooke, I'm sure Gemma's not cheating on you, she loves you too much. Plus if there was the remotest chance she was, then remember you've got us to turn to. We'll always be here.'

'Cheers Sloo, that's proper.' I've never heard Brooke take this much notice of Sloo in me whole life. When it's me, Sloo'll be like "fuck that Tina bird off." It's getting to me. I don't know why so much, but it's pissing me right off. I should be in a real good mood. I've got Tina and The Styx are going out. Sloo for some reason is getting under me skin more than usual. I'm swigging me beer like there's no tomorrow here...

As *Time* skips

I reach the door. Tin Lid stands there with only one carrier bag.

'Alright Liddy, on Whiskey tonight eh?'

'Nah mate I'm just 'aving a four pack before we go out.'

'JESUS CHRIST! What's the matter?'

'Nothing, it's just responses like that. Makes me think I should calm down a bit.'

Fucking hell, this is a bit much. I'm seriously considering swallowing a gram of speed right here, right now. Soon as Leg fucking gets here with it that is. At least someone'll be buzzing...

You can hear

'I bet it did, but remember it was just a dream and those things couldn't have been done by you. You're not that type of guy.'

Here we go, Sloo on his father figure speech again. Tin Lid puts his beers down without even cracking one open. It's fucking unheard of. I hope he's had a couple at home, then I could understand it. Still everything'll be cool once the acids come out. I know Liddy'll get on those bad boys.

'I dunno geez. The shop window and the bus stop were smashed on a Thursday night and you know 'ow pissed I get.'

'But you never get violent mate, you're one of the mellowest geezers I know.' Brooke joins Sloo in consoling, having had his own fears cooled by counsellor Sloo.

I'm starting to feel guilty now, me mates do seem shaken by these dreams; all I'm thinking about is having a good time. It's 'cause I've never known us not to. I live for these nights.

'Yeah Lid, we've seen you in your states a couple of times on the way 'ome. You've never done anything bad. Was there anything else you dreamed of?' I join in.

'Nah, nothing I remember anyway.' Tin Lid looks a bit embarrassed as he says this. Goes a bit beetroot. I'll leave it. Never told him about me Madonna dream yet...

The bells ringing

'Cheers lads.' Tin Lid goes, finally reaching in his bag and grabbing a beer. I reckon in about an hour, he'd have sunk his four and be asking me for a spare. No doubt about it. Brooke's drinking up as well, we're just waiting on Sloo now. Is now the *time* to change the subject?

'So anyone up for getting FIFA kicked off yet? We can set the teams up.' As I finish this question the doorbell rings. It's as though they're queuing up at the door. Coming in one by one to see Dr. Sloo, the dream interpreter, to help sort 'em out.

Next.

'If that's Beeke Crane, don't mention anything about Littl' leg's dream, he hasn't heard yet. I think I should break it to him.' Sloo says, as if I'm gonna fucking open the door and say "alright Beeke, d'ya know Leg dreamt you was gonna die last night?" I almost know it's gonna be Beeke now.

Sure enough...

The boat

Beeke has no carrier bag, as usual. He always carries his spirits in his inside pocket. As he enters me lounge I feel the tension eat at me stomach. Always do now when Sloo and Beeke are together. Wanna see Sloo's initial reaction to him; see if he really is alright with this Beeke being gay stuff. It'd take the slightest grimace or frown then I'd know.

By the time I get in the room it's too late though, Sloo already has the stupid smile on his face he came in with. It's really creeping me out. Still the numbers are piling up now and Littl' Leg and Moon'll be here soon.

'Alright lads?'

'Beeke.' Blah Blah... welcomes I shut out. Waiting to see what Beeke has bought to drink. From the inside coat pocket he pulls... a bottle of Malibu. Beautiful! Good old Beeke. I know he won't have a mixer either, geezer don't believe in 'em. How he drinks that shit straight though I'll never know.

Sloo doesn't say anything to Beeke about dreams, thank God. Brooke and Tin Lid seem to be cheering up a bit too, so I turn the music up slightly. It's too early to annoy Sloo by peaking it. None of us are properly drunk either and the loud ones ain't here yet...

Is almost

'Doorbell Crane.' Fucking beautiful, this has to be the boys. Last ones left.

The cavalry's here. Although passing through the main room, I notice the atmo's lifted anyway. Tin Lid's testing Beeke's Malibu, knew it'd be a matter of time. Brooke's laughing at something Sloo's said. Hope it weren't about me. Drugs paranoia. So maybe it's finally got going?

Open the door and see Moon and Leg, carrier bag each. The normal reaction at this moment would be a celebratory cheer and pre-*Time* joy written across their faces. Instead they're subdued.

'Alright son?' Moon says entering first. Leg follows with a raise of the eyebrows. Maybe I should be concerned about their grumpy faces, wonder how they are, but all I'm scared of is that Leg couldn't get the drugs. He's already told me he's got 'em, yet still a wave of panic washes over me. Maybe cause of his dream he ain't brought the drugs with him. Shat himself for the walk to me house. Surely no? I mean it was only a dream. Everyone has disturbing nightmares now and again. His may have been about getting nicked for possession and subsequently arse raped in the showers, but please don't let that change the lifestyle I know he loves.

I hold back from jumping straight to the point, these are my two best friends here. They've supported me in my times of trouble.

'What's up geezers?' I ask as we gather in the hallway.

'It's those dreams I was telling you about man, 'im, me, Sloo, Lid, Brooke all been visited by the same geezer on the same night. It's too fucking much.' Leg answers, Moon stares silently at the wall.

'Everyone 'cept Beeke's been miserable when they've walked in. Tin Lid even said 'e ain't drinking much tonight.' I try and comfort.

'It's 'im and Beeke we're most worried about.' Littl' Leg says. The conversation continues in the hallway. The Magic Number tend to discuss our problems together, before we share 'em with the whole group.

'What you seriously think Tin Lid's done those things what 'appened in 'is dream?'

''ow we supposed to know, we never see 'ide nor 'air of 'im from 'bout one onwards.'

'Yeah but it's Tin Lid man.' I try and reason with 'em. These people have gotta start seeing sense.

'What about Beeke then? I got told 'e's gonna die soon.' Says Littl' Leg lowering his tone.

'It was only a dream.'

'I'd say that if it was just one of us that saw this geezer, even two maybe, but five of us? It's too weird.' Moon supports Leg.

'Dreams are just your subconscious sorting out stuff that's 'appened to ya. They don't mean nothing.'

'Look ...' Leg holds his hands out in mercy. '...normally I'd agree with ya geez, but this bloke was a bit more than a dream, you'd know if you'd seen 'im. It's like you know 'im from somewhere, but can't put your finger on it.'

'Well the fact is I didn't see 'im, surely that's gotta say some'ing. This geezer's probably outta some programme you five watched and chatted about when you were pissed or some'ing. Your brains have reacted at the same time.'

I feel like some fucker outta *Nightmare on Elm Street* here. The one who's always got an explanation for everything, then finds out what *Heather Langenkamp* saying's true, just when *Freddie Krueger*'s slicing me apart with his spiked glove.

'Crane.' I hear Sloo calling from above. It makes me jump slightly, yet not noticeably. He obviously realises The Magic Number are having a chat amongst 'emselves. He never seems to appreciate exclusion from these. Tough shit Sloo.

'Still come on, can't we just enjoy ourselves tonight. We can talk about this tomorrow yeah; you might 'ave chilled a bit by then.' I continue to try comforting 'em.

Ain't gonna answer Sloo, he's only checking up on us. Anyway with Moon and Leg trudging upstairs now, he don't have to fear no more.

As they ascend to the cauldron, I stay at the bottom. There's something important I have to find out.

'Leg, got the gear?' I call.

'Of course, be careful 'ow you flash it around tonight though yeah?'

'Yeah.' I say like an obedient kid. I stare wide eyed as Leg reaches into his back pocket and pulls out a small transparent bag. This is the stuff. What tonight's about, beautiful. He throws it down.

Howzat-ta.

I stay at the bottom and inspect the different contents.

Then I realise what Leg just said to me. I never flash me drugs about.

Normally taken 'em all before I go out.

I grab meself a beer and head to the toilet. *Time* to get cracking on me fuel. My medicine.

I shut meself in the bathroom, open the goodie bag and check the goods. There's the acid Leg was going on about. He's wrapped it in cling film to stop anything damaging the small square of paper. Studying it carefully I see the tiny tree imprinted on it. I've had all sorts before, Purple Ohms, the goofy looking geezer on Mad magazine, Strawberries, Penguins, Smiley faces, Superman symbols. This is me first ever tree. Love trying something new.

Back to the contents. I pull a large wrap of speed from the bag. The Geez has used porn for his envelope, meant to be the sign of good gear. I unfold it. Oh nice. Pink champagne, the way forward. High quality whizz of which there's about one and half grams. I close it again. Soon my precious.

Wanna inspect the other package first. Gotta know what I'm letting myself in for tonight, work myself into a stage of highs, if possible. The other tiny wrap must be coke. Knowing I can't really afford bugle, Leg and Moon always sort me out a couple of lines worth. I take a peek in side. Snowy white lumps and powder, what the doctor ordered. I won't start on this yet, maybe save it for when I get home tonight. Keep the night flying.

I think of Tina and shake me head. Tomorrow's date's gonna be a nightmare, what a mess I'll be. Never mind, that's tomorrow. I'll not give up the good stuff just yet. She'll probably blow me out soon anyway. I got away with it the other night; I'm bound to fuck it tomorrow.

First the speed. In half hour I'll be buzzing me nuts off. I glance at the bathroom clock. Quarter past eight. Reopening the speed, I decide I won't take it all yet. Otherwise I'll peak far too early. They won't let me in the club with me jabbering away and dancing in the queue. No, half now, the other half when we're just leaving.

Crack open the Stella then lick me finger. Down it delves in amongst the sugar baby. Cling to my moisture, there you go. A toast to Tina, I smile then lick off the superior form of champagne. Swig of beer, swallow it down.

Although this stuff tastes better than normal Billy, it's still pretty hideous. Nevertheless I continue the process, unconcerned about retching a couple of times. I'm getting pretty used to this practice.

There's about half the wrap gone, one more for good measure! Eughh it gets worse. Now put it away Crane.

I wonder if they're on the dream discussion upstairs and whether they've told Beeke about his apocalyptic few days ahead. Oh no that's Sloo's duty ain't it? Stupid cunt. I close me bag of delights, shove it in me pocket and head off back to the "party"...

At port

Atmosphere's definitely improving. Tin Lid's hurrying down his tinny. More like it son. Leg and Moon drinking Kronenbourg, Beeke swigging his Malibu. I reckon he's had a couple before he got here too 'cause he looks well relaxed. I expected him to be proper wary of Sloo, but it seems like old times. They're sat on the sofa engrossed in conversation. Brooke's smoking a joint, one of Moon's pre-rolleds I don't doubt. This is much more like it. Tonight could be salvaged after all.

Let's get this show on the road…

Later

What a scene it is now. Beer cans begin to pile up. The room filled with spliff and fag smoke. People spread out. We've got Tin Lid in the corner, he's got that pissed grin on his face. Half nine and like I thought he's had to chaff a beer off me. No changing that bloke, it's what I like to see. Leg's licking his wrap clean, Beeke's laughing away. Don't know what at; don't think the others do either. Brooke's chalking a line. It's only Sloo taking it easy, only on his second beer.

I stand in admiration. Feel like a dance. Moving me arms around to the chilled Gangster rap. Not moving me feet though. The rushes are strong, but I'm in control. Can appreciate 'em without worrying about being fucked on the way in to *Time…*

And the lost souls

'Yeah, The Styx.' Tin Lid cries, obviously well on his fucking way.

'The Styx.' We all cry. Just like the old days.

Sloo jumps up right quick; I anticipate his move and turn the music down before he shouts.

'**OI MOON, THE STYX**.' Silence.

Then we hear a muffled cry of 'The Styx'. A raucous cheer in our room. This is it. The feeling I was waiting for. See what drugs do. The spirit lifter. Party maker. Drugs are my world. The remedy of all our problems. Medicine. Fucking beautiful. Getting merry, swaying but fresh.

I've had five beers now. After this much I'd normally be ready for bed. A tiredness sweeps over me when I've had a few. Speed changes all that. Suppose I've got a psychological addiction. Fuck it; if that's what is, then that's what is. What the fuck am I going on about? Escaping from reality that's what. Here I dance in me own little world. Where all the others ramble shit. I get the reefer, I'm smiling. Looking at all me mates. The boys, even Sloo. Love each and every one of them. Take a puff. This is what I'm talking about right here. Fucking beautiful. My hair feels like it's standing on end. Especially on the back of me neck. I wriggle me shoulders. Realise *time*'ll be jumping soon...

Will slaughter you.

Moon has called the cab, Leg's suggesting to get on the acids now. Get all the drugs out the way before we leave the house. Good idea. Sloo's saying we should do 'em even though the cunt ain't taking one. Still only seen him have two beers. I'm pretty mullered now. No more beers, but that extra bit of speed's kicking in.

Ten o'clock; sort out time. People are haring about all over the place. Getting up, reaching in pockets. Collecting coats, downing beers. Unwrapping acids. Putting drugs in shoes, downing the rest.

We all stand, I barely can. Gotta hold it together. Can't remember things already. Need this acid now. Should liven me, but I'm gonna be off on one. I know it. Fuck it. I'm gonna take me speed here too.

Got me wrap out. Lick. All gone.

'Take it easy Crane.' Leg's saying 'That stuffs hard-core.'

'Yeah, yeah... Moon 'ow'd your account end up?'

'Fucking shit mate. Don't even wanna talk about it.'

'Oh dear Moon, I see you're faltering before I'm even in competition with ya.' Leg's ribbing him.

'Fuck off Little bollocks.'

This is more like it. Just like old times...

The *time* is now.

I think we're all ready. I see Moon putting acid in his mouth, I follow, think everyone's there. All sucking slowly at the small bits of crazy paper. Letting the acid flow out, onto our tongues, into our senses. In about half hour it's gonna be bullshit all the way. Oh yes. Bullshit, bullshit, bullshit. At least I won't be flashing the drugs around eh Leggy? Done 'em all, that's right, done em all. Large and beautiful. The bit of paper. Certain it's acid, certain subtle taste about the drug. Takes a while for it to dissolve.

A cab sounds. We're all rushing downstairs.

Everyone's pissing 'emselves when Leg asks for "*Time* please". He had to mumble it as he didn't wanna drop the acid out his mouth. Sounded like a spastic.

Everyone buzzing in the cab. Hope I ain't gurning yet. Ask Brooke, he says I'm ok, he thinks. He's fucked on coke. His fucking jaw's twitching all the over the shop. Moon's slagging off Tin Lid about something boring he's just said. "Fucking drying me out" he's going. Don't know what I can contribute. Just sit at the back alongside Brooke. Put me arm round the boy. Great man.

He smiles at me. We're all gonna be so fucked here. Well all of us except Sloo. He's having a laugh, then I see him looking out the window all anxious like. What's he thinking about now?

Fuck it all anyway.

Here we go.

The Styx reunion.

This is gonna be one fucking biggun...

CHAPTER 18
JUST IN *TIME*

Time's Out

11.15

Nightly dance tunes enthrall a commercial public. A wide-ranging thriving mass of Essex youth, city workers, students and wide-boys converge as one. Soaking up the latest sounds whilst edging ever nearer that obligatory fight. The dance floor filled. People on chemical substances. Drunks flailing wild arms.

This is the centre.

Surrounding Surrounding

stand groups of friends amused at the expense of unwitting others. Cliques of men in late-twenties reluctant to give up their youth. Preferring the company of sixteen to twenty year-olds, because here they can show and feel superiority. A chance for them to ridicule those eighteen-year old chavs, or the girls less fortunate in appearance; or anyone else slightly differing from their norm. Way of release, weekdays over, now the serious business of supposed fun begins.

With belief tonight they will get that young virgin. The one in the skimpy black dress, doused in heavy make up. All designed to disguise her adolescence in order to gain entry. The fourteen year-old girl ready to allow her body to these men. The type that makes up around fifty percent of the club's female contingency.

Most older women choosing Romford pubs. Maturing before the men, passing off *Time's Out* as the "meat market" it is.

Proof given by couples hidden away in corners, strangers only going as far as the alcohol and their new partner encourages.

Masses line the understaffed bar. Thrusting forward previously rolled notes. Hopes of getting served within twenty minutes. Pushing in, frustration, tempers flaring already. Not drunk enough yet. The lightweight alcoholics needing complete inebriation to socialize/pull.

The remaining people are the wanderers, walking alone, circuits round the dance floor. Fuelled by speed or cocaine, looking for no one, but someone in particular. A person they know, someone to release their nonsensical thoughts on. The gibberish filling their head needing instant release, relief from their mouth. Drug induced noise, such essential knowledge to unleash on an unsuspecting individual. A break from the dance floor, a rest from being Travolta. A break from actually appearing like drowning wide-eyed drug addicts. Admittance refused.

The same scenario almost night in, night out. Week in, week out. Illegal acts in every dark corner. All in all, a standard, steady running nightclub with strong warnings against those consuming drugs on the premises. Yet mostly turning a blind eye. Gaining more money from the narcotic industry by jacking up prices on bottled water. Knowing turning away addicts would bankrupt. The idea of all these people putting up with loud garage and dance for hours without drugs; ridiculous.

Relative normality, yet unknowingly or not *Time's Out* was holding seven young men who's lives were about to be altered in very severe ways.

Flashing blue and red lights, strobes. Drones of a busy club, humming demonic. Chills waving over the club. A blanket of sea covering every individual it had to with its tidy possession. The outside is calm. Within boiled the cauldron of psychological ill health.

Ready

to

unfold.

Sloo heads back to the corner carrying two pints of lager.

Beeke waits, sits on the long green leather couches. Has taken the acid and popped two ecstasy pills procured on the premises. Bearing an expression that symbolises an enlightenment of life's meaning. Unaware that the sides of his mouth sag. Eyes searching about the club without valid focus. Unable to locate an area for more than a second.

Dressed conservatively. White Yves Saint Laurent shirt, black trousers. Nothing flambouyant, still wary of Sloo. Disguise the subject of homosexuality.

One arm outstretched over the vacant spot next to him. The other taps wildly on his raised knee. Spots his friend returning. Instantaneously clears the space beside. Doesn't want to offend.

Surprisingly Sloo shows little concern, hasn't all night. Chatting as though the last few weeks were non-existent. At first Beeke found communication difficult. What was a suitable topic for this unexpected reinstated friendship? Although Sloo was doing his utmost, talking incessantly about work and college, it was still tough.

Yet once the drugs kicked in the problem disintegrated. Mitsubishi and the tree. Knew it was a wild experiment, but this would see him through for the night.

No turning back.

'Cheers mate.'

'No worries! Sorry it took so long, it was rammed at the bar.' Both speak in high volume, but not necessarily shouting. This was the chill out area, recuperation zone.

'I just see Crane.' Says Beeke.

'Oh yeah, what's he up to?'

'Completely fucked. Think the acid's really kicking in with 'im now.'

'Shit. That boy's gonna do himself injury one of these days.' Beeke accepts this could be a shot at him too. Passes it off with a quick smile.

'Yeah, 'e was jabbering on 'bout that Tina bird and 'ow ecstatically 'appy 'e is.'

'Just hope he doesn't get hurt.' Sloo shakes his head. **Crane's friend will not be allowed**.

'Nah, she seems like a nice girl. It's about *time* 'e 'ad a bit of luck.'

'That's not the point, it's his own fault most of the time. Remember that girl at Leg's barbecue? He royally fucked that one up.'

'Yeah I suppose, 'e just needs a bit of belief in 'imself. That's why 'e keeps taking loads a drugs. Gives 'im the confidence.'

'He shouldn't take so much.' Sloo bringing forth the father figure, recognisable to Beeke.

''e's just enjoying 'imself...' Slight pause. Beeke's mind moves a pace ahead. Need a new subject, cloak awkwardness. '...What was up with Moon and Littl' Leg earlier? When they got round Cranes?'

'It's what I've been wanting to talk to you about, mate.' Sloo grasps his friend's full attention.

Beeke instantly suffers engulfing paranoia. Thoughts of a plan for his destruction cloud his rationality. Sweat more profusely now, preparing for a speedy exit, escape. Waits for the first move. How could he have been so blind?

'What is it?' Beeke asks. Trying to disguise his obvious tension.

'It's alright mate, nothing to concern yourself with too much...'

Hasn't worked, L.S.D. apprehends. Insanity drug taking a firm hold. Beeke remains poised to run.

'... You know earlier when we were going on about those dreams we all had?'

Beeke nods. Remembrance of the earlier eerie atmosphere at the evening's beginning.

'...We didn't mention it, but Littl' leg had a dream about you. Nothing major, look we're only worried because we all had these dreams on the same night.'

'What did 'e dream then?' Beeke asks, desperate for the point to be reached. Get it over with.

'The Police were after him because they'd seen him leaving The Geez's house. He had to do a runner to the camp. When he'd lost 'em he bumped into this bloke Moon, Brooke and Lid saw too...'

* * * *

Continuous flirting. Tin Lid's conscience struggling. The acid warming up, yet the beer in control. Should he go for the kill? No confidence, would remember this tomorrow. Terrified of rejection, last night's dream fresh in mind.

C R

R O

X

D S

S S

Needs one more drink, courage would be found. Frightened at the prospects. Aggressiveness, lashing out at each obstacle. Was getting too late though. Inebriated enough already. The hallucinogen? Soon be gibbering.

Last chance saloon.

'I fancy another drink, d'ya want one?'

'Yeah, I'll come over there with you.' Wendy answers with an appreciative smile at her company.

Sleepiness in her eyes suggests willingness.

* * * *

Beeke struggles to comprehend the news of his impending death. Was this a personal warning from Sloo? Or something that really did concern his friends?

Mind frying. Ecstasy and acid solution. Everything becoming unclear, untrustworthy. Now having difficulty concentrating. Wants his intelligence back. Shouldn't be told such things whilst drugs are the brain's monitor. Needs to assess the situation. Step outside his being. A short vacation to regroup. Then he could return to the land of the lost.

Too late.

Tripping on light effects. Love, paranoia, warmth, dread. The sun shines brightly over each emotion.

Sloo had been good so far. Understanding, accepting, surely meaning it?

If affliction was his desire, then it would be complete by now. No need to go through any charade. Over and done with.

Checking the dream, smoke eyes swell. The others wouldn't go along with some sordid plan; would they? This must have happened.

Dizziness, queasy, overwhelming urge, pleasure. Momentarily feels good. Gone. Anxiety now takes charge.

No the boys wouldn't hurt him. Sloo wouldn't hurt him. Would he?

Turns to face his friend, distorted image. Someone else. Focus. There he is. The whipping figure hard to keep still, concentration.

Sloo remains quiet, staring toward the dance floor. Must portray an understanding of Beeke's emotions, give him time to digest. Knows the time of narcotic hangover lay upon him. Genuinely looks upset.

Rushes of joy grow. Knowledge of Sloo's restored friendship flowing through. Spasm, Beeke shoots out an arm, without intention.

'It's alright mate, just a dream. I ain't gonna leave you that easy.'

Sloo suppressing the squirm with difficulty. Realisation of the touch. A treacherous hand clutching his arm. Wants to scream, hurt him now, but the boat's almost arrived. Flooding memories, Beeke had never tried anything with them.

Round your mates, don't usually view this in this sort of order.

No mistakes this *time.* Remain calm, friendly throughout. The plan will work.

Sloo's move is a hug.

Staring over Beeke's shoulder, fixed glaze. Gleaming, compassion disappearing. Embrace ends. Makes his excuses.

To the men's room, begin throwing up disgust.

Distant figures, arms long aloft swaying ever stronger. Pointing toward every corner. Hovering. Fierceness flowing through veins. Pulsating through the skies. Transported through the clouds. Rain, waterfalls crash upon the roof. Evil seeping in. The energy arriving. Frenzied attitudes transforming within. Dropping so hard causing the switch.

The long flowing river returning, direction change. Splattering, choking, gurgling. Hear the bells ring? Slowly it sails. Shadows twitching. Huge masts forced by gales. Cackling figures of reversed good, aborted back to Earth. Former selves lost in the whirlwind. New personas invented by a storm. Dangerous breaths, serpent minds.

To destroy, havoc approaching. Young leaves withstand the pressure. Cover the arrival. Red skies filled with blood, preparing to cleanse. Take over. The possession swears revenge. Disasters of old. The crew has been chosen, manning port/ starboard. Volcanoes under the ocean grumble. Tidal boiling.

Spell of hypnosis. Unaware. Scenes on repeat. Death is everywhere. The forest warming to the visions of old. Nature recorded vile actions. Outlasting time. About to replay all that has been witnessed.

Naked men dancing between trees. Digesting flesh under the claret rain. Drinking the bile of beast, the blood of fellows captured within. Lost and sent away. Returning to encounter the game. Reward for suffering. Act out their own Destruction on more innocents. Pictures, increasing hunger. Visions Deluding sanity. The river is restored. Souls vengeance. Dodging, intertwining, locked over time. Spellbound. Spirits Darting. All those Dead no longer resting. Danger spreading throughout the lands. Cumulus burst. Rest in peace shattered. Rest no more.

Arise to board the boat.

Laughing, a tall figure rises above commotion. Cast across the forest, and over the town. Inspecting his game board. All pieces in place? Checking on the progress of his resurrection. One concern, one thing out of tune. Something missing; must enter his protégé. Alter the situation.

Soon the real punishment begins. Sickening plans. The Styx will return to the camp by any means necessary. Surrendering. Shattering events to kill spirit. Sloo will be obeyed. ***BY ANY MEANS NECESSARY.***

Possession almost complete. First to the task at hand. Pushing through the air, into a vanishing wisp…

Entering back through the veins.

EXIT

Sloo feels warmth. Confidence on high. Renewed energy needed to finish this charade.

His journey back through the club leads him to Brooke, Moon and Littl' Leg. Movements orchestrated. A quick assessment. Has the acid taken hold? Will anyone remember tonight?

Brooke starting to lose control of his humour. Truly joyous experience, it's been a while. Laughter now. The comedown will soon come crashing home. Guilt trips like no other. Extreme Paranoia, doubting what has been and will be. Cocktail shaker, rattling Brooke's head. Cocaine, acid, alcohol mixes. Unused to this state for a long *time.* Appreciating the escape from a shaken reality that is about to grow far worse.

Sloo observes the three even closer. The mess they all look. Bloodshot eyes. Sweat drowning foreheads. Pupils wide. Zombies of pressure. Struggling so hard to fit in at eighteen; failing. Frowns at their disarray. Sorrow that they put themselves through this for leisure.

It will be ok my friends, soon life will improve. Live free and easy. No more fear. The father has come for salvation. Be merry now. Enjoy this evening. Appreciate the last remaining happiness outside the forest.

Being eighteen and popular?

'Alright Brooke?'

''ow's it going Sloo?' Brooke slurs, swaying before his friend.

Perfection. Sloo raises the volume on his voice.

'Pretty good son. You out of it?'

'Getting there mate; look at these boys.' Brooke points out Littl' Leg and Moon. Both of whom seem glued to swivel seats. Lost in a film, insignificant to the club.

'Glorious! They're out of it aren't they?'

'Yeah man, I ain't getting any sense from 'em. Keep talking 'bout paths and shrubbery and knights who say "Ni". They're fucked!' Brooke dances on the spot, without knowledge of movement.

Sloo smirks.

'Looks like you boys are in for it tonight.'

'Yeah man, why don't you get on it?'

'Nah, it's evil; besides who's gonna make sure we're alright?'

'Fuck that man, we'll be cool. Join us, join us.'

'Honestly I'm alright. I'm having a great time as it is. Getting on well with Beeke again.'

'Yeah, that's excellent man, much respect for that. Beeke's a top boy.'

'He certainly is.'

''ave you spoke to 'im yet? About the dreams I mean?'

Brooke looks at Sloo with respect never shown before. Had forgotten how good a friend he actually was. Missed these times. Good friends all of them. Loves Gemma, but now doubts her intentions. Could never do that with these people.

'Yeah he seems fine about it, but he's taken a couple of pills so I don't think he really knows what's going on.'

'Where is 'e now?'

'Round at the chill out. I'm gonna go back over, make sure he's alright. Where's Lid and Crane?'

'Crane's on the floor, I think Lid's upstairs with that bird.'

'Excellent, I'll leave you to your insanity then mate.'

'Yeah cheers Sloo, I love you man.'

'Love you too Brooke.' The pair share a parting embrace.

Although Brooke's wave of admiration recently overcame him, he now knows he must be with those tripping. The only sense.

* * * *

'Don't you want my loving?'

Felix. A classic. Chills down me spine and right back up again. Man I love this song. Really come flying up on amphetamines. A land of joy and love. Beautiful! Look at the people around me. All smiles, feeling the music. Total respect of an anthem. Am I smiling as goofy? Can't stop my legs moving. Buzzing, buzzing, buzzzzing. Fucking hell. I wanna hug all these geezers. Trying to smile at 'em all. Catch someone's attention, see if I get one. No takers?

All these faces, happy, changing... Is that Dave from college? No... it is... No. Oh fuck, it is... not. Like looking at that picture. The one with all those wiggly screaming black faces. On a bridge I think. Fucking brilliant, the acid's arrived.

Knocking on my door. This song then I'm fucking off to get Moon and Leg. Support gonna be needed. We have to stick together.

'Don't you want my loving?'

Whoa man. Me heart's racing, lights flooding in. Hair on end. Scanning the dance floor, people whooping with delight. What an absolute delight. Beautiful! Raised arms.

Thoughts of Tina. That beautiful soft kiss. Another date. West Ham battering the Arse tomorrow. Me mates. The boys love 'em all. Even Sloo. Top man. Delight, excitement; and all of a sudden I'm doing a fucking spin.

'Don't you want my loving?'

I feel like Michael Jackson. Motown days. I'm jiving, I'm grooving. I'm fucked out my fucking box. Eee he he. Wacko Jacko. Wonder if he did molest those kids? What about marrying Priscilla Presley? She was gorgeous in that Naked Gun. Oh fuck, the bit where all the fireworks are going off, the police telling the crowd "there's nothing to see here". Magic! That's a point, Airplane's on tomorrow. Wouldn't mind seeing that again. Maybe I should go tell Lid, he likes those films. I'll just wait till this song finishes.

'Don't you want my loving?'

Small section of reality, rambling thoughts. New song mixing in. Don't recognise it, but WHAT A WICKED TUNE. I'll have to stay on for this one. This is banging.

Is that bouncer over there looking at me? Better watch meself, must look completely wankered. Don't know how long I've been dancing for. Soon as I got in the club, couldn't resist. Sweating. Me hair must be fucked. Fuck it. I feel beautiful. That's what matters most.

Saw Beeke for a second. Getting a pill. Blabbed about Tina. Talk break. Splatter shit. Back to dance. Oh what a night!

The Styx back out together. Where's Moon and Leg? Fuckers. Suppose they're tripping somewhere. Ain't done as much speed as me. They should be here for this tune. Fucking mint. Moving me hands like it's robotics. What am I doing? The bollocks. Who gives a fuck? Love everyone. Love me. I love you. Thanks.

Where it's all happening. That bird's getting pretty close to me now, maybe if I push up behind her. What does it matter? Don't need to worry about that shit no more. I've got Tina, just enjoy the music Crane. Still got this itchy horny feeling in me bollocks though. Not yet. Still the whole night ahead of me. Loads `a fun to be had.

Gonna have to tear meself apart when companies departed though. No doubt about that. Gotta be careful though Crane you mug. Taking out Tina again tomorrow. No Mum and Dad, get her back. Shag her. Make love to her. Even if she feels me nob, don't want loads of blisters on me helmet. That'd fucking impress her, wouldn't it? Where can I take her if we go out? The Harrow, Henry Gurnet, Harry Hill, Harry Redknapp. Bollocks. Rambling bollocks…

'Yeaahhhh!' Littl' Leg and Moon fucked. I can only smile. They grin back. Hug Leg. Hug Moon. Bewilderment written all over their fucking boats. Brooke too. Absolutely beautiful. Don't see him on the floor normally. Give him hug too. More confusion than you can fit in one box. Yeah this fucking tune. Staying on for this one. Especially now the boys have arrived. Dancing like wounded animals. So fucking what? Blitzed and loving it. Me heart's a cannon. Firing signals to those unknowing. Boom, Boom, like the bass line. Totally addicted to bass. Yeah. Untouchable world of bliss. Wonder where Liddy boy is? So hope he's got off with Wendy. Sloo and Beeke the brothers. Getting on like the glory days. The never ending glory Part 2.

Listen to this... Crickets on holiday, chiming throughout the night. SSS. SSSS.SSS.SSS.SSSS.SSSS.

Put me arm round Leg. Celebrate good times. Come on!

* * * *

Tin Lid swigs, desperately trying to stave off the acid. Wants to talk about dragons. Can't do that.

Wendy moves in closer. The girl understands it's up to her now. She must make the first move. He never will. That's obvious. She rests an arm on his shoulder, talks into his ear.

'I'm feeling a bit drunk after that vodka.'

Not a great comfort to Tin Lid. Is she only coming on to him because she's drunk? Is she even coming on to him? The youngster watches some spiders drop from the ceiling. Mustn't show fear. Has to stay strong. Got to get something to concentrate on. Got to get and again and again. Can't even look round at her yet. Drunk too, but the adrenaline flowing from his heart through his veins. Nerves or love? Nerves or love?

Go for it, now or never. Not amazingly wasted. Snog her now and don't consume any more, no matter what. Then the dream can't come true...

That's it thinks Tin Lid. That's the answer. What is? Can't remember. Places his drink on the table in front. Turns to face Wendy.

* * * *

Sloo and Beeke. Same position. Normally on pills Beeke would be dancing. But the acid was rooting him to the spot. Hilarity prevailing. Not really at what Sloo says. His face, changes, knows he's being stupid. Funny in that way. Sloo turns and says.

'Beeke, how do you know if an elephant's been in the fridge?' Beeke looks at him with intrigue.

'How?'

'Footprints in the butter.' A few moments the punch-line sinks in. Beeke is unsure whether he even gets it. Just the way Sloo said it. Real deadpan. Then with a smile. Beaming grin that leaves him in a rout.

Sloo knows Beeke's gone. This joke showing how easy. Minutes passing in seconds. After midnight now. Staring, forgetting the company. Then back again. Beeke wails. Sloo sits beside him again.

'How ya feeling now?'

'Well fucked, but brilliant.' Beeke answers, intake of breath without control from mouth. One second grinning, the next a frown. Gurning.

'Everyone is fucked Beeke, everyone.'

'What about you, you taken anything yet?'

'I done half an acid.' Sloo lies. Pretence of instability coming naturally.

The time is now.

'Excellent, 'as it kicked in yet?'

'Fucking has it? When I bumped into Moon, Brooke and Leg they were well on their way too.'

'Where are they?'

In position.

'They were round near the toilets; that was a while back though. Don't know how long now.'

'Really? Suppose they'll be on the floor by now.'

'Surprised you ain't out there.'

'Yeah me too, I'm well monged though. Loving it just sitting 'ere chatting to you.' Says Beeke. Sloo spots the chance to make his move.

'Me too Beeke, me too...' Momentary pause. Beeke at ease. '... Look mate, I just wanna say I'm sorry 'bout the way I acted recently. I've been a bit of a nob.'

'What? No mate, that's alright mate.'

'No, really, I was a bit scared about it all, I suppose...' Sloo chokes back a speech bubble with convincing ease. Appears nervous.

'...I had these mad feelings about you and I was... well... afraid to admit anything.'

Beeke's heart rises to his throat. The mind not registering Sloo's words properly. Was he drunk or was it the acid? Could be imagination? That must have been it, he thinks. Don't get carried away. Things are almost back to normal. Don't read the signs wrong. Beginning to doubt once more.

Sloo counteracts.

'I just think something like this could change everything and it scares the hell out of me. But... then I think I could be missing out on something here, like fate. I don't know. It's hard for me to talk here.' Worthy performance. Overdrive.

Convincing Beeke, actions spontaneous. A hand moves on to Sloo's leg. Caring squeeze. Could be taken either way Sloo likes. Doesn't have to be the decisive move. Beeke feels numb, acid taking away sensitivity. Can't feel how tense his friend's limb is.

'What d'ya wanna do then?' He asks. Scared, excitement. A mixed up emotion of feelings inside.

'I think we should keep this really quiet, I know that. This is a bit mind distorting. Take our *time,* you know what I mean? Just chat about it for a bit. Are you alright with that?'

'Sure I am Kev...' Sloo winces at the sound of his real name. The amount of lost respect he feels that denotes. Sole aim now is to regain it. '...You know 'ow I feel about you, you're so special to me. I'll wait for ever if I 'ave to.' Beeke can't believe he's saying this. The drugs, the moment. Sloo's words pushing him forward.

#

Knew the queer cunt fancied me. Just you wait faggot. False smile Sloo, that's it. He's in the trap. He's opened up. Totally understand what the Lord is saying now. Can't have this in our camp. It's unnatural.

Disgusting. No room. I've got more power than you Beeke. This charade is becoming easier. The more you fall. The higher I feel. The more I know I must kill you.

Patience nearly over. Being told to get this thing rolling. The storms are coming.

I know father. The *time* is almost here. My final task. This will save The Styx. Sacrifice.

'Listen, I've got an idea. We'll probably get cabs home, most people'll go to Cranes, we'll say we've had enough and get dropped off at the top of our roads. Don't go home, but meet up over the park with me. We'll take a walk. Have a chat.'

Ecstasy joy, acidic mirth. Rushes of disbelief. Overwhelmed by the words. Spelling out Beeke's once abandoned dream. This was true astonishment. Runs a hand through his sweat drenched hair. Looks at Sloo with delight. The best feeling in his life. Forget the drugs. Forget Ricky. This could be the start of ever after. Knew complications were out there. It was always gonna be difficult, but with Sloo he could work through these. Desire!

'Sure I will.' Gazing into each other's eyes.

Sloo doesn't want to push it. A period skips. He turns away.

'As I said, got to play it cool for a while yeah? Just a walk and a chat.'

The tree positioning, grabbing.

* * * *

'Take your top off Brooke.' Moon's shouting. Brooke's doing some mad shit dancing. Like some raving lunatic. Not even on the dance floor no more. Found Beeke and Sloo. Got a little section of seats to ourselves. The Magic Number is having a break.

Brooke looks like a mad fucker. A waving windmill on acid. I have to get up and hug him…

'Don't forget the kettle next *time*.' I shout in his ear. Surely that's what I wasn't meant to say? Or was that what he heard? Brooke's looking at me and laughing anyway. Could I say anything? Will I say anything? It's hard to think. Nothing's on the narrow. Only those little men that stick their heads into lampshades and pretend to be Martians.

Have to talk to Leg, forgot to tell him those fucking dvd's have gone missing; again.

'Leg I saw the Sky Sports satellite the other day.' Was that it? Fucking hell.

'Crane you're driving me round the fucking bend. Everything you say is complete bollocks do you know that?' He shakes his head, but then looks at me a bit guiltily and goes:

'I love ya man.'

'ME TOO.' A lazy Moon raises a limp arm. Not looking anywhere. But here.

'There's somebody at the door.' I've turned like a shy mouse to face Beeke. He's pissing himself. Seems well happy. Think Sloo is the dog of the tyre. Well happy, well buzzing. Back to mine soon. More bollocks. Cocaine. Drinks cabinet. Geezers, geezers, geezers. Lend me your ears.

'When John started saying some'ing he was right badly on the old salt and vinegar.'

Leg's looking corrupted at my ramblings. Don't mean it, any of it. He has to put his head in his hands. Tear a small clump of hair out. Moon's fucking with his mind too.

'Alright Leg?' Sloo shouts. I dart round like the weasel. Leg looks up.

'Insanity geez.'

Jumping, Jumping.

'Look...' I shout '...There's some geezer there wandering around wearing rags. He looks well lost.'

* * * *

'Tin Lid you fucker, what's going on?'

'Alright Leg, this is mad.'

'You look peaky.'

'Eh?'

'Don't matter, what's GOING ON?' Littl' Leg screams at the end. Tin Lid undisturbed.

'I've been getting off with Wendy for ages. She's well into me.'

'Wicked. Nice one mate. Where's she now?'

'She's gone to the bogs, what's 'appening with you?'

'Well mashed geez. The others are all downstairs talking shit and dancing. Real fucking party *time.*'

'I'm trying to 'old it together.'

'Not feeling that acid?'

'Totally. Been trying to talk to 'er, but nothing's coming out right. So I keep snogging 'er instead.'

'That ain't a bad thing geez. You're doing well my son.'

'Could do with another drink though.'

''ere 'ave this. I've only just started it. It'd take me about a year to drink anyway.' Leg hands Lid a bottle of Becks.

'Sure?'

'Yeah man. It's my present for ya. For getting 'old of Wendy.'

'You the man Leg.'

'No you the man.' Another couple embrace.

'Look Lid I won't cramp your style. Us lot are 'eading off in a minute.'

'What? What's the *time*?' Tin Lid shifts in his seat. Expression of a frightened rabbit.

''alf one.'

'Fucking hell, I thought it's about twelve and that. What the fuck's been 'appening?'

'You've been getting 'old of Wendy man.' Leg laughs.

'Oh yeah. Fucking night.'

'We don't wanna get caught up with the crowds. Gonna get a cab and carry the night on at Crane's.'

'Nice one. I've gotta stay 'ere though. Bird an' all that.'

'Well look we'll wait round for ya then. No big shakes. It'll be a fucking giggle in the cab office anyway.'

'Nah yous lot go. Wendy said one of 'er mates 'as got a crowd going round there and I could go with.'

'Whoa! Serious?"

'Yeah, can't fucking believe me luck. Only worry is if I embarrass meself.'

'Nah that ain't gonna 'appen. You're doing well so far. The acid's gonna be a fucker though. Just don't drink anymore after that and you'll be alright.'

'Not sure.'

'Look d'ya want one of us to go with ya? I'll come if you want?'

'Oh nah nah, God bless ya though. 'onestly it's cool. You'll be a gooseberry anyway. Crane's'll be far better and that."

'You sure, coz you know I love ya don't ya Liddy boy.'

'Yeah I know that. Everything'll be ok though, I'll take it easy, 'ere she's coming now.'

'Right I'll chip off and leave you to it then you lucky boy. Take this though.' Littl' Leg stands, reaches in his pocket and pulls a twenty pound note from it.

'You don't need to worry about that geez. I've got a bit of money on me.'

'Please take it, that's a just in case. You can pop round Crane's then. If you feel fucked at this do that is. Get out while the going's good. Know what I mean?'

'Nah I can't take it geez.'

'Lid, take the money please. It'll ruin me night if you don't.' Lid smiles and accepts. Knows he could do with it. Cash running a bit tight for a student aiming to impress.

'Thank you man.'

'No worries geezer, you take it easy.' Hugs between the pair one last *time.* Leg turns. Wendy stands a short distance behind.

'Wendy.' He proclaims before embracing this stranger to him.

'Hiya.' The surprised girl looks over Leg's shoulder at Tin Lid who can only shrug.

'Right see ya boy. Good luck.' Littl' Leg leaves with a wink.

Wendy sits beside her man.

'Who was that?'

'That was Littl L.. Tony.'

'Little Tony. 'e's not that little.'

'Just a stupid nickname and that.'

* * * *

'Don't go Beekey, don't go Beekey, don't go Beekey, don't go.' Loud chanting from the cab remains ineffective. Beeke's mind made up. A decision easily reached. Conversation with Sloo confirmed their meeting. Wouldn't miss this for the world.

Fears being alone for the few minutes before they rejoin. The dark night, wet weather. Alone on acid. Would all be worthwhile. Eventually. Once he's by Sloo's side.

The awkwardness they felt in having a gay friend; soon disappearing from the minds of The Styx. The boys want everyone together.

"onestly lads. I've gotta get me 'ead down.'

'Ai, Ai.' Crane shouts, oblivious to the implications. The others can't help but laugh. Then through their little remaining collective intelligence figure Beeke may have a boyfriend to go back to. Why not? He's keeping it quiet, doesn't want to offend. Whereas before "no" was not an option, Beeke acquires the rarely accorded "benefit of the doubt", allowing him to leave the taxi freely.

'Cheers lads. It's been a great night.'

Sloo, hasn't taken anything, didn't drink much; doesn't want to put up with their madness. Granted permission to also abandon the final leg at Cranes'. A short way farther, once more they say their good-byes. Sloo hears his friends singing into the distance.

Soon, he thinks, they'll all be able to celebrate together.

First there's some business to take care of.

Bitter air. A strong breeze. Summer closing in, yet heavily disguised. Drizzle. Nothing could affect Sloo's plan. He must be unhindered. Little to stop Beeke from attending this meeting. Brewing storm; still being held at bay. Dark clouds rush fast past the moon. A glowing eye inspecting the movement. The thunder, lightning awaiting a sacrificial repeat, then it may not end. A return. Weather controlled. A horrific force waiting in the wings. Presented before as mischief. Soon mayhem.

Misleading, possessing a young man. Once thought the world of all his friends. But now wary and hateful. Thoughts of their protection a part of the destruction situated beneath the trees. The site once a shrine to an unwitting cannibalistic tribe.

Sloo believes he's realised his purpose, a born again Noah. Instead fooled into re-opening the gate for a depraved leader. He that drugged his followers to conceal his sickening acts. Here to collect fresh meat. Enhance power with every meal. Reinstatement.

The beginning of the feast would bring forth the power of *time.* Take over nature, then the world. Reverse the River Styx, those lost souls would return as a new population. After wiping out Earth's inhabitants.

Kevin continued, being led towards the loss of his own personality. To obey Sloo and kill Beeke. Then Sloo forever.

A bench. Beeke waits, shaking movements. Rapidly rubbing his hands over his legs. Trying to stop the shivering. Numbness against cold, but nature to explore it. Needs company; scared of the shadows. Disfigurement animated. Lights flowing through the landscape. Swirl up, meet as one. Change constantly.

Struggling to overcome the shock. Sloo's confession out of the blue. Needs confirmation. Wants Sloo to keep him warm. Sitting in wonder. Makes out a figure in the distance.

Walking towards him...

THE BIBLICAL DIRECTORY
(iv)

'...After centuries of having to command evil souls, Thanatos gained awesome leadership skills. Soon he had inspired the group of magicians and philosophers to achieve a massive breakthrough. Two men in particular delivered what they believed to be the definitive answer...'

It's the old directory again and still more of these fucking names.

First row, lower middle

#248 Asmodeus and

first row, upper middle

#130 Solomon.

'Eh is that 'im off of King Solomon's mines?'

'If I say yes will it help you follow?'

'Suppose.' I shrug. Gotta have some context here innit.

'Then yes; but I'll give you a quick account of Solomon and Asmodeus...'

Oh please do!

'...Being the son of David, Solomon became the pre-ordained King of all Israel. He made a promise to our Lord to rule the land justly, if he was given the wisdom to do so. Our Lord believed greatly in the man and so granted extensive knowledge for his task.

Yet once again greed reared its ugly head, and this wasn't enough for Solomon. He got clever, but still wanted more. He soon fell in with the magic crowd; in order to obtain even greater acumen. It grew and grew so much he soon became arrogant, or I should say complacent. His dealings with the demon Asmodeus..." Ooh demon.

'...led to the astronomically quick erection of a temple for the King that would reflect his great wealth and power. It certainly did that! Once the building was complete Solomon... how can I put this to you? Erm... Well you see this was a rich bachelor here; and King to boot. With his own temple! So he... he had no trouble with the ladies.'

'I getcha! Like me mate Brooke? Except for the King and Temple bit anyway.'

'Exactly. Like Brooke. Glad you're following me.'

'I'm doing me best.' Feel a bit proud of meself now.

'Eventually Solomon had become husband to many foreign women, who he then allowed to worship other false Gods; within his temple. For betraying The Lord and belittling his vast position as King, he too was banished to the Underworld...'

Another one bites the dust.

'...Asmodeus, a conniving little demon, was destined to go there anyway. But these two, with their exceeding cunning, were a dangerous pairing. From the group of mathematicians and philosophers, Hades and Hermes held out most hope from them to devise the final equation to make their plan work. They were not let down as very soon in his calculations, Solomon had developed the "*Tree of Life*" and the arrogantly named "*Seal of Solomon*"...'

He hands me a diagram of a six pointed star in a circle. Got loads of writing on each point:

TE GRAM TON T MA TRA. I can't make head nor tail of it.

'...This seal signifies the unity of man and his universe. From this point on the mystical significance of numbers flourished in its entirety. Note there is six points to this star. Interpretations suggested that they had to find a sufficient member of the directory, with a six in their number. That was the easy part, who could be better than the fed up Charon? Seven, SIX, Eight.'

'The devil?'

'Satan's got his own "end of the world" thing going on in Hell. No need to concern yourself with that...'

Like I'm not gonna now he's said that.

'...No Charon was perfect. Because of his job, he was the only one who could get close to Earth on a regular basis. So our unruly group agreed; Charon would become the new leader and he in turn could release them from the Underworld and its unearthly shackles…'

I'm getting a headache. This is truly blowing my mind.

'…So they knew how the six was vital, but how to utilise it? That was the big question. This is where Asmodeus showed his worth. The evil being pointed out that "the mind of man was the source of true magic; and that it was man's destiny to reconcile the forces and elements of the universe within themselves".

As hard as it is for me to admit: Genius! The gang got to work and had soon figured it all out. Charon should eat the brains and hearts of six agreeing friends and disciples. With this he would take on all the knowledge and hope contained by mankind and break the circle of existence. Do you know of Cannibalistic tribes?'

As much as I'm completely lost, the geezer's speaking my language now. It sounds like some real horror film shit here.

'I've seen *Cannibal Holocaust.*' Great film. Like the original *Blair Witch Project*, but with gore.

'Does that state that to devour someone leads to inheriting all their knowledge?'

'Err…'

'Well anyway it does; and has a major subsequent power transfer.'

'Cool.' I goes, but he just shakes his head a bit, like he dunno what he's dealing with here.

'The scheming crew knew that it couldn't stop there. Just by eating six people's hearts and minds would be too simple. There were two more numbers to decipher. The seven and the eight. With the six in the middle it had to be something that sandwiched humankind in its existence. No problem to these masterminds, it was obvious…' He's looking at me, like he's waiting for me to give the answer. Fuck, should I know this?

'Err…computers.'

'No Crane, nice try though. The answer is the Universe and *Time.* Because you see the Universe is a large clock.'

'Large Clock?' I'm hoping that's what he said anyway.

'…Each element serves a small, but significant function within the overall mechanism. They had to figure a way to destroy this clock.'

Thank God, but woah there wierdo.

'I definitely don't get that bit.'

'Don't worry it's not important to you, I diverse sometimes...'

'Sometimes?'

He has a little chuckle, but carries on regardless.

'With this in mind they soon discovered the second clue and fortunately for them, it all related to Charon...'

Well what do you know!

'...Now the eighth year of any millennium, is the year that the River Styx' tide turns for one week only, in order for Judas here...'

Points at second column.

#445 Judas Iscariot

I've heard of this geezer.

'... to carry out a complete clean of the river. Jobs like scraping body parts from the surface and such. This is the only week that Charon has off.'

'Oh.'

'Now Judas and Charon were good friends and shared many a conversation when their paths crossed. Charon mentioned one to the plotting gang. One that he felt may be of some importance. The traitor had told the Riverman of Lord Christ our saviour's teachings. Christ was a brilliant prophet, but on one or two occasions, would perhaps, divulge a little too much information. So trusting was he...'

He makes the sign of the cross that Italians do when they run out on the football field.

'...The Saviour told Judas that the seven days following his future resurrection, would also be a portal for evil to enter this world. His re-entrance so big, that there would be a gap for someone else to seep through. After that or before, there is none. The scheming scoundrels wondered if this applied every year. Whether this portal would always be around as a reminder. Then **EUREKA!...**' He shouts. I'm positive only to make sure I'm still awake. Lucky really I was just going again there.

'...To carry out his job Charon was allowed, by Zeus the God of weather...'

Obviously one of the top boys:

#003 Zeus

"...to have charge of the skies bordering his river. In order there were no troubles for Charon's boat whence setting off from the shores. This meant they could put their theory to the test. Solomon had already taught "that magicians were profound and diligent searchers into nature; they; because of their skill, know how to anticipate an effect, the which to the vulgar shall seem to be a miracle"...You see?'

'No I can't see, wha...'

'Charon could use storms and their magnetic fields, along with Hades' number three- two-seven, to enter Earth on his week of vacation. The seven days following the anniversary of the resurrection.'

'Oh!' I pretend I get it now. Maybe somewhere down the line I'll fall in.

'Their first test worked and the three numbers all had their meaning; subsequently Charon and Hermes had means of influencing events on Earth. All they needed now was a little help from friends to disguise their actions. This brings us neatly back to the tree of life...'

I wouldn't really be giving it all this "neatly" bollocks. This is more messy than me head after a massive speed binge and horror marathon.

CHAPTER 19
THE RIVER RUNS RED

'DRINK ONE LAST TIME AND BE MERRY.'

Five naked figures run amongst the trees. Smothered in dirt. Their feet bleed. Clogged with thorns, shards. Lost faces. Distant minds. A pretence. Role playing. Like children imitating adults. Break time.

Wadard Mooning skips, sings. At times stops over piles of twigs.

Bends down. Exposing bare arse-hole. Pride evacuated the scene. Testicles swing freely, hang low. Cuts and bruises mingle with bodily filth. Skin peeling. Dry, scabby. Gaunt, but well fed. Hair greased back in animal fat. Sunken black eyes. Energetic, yet without sleep in days. Delirium.

Spotted some berries.

Picks up the leaves. Glory in more useless work done. No food in the dank camp surroundings. Soft muddied ground, shadowed. Trees block the sun. Nothing grows underneath. Impure earth host to insanity. Only visions of red fruit for drink here. Now a handful of damp leaves handed to Hevey Little.

He'll prepare the berries for a succulent meal. Mooning feels proud. Job well done. Much easier here. Collecting ingredients. Singing in the vast light glow. Out there arduous work on fields. Here laugh, dance. Collecting for the community. All help each other. Atmosphere euphoric. Better surroundings. Fine embroidered cloaks line the trees as walls. Golden berries, buds grow from the branches. The sun warming their spirits. When rain arrives, protected by rooves of twigs and crisp leaves. Yes much easier here.

Scurrying like rats in the black undergrowth. Animal skins hanging from the limbs of perennial plants. Drip steadily with blood from freshly slaughtered wildlife. Gaps, thin, hardly protective. The sky a mishmash of locked branches. Holes, hardly shelter. Mound of bones. One night Mooning chewed on one. Momentary hallucination. Believed he was a dog. Sloo patting the head of his follower.

Each figure wears warm cloaks. Varnished with glittery leaves. All wear crown of thorns. *None wear anything. Skin torn, ragged. Scrambling on all fours. Sniffing, rolling like pigs in mud. Red trickling down their cheeks.*

The steady flow of thick liquid; a beautiful shower to cleanse their skin. Looking to the sky, pure water falls.

Washing each day in vein juice.

Faint music in the distance. Melody creating a harmony. Makes Mooning want to dance all day long. Lovely angelic choir. Humming below. Collecting berries to fill his bowl. Spring in the step. Non stop harmony.

Creaking twigs, injured wolves howl. Constantly determined to crawl back to their feet. Wounds so severe and deep make that impossible. Screaming delusion taunts. Wind spanking each trunk.

Nothing is certain here.

A summery smelling forest, fresh with spring growth. Beautiful fruits bringing forth an emphatic aroma. Take in deep breaths. Huge lungful of freshness.

Reek mix blood, faeces and urine. No escape from a foul stench of death.

NOTHING IS CERTAIN HERE.

At least not in the mind of six men. Tempted from a harsh existence into a false one.

Hevey Little laughs. Just seen a small animal darting around in hot pursuit of its mother. Squeaking yipping. Cute innocence, in slight terror of its new habitat outside the womb. Could watch this side of nature all day.

A limbless sheep rolls in agony, screaming. Trying to find stability. Complete disarray, too naive to comprehend why it no longer stands.

Could watch it all day, but no time. Must squash berries into a jug. Fresh juice for their meals. Plenty to go round. Squeeze.

Oozing red. Draining the pigs heart. A sodden muscle bursting of its contents.

The food, Little cuts at wild vegetables. Share the cuttings equally. Veritable feasts placed on their dishes.

Scabbed worm filled fingers to chew, devour.

There's Mooning skipping past. Takes the attention. Smile.

Inane laughter. Psychotic cackle.

'How are you today?' Little hears himself say.

Dribble falls from his chin. Saliva bubbles from hanging lip. Speechless.

'Thank you for more fruit James, wonderful.' Will go nicely.

Break it apart with grotty dirt fingers. A slice of eyeball for each. Keels to the ground. Staring blankly. Continue the preparation.

Hand to the forehead. Imagine a sailor crossing the seas. Sees the beauty withheld deep in the forest. Petals float like snowflakes. Colours from blue to red and green to yellow. Decorating logs, puddles of clear water. Picture a clear reflection. Well looked after. The face of health. No danger here in the North side. A few metres away from Tilnid. Keeping protection over the land. So deep, unexplored yet. Insects flutter between wild plants.

Nothing occurs. Except rapid movement within his sockets. Wide eyed. Eyelids cut from his face. Slept peacefully one night. Unconscious, Sloo sliced them. Driven insanity. Almost blind. Black lifeless forest.

Visions of beauty.

Nothing to be seen. Destruction, a hollow clearing of desperation. Screams, wailing, psychotic babble. Mingling with deceased nature. Spring not forcing life. Resurrection waiting for a command.

Still Tilnid stays put. Dinner soon. Revamp for the nights festivities. Dancing and singing.

Mindless prodding. Sickening gurgling fits.

The final night.

Brooks lay next to the river.

Standing by the edge of the clear water. Sharp ended branch in hand, poised to spear the oncoming fish.

Spittle bubbling, running down his chin. Small puddle on the floor. Brooks' urine. Holds his penis.

A large one this time. Drives the weapon into the fish. Feast for a million.

Feast on six.

Punches a fist in the air. Congratulates himself on another fine catch. As big as Brooks' outstretched hand.

Flaps an arm up to the sky. Twitching. Brain-dead. Jostling his organ back and forth. No idea of sickly white semen spreading over his fingers.

Beautiful pure spring water. Plenty to drink and cleanse with after meals. One more fish and then collect their refreshment in jugs. Take it back to the camp.

Excrement clogging on a detached leg.

All around Brooks pretty flowers grow.

Urine drowning the area. Piles of faeces trodden by a heel.

Robert Cranley head in hands. Seeing bright lights in every direction. Flashing extreme violence. Probing. Lost in various colours. Closing his eyes, worse there. Insanity creeping in. Has to cut out the glare. Seeping through the gaps. Clawing in to his world. A land of uncertainty.

Hands away from his eyes. Only the bathroom. Checks the mirror. Glory at the saucers that are his pupils. Could stare at the changing shape of his features all night. Distorted images, loves it there. Loves this feeling. No matter how obliterated, Crane can always pull through. Adores the insanity. Becomes one within it. Encourages it, sees it. Never once letting it bear down and suppress him. One more time before going back to the others. Head in hands.

Wants to sing like the others. Be able to skip, dance amongst the trees, but losing senses. Can't experience the joy as the others say. Aware of something wrong. Senses a presence...

Final twitches. No vision of delight. Strictly no sight at all. Eye socket empty, red, swollen. Nose removed. Gaping messy hole. One leg remaining. Both hands cut to the wrist. Wounds wrapped enough to stop hemorrhage. Blood stained. Alfred Beech still breathes, yet knows nothing of the torment. Given up on pain. Numb. Drugged from the vessel. In a land of nowhere. Black, searching. Being called towards a distant river. A dimmed huge man stands. Beckoning. The next boat is about to leave. Room for one more. Must make it. Remembers a good life. The figure solemn. Bony fingers reptilian, curling. Drawing, hypnotising Beech to his last voyage. Bodies on board. The *Time* is up.

Last moments were joy.

Then trapped. Others hadn't noticed disappearance in days. Still believed they talked to their friend. He was there in their eyes. Reality. A battered mess just yards away from home. Beech forgotten. Sloo towering. *The time is now.* Shadows fill the trees. Looming large. Beech's final day, the poor weak man naked. Balanced against a tree. Drugged on raw flesh and blood. Final minutes of coherence. Ripe for the taking. Entrusting to his leader.

' Do you agree to obey me for the remainder of your life and then on?'

'Yes my Lord.'

Blackened face, lost eye.

Full of wonder. Respect. This lord had given him tranquillity. Of course he'll obey. No sense not to.

Head controlled by cannibal urges. Overpowered. Beech crumbles to the ground with the final dedication. Leg and mind not strong enough to carry him. Sloo begins draining Beech slowly. Still alive. Resurrecting energy for the benefit of the final five, for now. Tonight Beech will be finished. The others can feast. So brainwashed now they will celebrate the exquisite food. Still obey their master. King of Kings. Then one by one willingness to submit their all to his power. No opposition. Sloo is good. Then they will be carved. The final feast. The dismemberment of six bodies. Six given brains. Six awarded hearts. Sloo will eat well. The meal for eternal power.

Nature will become his tool. Trees alive to his power. Rain conjured at a demand. Floods tirade. Winds of tremendous proportion, mountains will be moved. Earth destroyed for his own rebuilding. A new God ruling his own dead inhabitants. The River Styx in reverse.

Power over lost souls. They will build his new kingdom outside the forest. Rest no more. Where everyone dead is led. This was the future. The forest? This would be his haven for now. Nothing could touch him.

All power will be Sloos. Come the feast.

Lights flashing. Penetrating the area. One last hope. Someone whose will is stronger. Not ready to give up in the face of adversity. Someone able to challenge, accept all that is horrific. Not shy from disaster. Who may appear the weakest, yet the mind stronger. Robert Cranley stares at the apparition. Golden glow. Hair blowing away large and proud. Colours of the sun. A face that lights, sending out warm belief. The smile creating hope. Cherry red lips. Trust in the eyes.

Maybe he will see now. Through this angel that has arrived.

This beautiful angel.

The first course is about to be served...

Time Is Momentarily Ending

CHAPTER 20
TABLE FOR TWO

Sloo and Beeke continue their walk. From the park, down the long darkened main road. Tranquility sets over the area. Halcyon in Beeke's senses. A slight drizzle dampens the ground, the trees blow softly.

Sloo looks at the court house. Reminisce. The orchestra begins again. Violins, cellos slowly soothe. No anger in their sounds. For now he remains in peace. Waiting for his father to inspire. Enduring this conversation until the big band strikes the match. Drums, bass will enter. Ignite the fire.

They had sat for a while, the increasing rain giving Sloo an excuse to move the pair for cover. No mention of his admission in the club yet. Talk ranged from the state of their friends to old times. Beeke in hysterics at each tale. Sloo had him fully at ease. Working hard to find the right time. Then the idea. Get protection from the woods. The weather appears to be getting worse. The journey proceeds.

Beeke experiencing slight frustration. The subject he craves not being discussed, though he waits patiently. Sloo asked him for a walk and a chat. That was all. He'd give him his request. As long as they were talking again. He was happy. Rediscovered his best friend and maybe more.

The acid. Beeke can almost feel the loss of brain cells. Revision tomorrow already a write off. Today even. Hopes he'll spend it with Sloo anyway. Willing to talk all night and day, if that's what it took. Nothing fades him now. Ecstasy pills taking a back seat. Making way for a humour invoking experience from the prominent drug in Beeke's system.

He considers the miserable nights endured recently. Lying awake, moping for himself. For his lost friend. All that over now. His wildest dreams answered. Never thought it could go this far. Still giggling. Not sure what at. The houses, a thought of Upminster manor hall past. Streams of ideas and concentration mingle into a looseness of thought. A few days ago suicide crossed his mind. Now a thousand things storm in and out his head. Not one covers the area of death. Beeke's looking forward to every second of life now.

Every precious second…

'I'm sorry mate I'm talking rubbish here, I'm just really nervous.'

'It's ok Sloo, I'll 'elp you through every step of this.' Beeke experiences his first charge of power over his friend. A new found confidence. Coming out the closet first, shows he had most courage of the two. Now he and Sloo both knew it, Beeke thinks.

Sloo waits, **RIVER DRIVE** nearing.

'Thanks mate. I still feel this is too public. I dunno if it's all the drugs I used to take, but I've got this terrible paranoia feeling.'

'That's pretty sensible. Essex ain't a pleasant area is it? You never know what'll 'appen if we bump into a group of blokes on their way 'ome.'

'That's what I'm scared of. D'ya fancy walking through the woods.'

Beeke admires this nervous side of Sloo. Rarely shows vulnerability. Must be the acid. Should have spotted Sloo's error. Last chance?

RIVER DRIVE.

Those peaceful houses. Sloo could stroll the road with eyes closed and still describe each one. Most lights are off. Residents sleep whilst only a short distance away, terror was about to unfold.

The opening.

Two gaps beside a short pole. Sloo slides through first. No sooner under the first shelter, warmth envelopes him. He is at home. Trumpets sound. He's here. Can feel the power resurgence. His Lord is near, watching. Knows he must impress. This was important to his father. Once he'd slaughtered Beeke, could he then lead his friends to safety.

Beeke follows. Unafraid. Here with Sloo. Wary, the acid confusing, but mirth to be found in the situation. Already the growing storm a distant memory. Sloo leads, naturally zig-zagging amongst the trees. Travelling the same path that led The Styx to the camp exactly one decade before.

Sloo knew the anniversary was here. He hadn't mentioned it to the gang, for now. Sensible enough to know any coincidental events linked with the disappearance of their friend could raise suspicion.

An owl sounds. Crunching. Sloo builds with every step. In stature and confidence. With the music building to a crescendo. Looking forward to the sacrifice.

* * * *

'So we're all hats! Now what the fuck is that supposed to mean Crane?"

'Fuck knows that's what Brooke just said.'

'Did I?' Brooke looks up, confusion engraved upon his face.

'I asked you what Leg was going on about, and you said 'e said "we're all hats"'

'Are you sure?'

Moon, Littl' Leg and Brooke have scattered themselves about Cranes' parents living room. Moon and Leg claimed an armchair each. While Brooke is laid flat out on the sofa. *Jazzy Jeff and The Fresh Princes 'Code Red'* the chosen sounds. It suited the happy mood.

The night seemed to be moving at a rapid pace. The acid creating a warp. Hours would soon pass with nothing acheived. They all knew that. None of them cared. Crane even looked forward to it the most. Loved to be lost in *time.* With his friends talking nonsense, but guffawing at everything. Nothing finer.

He'd found some wine in his parents drink cabinet, didn't think twice about opening the bottle. All four had a glass of Cabernet.

Crane was laid out across the floor. Head resting on a stool. The others had been pushing him to prepare some lines of cocaine. He managed to show such complete ignorance of the process that one friend gave up hope. Littl' Leg now sits with the bread board on his lap. Credit card in hand, organising four stripes of the drug. He figured it was an easier task than making a joint. Something that Moon had also passed on, for the time being.

Inanimate objects move without warning. Focus spreads across three times. Ghosts around each person. Everything was difficult in this room.

'So what hat are you Crane?' Moon laughs. Normally he'd not encourage Crane's insanity. Tonight he was in the same zone.

'I'll be a bowler 'at.' Crane's serious in his answer, truly believing this to be a significant event. Proud at his choice. The competition heats up.

'You Leg?' Asks Moon.

'Err... a sombrero.' Leg decides if you can't beat 'em, join 'em.

Crane murmurs jealousy at a great choice, wishes he'd chosen the Mexican hat himself.

'I'll be a cowboy 'at...' Moon continues '...Brooke?'

Brooke looks up in shock. Not up with this one. Not up with anything anyone's been talking about since they got back.

'I'll be a werewolf.' The others can't contain howls of laughter. Unstoppable. Crane tries to control himself. Needs to say something before the discussion moves on to something else. A subject even more random.

'A werewolf 'at? What the fuck's that?'

'I really ain't got a fucking clue what yous lot are going on about. Can't I be a werewolf?' A childlike quality shining through. The acid dissolving sense and poise. Brooke reduced to the level of his three friends. This would be standard for them. Brooke had been out the game too long.

'Yeahh you can be a werewolf 'at...' Considers Leg '...It's good to 'ave you 'ere that's all geez.'

At these words Crane jumps to his feet. Sudden burst of energy.

'Yeah, I've been dying to say that all night. Brooke you are the man. We need you 'ere more often son.' He goes over and hugs his friend.

'Good to be 'ere. Even though you are all fucking nuts.'

* * * *

Underfoot dead leaves and twigs transform to solid earth. The journey at its final stretch. Toward the camp. Sloo can hear it calling. Beckoning whispers. Tempting, luring the visitors. Play it all again. Process cycling, going around, coming around. Promises fulfilled. Revenge uninhibited. Waiting in the dark. Patience. Almost *time.* Watching for a return. Closer. People swimming alongside. Overflow of lost souls. Party of new chances. Wind blowing ever stronger. Masts high, pushing the boat on. Wailing. Screeching. Jibes of lust. They have life. Tormented to grasp what used to be theirs. Coming back to inherit the earth. Out with the new and in with the old. Death is upon us.

Beeke acknowledges the route. Knows this is the camp trail. Is this romantic? Forbidden love in the reluctant's haven. Giggling.

Sloo laughs along. In front, eyes wide. All part of the plan.

Beeke feeling nervous, acid love. A novice himself. Nobody since Ricky. Do you make a move? How far would Sloo allow him to go? Wait until he was ready. Was Beeke ready? Maybe nothing would happen tonight. Just a chat, Beeke tells himself. Just a chat.

Growing darkness. Hovering above. Spirits fly. Visions held in time. Paused. Longing to be released.

Beeke doesn't remember the camp being this deep into the woods. Comments. Sloo agrees. Blames the acid. Spreading further and further. *Time* lapses.

s

p

m

u

J

Beeke unsure of Sloo's words. Puts it down to L.S.D. Only understandable solution. What was going on? Sudden fear. Middle of forest on hallucinogens. Could be something nasty here. Calls out. Sloo stops. Calming words. Difficult to see for Beeke. Near impossible. Sure where they're going?

Comforting. Sloo sees all. Nearly there. Just the acid. Everything's all right. It's the drugs. I'm here with you. No one else is around. There was a light in the camp. Always had a torch hidden. Beeke confused.

Fear growing with each step. Holding hands outstretched. Feeling his way forward. Touches something. Sloo's back.

Shudders.

Keep it going. Don't fail now. Steps back, puts an arm round his friend. Beeke returns the gesture. An extremity in paradox. To one a symbol of safety, to the other a representation of depravity. The world should punish without sympathy. Home draws nearer. Black air hides the long *time* banished evil.

It's ok, few more metres. Why the torch? Comes here every so often. Get away from Mother. Hideout for a joint. Perfect getaway. No hassles.

Beeke soothes. Plausibility. Sloo knows what he's doing. Beeke would never dream of coming through here on his own. Sloo was like that.

Possibility of monsters/ ghosts/ murderers never phased him. Second home now. Since a kid. His own private hide out. Beeke respects that. Adventure. Enjoying Sloo's arm round him, leading the way. Something would surely happen. No doubt. Maybe a kiss. That would be perfect. Longs for a kiss. Safety in Sloo's clutches. Fear of a watching wraith however. Every move intimidating. Must be the acid. Chill out, with Sloo now.

Darker, deeper. Leaves rustling. Childlike whispers. Wind shaking branches, almost laughter. The storm builds. Sloo stops. Takes his arm away. Beeke shivers. Hears Sloo bend and rustle. Must be the torch. Sensory, this is the camp. They're here. Sloo stands.

'Right I've got it, here we go.'

* * * *

'You're 'aving a laugh ain't ya?'

'Nah.'

''ang on a minute, the geezer's in the shop and what?'

'I was behind 'im...' Brooke is in tears reporting the recent event. Laughter stalling each triviality as if four comedians battle for air time. '...There was no one behind the counter... and he turns and goes... "You just can't find the staff these days."'

Crane rolls around the floor clutching his stomach. Trying to stop the pain of incessant hysterics. Leg struggles to grasp it, but chuckles anyway. Normality, this story would raise a murmur of approval. On acid, the world's funniest joke has just been told. Moon gets up, trying to suppress laughter, only manages to shower his feet with saliva. He opens a cabinet draw, looks in.

'No.' Shuts it. Next drawer down does the same. Crane losing control, trying to speak, can't mouth words. Losing breath. Leg knows what his friend is attempting to say.

'What ya doing Moon?'

'Trying to find the staff.' More seconds drowned with the noise of mirth. Brooke speaks:

'Look mate I told ya. You can't find the staff.' The penny begins to drop with Leg. He collapses from the armchair onto his knees. Takes a similar position to Crane and begins rotating on the ground.

'It's 'ere somewhere, I know it is.' Moon continues.

Soon all four are darting about the house. Opening cupboard doors. Looking under furniture. Lifting bin lids. Looking in mirrors. Out of windows. On top of sideboards. Under paperwork. In drinks cabinets. All with the same replies:

'It's not 'ere.'

Moon becomes so engrossed in the game he stalls at one cupboard and repeatedly slams the doors whilst shouting.

'I can't find the staff. Just can't find the fucking staff.'

* * * *

Sloo switches the torch on. Camp lights. An inner glow. Lamps burn. Lit as before. Dancing, singing. Joy. Visions disintegrate before Beeke can adjust his eyes. The camp Styx. Been so long. Beeke laughs. It's hardly changed. Sloo shines light on the old carpet.

'My God that's still there.' Like a guided tour. Sloo proud at keeping the settlement presentable. Treated as if it were an abode. It was his home.

Push aside thin veil of branches obstructing their entry. So neat. Something new. Even Sloo is surprised. A present from father?

Set the scene. Two tree stumps placed side by side in the camps centre. Every piece in position.

'I came over here earlier today, had a reefer, make sure it looked all right...' The final mistake Sloo would make? Drugs clouding Beekes' intelligence. Forgotten their earlier conversation. Sloo had been home all day. Last chance?

Beeke lifts his heavy eyelids. All seems familiar, yet vision unsteady.

'I hoped we'd come 'ere.' How sweet. Beeke smiles.

Sloo copies. Then watches Beeke walk across the tramps grave. Holds back humour. Beams the torch about the camp. Like a log cabin. Sloo couldn't remember it looking so good. As if walls appear. Set for a wonderful dinner by the Lord. He grabs Beeke's hand. Knows what he has to do. Take this further. Beeke must give in, obey. One option. Leads the ex-friend to the stumps. Like a gentleman waits for Beeke to sit, then mirrors. A glimpse; notices the weapons stored behind his seat. Perfect.

Sloo turns to Beeke.

'Well... I suppose I've kept you waiting long enough.' Broad warming grin. Gazing into Beeke's eyes.

Shyness, stomach lifts. Heart beating fast. All a dream? Has to be. Sloo loves him.

'It's ok. I know it'll be worth it. To tell you the truth I never expected this at all.' Beeke answers.

Sloo leans a little closer towards him. Idea hatching. Puts left arm on Beekes knee. Knows Beeke will look upon it. Sensations, acid rushing. Feeling intensity of situation. Sloo lowers right arm. No fumbling, takes hold of the screwdriver. Grips the handle.

'Are you sure you want to do this already Sloo? We can take our *time* over this.'

'Do you promise to take it easy? Go with whatever I say. If I want to stop, you stop yeah? And not say a word of this to anyone, 'til I'm ready?'

'Whatever you say, I'll do whatever you tell me to.'

Trees glower, word spreading fast. The boy achieved instant success. Received total commitment within the camp. Waves of nostalgia. So proud. Shame the boy will have to leave.

Now the sacrifice, then Sloo can begin again.

'Perfect. I think the *time* is now. I feel safe here with you Beeke.' Sloo raises his left arm. Places his hand on Beeke's cheek. Loving tender strokes. Moves his face a little closer.

Beeke wanders into Sloo's gaze. Lost. His own eyes wide, pupils dilated. Sloo looks different to Beeke. An older version. Acid plays tricks. Remembers once being convinced that Tin Lid was ninety. Vision. Safety, comfort. Six inches away from the dream.

Sloo moves his left hand further back, fingers rummaging through Beeke's hair. Slowly drawing in. Both hearts sprinting against one another. One mind lost in make-believe, the other focused on horror.

The ultimate fantasy. Pills, acid. Mind bending alterations. Adrenalin pumping. Beeke expecting to wake any minute. Back in the miserable existence he'd grown used to. Doesn't happen. Two inches apart.

Sloo tilts his head to the left. Needs full force in the planned swing.

Beeke leans in, slightly to the right. Alone. The woods. Rain. Sloo's protection. Romance not dead. Lips touch ever so gently. Prepared. Stays there. Paralysed in *time*. Beeke's breathing growing heavy. All a little much. Wants to delve deeper. Explore the senses. Takes his *time*. Gently. Mouths open slightly, then close in a kiss.

Sloo's embrace becomes firmer. Mouths open again. Beeke losing himself completely. Tongue entering Sloo's mouth.

Sloo feels it, tastes it. Sickness rising. Must endure. Prove his commitment to his father, once and for all.

An acid twinge sends uncontrollable desire into Beeke's loins.

Sloo holds back slightly. Must swallow vomit without suspicion. Difficult. More courage. Power through the veins. The passive, let Beeke feel in control. Let his tongue come further inwards. Probing. Captured in the moment.

Beeke loving every second, yet wants perfection. The stance was a little awkward. No longer paralysed. Shock is being overcome. First things first. Comfortable kiss. Wants Sloo to become the aggressor, how he'd imagined it to be. Understands the intimidation though. Remembers Ricky controlling his own first experience. Needed it to be that way. To encourage Sloo. Has to take on the role of Ricky. A minimal shift. Better. Relocates his arm round his friend's back. Caressing carefully. Then the other hand. Copying Sloo's move. Rubs the back of his head. Much better. Tasting Sloo, engrossed in the saltiness. The sweetness. A side Beeke knew was there. Thoughts about his femininity clouding sight. Covering minds vision. Doesn't sense where Sloo's right arm is. An opposite from thinking negativity.

It rises higher into perspective. ***The time is now.*** Sloo forces added pressure onto the kiss.

Beeke experiencing Sloo easing into the situation. Must be more relaxed. This is it.

The tip of the screwdriver a short measure from the side of Beeke's head.

Beeke moves closer into the kiss.

Sloo's hand raised level with Beeke's profile. He waits, allowing Beeke's overexcitement. Tongue DEEPER, entering lavishly into his mouth. Sloo withdraws his tongue from the tension. Beeke enters further still. Pushing his fleshy muscle so far in...

Sloo shuts down with teeth. Not to cut or remove, but hold steady. Terror first. Real pain later.

An incapacitated nerve racking second. Beeke's eyes open. Sloo's too.

Watches the fear develop. Smiles whilst clamping Beeke's tongue like a vice…

Then with power smashes the screwdriver into Beeke's temple. Burying the end.

* * * *

An attempted discussion moves rapidly onward. Two secretaries at Moon's work were now under scrutiny. The four back in the living room, laughter calmed. Moon had set about describing the events of a company night out a few weeks before. Brooke, Crane and Littl' leg sit enthralled in the tale.

'I could tell Sally was getting the 'ump, she's 'ad it in for this fat bird for ages. Said she's always ordering 'er around as if she was the boss. I mean they were both just fucking skivvys, but this fat bird's like "do this fax for me", or "type this letter, while I eat me big fat lunch." Anyway the old booze's flowing through Sally like nobody's business. It'd make Tin Lid look fucking sober, you know what I mean? ...'

Listeners once again in hysterics. Crane trying to suppress himself. A vacant looking Brooke quickly exhales. Belly humour. Leg was preparing more lines, struggling against blowing the cocaine away with his chuckles.

'... She was getting loud. All the bosses were there and everything, they was trying to turn a blind eye, like they do. Snobby cunts. But not me, I went over, wanted to see a bit of action. Fucking love things like that. Especially birds man. So I was saying "what's a matter Sally?" all that bullshit. Pretending I was trying to diffuse the situation or some'ing, but keeping 'er mind on it really. She started getting louder and louder with 'er rants. You know women "bitch this, bitch that."

So fat bird, can't contain it any longer. She comes barging 'er way through the crowd in the pub...'

By now Moon is up on his feet. Knowing he has full audience attention, he begins mimicking the movements. Puffing out his cheeks and knocking imaginary people out of Crane's living room. Then with a high pitch female imitation

'..."'ave you got a problem with me Sally?" She was going. I was thinking lovely, this is kicking off 'ere.

Sally's pissed and 'er balls are fucking large. Thinks she can 'ave this fat cow. So she's going: "Yeah I 'ave actually." Then fat bird only fucking shoves Sally backwards into me. I sort of steady 'er, 'ave a bit of a feel at the same time, know what I mean? Then push 'er back again.

Good old Sally. Looked pretty fit when she was angry. Steamed straight back in there. Grabbed fat birds 'air. Started leading 'er around the pub by it. Me and the other brokers are fucking loving every minute of it, know what I mean? Fat bird's screaming: "What's ya problem? What's ya problem?" And Sally's going: "You really wanna know me problem do ya?"...'

Moon stands eagerly. Looks around at his three wide-eyed friends. All clinging to the story like it was sanity itself. The only thing they've managed to follow that's lasted longer than a minute. They need this tale. A moment of clarity. Sensibility in a night of mind mayhem. Moon clasps his hand onto imaginary hair and starts talking to it.

'... "D'ya really wanna know me problem?" Sally goes...'

He looks round again. Crane's even nodding with eagerness to find out Sally's problem.

'... "I'll tell ya." She goes. Taking a right grip on 'er 'air and everything. Thought she was gonna rip it out, know what I mean? Brings 'er 'ead even further down near the floor. So that this fat birds 'aving to look up at 'er, while Sally's baring down, this right angry face on. She goes: "You really wanna know my problem? I'll fucking tell ya. My fucking problem love is...

I just can't find the fucking staff.'

That was it. Absolute chaos breaks loose. Leg has to put the board down. Crane manages to knock his wine all over the carpet. Brooke tries desperately to keep his stomach down.

Moon runs off.

Distant banging soon heard.

BANG BANG BANG

'Can't find the fucking staff. Sally can't find the fucking staff.'

Acid insanity.

* * * *

It's fucking dark. The only light's coming from a barn about hundred yards away. Where am I? Can't remember the last hour. If it's been an hour. Fuck knows. Could be a whole day for all I know. Nah, can't be. The acid's working like a goodun and I'm still in me *Time* clothes.

The bottom of me trousers appear to be all muddy, because I'm sinking into a swamp and that. Eh?

I am almost. I'm standing in a sodding field for some unknown reason and it's boggy as shit.

Last thing I knew I was in the club with Wendy. Littl' Leg, I remember him coming to speak to me. Then Wendy came back. Was meant to be going round her mate's house. What happened there? I can't remember leaving *Time* for the life of me. Reality's come crashing in.

Come on Lid. Manage one step out the mire. I bet I've been stood here ages like a scarecrow and shit. Now I've got to work out where I am.

Flowing water enters me senses. Which one? Your ears Lid you tool, come on son get it together. I look around then see the blackened river, gushing alongside me. It's raining. All pretty heavy and that. I'm drowned. How the fuck have I not noticed this? There's the woods too.

This must be the opposite exit to **RIVER DRIVE** Ain't that far from home sweet home. If I walk through the middle of the woods that is. On acid and shit. Not sure about that. Must have been taking a short cut to Crane's through the field and forgot to turn off. Now I'm nearer home. In two minds, lost. Dunno why I didn't get no cab. Maybe I did? Maybe anything? Who knows?

Gotta get it together. Home or Crane's? Bit of a trek to Crane's now. What with this rain and shit, I might be better off calling it a night. I'll catch me death. Only quick way to mine is through the woods though. Just a bit of acid paranoia to contend with. That's all!

It looks dark man. The trees are blowing like in some sort of slo-mo. A rushing waterfall, the sound. Dizzy lights in me head. Changing shapes, colours. Reckon I could walk through staring at me hand. It'd take me mind off the journey and shit. Looks pretty covered from the rain in there.

Fuck it. I'll do it. I'm still buzzing, but I know a real downer's gonna come soon. Can't lay that on the boys. Once this acid wears off, it's gonna be like: "What happened with Wendy?" and "have I done any damage?" and all that. Bollocks to that. Get home now. Have some booze. Then crash, hopefully. Nothing else for it. Through the woods.

'If you go down to the woods today beware of a big surprise.' Don't sing that Lid you fucking moron.

* * * *

Beeke manages to force Sloo away. A tough scrape burns his tongue, blistering it as he pulls free from the clench. Stands in utter shock. The screwdriver still lodged about half inch in his profile. Off balance.

Delirium. The weapon caused damage, not yet fatal. L.S.D. power taking away pain.

Looks down at Sloo, the vision creates utmost fear. Face aged about ten years. A crooked smile. Eyes glowing red. The expression. Real horror. Lost in the woods with this. No *time* to figure it out. Has to act fast.

Grabs the screwdriver, pulls it from his head. The first searing discomfort. Small squirt of blood with release. Run or attack *time.* Yet seconds of shocked hesitation passes.

Sloo has already picked up a Stanley knife and is now too standing. Prepared for Beeke's next move.

Lacking confidence in his own strength. No challenge for Sloo. If this was Sloo. L.S.D. an uncertain creature prowling the brain. *Time* to run. Flee into the darkness of the trees. With the commotion Beeke drops the screwdriver. No *time* to re-arm himself. Has to get away. Vision blocked. Woods in black. Figures scattered in his way. Solid shadows ready to block his path. Reaches his hands out in front. Aims to protect his head from the oncoming obstacles. Heart beats twice as fast as the kiss. Ecstasy overtaken by terror. True trepidation, like nothing ever experienced. No knowledge of a path through the trees, not like his pursuer. Unable to visualise anything. Disadvantaged without a torch.

Doesn't realise Sloo had discarded the unnecessary tool already. Sloo walks casually through the dark. Led by an outstretched grasp. Blade shimmers in the rain. Ready for surgery.

Beeke looks back, expectant of a following light. Nothing. Doesn't know where Sloo could be. Feels lost under the trees. So huge. All seems much larger than when he was small. As if expanded. Ought to be the opposite. Enemies all around. Changing shapes. Seemingly springing to life. Severe distortion, tremendous joy to extreme fright; the drugs make a savage downturn. Bad trip. Beeke wishes that's all it was, imagination. Hallucinations. A dream. He'd wake soon, just as he thought before with the kiss. The dream had turned nasty. Nightmare moment, should come round at any moment… Shuts his eyes tight. One second, two. Hoping, praying. When opened expects his bedroom…

Open. Instead, still lost deep in the woods.

Sloo enjoying the chase. His Lord was here. He knew. Forcing the trees to form a path, a direction guideline toward his once friend. The perennials sway on his approach, avoiding. Sloo had ultimate knowledge of this locale. Been here so long, waiting to show his deep awareness of its exploration. *Now is the time.* The omniscient master had returned. Let the storm find its way through; add to Beeke's misery as he seeks exit.

Struggling to run at pace. Couldn't see. Constantly his hands hit blockades forcing him into another turn. Blood trickling from his fresh wound. Something out there; could smell it.

Wanted the taste. Been hungry for a thousand years. Savours Beeke cooking in fear. Screams easily drowned by strong wind. Torrential rain. Doesn't know which way to go.

Looking desperately for the light of suburbia.

Suddenly catches a glimpse of hope to his left...

* * * *

Tin Lid runs his hand through his hair. Drenched, it sits back. Treads carefully along the muddy path. Desperate not to slip.

Singing. Something to take his mind off the journey, a trek he so now wishes he hadn't started. Too late.

Tries to focus straight ahead, but acid invokes strong suspicion of his surroundings. An eerie feeling forces his head to the right. Branches high above sway from side to side, shaded by the ever increasing rain. Something's out there, Tin Lid knows it. Feels it. Harsh terror. Skin tingling, wants out. Presses on at a rapid pace.

* * * *

Beeke had seen hope. Quicker movement towards it. Every step taking him nearer a chance of survival. Still the storm drowns his call for help. Yet the trees were growing sparse now. Prospects increasing. Can't hear what occurs behind. Knows he shouldn't look back. Maybe Sloo didn't follow?

Crow flight route through the remaining woods. Beeke within his senses. Slashing footsteps. Willed by everything surrounding. Let Beeke have his optimism, for now.

Approaching the edge. Doesn't see the intertwining twigs unearthed from the roots of the outer trees. Trapping his left foot. Face down into a muddy leaf swamp…

* * * *

That was definitely something near me. Fuck it. Fuck it. Tin Lid why have you come this way you mug? On acid, walking through the middle of woods. What a prick. It's gotta be a fox. That's it, a rapist. Shafting rapist coming after me. Hear something muffled, like a child crying. Probably already getting raped. Could save it. Nah, it's a trick. Could be anything. Get the fuck out of here.

Run.

* * * *

No chance to look up and see his friend sprinting past. Thunder cracks masking the footsteps. Two strong hands grab his ankles. Restraining movement. Drag him back to the darkness.

Beeke tries to swivel, face the attacker, but the grip too strong. Reaches out, desperately clawing for a hold. Something to counter the pressure. A tug of war with his body. Can't find anything. Still the forest remains against him. Cutting palms on sharp twigs. Pulled further and further away from the diminishing light. Screams are no good here. Not at this *time.* Not in this weather. Clothes ripped, muddied. The front of his body scraping across the harsh ground. Singe his stomach, soon hurting him.

Branches swerve, allowing Sloo to drag his captive deeper.

Beeke tries to search the area. See any form of salvation. A darkness, only revealing figures that hide behind the trees. Bursting with shrill laughter.

* * * *

'Fuck it, leave it.' Brooke tries to clean the wine stained carpet.

'I can't see it anyway.' More merriment, the night becoming unbearably funny. Each person hurts through excessive humour.

* * * *

The camp.

This *time* far from romantic. Beeke laid face down on the carpet. All that effort, only to find himself back from whence he came. Only now cut, bruised and petrified. Head throbbing with pain. Pressure on his ankles thankfully released. Force of two reduced to none. Beeke flips himself over. Focus, eyes steadying. Hard to know reality, tripping. All is lost…

Then through the pitch Black bares an outline. Aims to lash out; kick it. His foot disappears for a second. Enters a different dimension; no connection. Couldn't even see where to attack. Or how near this thing was.

One blow does connect. Yet not in Beeke's advantage. A kick cracking a rib. Invisible assailant, Beeke crippling with pain. Blind to the ambush. Fetal position. Wishing this was the womb. Surrounding darkness, his mother's innards. Boy in a bubble. Protection. Now nothing fends away the outside world.

The return. Setting sail for home. Lead the mission.

Winded. Beeke relenting. Swarming, a body pounces on top. Wants to give up. Surrender. Longs for release.

'You queer cunt, thought you could have me faggot.' Hears Sloo; anger extremity. Spitting venom. Fierce words; terrify. Loss of bladder.

Sloo lifts an arm to the sky. Stanley knife remains in clutches.

Swiftly charging, dug in Beeke's side. Released. Blood escapes the wound. Cries of pain. Tears well, discharged. Highest hopes diminish to despondency. Death a reasonable resort.

Sloo wouldn't allow that, not so easily. *Time* for some torture. Inspiration, last offering. A second stab, this one to the chest. Thick red splashes eject. Wetting Sloo's grinning face.

Cries. Paralysis. A foot stamping head. Someone else. Abscond to black…

* * * *

Fucked. Signals/ signs ripping through from nowhere.

Can't get down the stairs. Why was I up here? Cd in hand. That was it, music. I dunno if it's me, but I swear these acids are getting stronger by the minute. Must be about five hours since we took it. I'm only just now getting dangerously near the level. No one can be fucked to skin up. We need resin, bring us down a touch. Who could even see it though? Wits not about us.

There's no way I'm getting down these fucking stairs. Banisters folding down. Exposing the room below. One step out of place and I'm over. Fucked. Look like they're leading up then down. Mismatched.

Gonna take me forever to get up or down these stairs. Maybe I'm at the bottom? Trying to get up? No there's the cd. Must have got up, surely? The ceiling comes crashing down. Cower, awaiting impact. Nothing. Devils call from my room. If I don't get down they'll be coming for me. I just fucking know it.

How will I get through this obstacle course though? Fucking lines drawn from wall to wall. Tripwires, no question. I'll set off all the fucking garages in the world. Tune in. Turn on. Humming. Nearer. Breath on my neck. Sharp turn. Nothing there. Den of goats. Chipping. Chip chip chip chipping at the wood.

Get me fucking down. CALL.

'HELLO.' My voice is the Big friendly giant. Tall and long. Hollow, in a cave with insects. Fucking buzzing about me head. Eurghh. Get off. Someone in view. A friendly face.

'You alright Crane?' Think its Moon.

'Nah, I can't get down the stairs.'

'Well I'm not gonna be able to get up em mate. I can 'ardly see down 'ere.'

'Well then we're fucked ain't we?"

'Totally.'

* * * *

Vessel of souls watching. The leader is almost at land. Poised; witness the sacrifice.

Beeke, land of living. Bound. Struggles. Short jerking movements. Arms and legs spread, strapped by loose branches to a tree on either side. Marred recollection; worst trip imaginable. Weakened by loss of blood. Still sightless. Yet hearing intact. A muffled voice. Disturbing ramblings: Sloo. One half of a conversation.

'What should I do with him?'

'What first?'

'Of course father.'

Beeke cannot hear the answers. Yet the questions were frightening enough. Wants to call to his friend. Reason with him, or beg forgiveness. Not possible, mouth plugged by twigs and branches. Sick congeals with bark. Can't loosen Gag. More retching. Swallows vomit. Choking. Leaves clogging throat.

A bright light aimed at pupils. Dazzling. Beeke averts his eyes. Steadies focus. Looks back. Sloo stands with torch. Clothed in a dark tatty cloak. All alone. Smiling at the captive. Evil portrayed through friendly gesture. Beeke trapped, petrified. Trying to wriggle free. Difficult to breathe. Last gasps. Turning blue.

Swipe. The knife appears two inches away from his face. Small relief. Sloo cuts the branches tied round Beeke's face.

Manages to spit the woods from his mouth. Then yellow/ red bile flows. Coughing, spluttering. No time to plead.

'What shall we dine on first?'

'The tongue. Don't want to hear the faggot blubbing.' Answering himself in a menacing gravelly tone.

'Good choice.'

Sloo approaches Beeke. Last minute. Can't be real. This isn't his friend. Something inside in control.

'Kevin, mate. Please wake up. It's not you. PLEASE.' Blood, puke, spit, tears and urine have all evacuated Beeke's body, as if they saw no hope. Knows this is it. If he couldn't get through now, then forever hold his peace. Watches in terror. Sloo points the knife at mouths entrance.

'Please, Kev. Please.' Wailing becomes gurgling. Once again gagged. Desperate scrambling.

'My name's not Kevin. It's Sloo...'

Pain. Trying to wriggle tongue free from the sharp twinges.

Light shines back on the attackers face

'...Or is it Ricky?'

Beeke's comprehension in disarray. The twitching reverberating face in front; now becomes that of his virginity snatcher. Tears and venom. Drained belief, horror. Nothing makes sense.

Beeke concedes.

Sloo unrelenting, the knife slowly dropping. Cutting several tears into the muscle. Shear anguish. Tongue hanging in pieces. Choking with liquid. Spits; dribbles red.

Pulls the knife away and once again moves in for a kiss. Tasting the blood; lets it swim down his throat. Enjoying nutrition. Licks at Beeke's damaged face. Then grabs the hanging tongue in between his teeth. Sharp twist of head rips the organ free.

Beeke's eyes close in suffering. Rapidly Sloo slams the knife into one. Squirts from eye vessels. Staining Sloo's cloak. The sky rinsing rain. Lightning flashes throughout the woods. The scene lights. A stage, humdrum. Chequered flags. Thunder replacing life. Beeke's head dropping. Unconscious.

Something willing the attacker. Spirits whispering encouragement. Sloo dances like a boxer. Assessing the wounds. With every injury inflicted feeling stronger. Beeke on the ropes. Sloo has him tied. One eye out. Tongue lost. Holds the knife. An extra power filling his soul. Never felt so strong, so alive.

'Remember the other tools.'

Sloo grabs the hammer. Re-approaches Beeke, lifts the injured head, blood dripping from the chin. Hair in left hand. Swings his right. Connects the head of the hammer across front teeth. Shatter instantly.

Beeke opens his remaining eye. Gasping for air. Mind escaped. Only living through the blood in his veins.

Must stop the flow. Sloo grabs the pincer. Searches for the spot. Lifts arm then slams it sharply into Beeke's chest.

Gurgling; wasted screams. Useless bursts of remaining energy. Ripping through his torso, the sharp pincer moves like a compass, tearing through skin and flesh.

Sloo tears a circle around the life creator. Claws at skin and bones, in way of the view. There it is; Beeke's dedicated heart. The one he'd given to Sloo. Awarded along with his brain unto his companion. Once received the transaction would be complete. The job would be done.

Sloo/Kevin unsuspecting of the consequences. Believes this is his last task for safety.

Air entering. Beeke's head drops for final time. The heart beats, flaps. Before its last splutter, Sloo reaches in and rips it from the cave. It heaves with a couple of remaining bloodied chokes before lying still...

Beeke escapes for now. Over.

Kevin spasms. Convulsing with the heart.

'This is it young Sloo, take a bite and I will arrive. Then you and your friends will be led to safety, while the world is wiped away.'

Kevin puts the heart to his mouth. Closes his teeth around the slimy softness. Juices flow. The drink, potion.

You were not a part of the past. A useless pawn in my revolution.

Another whipping lash of lightning strikes through the trees. Firing into the camp. Hits the boy. So young...

Jolting, fits.

Sloo makes a full entry into the body.

* * * *

On Crane's return from the bathroom he re-enters more confusion

'I think it says three, something, oh fucking 'ell, I dunno.'

'Let me have a look...' Crane kneels then rolls across the floor. Away from obscuring the digital *time* on the dvd player. Littl' Leg takes his place.

'...Nah 'e's right, it's fucking impossible to read. Three... Two...' Leg squints desperately for a reading of the final number. '..seven, I think.'

'Well what does that mean then?'

'It means we've been back 'ere nearly two hours.'

'Fuck me, what 'ave we done in that *time?*'

'Well you was stuck upstairs for about 'alf hour.' Moon answers Crane.

'Jesus I'm fucked.' Brooke curls into fetal position upon the couch.

'Tell me about it, me 'ead ain't right. The whole room's spinning like a cunt... And Crane looks like a fucking werewolf.' Crane giggles, then rests his head on Littl' Leg who lay motionless on his back.

'Your ceiling's got all scorpions 'anging from it.' Says the headrest.

'Don't start with that. This ain't even funny anymore.' Brooke states, shivering.

'It's 'it that fucking 'orrible stage innit!'

'This is why I stopped doing this shit.'

The winging provokes Crane. He jumps to his feet.

'Lads, Lads, Lads. You're losing the spirit. This is meant to be funny.'

'It's fucking mental.' Moon complains.

'Right, I'll knock up the final bit of coke. Then I'll try and get past the horses in the hall way for more wine. Moon you're gonna 'ave to do a reefer. Then I'll get a nice film to watch, yeah?'

The question is met by several groans.

* * * *

'A thousand years of toil. A whole world of revenge.'

Sloo picks up the knife then sets about carefully skinning Beeke. Eating various body parts as dismemberment takes place. So hungry. With each bite his strength mounts. Breaking the young man apart like a chicken. Sucking dry the bones. Muscle, flesh all devoured.

Buries the remains then drapes the skin over some trees a short distance away. Notices blood splatters across the camp. Stands back to admire his work. New decoration as old. Soon the place will be like home.

The first part of the plan achieved. Sloo had returned. A new reign of terror. This *time* confident there would be no mistake. He would draw the other five to the camp. Have them give in to him. Then the river Styx would return the travelling souls and the Earth could be destroyed by nature.

'Ah! The new hell. Beelzebub, bow down my friend. Worship the true King.'

A home for the dead.

The riverman's reign as God.

'Who's next?' …

"On the second day, God created the angels, with their natural propensity to good.
Later He made beasts with their animal desires.
But God was pleased with neither. So He fashioned man,
A combination of angel and beast, free to follow good or evil."

Midrash Semak (Hebrew Biblical Text)

PART THREE

CHAPTER 21
COME DOWN

LIFE DETERMINES DEATH
DEATH DETERMINES EXISTENCE

////////]#768[////////

His original idea brought forth the ruckus. A re-energizing halted the film's beginning. More stinging white powder, vein-splitting red wine. Four young adults engrossed in the Magic Roundabout. Episode after episode: confused, humoured, shocked and terrified. An omen-warping theme tune so distinct. Littl' commanded:

'Will someone please turn this off? It's driving me mad.'

Soon eyes narrowed, laughs dwindled. Crane had his way, collected the waiting twin sisters. A duo ready to inflict formidable mind alteration. Moon sat in shocked silence, disturbing rivers of blood gushing from elevators. Littl' and Brooke didn't object. A new ideal; concentration of a story that flowed. Unlike within the walls. Events uncontrollable. Percipience disturbed. Three needing time for ostrich hide-and-seek.

Bring forth serenity. Crane glued whilst Jack Nicholson portrayed the room's mood with magnificence. A quiet hotel depicts the sleeping town. Slow insanity intensifies.

Darts to repugnance............ Cleanliness becoming unsightly........... Locked doors.......... Rabbit-costumed men providing oral pleasures.......... Axes hacking at doors......... Ghosts of old........ Twisted frozen mazes....... Pages upon pages of repetition...... Bruises..... Murdered caretakers....A finger for a friend...Redrum.. Redrum. REDRUM

Hallucinogens thistles, worthwhile A befriended
diesel horribly Thin theirselves Scampers.

Crane's mind programmed on repeat:

Hallucinogens thistles, worthwhile A befriended
Diesel horribly Thin theirselves Scampers

Again:

Hallucinogens thistles, worthwhile A befriended
Diesel horribly Thin theirselves Scampers

And again:

Hallucinogens thistles, worthwhile A befriended
Diesel HORRIBLY THIN THEIRSELVES SCAMPERS

HOW MANY FOR YOU TO TAKE HEED?

HALLUCINOGENS THISTLES, WORTHWHILE A BEFRIENDED
DIESEL HORRIBLY THIN THEIRSELVES SCAMPERS

HOW MANY WARNINGS?

HALLUCINOGENS THISTLES, WORTHWHILE A BEFRIENDED
DIESEL HORRIBLY THIN THEIRSELVES SCAMPERS

I **EVEN *GAVE* YOU *AN* ANGEL.**

HALLUCINOGENS THISTLES, WORTHWHILE A BEFRIENDED
DIESEL HORRIBBLY THIN THEIRSELVES SCAMPERS

Yet drugs rule you again....and again.....and again.......and again.......and again.........and again............and forever.

Crane sits mirroring Daniel. Head drooped to one side. Spittle bubbled.

Snapped away:

'Woah, what a fucking trip this is man.' Wind vacates like the sighs of death.

Designer acid tabs. Created by the Riverman. Invented to distort your warnings.

It's over Cranley, you will not succeed.

So why try and escape? Purgatory and maximum joy are one of the same. Remember that.

Let me

T.I.N.A. t.I.N.A. t.I.N.a.

'I'm gonna get off. Gotta go and stare at a wall.' Trees are breaking Brooke's resistance

'It's your fault Crane.' Moon's dismay, fears the sky's collapse. Clouds of blood weigh heavy on his mind.

'Ah Brooke, come on geez, I'll turn it off.'

'Nah, it ain't that...' Sentences jump. 'This whole fucking room scares me...' Drip, drip, drip the river, congeals throat. '...ain't even been watching the film.' Branches reaching inwards. Twigs pinching him like fingers.

'I want you to turn it off.' Littl' Leg sinking in to leafy swamp.

'Shut up Leg, you ain't been watching it neither. Jabbering bullshit about Scorpions.'

'It's true Crane... You're the only one still fucking enjoying this acid... I can't shake it out me head.' Moon under great pressure from above.

'Shake what out ya 'ead geez?' Brooke asks, now sat upright. Fearful of possession.

'This rain, I can't get dry... Oh fucking hell man. There's nothing in me head. Just this acid.' Hands massaging deep. Temples and face kneaded-no fewer penitents.

'Well I ain't seen ya shaking your head.' Belligerent confusion dictating trepidation.

'Shut up Leg, you've been staring at the ceiling.'

Return of conversation, instigating Crane. *The Shining* is paused.
As is the life of a friend.
Yet not over.
Swims to the boat as it's not far away now.
Ready to board and serve his killer.

Acid calms too. Executed its destruction.
The woods have entered civilization.

////////]768[////////

Time is halcyon for senses

Of what is left

AN ERA s I s

K P

Quarter PAST six. Brooke deciding enough's enough.

'Seriously man. This fucking stuff plays with ya mind.'

'This film's done that job.' Moon says rubbing his eyes.

'Good innit?'

'Crane, you're fucked man, absolutely fucked. I worry about you sometimes.'

'Yeah, Crane's gonna kill us all one day, any money you like.' Leg arrives again. Can look at his friends. For now. Not literally behind his statement, shows no sign of this though.

'Ah Leg, man, that's out of order.'

'It's true Crane, you're a nutter.' Moon's opportune.

'Listen boys, this is all by the by. I'm gonna 'ave to leave you to it. Gemma's give me 'er key so I'm chipping before she wakes, sleep a bit off… At least.' There would be no respite of guilt for Brooke. His sentences lean toward the shore.

'Will she be o.k. with ya then?'

'Listen, it was 'er idea I 'ad a big night. She knows you lot. She knows drugs will 'ave been consumed. She'll be alright.' Almost toppling under falsities.

'Unlike Crane.'

'What's that supposed to mean Leg?'

Littl' Leg starts laughing. Humour, been missing so long. Strong characters pushing it back in.

'I'm only messing geez.' They shake hands high in the sky.

'It's true though, you're not right in the 'ead. Tina'll never put up with ya.'

'Least I've got a bird now.' Crane rubbing his hands in glee. Cackles medieval witch style.

'What the imaginary Tina?' Moon's finding those old dancing feet.

'Lads, Lads, Lads. You're missing the point. I'm off.' Brooke stood in desperation.

'Shit sorry Brooke, it's this wanker Crane messing with our 'eads.'

'Yeah.' Leg, the apprentice wag. Some things **will never change.**

'What 'ave I done?'

'Lads!'

'Sorry Brooke...' Crane springs to life. '... I'll see ya out.'

'Cheers, see ya Lads.' A quick swivel and glance from Brooke. Wants away from the deteriorating fracas.

'Cheers Brooke, see ya tonight, few beers?'

'Dunno.' On his way now. Can't be certain of anything.

'Ooooh, coooeee, see ya then gay boy.' Outside in. Moon can joke again.

Brooke laughs, reverberates his head.

Then sets off on foot to Gemma's abode. Certainly no haven. The next episode.

Ba da da da da

Morning shines through, empty streets. Brooke's lowly walk home. Not his home, he doesn't reside anywhere now... A cat screeches and jumps a fence, Brooke almost jumps from his skin... Few cars pass, yet each consume paranoia for fuel. Passengers pinned to windows as they pass. Bearing bewildered expressions. Watching him. Focal point... The next could be police? ... Or a drive-by? ...

Drizzle, lightly blanketing Brooke. The storm subsides. Agonizing light, adjusting eyes to this forgotten entity. Everything before was that one room. Now realization dawns. A contorted sense of normality arriving. Unlikeable, yet what alternative? There is one. Brooke must now comprehend.

An ice cream van chimes in the distance

A slowed version. Brooke keeps in time:

'If you go down to the woods today, beware of a.......'

But who wants ice cream at this time of day? He wonders.

* * * *

'Tin Lid,

Tin Lid,

TIN LID, TIN LID'

Ooh ya bastard head. Gotta keep straight. Ain't moving. Slightest twinge and it's coming out me stomach.

So where am I?

Open eyes slightly, nothing too sudden. Blurry and that. Tears, one drops down me cheek onto the pillow. Must clear the view. Senses joining the action. Hello light…

My wall. I made it home then. Now it's the *time* we've all been hating for. *Time* to figure out the events:

i) Round Crane's. All of us there.

ii) Getting pissed. Said I weren't gonna. Well that was never gonna happen.

iii) Got to the club in one piece.

iv) Wendy… Wendy… Wendy, Wendy, Wendy.

It fucking happened. Snogged Wendy, that's fucking mint. I can lift me head. The memory serves up like a cure and shit. Turn to face the front. Still a proper pain right at the back of me skull though. No I was never gonna get rid I suppose.

Who gives though? 'Cause I snogged Wendy in the club. Could do with a knees-up right now. Bbbhhwoooo, if only.

v) Stayed with her a while as well.

vi) Vaguely remember Littl' leg coming over. Gave me a beer. The one that must have sent me over the edge. Especially as I took that acid as well. Man how did I hold it together? Did I?

vii) Told Leg I was going to Wendy's… No Wendy's mates. That was it! Then...

Nothing, fucking nothing. As soon as Leg left me I can't remember nothing. Come on Lid, this is vital, you gotta get something out your memory this time.

Come on brain. Please something.... …… ……………….. …………………..

…………………………………….The Woods.

What was I fucking doing there? Running through the middle on me own. What a dopey bastard. Then… Now… Then is Now.

So from *Time* to the Woods. That's it! You've got nothing else up there for me brain?

Such a wanker. Had it in the grasp of me hands and I had to go and have one more and that.

Need to know what the *time* is. Me throat feels like someone's been sandpapering me tongue. Gotta sort some water and Ibuprofen out. Essentials. Raise meself higher up. Hands on me wet pillow. Soaked with dribble and sweat. Digital numbers shake like little bastards.

AN ERA s / S

K P

Then steady. Jesus. Only six-thirty.

That's gotta be bollocks. Surely? Still, least I've got plenty of sleep ahead of me, once I get me pills in.

Treading carefully down the stairs. One at a time Liddy. Don't wanna wake the parents. Don't wanna fall down the stairs and break me fucking neck. Swallowing early remnants of puke. Reaching the bottom, I see the answer machine light flashing. First things first though. Need me remedy, before I collapse.

Pour some cold water from the tap, have a couple of swigs from a pint glass. Then scramble around me Mums medicine box. Ibuprofen Plus. Lovely! Push out four of 'em. Don't wanna overdo it now do I? One after the other they slip down. Don't even need the twenty minutes they should take to feel better. Just to know it's fucking in there sends a psychological message to me mind and shit. Once more the land of the living seems ever more plausible.

Not while I'm here.

Can go back to bed now, sleep the rest of this bastard off. Feel right as rain and see who fancies the pub this fine Saturday afternoon and that. Just wish I could remember what happened. The boys won't be able to tell me though, they done one before me. Sure of it. We never thought we'd see the day.

Pass the answer machine again. Still the red light flashes. Like a hypnotic pull. Sure it ain't for me, but knowing something's sat there waiting. Like a parcel at Christmas when you're kid or something. Well I just cant fucking resist. Lower me finger over the play button.

Click. 'Message received at three twenty-seven a m on Saturday the eighteenth April.'

"This is a message for that wanker Adam…" What the f… "…This is Wendy's mate Tanya, I'm 'ere with 'er now, she's crying 'er eyes out 'ere. If you touch 'er again you little prick I'll fucking get everyone I know to come and kick your fucking 'ead in." click. 'Message ends. There are no more messages.'

• • •

Several moments without movement or thought. **BANG**. Did that just fucking happen or am I dreaming here? Poised over the machine. Once more, surely that didn't just happen. Please. Still can't move.

Dunno if I wanna hear it again. It all seems pretty fucking obvious. I've gone and fucking done it again… I'm like a statue here.

I had the warning from that geezer in me dream…

Oh No, that dream, don't say I've fucking had a go at her. Fucking hit… Nah, that ain't fucking happened… I see me dog. Spanner. Oh fuck this; I don't think that acid's gone away yet. Think it's coming back with a vengeance. In fucking fact.

One last play of this message and I'm gonna have to disappear in me room, deal with this fucking incident and that. Rewind. Click. Oh fuck it, I've fucked it.

Pressed record and deleted the fucker. I stop it quick like, rewind it again see if I have. Press play.

Room silence • • • Stop. ERASED.

From the machine, but not from me mind. If I'd have listened to that bloke and not that voice in me head.

I am that voice

I should have stayed off the booze. It's a crime. A set up, framed and shit. It ain't me. There's someone else, takes over me body. Must be? Everyone knows I'm not like that.

I trudge upstairs. Which start moving under me feet. Now I've gotta deal with this.

The acid had never stopped waving its wand over Tin Lid. Sap drained from the trees that Sloo empowers. A wounded soul, lapsed memory. No true recollection of the previous two and a half hours.

Sat stationery on bed, head buried in hands. Not wanting to look at shadows dancing mindlessly about his room. His usual waking state a fabrication. Imagination – that's all. The drug relentless; the hallucinations only for a calculated moment. His decline downstairs, an eye in a magical storm. All so he would believe the answer machine's debilitating voice. The acid swapping senses without a noise. Left the vision to distort the hearing. A sensual explosion Styx bent on crippling his friend's. All at the very same *time.* Poor Tin Lid doesn't recall the message he left before half three in the morning. One that told his parents not to worry, he might not be home tonight. "Leave a key out, just in case." An unheard tiding now wiped from existence.

* * * *

I'm shaking like a leaf. Yet clinging on to the branches, just. The room is encased in Black. I can make out a Television screen. The blood falls from the stairs. Out from the elevator shaft. Gushing right down the corridor towards-- ME. I shudder, who's walking over me grave? Don't even think about that shit. Thought the film had finished, was certain of that. I can put me head in me hands. What will that prove? The visions are fucking worse there. Last time I managed it, there were those fucking scorpions… and Leg blames Crane.

Scorpions crawling all over the room. Up the walls onto my hands. Don't even think about it Moon. Need to speak, I don't even know where the others are. Just to hear a voice would mean comfort.

Hear mine

What the fuck was that? Oh man.

Crane's probably fucking engrossed in this. That devil, demon whatever the fuck it is you wanna call him. See the bloke in a rabbit's costume, again? Giving the geezer in the suit a blowie. Just looks up at the woman holding the knife. All the while Jack's walking round with his axe. Look at screen again, blank. Nothing even on, I knew it. Then a tree appears. A whole forest being created slowly behind it. Everything's dripping red. Horrible whining noise. I jump again.

Where can Leg be? Is he even in this room? He could have fucked off. Maybe they've both fucked off. Switched off the lights, locked the door and are laughing outside. Laughing at me alone in this room. With that fucking film.

This room.

The room that changes to fit with the demented visions of my mind. The mask that sits above, staring down. Watching my every move. Blood dripping from his eyes, splashing my head. Pitter patter, pitter patter. Feel it saturating my hair. Soaking me, as if I'm standing out in those woods. Those woods on the screen. *The forest was always dry. Protected us from the weather. Here I am. Where am I? Quivering like a wounded lamb, under the trees. Each one comes alive. Waving each of their branches. Filling the sour mood with hideous laughter. Drilling fear into my skull.* Take down this thing above my head someone. I'm gonna drown here. The blood is rising. Reaches my waist line. The freezing cold. A maze a kid runs. *The kid is me. I'm eight and the maze is the trees. Through my heart. Blowing a chill from beneath my feet.* The screen begins to twist. *It tries to zigzag in amongst the bushes. Ever running. How do you escape from here? Escape from these woods? It's me running not the screen. Running through the trees from something. The scorpions, the mask. All the while I run. It seems as though the Jack of Clubs has finally found me . Led his wolf people into my domain. They'd been chasing me through the streets earlier. Thought I'd got away. Now here I am trying to flee the forest. From the wolves and something worse. Much worse. But I can only wade. The water's rising. The river runs red, breaking its banks flowing throughout. Like a sea now, my strength as a swimmer lacking. Beginning to flounder. Regretting that sandwich I had on the beach. Ibiza, delirious every night, trying to swim back to the shore. The griping pains in my stomach tightening, worsening. Don't panic. Last thing to do in this situation. I'll drown if I do. There's people after me, all sorts. Owls' playing cards, reptiles. The mask forever hovering over me, replacing our vanished sun. Or the moon? Couldn't be light in this darkness. The moon, like me a glowing diver into this red sea. Closing in on shore. Rooted trees still act as blockades. Ducking, diving. The voices are calling for my head. Need something to cling to.*

Life maybe? There is no sign of reality. I know I'm finally trapped. Finally lost in the state of subconscious. Driven away from the evil into Styx. Someone's calling for me. Don't know if it heeds from behind or in front. The tide is against me. The steady

waterfall from the moon ensuring a heavy push. Don't think I can go any further. Could almost be time ***to give in. Stay in this land of insanity. The sea of delirium. The boat coming from one side. People are falling off the side. They're swimming towards me too. They're purpose is to take me. Another one for their army. The bell sounds. The haunting tones of warning. When the boat reaches shore they'll be hell to pay. If only I could make it myself then I'd warn everyone. Know nothing will get me there. Cannot muster the strength. The water rising above my shoulders. Up to my chin. Seeps into my mouth, drinking the blood of these souls that chase my plight. They're on their way. If only I could find the others.*** *I'm sure I can hear them calling. Standing at the shore . Littl' Leg and Crane, waving their hands, screaming me on.* ***Thousands of the dead chase me through this dark red liquid. So thick, so difficult to wade through.*** *They're calling for my safety.* ***But it's too late for me. Save yourselves lads. I'm gonna flounder and die here. The bodies swarming ever closer…***

'Moon, MOON.'

It's too late for me now. How can you stand there watching this? Not drowning in love. ***A hand gripping my head, pulling me under. I can't breathe. Encased by blood, trying to claw back up.*** *One of you please save me. I'm drowning. No hope, with hands gripping my ankles, they've got me.* ***Captured by the souls.*** Time ***to give up.***

That time ***is now. There'll be no return to reality after this. What is reality?***

'**MOON**'...

* * * *

Brooke cancels all hope of sleep. Figures dart in amongst darkness. Worse than any sleepless night he suffered before. In bed with Gemma. Experiencing her warm breath on his neck. Feels like serpent's spittle drowning his faith. Clouding any intelligence.

He closes his eyes but can only picture that dream. *Can only see his beloved girlfriend's face. All satisfied and dripping with another's come. She had rinsed her face within a pool of semen. Flowing freely down from the hillside. The spring of come. Bottle it up, rinse clean with the sperm of a traitor.* Eyes snap open. Morsels of thunder. Ascension.

Visions breaking the blindness of the room. ***Time*** must be moving, but not here. Those people constantly transcending. Brooke doesn't budge. Trying to remember something, anything humorous. Dismissed as improbable. A mind un-repentant. Always returning to the same location. Always him. That man. Paul. Gemma's putrid colleague. Like a sad little duckling wandering behind the goose.

Remembers going to London. A surprise, take her to lunch. Admission to office granted. Spots her sat behind a desk. A man mid-twenties. Good looking, stood next. Says something. She looks up laughing.

How does it make you feel?

SICK

The vaginal passage of a person looks at him. Guessing immediately the newcomer's role. Head hangs low. Lack of eye contact. Brooke knows the game. Lived it. Can't portray jealousy, never experienced this vicious emotion. Paul murmurs upon fleeting. Just in ***Time,*** knight arrives. Had to swallow venom. Female comprehension of inter-gender friendship useless. Men were out for slippery stinking action. Brooke knew. Defied anyone to deny. Even for a glimpse during masturbation. Every straight man would at some point consider a female friend. In the art of lust. Temptation unrelenting.

No Christ walked this earth. No chance. Women clueless "just a friend." Falsehoods. Brooke knew. Yet guilt plagues his intelligence. His own disgraces of unfaithfulness. Payback time. This earth will always punish cheats. Haunting pasts re-align and crawl at the feet. Keep searching.

Brooke's cranium is churning like a cement mixer. Sins sticking upon the side. Dissolving the walls of skin. The acid that disintegrates his sensibilities. He hadn't mentioned his fear, yet. Would never again.

Pretty young thing. I look forward to what I must subject her to.

Volcano's beneath the surface. Tsunami sweeping forward. A pace that will destroy

. . .

Brooke shifts, must calm his over-active mind. Gemma cuddled up to him. Had managed to creep in without disturbance. Yet the darkness confuses him. Morning had activated. Cold draughts, window slightly open. Callous storm. Brooke pulls himself carefully away from the clinch. Goes over and closes a passage of air. A room now freezing. Covers arming, protecting. Unnatural out there. A short vacation from White noise. Sensibility come alive. Cuddles his girlfriend. The movement enough commotion for the window to reopen without notice.

His raw confusion instigated by the pitch black. Must look at the ***time***. Arches his neck.

Bedside table. Digital clock. Focal adjustment

AN ERA S I S

K P

3.27

on Gemma's digital clock. Doesn't calculate with Brooke. ***Time***, light, anything. Nothing adds up. Must be the storm. Power cut he reasons. Dark clouds obscuring light.

HAS TO.

Gemma pushes up tighter to him. Brooke weary. *Drifting away, required sleep lurking . Until he hears:*

'I love you Paul.'

* * * *

"MOON"

Still calling me, but cannot see me. ***Cold at the foot of the river. It's all become so much clearer now. My lungs soon filled with the red, red blood of the dead. This is their river, their sea. Where everyone that dies must travel. A one way voyage from Earth to the other side. Whatever that may be. Yet the tide is now turning. Above me a boat hovers. It's not far from shore. But something holds it back. An army under new command waiting for the signal. Patience a virtue now, the souls know it's just a matter of*** time. ***They swim and prosper in their future. I am one of them now. It's over for me. There is no other reality.***

'It's fucking me up Crane. I've never seen anyone get like this, especially Moon. He's fucking lost it here.'

'Well I dunno what to do, do I? Shall I get him a drink?'

Drink? Who needs drink? Heavyweight consumption of blood, I need no more. ***Moreover so much murder, plenty more refill. There'll be no parting of this red sea. Too thick you see . Soon it will swamp our lands, Haemoglobin rising. A boat that sways. Anchor rooted. Under careful instruction. The General? I remember looking, catching a glimpse as I was pulled under. That famous face. The laurel. Golden attire. I know him, we all do. He smiled and with it came peace. This is our future, a better one. No point in resisting the inevitable. Apocalypse always approached us rapidly . Asylum seeking dead. Illegal un-living immigrants. Why not Re-inhabit the Earth? Then there would be no more dying, no sickness. Vitally, there'll be no more murder.*** *You hear me?*

'No more murder'

'What was that he just said?'

'No more… murder, I think.'

'Crane, this is all your fault. These acids are fucking mental and you go and whack on *The Shining.* I'm gonna be sick in a minute. It's fucking my head up."

No, no film, the blood would always enter. From the hotel in fiction, but in reality it ***flows through our forests. A river greater than 10 times the magnitude of the Nile. Right here on our doorstep. Here I wait, deep within. There are the bodies of Romans, they couldn't withstand the power. Who would even try? No one could change their expiration date. Our demise is guaranteed. Then it's off down the river. We're all stuck here now though. Someone is changing the pattern. Bringing good and evil together. Uniting all religions as one. Each God a useless tool. There will now exist only one. Of that I guarantee. He will take over. No heaven, no hell. Sanctuary on earth. War a waste of energy, victims of genocide, famines all to be returned. They're coming back for you. Like I Wadard Mooning. I know those murdered are Styx-bent on revenge. Then harmony take your seat. Under our new red sun.***

'I'm thinking about getting an ambulance 'ere, 'e's dribbling and everything.'

'Fuck it, I'll get some more water, keep throwing it at his fucking face or something.'

"urry up then. Fucking hell I feel sick."

The deeds of* time *will turn back round. All that power, all the hatred. Come back to break their silence. We will become one, within one person. Itinerary for God. Someone that owns everything that ever was. Inhabit every person that ever lived. That man is the one who controls death. The Riverman has discovered a route back. Transporting a loaded ferry back. Numbers that crucify those here on earth. Shadows will wait behind every corner. Once they find you, they are you. No fight against those deceased. Victory unachievable. Who would you be defending? Your friends? You will be battling those. You must now stand with your enemy as your empire falls. When it's too late the world will rally as one. Against a hidden army. I am going to be in the first row. One of the six disciples to lead under Sloo.

'Got it.'

'Well throw it over 'im then.'

Pulling me up from WITHIN. My time *has not yet arrived. He must pluck me from the forest. Then the war may begin. Fucking salvation now.* No cunt's taking me just yet. Lung capacity increasing, beginning to breathe.

RISING UP
Up UP
UP up UP
UP
Hit the fucking surface with UP,
fresh......

AND FUCKING WELL UP I COME – HOW DO BOYS?
'AAAHHHH, fUCK'

'Moon, it's us.' Crane's looking at me with fucking fear written all over his mooey. Leg's just behind him, looking all white as a sheet. What the fuck's wrong here? The room's bright. I thought we was watching this film in the dark a minute ago.

'What's up?'

'What's up? What's fucking well up? I thought we'd lost ya geez. Jesus you feel alright?'

'Fucking dazed, bit trippy. Must have nodded off. Seen some crazy shit man' I rub me eyes with me palms. I'm not sure what I saw. Quickly I look back up. Make sure I'm still in with Crane and Leg. There they are. Bright lights.

'Weren't it just dark in here, what about the film?'

'I turned the film off ages ago geez. You've been nattering about floods or some'ing Thought you'd lost it there son, maybe become a spastic or some'ing.'

'Crane, don't say that for fuck sake.' Littl' Leg gives it, real shaky terror in his voice.

He's clutching his face now. Looks like he's pouring with sweat. White as a fucking sheet.

'I do remember some'ing about drowning as it goes, these fucking dead people

with me, then this blood was rising...' I start laughing a bit, got to innit. '...Really thought that was it. Reality had fucking gone.'

'Shit, shit, shit.' Littl' Leg's muttering. He goes and takes a seat, starts rocking back and forth like some kind of fucking nutcase. I've really fucked him up here.

'I'm all right now Leg, I think. Don't worry mate.

'I'm not though, thought we was off to 'ospital with you then... Oh bollocks... now 'ere come those fucking scorpions again.'

* * * *

Nine-thirty. I've managed no sleep. Don't think so anyway. Soon as I feel I'm going, keep hearing me name shouted in me ear.

" **Lid"** It goes. Banging me wide awake again. Makes me heart beat massively and shit. Makes me head spin too. I'm trying to escape reality. Just for a bit, anything'll do mate. The acid ain't having it. Evacuate my mind YOU LITTLE BASTARD...

Not with what's weighing it down it ain't. Don't need to have done nothing for guilt to show its ugly boat on acid. What the fuck I've done to Wendy I'll never know. What would suit me now would be to sleep for good. I never wanna face up to this corrupt reality.

Anything's possible

Woods still playing tricks, keep seeing things in the corner of me eyes. Keep double taking and shit. Reassure meself it ain't no orange totem pole in the corner of me room. In fact as always, ain't nothing at all. While this acid survives though I can never be sure. Just gotta lie here wanting to puke it all up and that. But it's taken root inside me. I'm certain of that. I try and dig, claw for things a bit happy like. Anything, what is there?

There's only one fucking thing that bangs on me brain's door. Like an irritating fucking drum. **BANG.......**

BANG.........

BANG.

More raw fucking panic. What the fuck have I done? That message petrifies me. Sounded so vicious, never had anyone talk to me like that. Fucking voice, "gonna get you if you hurt her again." Ringing in me ears.

I didn't touch her surely?

Fuck, I thought that was a dog jumping in me window then. One of those big fucking St. Bernard's. With those tumbler things filled with Brandy and that. That's just what I could do with too, a nice soothing Brandy. I know that's what's got me in this shit in the first place and that, but it's done now. I've proved I ain't worth a light. Why do I have a right weird prophecy of a scary shit dream, telling me what I'm like when I'm drunk, then go out the next night and get wankered? The answers clear. I'm gripped by the demon shit. This is it though.

I should really learn me lesson from this one. I actually pulled her, had Wendy there.... Maybe that's it, maybe she went off and snogged another geezer, like in me dream. Then she deserved what she got.

How can I say that? I don't even know what I've done and I'm justifying it. All so's I can have another booze up. If I've hit her, there's no excuse. Just well out of order. Can't go round hitting birds and that. No matter what.

I've gotta stop drinking now. Learn me lesson, fresh start. I could so do with a drink now though.

Drink and be merry.

Something that'll knock me right out.

Experience the beauty within these woods.

Otherwise I'm stuck here looking at... What is that? Looks like a fucking mouse cowering in the corner. Not a real one, a king cartoon one. Like itchy. Starts looking like Beeke over there now...

There's nothing there Tin Lid. I'm gagging here. Ain't heard the old man get up yet, could sneak a special combo. It's gotta knock me out, what with those painkillers an' all. Wish I knew what was going on here. Woke up this morning with hangover, sure I did. Remember walking through that fucking forest, then nothing.

Thought I'd just been asleep, but the way this acid's going I'm not so confident. Reckon I've got another few hours to account for. I'll get that drink and have a think and that. Shit, Shit, Shit. I can't. I've gotta. Need something now. I've already fucked up, one more ain't gonna hurt me. Bollocks. I'll go.

Yes, I'll hold your hand on the way.

* * * *

Staring at a wall. All my life's become. I can feel her arm around me, don't even wanna touch her. I know I heard it. She said Paul. I understand this acid's working overtime, but man I know what I fucking heard. Can't be just hearing things off this shit.

Don't wanna go outside, but do. Must be light out now, her fucking curtains black out everything. She loves it dark, I fucking hate it. Those shadows are behind me still, guaranteed. Hanging round, looking at their watches. Waiting for me to change them into hideous creatures or something. Forever approaching me, without quite reaching me. Lunging forward with their disgusting filthy hands. Well they can fucking well wait there, the bastards.

We're not waiting long

Wish I never took that whole acid.

You will have to face us

I don't need this now. I would get up and just fuck off out of here, but I'm afraid. Very afraid.

Gemma, what have you done? I trusted everything about you. Thought this was it. The one, all that bullshit. What goes around comes around though eh Brooke? You've deserved this. All those birds'll be pissing 'emselves if they could see me now. Payback time. Well two can play at that game, bitch. I'll get back out there and pull a bird of me own. You're messing with the master here.

Soon as I shake this acid off. I show you what I can do yeah?

Dunno where I'll stay from here on in. I've gotta tell her later, what she's done, no doubt about that. It's gonna cause a scene, but I'll tell from her face. I'll know if she's with this geezer. Then I'm fucking off. One of the lads'll put me up for a bit. They're the main people in my life, they are what matter. Always be there for me.

If that bloke comes and visits me in me dreams again, I'll say where d'ya want me to sign mate? ....**X**............

Turn to the boys and Sloo, too right. Whatever the fuck they do, I'll stick by 'em.

Guaranteed.

* * * *

I think Moon's sorted and now Leg's on his way back to reality. What a fucking immense trip for those boys. It's hit me hard, but no more than usual. I've proved I can handle the acid better. Those boys always have a go at me for being the most fucked. Now take a look.

Maybe I should hold back with the films though. Reckon I'm immune to it all, amount of horrors I watch. For them though it must be a bit of a mind fuck. I'm skinning up, thought I'd make meself useful. Moon's sipping at his coffee. Leg's muttering but he's shown he's with us now. More than we can say about Moon earlier, that was a tad on the scary side. Gotta admit, thought he was a goner for a bit.

But what can drugs do? They'll always wear off. You'll always get the madness, always get the paranoia, but you've gotta enjoy it. Then it'll never take over. Use it to your advantage.

One thing that I'll always remember is; drugs are only drugs. They ain't powerful enough to swamp your mind, unless you allow it. Let the confusion in, respect them, but never show no mercy. Soon as you panic, the drugs'll smell the fear. They'll take over and have you thinking all sorts of crazy shit. I mean they do that anyway, but I'm talking real crazy shit. Lost in the land of no man. For heaven's sake go and have a look round that land, I do, always go and have a little exploration. Little further each time, but I'll never get fucking lost there. That's the biggest mistake you can make.

I've lapped up most of tonight. Seems I'm pretty much the last man standing. Granted no fucker'll be sleeping, but I bet no-one could go another round like I could.

'Are you alright Leg?'

'Sure they've got the fucking door knobs on em now.'

'Cool; Moon?'

'Eh?'

'You alright? D'ya need anything?'

'Nah mate, I'm getting there, keep getting lost a bit man, but I'm alright.'

'Explore man, never get lost.'

'Yeah.'

They ain't even got the energy to rip me apart for once. It's weird, these acids seemed to keep getting stronger for everyone, bar me. When Brooke was leaving I hit that confused level. I'd had the trip out. That shit in the bathroom when I looked in the mirror and could see this angel in the middle of the woods. Then I had the pissing meself then there was the sheer confusion. Your standard acid trip.

I thought the others'd level out, but Brooke had to get outta here and these boys, well they just went into oblivion. Hope Brooke got home alright.

Then there's Beeke he reckons he was coming down on the way home. Don't believe that for one second. Then Tin Lid, fucking Tin Lid, anything could have happened to him. I wish I could pop down the pub with em all later. Get all this sorted and straightened. We'll piss ourselves at this eventually I'm sure of it. But no I've got me date with Tina first.

I feel pretty damn good now, that's cause the speed's still working. I must sort out a bit of sleep though. Got all day to do that; bonus! Hopefully I'll be sorted for later.

Now these two boys are chilling out, I could leave 'em to it and go for a wank. Can't stop thinking about some of those birds at the club. There was one dancing right near me with this little pink outfit on. Blonde bird, lovely tits all pushed up, only tiny as well. All petite and totally dirty looking.

NO. No fucking way Crane. Date tonight. There has to be a morsel of will power inside this brain of mine. Tonight could win it or lose it for me. With a beautiful girl.

I'll manage to withstand your lure Gabriella; I'll probably not get anywhere anyway.

I'll spark this reefer. Want it to knock me out, then I don't have to fight these demons. For these boys too. Try and knock 'em out as well.

'How many Smarties would it take?'

'Not sure Leg, I'm really not sure.'

AN ERA *K* ....

S */* ....

A man chewing a leg. Now he's running, right round a track. Above him fly dragonflies, each squealing in dance that suggests everything is on ***time****... The chair swivels round and the lion pounces against my shed... A land becomes clear, I fly away over this desert. Gone, Gone...*

Don't let that thing find me Crane. I'm not sure where I am, but you know. If you lead him here, it will all be over. Either one of us will do... Excuse me mate but you're fucked ain't ya? Listen I told you once before I don't belong here. You certainly don't sonny, but management ain't letting you out, so behave... Please Crane, get me out of here... **OUT**

Wake, sweating like a bastard. What the fuck was all that about?

Me bed feels like it's been pissed.

Only half ten. Jack shit times moved.

Vast drug consumption. A voice:

'**fear him.**'

Yeah good one.

CHAPTER 22
WHERE YOU RESIDE

Sloo picks at the crusted blood buried beneath his fingernails. A triviality in an arduous process. Now to the mirror. Another inspection. All new features seem whimsical. He'd taken many appearances before. This would be his favourite. Heartfelt in adolescence. The correct choice had been made. Difficult at eight to perceive how a child would grow. Maybe good fortune? Perhaps thousands of centuries of human knowledge? Whatever it was, this was perfect. A Stalwart exterior, yet inside an extremely fragile soul resided. A boy disillusioned by his parents. Desperate need of a role model, a father figure. Once the weakness became apparent, Kevin was easily convinced.

Young Kevin's diary. A protégé to be proud of:

Monday January 1st 2008

This is going to be our year. It was a big one last night for The Styx. Such a laugh at Trax. We was all well gone. Ended up at Beeke's Mum's party till about three. We was on the speed, but not too much. No one went overboard because we knew we had to face Beeke's uncles and aunties and stuff. But we had enough to keep us all going. Drinking and getting pissed but all still wide awake. I love those boys, seeing in the new year with them was the one.

The best bit though was when I got home and started to crash. That's when he visited me again. What a geezer. He told me the plan. I knew we was all special, but now me and the boys are gonna save mankind. Absolutely blinding. He warned me about the end of the world. All these floods are gonna come and rip the world apart. Except for a few forests.

This is where existence is gonna restart, with our help. My man (my God) said he's gonna take us into River Drive woods, where we'll be protected till it's over. Then it's up to us to rebuild. We'll be Gods in our own right. Me, Beeke, Tin Lid, Crane, Moon, Littl' Leg and Brooke. The Styx. It's all come together. I love him. He's my dad now. Protecting me like this. I'm so excited. Gotta keep it quiet for a while yet, he says it's gonna be difficult for the rest to believe. Only for now though. Once the storms start they'll soon follow. Then we'll be together forever. In the next few months he reckons. I can't wait. Just me and the boys and our father. This is the best New Year ever. I'll keep you posted. Sloo

THE STYX

OUR FATHER	*SLOO*	*BEEKE*
		BROOKE
		CRANE
		LITTL' LEG
		MOON
		TIN LID

FOR ETERNITY - THE NEW WORLD
Yeeeesssssssssssssss

So straightforward. The one thing the boy adored was his friends. Lacking the male progenitor in his life, The Styx became his own children. Persuasion then, that these very people were the salvation of earth, simple. Not a chance these claims be dismissed. Now Kevin's stranded in the River. A lost soul. His role not over though. An important prospect in my recreations. Warrior of the dead. A reversed spirit intent on cataclysm. No longer is personality trait a chosen factor: Good and evil a circumstance of society?

Everyone's soul is good. Overthrow this and reverse the passage of *Time*. Then Evil will rule incarnate. I have returned and now I'm in control.

Not difficult, once my acid poisoned their minds. Brilliance of intelligence. If they won't come to the woods, then bring the woods to them. Answer machines? Basic technology. Whispers in dark rooms?

When isn't there? There is harder to come, but the prospect fills me with delight. **#768** The Riverman. I've spent the whole of *Time* dealing with death. Evolve insane? Mentally unbalanced? None of these. I'm immune.

Lord **#001** removes humans all the time. So what have I done that is wrong? Transporting souls across the River Styx: heavens oppression. I understand the plight of mankind. People exploited throughout life are those easiest to lead with a promise of salvation. Crushed by society's corruption. Only with death to look forward to. Heaven or hell? Remember those sins? Can you really be sure where you're headed?

Anyone would soon agree to follow a new leader. Immortality here. So why not stay? No labour for living now. I will rule without tyranny. Just defend my forests and he that saved you. Roam free.

My disciples set in place. Tilnid, alcoholic at eighteen. A boy convinced his actions to be abusive under the influence. Destructive. No doubt he would crave help. Mortals convinced far more conclusively now than ever before.

Brooks' relationship with Gemma lay in tatters. The young girl alone tonight. I will finish them for good.

Like you say young Kevin: FOR ETERNITY – THE NEW WORLD. It's all upon us. Mooning and Little entered my world of paranoia. Effects of drugs heighten the mind's most fatal disease. Attacking each cell. Rapid victory, spreading gloriously today. Soul destroying trips.

There is one however. Crane, an escapee, a sick mind. Horrific influence. A nemesis. I intend paradise. Crane rapes it from people's grasps. Yet too corrupted for his own good. Should never be allowed to subject his race to a disgraced world.

'You win Crane, you lose. Fighting for the real devil. I know a better one.'

I know your weakness, so this is highly unlikely. The Magic Number.

Find your closest friends in extreme danger? Trust the nearest person who says he can liberate them.

Old Sloo

Old **#768**

The Riverman.

No matter whom you send now **#001**. He's tasted the woods and is under my influence. This *time* it's over. Then we'll re-write the numbers shall we? Oh no need for panic. I'll assign a job just as fulfilling as the one you accorded me. You can be **#445**. I'll promote Judas and leave you his work.

Clearing the layers of flesh that skin my River.

Genuine reunion has arrived. A thousand years from the last opening. My River's tide turns. Once again six willing disciples needed. One down, five to go.

Now to inspect your toolbox young Kevin. Tonight its usage will be compulsory.

Let the diminution commence…….

Broken from the trance

'Kevin, are you getting up yet?'

'Yes mother.' Sloo sits. Smiles, wants to cry with laughter, but he knows that would wake the dead. Louder than the trees. Must wait. Soon he can scream and wake the forest. Bring forth harsh weather under command.

It was beginning. Storms loom over one locale. Soon he could land them everywhere. Destroying islands, continents. Washing away land's materials. Recommence. Sloo could labour no more. No need to transport the defunct. They'll all exist again and be here under one roof.

A mist blankets red waters… Swim or fly through…
Zooming in
CLOSER CLOSER

The distance displays a BOAT.

Flaking hands grab at curtains Flaking hands grab at curtains
EXPOSURE

Damp rotten wood. Soaked unremittingly in red liquid. The people that hang from the sides. Open wounds. Missing limbs. Haemorrhaging profusely. Stench of maggots. The backlog of deliverance. Bodies lay underground. Waiting, longing to be released. Disease and famine writhe. Too many dying, dead. Capacity inadequate for death's toll. Back and forth across the River. No rest for the wicked. Riverman toils as penance. No more room.

WAIT THERE IN YOUR GRAVES.

Let Earth's creatures feast on your remains.

Coming for your soul in infested capsules. One day, one load at a time. Some deceased for centuries. Boarding passes at ready. Suffer the itching. Blind to its cause. One day your turn will arrive.

CLOSED - BOAT IS FULL

Cannot cope with the barrage. Aids, cancer, old age, heart disease, murder, accidental death. There is no order! You must wait there. Worms, ants, slugs, rats, anything that may find you first. They're your company now.

THE BOAT OF SOULS RETURNS AND RETURNS AND RETURNS AND RETURNS AND RETURNS AND...

Lingers at the Earth's end.

RIVER DRIVE

View the PORTHOLES.

Bruised cheeks. Eyes breathing menace. Veins penetrating the white. READY TO BURST. Filthy Hands, blood print smears. Moulting, mutating, maimed. Foreheads knock repeatedly on glass. BANG BANG BANG

BANG BANG BANG.

Hear them knocking in your sleep. They will wake you. Wanting your place. Suffered long enough. Crave your life. Hell's passengers. No anticipation at their prospect. Coming for you.

Heaven will let some in eventually. Expansion first. Limbo, purgatory on water; Or under the earth. Covet your homes. Lust for your beds. Satisfaction guaranteed. No more certainties in the after life.

Clambering torsos, ugly hills of corpses. First to the shore. Into your rooms. Waiting in every shadow. Behind those closed doors. Creeping up the stairs. You're next on the list. No hiding place. These are the experts. Beware the street corners. Dead babies scream in your ear-holes. Grandfathers stamp on your necks. Little sisters rip out your hair. No stone left unturned. What becomes of the new dead?

Your future lies in the River. A mound of you. A new volcano deep in the bloody waters. No longer active. Left to drown for existence. Every time **like the first. Feel your lungs filling with blood. Your noses, mouths blocked.**

YOU **YOUR**
ABOVE **ORGANS**
LAY **CRUSHED**
THOUSANDS **SPLEENS**
Emerge like tapeworms.
Each will turn upon you and feast on
your screaming faces… again… and again
AND AGAIN… **DO NOT LET THE**
SHADOWS IN. STAY LOCKED AWAY.

THE BOAT IS COMING TO PORT.

* * * *

'The *time* is now. You have to show him. The only way he knows how.'

'I will do anything.'

'Tonight he will strike again. Make your move meanwhile. He feels he has the boy now. We know different.'

'He is easily influenced. Open a young man's mind and a place in their heart soon follows. I will give him something to live for.'

"Then you must bring him here. Perhaps my final words of encouragement can end this once and for all. We cannot tell him anything until then. They're the rules.'

'I will go immediately.'

* * * *

'Alright lads?' My state's much better than Leg and Moon's here.

'Dunno yet mate, it's been a bit of a couple hours 'ere.' Moon answers, they've got *The Simpsons* on, mood lightener any day of the week.

'Are you all right now Leg me old mucker?' I look at the poor wreck that is Littl' Leg. He grimaces. Incapable of forming words. Never seen the boys like this. They need my help.

'Nicholas Kiefer anyone?'

'Yeah nice one.'

'What about a line or two? Got any left?'

'Fucking 'ell Crane, 'ave you seen me? Let alone this geezer here. I've been to 'ell and back and 'e ain't said shit in hours. Do we look like we want more drugs?' Moon rants, all despondent looking.

'Well you want a reefer.' I argue

'That's different. Look there's some gear left on the chopping board, go ballistic. Just leave me out of it, alright!'

'Leg?'

'Pffsss.'

'I'll take that as a no. Right I'm off for a clear out. 'elp it along.'

I find everyone's remainders out on the board. Coke stacked in a miniature *Scarface* type scenario.

'Maybe can I 'ave one later? Before me big date?' I ask trying to appear all innocent and childlike or something.

'Yeah, knock yourself out.'

'Safe! Cheers.'

I head off to the bathroom and collect some bog roll. Pull off a couple of sheets. Twist one corner into a thin straight line and push it into me nostril to tickle right up inside it. Sneeze comes instantly.

Repeat the process with the other nostril. Spray even more snotty liquid about me bathroom. I feel a big globule up there now, ripe for blowing. A quick loud blast and I feel it plop out in the tissue.

On inspection I see the specks of blood suggesting major unhealthiness up there. The rest is a dark green almost solid lump. It's fucking evil. Like... like I just released a fucking alien from me brain or something...

Instant impact with air has left it lifeless.

I grab me Vicks inhaler from the cabinet and have a quick double bang.

I can breathe again. The coke should fly right up there.

Keeping the tissue in hand I head back to the living room. Must show Moon the state of me sinuses. Need a second opinion...

'Look at that Moon.'

'Oh geez, you sick fuck. Just what my fucking 'ead needs right now, you clown.'

'No problem.' I ball up the tissue and hurl it in the bin. Straight in first time.

Feeling surprisingly ok at the moment. Totally dazed after that acid, but I think not having a speed wank last night has saved me heart, and mind, from complications. Plus a couple of hour's kip has provided slight relief. I'll chalk up a line now, then I'll do the Nicholas. A couple more after that, bit more kip and I should be sorted for the big one with Tina. Beautiful!

* * * *

Staring at the ceiling. The first thing on Brooke's mind as he came to was Gemma's agonizing words.

"I love you Paul." Leper's bells crushing an already downtrodden spirit. An oblivious Gemma remains curled against him. Doesn't know what his next move will be. Never anticipated something of this magnitude happening. Fully convinced now, his girlfriend was a cheat. For the first time in his life, he knew what it felt to be on the receiving end of such hurt. Pre-eminent love. Life's most magical experience had now devastated him.

Previous flings enter and leave his mind like children in Santa's grotto. How he mistreated them. Never with intentional harm. He was only utilizing an extensive charm. Still young, any adolescent would kill for this lifestyle. Usage and abuse of women demanded respect from male friends.

Now he regrets each and every ill-treatment of young ladies' emotions. So this is how they felt. He supposes Gemma had the upper hand all along. Every notion that her incalculability was a charm is now just plain ignorance. She didn't want to be worked out. Simply playing Brooke at his own game. Can see it all very clearly now. The fact sex never took place on those early dates, served to confuse Brooke. Make him want her plenty. He's sure of that now.

Brooke spent more and more time with her as he aimed to conquer this mountain. An Everest to those so young. These extra encounters changed his priorities however. With each meeting grew a deeper admiration. Her refreshing outlook on life, high spirit and sense of humour. No problem too big to handle. Lived care free, her life her own. She would live it the way she wanted to.

To Brooke now, traits that obviously meant he was a burden. Since the row with his parents, his heaped misery must weigh heavy on her shoulders. She wouldn't want that, she wanted fun. Now Brooke couldn't provide this, it all becomes clear. To him alone. Gone through every scenario. Couldn't get the damn situation out of his head. Negativity, guilt, jealousy; the concoction toward instability of mind.

Desperately searching for an answer of what to do. Already thought about waking her and arguing it out, but she would only deny it. She had been good to him. He loves her. Maybe he should just leave now. Could go and stay with a friend. No irreparable damage done. If she really wanted him, then she could come find him. Perfect, he reasons.

Brooke eases himself from the bed. It was now gone eleven. A Saturday morning lay in? Gemma would normally be awake by now.

Yet Brooke could no longer be sure of anything.

Eras s l p n

K p l g.

Immobility come alive.

Very careful not to wake her. Cannot deal with the situation at present. Not with an acid hangover. Hasn't a lot to collect together. Still has possessions waiting patiently at his parents, due to his rapid departure from there. Just needs his wallet, phone, some underwear, a couple of shirts and jeans. The traveler would cope. He bundles the clothing into his sports bag and gets dressed in last nights' attire. There are more of his belongings here: cds, dvds, nothing of great importance. He knows Gemma will surely wake soon. Must leave quickly.

Doesn't comprehend the game she is also involved in.

There would be plenty of *time* to sort things out he figures. It wasn't as if he would never speak to her again. Give it a few days though. *Time* for calm.

Decides upon a short note, to make it official. Grabs a post-it from her desk and scribbles:

'You said 'I love you Paul'
in your sleep last night,
so I've gone'

Takes one last look at Gemma. Sleeping peacefully. Then makes his exit.

* * * *

Shortly after Brooke arrives back at Crane's. The scene of his destruction. He wonders what sort of wreckage would be left inside.

As Crane leads Brooke through to the main room, a waft of skunk hangs heavy in the air. A fog fills the room, dreamlike landscape. Tries to cancel the image of such. Of Gemma dripping with sperm. He can't.

Fans his way into the dimly lit room. Littl' Leg crashed on the sofa. Moon looking sick. Confusion resides here.

'Alright Moon?' Brooke asks.

'Fucked.' says Moon. Recovery a marathon distance away. In-depth conversations even further. Brooke drops his bag on the floor and sits up against the wall.

'What's up mate?' Crane says returning to his seat. Sniffing. Searching for the comfortable position he'd just vacated.

'It's fucking Gemma. She's got another bloke.'

'Nah.' Moon, back from a far-removed planet.

'Are you sure?' Crane asks.

'Yeah she said: "I love you Paul" in 'er sleep this morning.'

'Come on mate, are you sure? That could mean anything. I've 'eard Crane say 'e loves Michael Douglas in 'is sleep before.'

'That's 'cause Crane's normally on serious amounts of drugs.' Argues Brooke

'True.' Everyone except Leg found the amusement in this. Brooke returns to the sorrow of his inner feelings.

'It's the same fucking geezer she was with in me dream the other night. The one I knew who fancied 'er when I went to 'er office.' Brooke raises his voice to promote certainty.

'But are you sure she likes 'im though geez? You might 'ave dreamt that too!'

Crane takes one last toke of the reefer before passing it onto Brooke.

'Nah mate. I couldn't even sleep at the time and when she says things like that in 'er sleep; it's a bit fucking sus innit! I just dunno anymore man…' Everything falls momentarily silent as his friends digest the information…

Brooke doesn't like it. '…I've left 'er a note saying I've left 'er. That should sort out whether she wants me or not. I'll wait and see if she's bothered in trying to find me.'

'Yeah, she'll probably call later and it'll be nothing.' Consoles Crane.

'Maybe... Still is it all right if I chill 'ere for the day though geez?'

'Yeah course, I've gotta date tonight though. So I'll be getting ready about seven.'

'It's alright; you can stop at mine tonight if you want geez. Pop out for a few beers as well, 'elp take ya mind off it.' Moon assists

'Nice one lads.'

* * * *

I've spent the last half hour trying to get some kip, but me head's fucked. Every time I drift I think someone's calling me. I've already been down twice to see what Moon wanted.

Desperate to get some sort of sleep. Probably too desperate. Thought the reefers would have knocked me out, but I'm edgy with the Charles.

Stupid idea. I'm full of 'em at the moment.

It's half five now. In bed once the final whistle had been blown on Essex FM. A dismal four-nil whooping by Arsenal, not that we were that bothered. The football reflected our downbeat emotions.

I'm meant to be meeting Tina at half eight. Alarm's all set for seven. Bit of *time* to wake up and get ready. Another line of coke too. Level out if it's the last thing I do. Tina seems pretty keen on me and I don't wanna be a mess later. I will be if I don't get a couple of hours here though.

Why the fuck did I take so many drugs last night? This will all end if I start getting serious with Tina. I wouldn't need drugs for enjoyment 'cause I'd have her. I still gotta build a defense against falling head over heels though. I've been hurt a few times, pessimism could be a blessing on this occasion.

I'm just an immature druggie that needs to be pissed before I can even chat a bird up. That much is true. Such a loving review of myself. One thing's for fucking certain, I'll need to get a couple of beers down me before I meet her later.

What is wrong with me? Why do I find that I can only be funny and likeable with alcohol? In college I get on really well with her, and I'm stone cold sober there. She must like me or she wouldn't have gone out with me. Snogged me even. Why can't I accept this?

I know full well why. Excessive drug consumption and alcohol dependency anyone? Me mind's possessed with insecurities. Still that'll all change with Tina. Hopefully!

Probably not.

Come on Crane sleep. Close your eyes, think of some strange thoughts. It normally gets you off. Let it flow. Clear my mind of all thoughts...

Mystic Meg coming down a helter-skelter singing 'Snow Patrol's: Chasing Cars'. Again and again. Holds a flag. Reads:

'Do you like good music?
yeah yeah'.

Wanna get closer as there's a PS. I can't quite make out. Someone's barring me way. It's a thin tramp like geezer. Now I've gotta follow him through lands of time. Apparently.

A dark horizon through trees and rain. Vision's clouded. Wailing and burning screams that wisp in a black wave around the edge. Through this I hear a voice:

'Crane, you must listen to me. Your leader is not who he says he is. He is very dangerous. You must slay him or he will rule again. I have escaped to tell you this, save my soul and all of your friends from a despicable future. For one it is too late, but you can still release him from a murderous oppression.

Crane, Crane,

Cranley. Where are you? I will find you. Cranley,

CRANLEY

CRANLEY... *louder and louder. Horrible voice .*

I gotta get away from it.

Don't bode too well............

* * * *

It's got to the point where I fear for anyone who knows me. For me to hurt the girl I'd fallen in love with? Who's next?

I'm too scared not to have a drink now. Need to escape reality man. Living with the knowledge of being dangerous is hell. So I become that problem once again. My only chance to get away from it: drown me sorrows. Homer's right. "Alcohol is the cause and solution to all life's problems".

What am I doing here? Drinking again. Alone! I should go and confide in someone. Take some booze round to theirs and that, get pissed together. But what would I do to 'em?

Maybe on me own is the best place to be. I could hurt someone bad. That beer makes me step over the edge and that. Violence! How could I do it? Hurt me mates? Surely not! I know I ain't touched them yet, but that's probably 'cause they ain't around when I'm in me state. If I leave *Time* early to do me damage, then the boys don't see it. Simple as. They're still in the club, safe from me actions.

If they were there would I start on them? Don't see how I could, but now though I don't arsing know nothing.

Never like this before. When did it change? All I can put it down to is the drugs. Instead of the passing out bit, I'm conscious. Acid, Billy, Muswell's? Whatever. They all keep me awake so I can drink more. The more alcohol the more bother I get.

That's it! There's me answer. Drugs! Can't be the alcohol. If I just stuck to drinking I wouldn't harm nobody.

So I can have this drink now. Staring at me. Almost calling my name. Got meself a bottle of Bells. Not opened it yet. Been figuring this stuff out and shit. But I can now. If I don't do no drugs then I'll be alright man. This could be a sort of experiment and that. Drink this bottle of scotch. See what happens. No trouble; then that's problem solved: No more drugs. I reckon I'll just pass out.

It's been messed up after that acid last night. Seeing things in the corner of the room and shit. Having to double take all the *time.* Not certain it's left me yet. Not fucking certain at all man. The strongest thing I've ever taken. Spent nearly the whole day in bed. Too scared shitless to face me Mum and Dad. Don't know what I'd have seen in their faces. Probably would lash out if me Dad suddenly turned into the devil or some shit.

Managed to make it through though. A bit of the drink done up the weirdness. Had a couple of me private stash of tinny's and that. Got to get to that state of out of it again. Me place of safety.

Feels so good to be drinking. Spoke to Crane a bit ago. Knowing the lads are in the same boat as me helps a bit, I suppose. Moon and Leg especially. They had the worst trip of their lives off that acid. Brooke too, split up with Gemma and that. Man I never see that coming. Things are totally fucked up in this world.

Wendy.

That's all me head ever comes back to. It's like an horrible bastard circle. Just getting me mind off it, then Bam! For all I know I could have tried and raped her. Took things too far and shit. Didn't hear her say stop. I couldn't though. Could I?

No come on Lid, it ain't possible. The dream showed me that I caused a bit of damage, bit of vandalism and that. Starting on people, all that shit. It didn't say I'd ever raped nobody.

But it did say I'd smack Wendy one. So why not take it one further? I was that out of it. I really could have fucking tried to rape Wendy.

What did the message say?

"If you ever hurt Wendy again I'll come and get ya."

I really doubt meself now, doubt me actions. Scared of my capabilities. Man this is getting a bit much to handle. I need this drink. Need to get away. Run away from all me problems. For another night at least. I need this drink.

College starts again Monday. All those A levels and that. Can't face up to them. I need this drink. Have to have it. Unscrew the top. I need this drink.

Calling me.

"Tin Lid drink me, drink me Tin Lid, it's what I want. It's me duty to get you battered and that, away from the disaster that is your life. Trust in me. Drink me"

Fucking hell. What is going on in my head? What is wrong with me? Sat in me room, talking to a bottle of Whiskey for fuck sake. All on me own. Can't force it on anyone else though can I?

'**Adam**.' Fuck! Me mum's scared the shit outta me there. Was right in me own little world.

'YEAH?'

'Kevin's on the phone.'

Sloo. Now there's a possibility…

* * * *

Gemma closes the novel. Re-reading the pages three or four times becoming a little tiresome. Concentration elsewhere. Andy circles her mind. What had happened? Sleep babble destroying something special? Even if it had happened at all.

Wonders about her boyfriend's state of mind. The family feud left him wearisome. Must have been dreaming himself. Paul was a friend. No, colleague at best. Andy was her man. The first true love. Everything had been going so well. Must have been the drink; or drugs. Gemma frustrated, annoyed that he had not considered these factors.

Debates a phone call. This was all a misunderstanding. Has to entertain the idea she may have said "I love you Paul". This meant nothing, but the reaction justified. Unlike Andy to display a jealous side. Life was hard for him at the moment. Benefit of the doubt.

Time ticks by. Would Andy even answer his mobile? Maybe call one of his friends. Reason with them. They could put a word in. All seemingly well natured.

Tony.

Two rings, clicks into answer machine.

'Alright people? This is Leg's phone. I'm not 'ere… or I'm down the pub and can't hear ya or something. **BO**'

Gemma smiles. Innocent immaturity. Doesn't leave a message.

Sloo sits waiting.

Who now? Maybe Kevin. He had helped Andy a couple of nights ago. After the bust up. Finds the number…

Ring, Ring…

Not the first time, too eager.

RING, RING.

One more for good measure.

RING, RING

#

Gemma had always struggled to talk to Kevin. His mannerisms strange, his distancing effective.

'Hi, it's Gemma, sorry to bother you, but you haven't seen Andy have you?'

'Andy? Brooke you mean?'

'Err yeah.' Gemma knew her boyfriend's nickname, but couldn't imagine why his best friend would confuse the two.

'Yes I have actually. He's here with me now, do you want a word?'

'Err yeah please, if you don't mind?'

'Here he is, just give him a second.' Sloo shrugs

'Oh thank you.' Gemma's heart skips.

Sloo breathes in the aroma. Changes the phone from his right to left hand, and then counts the number of people he must now eat.

One Little. Two Mooning. Three Brook. Four Cranley. Five Tilnid. Quick succession. Then:

''ello Gemma' A smile. Split the jugular vein.

'Hi ya...' Gemma pauses. A nervous experience, un-encountered with her man before.

'...Do you wanna talk?'

'Yeah. I think we should.' A mirror opposes. Sloo admires his poise.

'See, I dunno if I did say anything in my sleep or not, but I promise you if I did, it really, REALLY never meant a thing.'

'I don't think we should talk about it over the phone. D'ya wanna meet up later?'

'Course, where?'

'I'll come round later, if that's alright? Will ya Mum and dad be in?' Juvenility, swift recital. A pleasing menace.

'No they're out tonight, why?' Gemma's concern grows at her boyfriends' aplomb.

'Just for a bit of privacy.'

'Well, no they're at my Uncles' 'til late, so the house is free.' The fear rises. The old Andy. Was he going back? Was this their break up?

'That's good. Listen, I'm out with the boys for a couple. I ain't gonna drink much, so I'll shoot round about half eleven.'

. . .

A thumb to a red phone. Sloo appreciative of his own deviousness.

How times have changed. Ripped Brooks from his loved one once before.

Now he would tear Brooke's loved ones life apart.

* * * *

I arrived at Sloo's with the full intention of not telling him nothing about me drinking worries; or what happened with Wendy. But as the drink flows it can't be held in any longer. I'm desperate to tell somebody and Sloo's been right understanding of late. What with Brooke and that.

Now I need someone's help. I'm not really listening to what he's saying. Just waiting for me chance to speak. Was gonna say it a bit earlier, but when I got meself all prepared, he started talking about something. Normally I register this as a sign to not say things. Yet there are times, usually drunk ones, where I just gotta. Sloo finishes; I don't really know how to respond. So fuck it…

'I'm sorry mate, I'm in a world of me own 'ere.'

'That's alright Tin Lid. I can tell there's something on your mind. You can tell me anything you know?'

'Cheers mate, 'cause I feel like this is one of those times.'

'Go for it mate. I'm all ears.'

I try and steady meself and take another gulp of port and lemonade. We're over halfway through this bottle now and I can feel it. Sloo's been steady drinking the strong red stuff from a glass, but seems untouched. If anything he seems more aware of what's going on. Or is it my state that's making it seem this way? He's been a right good host anyway. Keeps going down with me glass to fetch a mixer when he fills his own and that.

'You know I had all those dreams telling me what I've done when I've been drinking and that?'

'Yes.'

'Then I 'ad that one where I smacked Wendy at *Time*?'

'Yes.'

'I think I might 'ave done something like that, but I'm not sure.'

'What you hit Wendy?' Sloo seems right shocked at this. Maybe I shouldn't be saying anything. No-one likes to hear stories of blokes hitting girls and that. I dunno who else to turn to though.

'I dunno man. Don't think I would, but 'ow the fuck should I know? The dream taught me that. Then I get this message from one of 'er mates this morning, saying if I 'urt Wendy again she's gonna come and 'ave me.'

'Shit.'

Sloo doesn't really look astonished as I say this. Maybe he even believes that I could have done it now. Me own mate seeing the dreaded alcoholic I've become. Look at me now downing this port and that. Things are starting to move around me too. Starting to feel pissed. Coming on quite strong.

'Sho, I'm not sure what to do…'

#

Tilnid. Easiest of all. Not so bright are you young boy? Falling into place like I knew the weakest one would. Any drug, any escape, I will force my way into your world. Already draining your self confidence. Humans turn to anyone in times of trouble. Who better than me to come and take those aches and pains away?

I can see you swaying now. The extra touch to your drink will have you following everything I say. Lost to the notion of belonging. The blood will come your way Tilnid, never doubt that.

Back to the woods. Back to my work.

'It's a difficult one, you must be afraid. I can't sit here and argue that you haven't done it. The only way forward for you now is to accept that you have...' Now you believe anything. Your head drops. Realisation of your own destructive nature. Instigated only by feats of the new Lord. Acid annihilating the senses. Tree extract. My own special potion. '...It might help you to curb your drinking. I mean look at you now, it's no state to be in already...' Shrug your shoulders. Bewildered at the sudden change to consider why. '...We have to set off for the pub now. You'll have to ease up a bit. Can't have you walking about in a mess can we?'

Poor Adam Tilnid, shakes his head, almost ready to cry. A depressant to instigate conjecture of his malignant prophecy. I own you now. My command will gain acceptance. You won't even realise where you are when you grant it. You are just easy pickings for someone of my sagacity. The portion of *Time* lay resting in my lap.

Plans have been made for the arrival. The tide has turned already. My boat is fully boarded. Hungry souls look to wreak unprovoked revenge. Their peace is shattered, waiting almost unbearable. Ecstasy for them to arrive back on Earth. Me as their guide. A modern hero. Awards of immortality to reside under my rule. It's all becoming so simple. If I plan it right I'll be rid of Tilnid in time for a visit to Gemma.

Who am I to say "if I plan it right?" I'll perform it to perfection. No mistakes this *Time*.

Then once I have his friend's lives in danger, they'll be no stopping Cranley from buckling. He was strong enough once before. It's what makes him the most difficult to poison now. The rest: I've killed you already. I've full access of your hearts and minds. I know all about you.

You're destroyed through my visitations. My continuing depression into your very psyche. Fold under my power like I knew you would.

To Cranley: the hope for existence has come too late. He'll witness the carcasses of Tilnid, Beech and Brooks. Then his special little 'Magic Number' begging for mercy. The angel's work will be worthless. I'm in charge now. This *Time* I know you have come to save him. Last *Time* I did not...

Still, there's a pressing matter to attend to first. That familiar journey to rip someone to shreds.

It's your turn Tilnid.

Step into my arena…

* * * *

The Plough. 10pm.

Tremors ceaselessly run through pavements. Streetlights flicker. A howling wind slowly opens gates.

Then slams them shut.

Mauve clouds rampage through the sky. Late for their positions. The first drops of rain hit windscreens. Wipers turn on. Left to right, left to right, left to right. A march through the ages played out on different surfaces. Dogs bark in conversation. Desperate shuffling on deck. Anticipation scratches at patience. Long awaited damnation. Only one more day. A thousand more years of preparation. Stolen armies of souls.

Every second that passes beats a jolt through pedestrians. A police siren sounds. Screeching tyres. Car horns beep. Shouts on street corners. Lights switch on. Lights switch off. Tireless existence heading towards its destiny, without the slightest change of pace.

Do not look into the portholes. The sight of mangled faces will strike you frozen. Episodes of indignation. Desolate landscapes. A cloaked man scampers. Sheep flee in terror. Long sharp skewers. Spikes one animal. Lifts it to the sky as it wails in fright. Head in wide mouth. Clenched teeth. Head removed, spat to the ground. Saliva intermingled with blood. Fingers that scrape, bending back nails. Eruption of the skin, more red oozes down the glass. Hear the laughter surrounding you. They're coming.

Coming to devastate your family. Devour your loved ones. Dissect your children. No stone left unturned...

They're watching you.

For ten years I travelled along the path of a young boy's life. Watching his movement. Understanding his lifestyle. The choices he made. Speech patterns, body language. Interpreted his strengths and weaknesses; following his attributes. I know his family, his friends, everyone that ever met him. Chance encounters with me attending in the wings. Each is a life on my waiting list. They will all cross the River. All a lot sooner than they could ever imagine. With each spare moment I witnessed, visited and indeed influenced my young apprentice. This is why my list grows. Why acquaintances rot in limbo. **#001** knows. Little **#001** can do now.

Why would he not leave flaws? Has to present an enigma to everyone. The meaning of life? To excel above he that created you. That's all you're here for. If you succeed then you become God. If you don't it's a trip across the River with me. Two stops only. Neither that interesting.

That's the game. It's so difficult, so brilliant, who could ever figure it out? Created in the same image, erected from his making. Why would you be able to? He left us all a clue. Designed a route to the throne. Yet gave no-one the intelligence to even determine there was a way. No great leader led without taking a chance.

This was the gamble. A way of having fun at our expense. Even with defeat came the chance to rest. No one ever satisfied with their lot. What fun in settling? My sharpness, greater intelligence. It would always be old Sloo who would master any challenge. Yet I will not settle. The task I was assigned has left a bittersweet taste. Couldn't reckon upon me changing the rules. Because if I win then **#001** will not rest. I will not follow in anyone's footsteps. Things will be done my way from now on. My followers will come back.

This is not how it was meant to be. Reversal in the image. All those evil humans were good in the beginning. They only chose a wicked route. I'm not a pleasant person. That's #001's fault. I've chosen my path of destruction and I will choose that for the people who follow me. They will all be created in my image. You will all be evil. Together we will destroy this earth. All except for my forest. There I can retire and once again enjoy the simple things in life.

There'll always be an opposer for me. Someone sent to try and alter another's way of thinking. To deny me from winning. That's all he can do now. He set the challenge, but cannot alter the rules. Never envisaged the Riverman figuring it all out. Puerile person. Couldn't comprehend someone unsatisfied to continue his reign, even if they did. Big mistake.

I want to make **#001** pay. I will take down anyone to get that. I'm not liked, but so what? I won and now all those that sit before me are my way to greatness. The way to re-write the history of the Universe. Once I'm done here, my disciples can go to another dimension and destruct what they see fit. I've had enough of mankind. Day in, day out I deal with their complaints. Woes, fears, questions, desperation. I'm sick of it. Tired of it all. I need my rest.

Everyone needs their *time* out. So here I sit. Under the guise of my young protégé; whom I know so well, I can portray with ease. Joined by his cronies who will all soon be my dinner. One pace at a *time* however. The next part of my plan has come into effect. One languishes, afflicted under my torment. Each sip he swallows, containing the secret.

How good Beeke tastes don't you think?

'What's up Lid?' The young boy Mooning is asking.

'I dunno man, but I feel sho washted.'

'Nothing new there though mate.' Brooks is laughing. Feels at ease for a short while. This will not last.

'What you been drinking?' Little asks him.

'Man, I've been on the port, whiskey, few beersh and that.' He's swaying as he sits. I've made sure to obtain the drinks. That way he will continue to feast.

'You wanna go steady. You don't remember fuck all of last night.' Mooning adds. Poor little Tilnid he hasn't divulged his received message to the others. Only entrusted old Sloo, with this information.

'Yeah mate, you ain't even spoke to Wendy today 'ave ya?'

'Nah. It'sh alright though.' The boys sit round me in mirth. Acid a distant memory, but a dormant ingredient ready to explode.

'Where's Beeke tonight anyway?' Brooks is asking. Bring forth those wonderful memories.

'I phoned 'is 'ouse earlier coz 'is mobile was off. 'is Mum reckons 'e's gone to see 'is Dad. Must 'ave set off early or some'ing 'cause she never see 'im.' Little answers.

''e probably done one before she got up. Use the train journey to shake off last night's acid. Gotta be better than facing your old dear innit?' Mooning adds. I have to take a moment to reflect on a job masterfully done. The Riverman shining through.

Tin Lid falls from his chair. *Time* for me to make my move.

'Woah there Liddy boy! I think it's time I got you 'ome...' I say. Like clockwork the barman appears on the scene. Before he can speak I assure him of my control. '...it's ok mate. I'll get 'im out of 'ere.' My accent's coming along just fine. The others are laughing and asking if I need a hand. I tell them to worry no further, I'll be able to manage on my own. They don't offer their assistance too much. All settled in ready for a bit of late licensing. Well who can blame them? With Tilnid's arm round my shoulder we say our goodbyes.

His is forever...

* * * *

If I keep up this form I'm gonna get lucky, I reckon. Had her laughing; enthralled. I've listened intently to everything she's had to say. So far it's been blinding. The way she looks at me sometimes. All starry eyed, like she's fallen for me.

She don't half make me feel good too. I've never felt so relaxed and comfortable around someone in me life. I've only had three beers while we've been out too. Two before hand and the schnifter, I'm on top form and I'm not too bothered about drowning too many more. It's going lovely.

She's even insisted on going to the bar. Beautiful. One of these modern day dates. Going Dutch. All that bollocks. Oh Tina I love you. Shut up Crane.

'Here you go.'

'Cheers.' The girl of my dreams hands me a pint of wife beater. Can things get any better than this?

* * * *

'If you go down to the woodsh today beware of a big shurprishe.' Tilnid slurs.

Don't think I didn't hear it when I was about to mutilate your friend little boy. It wasn't quite your turn then, just a bit of fun. Just to let Beeke have a little hope. Made it all the more enjoyable for me.

'We'll take the footpath through the woods, ok Tin Lid?'

'Sure Shloo anything you shay.' At least he's walking on his own two feet. The calculation to my concoction inch perfect. As always.

Admire the beauty. The remainder of my forest. Trees that tower, locking horns to create a force-field of a haven. Fresh smelling air. Dank foul smell of death.

Witnessed a lot haven't you? About to replay some horrific scenes. Seen so much bloodshed and slaughter. You must be addicted by now? Craving the purification of red liquid. Blood extracted from veins to drain life from one into another. Affording you with something more obscene, more plausible than that of human existence. Come alive under my reign.

You long for me to preside. Turn on the race that destroys you. Tearing you down for its own meaningless gain. Reduced to discarded paper. You could believe your life is purposeful. No. Years upon years you stand, through generation after generation. Then within a heart-rending second yields the chainsaw. Lopping you from your majestic position. Harmless to those that cut you down. Life-saving even. Your oxygen breathing life into their very lungs. Their existence that then brings you to your knees.

I know you watch me now my trees, urging me forward. Your roots murmur under the soil. I hear your whispers, your laughter as one by one my victims fall. It's *time* for revenge and as always you play your part. Keep faith. I will help you reign again as an untouched existence.

Remember how vast and proud you once stood together. Such little left of you now. Yet be proud, you are the remaining soldiers in my battle. A war we will not lose again. Keep those souls within. Tonight I want to utilise your strength, your power. Let you join in my fun and games. One fortunate will have the benefit of dismemberment.

See this sorry creature that follows behind me. A poor insignificant, next on our agenda. Help me destroy this weak imbecile and your future safety is sealed.

Untouched everywhere, your ancestors will stay safe. There'll be a new way of life. People will sing and devour within your chasms. Observe as they slay your betrayers. Laugh once more as each member of my army chews their way through negligence. Your *Time* has come. The *Time* is now.

A tide that turns. My boat is coming to port. Returning to earth as baneful shadows. The river runs red my children. I shall not fail you again. This Earth will soon be ours to do as we please.

You can move as before. Free to coalesce as one with nature. The definitive power on this meagre earth. Riverman in charge of wildness. My tool to liberate. Be used once again in entirety. Pride to be restored worldwide.

Weary of this human belief in its own importance. The hour arrives to show them everything was worthless. All their petty wars, dire religions, leaders, laws, love and hates; meaningless. A new breed is coming.

'Keeping up with me Tin Lid?'

'Yeah mate, we nearly 'ome yet?'

'Very nearly my friend, very nearly.'

I can feel the warmth here. An eager audience supporting me on my next venture. An encouragement belittling my opponents. Spurring me further into the lead. Can hear the wonderful music. Tortured souls wreaking vengeance on the pitiful collaborators of death. The *Time* is now.

'Shloo mate are we in the f-f foresht?'

'Yes, wonderful isn't it?'

'It'sh great, but what we doing 'ere?'

'We're here to solve your drinking problem Tin Lid. You'd like that wouldn't you?'

'I'D LOVE IT Shloo, absholutely fucking love it.'

'That's good news.'

Ever nearer to my shrine. The setting of pogrom. What joy we had massacring those slaves. Shredding them to pieces in the presence of each other. Yet still they willingly gave themselves unto me. I enjoyed myself too much. Lost my concentration.

That will not occur again. This *time* I am focused. Leading another lamb to its slaughter. Death is upon us.

'Shloo 'ow is coming 'ere gonna sholve my drinkie problem?'

'Just a little bit further my friend and I will reveal all. Remember to ask that question again when I tell you to.'

'No prob- problem mate.'

Feel your energy. Thank you my friends. My stamina increased to its limit. If only these humans could interpret your power. They would not neglect you as they do. You're so trusting, I know you'd help them too. But they've let you down too many times before. I cannot see them harm you further.

That's it open the way to the camp. Be my guide. Move aside for the show is about to begin. Tonight my companions, is audience participation night.

The row of the sacred. Arched together, the scene of the most memorable torment. You've enjoyed the recent executions. I've heard your amusement as torture takes place. Stood almost dormant for a thousand years. Gave you a few tasters. When I found time to escape my job, I gave you something to muse over.

Floods, tirade on William Smith. My river overflowing. Water crashing and expanding the lungs. Bursting like the banks of the Brook. The bird scarer. Life sucked from his existence. Diagnosed as natural causes. See how my interferences excel.

Behold my closest friends. Your branches will become vital. Revered by every other living organism. Once again exist as the perennial plants that provided the kingdom back to the trees. Tonight I have saved for you.

Push aside the THIN veil of branches. Here once more. Put your hands together for Tin Lid.

'Sit down mate, are you ok?'

'Shorted Shloo, feel a bit better now. Shtill pissed though man, but your gonna sort it and that, ain't ya mate?'

'I'll not let you down. From tonight you'll never drink again.'

'Thatsh wicked.'

'Now what was it you wanted to ask me?'

‘What?’

‘Do you remember your earlier question?’

‘Err…’

‘About your not wanting to drink?’

‘Shit…’

The poor boy sits shaking his head. Unable to recall something so recent. Shocking waste of an organ that could be used for so much. Humans waste their brains on trivialities. Use it like a toy. Never realise its full potential. There is so much power within them. Wasting a vast percentage by not even using it? Well I have a better use for it than you Tin Lid, especially you.

Still you will remember your question…

‘Oh yeah, how ish thish place gonna cure my drinkie problem?’

‘I can show you Tin Lid, but first you’ve got to think back to your dreams. That man that told you about your destruction. What else did he say?’

‘Err…’ No more *time* for this, I’ve more work tonight.

You will remember.

‘…Oh yeah ‘e shed I must listen to you. Do what you shay, shome shit like that.’

‘Well my good friend. To help cure your ailments you must do exactly what I say. Agree to my every command. So will you obey me Tin Lid?’

‘Yeah of course I will mate, but…’

‘It’s too late for buts. Unfurl your legacy my watchful colleagues.’

Branches extend, slowly twisting nearer to the visitor. Roots hum underneath. Tin Lid looks about himself. Curious at the disturbances. Doesn’t feel the vines wrapping about his ankles. Looks up at Sloo to wonder what was meant by his friends’ words. Sloo looks back with a caring smile.

‘It’s nothing personal. You’re just a useless disciple. Incapable of your own help. A reincarnation of someone who obeyed me once before. You’ve done no wrong, but nothing must stand in my way. I am to become ruler of this land. You will return with me Tin Lid I’ll have a special job for you… For now though… Goodbye.’

‘What the…’

Before he can finish his sentence, the young man is whipped from his feet. Stranded upside down in the sky. Seeing the world from a different angle. The earth that would soon too, become inverted. Alcohol no longer potent enough to conjure any disillusionment to the current situation. Droplets of Beeke's blood with each sip flushing the impurities.

'Everyone will drink the blood of each other. This is the new alcohol. I have many people craving the liquid on their journeys. Feeding my travellers blood, so when they return they'll be desperate for more. An addictive quality like no other drug experienced. I found a way, been working tirelessly for too long now. The River Styx is returning and I am the conductor...'

Tin Lid begins to scream. A panic at his friends' words. This was no longer Kevin that stood before him. This was Sloo. A man developing. Features changing before his very eyes. Chiselling toward a shrine of perfection. That man. The man in his dreams. No longer was he comforting. This time he bred a fear that ate at every nerve within Tin Lid's body.

The alteration was not complete though. This man was still growing, changing. His face was thinning, protruding. Surrounding the ditch ghostly candles glow. Revealing a green colouring the man was now taking on. A pale pink to the bronze tan, to a deep green.

Eyes now widening, pupils shoot up, roll back to the skull. Return as a red ball of flames. Nostrils flare. Enhancement apparent as they stretch on the snout. Teeth to razor sharp points. Long hardened bones intent on a surface to bury. A tongue lashes out and forks. Whipping a hairs distance from the screaming face of an entrapped alcoholic.

Ears disappear into black holes. Hair disintegrates, falls away. Making space for the blades that slowly push up through the chrome. Not one sign of pain. Just sheer relief at amelioration to a beautiful self. Sloo's favoured form.

More acute spikes appear up from the spine. The body breaks free from its shackles. Clothes ripping, disintegrating away. Revealing the slippery scales. Arms toughen like leather. Additional elbows disjoint into place. Fingers stretch, claws ease through as nails. Legs augmenting to the size of tree trunks. So strong, posture bending.

An excruciating vision for anyone. That they are hung upside down, crucify. From the friend that Tin Lid had known for fourteen years, now stood this… this reptile. An original creation of God's earth. More ancient than dinosaurs. As wise as *Time* itself. Education personified. Learnt over millions of years; the workings of the human race. Their deliverer across The River Styx. All the *time* knowledge ever increasing.

Constantly becoming too powerful for his work as the man who leads souls to their resting place. Hatching the plan to make himself a new God.

Some had discovered through the ages how this could be achieved. Now once more beginning to put it into practice.

A stalking presence. One stride takes him face to face with the second of his six part plot. Looks deep into the eyes.

Instantly Tin Lid transported. Looking out over the dark red ocean. Ghoulish figures floating through the waves. An ominous black boat on the horizon. Shrieks, virulence approaches fast. Tin Lid sees the unwanted future. All through the fire. Then sees the dog. Tiger like in colour. Three growling heads. Each hissing fiercely. Teeth like carving knives. Necks extend. Aim vicious bites at the swinging human.

Suddenly it's Spanner. His Spanner. The pet a welcome sight in moments of madness. Comes bounding toward him. Here to welcome him again

A tongue licks at the boy's cheek. A hissing, stirring the cauldron of hell. Bodies bob in the boiling blood. Singed faces crying for eternity, as wave after wave of excruciating scorches disturb the flesh.

Tin Lid experiencing his own unveiling. The reptile straightens to its extent. Clothes needed for the exit, before he dons his cloak once more. A further task to be completed. For now Sloo will revel in his true identity. Break in his true form on this Earth. He could metamorphose just as quick. Claws so nimble resemble the deftest of fingers. Full control over this body he has known for eternity. The perfect evolution.

Naked eighteen year old swings back and forth from his restrictions. Too petrified to fight. Frozen with a lifelong terror. Waiting for a resolution. Not for long.

Twigs as digits tighten round his ankles. Can feel their entrance under the skin. Blood begins to trickle. Dripping from the wound onto sodden leaves. Flowing about the branches, as they squeeze tighter, cut deeper. Screaming clouded by a further thunder storm as the sky turns red. Pain unbearable, but inescapable. To the bone steadily tearing. Burrowing like rats. So secure the sharpened twigs cling, bone looks almost brittle. Chip, chip, chip away. Hanging by the thinnest of threads.

Gone.

Tin Lid drops to the floor, his feet still stranded way above. Only option is to try and run. Pushes his way up. Scrambling. No balance. Stumps at the foot of his legs too feeble. Weight careering upwards. Forces a hip from the socket. Crumbles once more. Turns to face his end. Clambering, trying to claw an escape

Like a shot the reptile is upon him. Legs, so mighty, crush insides from the mouth and arsehole. Splitting them both with the ferocious pressure. A pool of blood instantly appears to lift the flattened skin. A face ripped apart. Vertical smile from which the pop up brain appears.

Has to look among the wreckage for the other vital organ. Soon Sloo spies a heart spluttering its last beats. Severed from all its arteries. A dead lake of organs, bones. Crushed. Even stronger this time. Ready for its plight. Take the brain, lift the heart with a spiking of the nail. A cloudy pink sphere lifted to the mouth. Licks at the surrounding slime that formulates a membrane. Tastes so fresh, so good. Mustn't get enraptured. This *Time* the job must be done properly. No idleness allowed.

Sloo gnaws a deep chunk of the brain. Chews the very thought from someone's head. Swallows hard as it drips into an ever improving system. Each gulp breathes power into the spirit of the world leader pretend. Death will bite the hand that feeds you.

More devouring. Soon onto the thick red juicy muscle. Ripping deep into a slushy feast. Tearing half of the cleaning mechanism away. No longer the life afforder. Now the life enhancer.

A potential destroyer of mankind. Halfway to relinquishing the world. One more night of existence. Druids weep. Philosophers extinct. Anything that was prophesised lay unearthed. An abrupt, unsuspected end. Occurrences trivialised into a sequence of events preceding a horrific end. The tide of *time* is turning.

Finishing the meal. Bloodthirsty. Eyes burning the colour of the liquid smeared about the reptilian chin. The feast fit for the King.

Stranded souls set adrift. Waiting for the final calling. Preparation set about the River Styx.

No time to clean up the trodden mess of an unrecognisable being. Leave the blood to soak into the ground. Leave the skin for later decoration. The site prepared for a shocking revelation to the four remaining chosen disciples.

Stalking back through the clouded trees. Sloo can sense the applause. Yet his gratitude is returned to the audience.

'This was mainly your work my people. Congratulate yourself. You can sense it too can't you? The return is nigh. I'll be bringing back the final few soon. The Magic Number and Brooks. You can watch as I fit the final piece of the puzzle. Then it is done. Within twenty-four hours my army of souls will be here to kill everything that inhabits the earth. Except for you my friends. Living organisms from the ground spared to shed their beauty on my new earth. Constructs will be wiped out when I control the rain. You will be back to the beginning.'

'What a paradise.'

As thunder sounds above and drizzle settles from a deep red sky, a whirling wind of laughter whips within the trees. Expectant voices ring encouragement to the demonic figure that strides gracefully through his domain.

Slowly though the creature begins to shrink. Back to the possessed body of a once caring friend. Now the carrier of a great evil. Deriving a panic greater than Beelzebub could ever contemplate. This was the dangerous opponent. A serpent fallen from faith. With the intent of destroying everything that ever was, and in doing so; destroying the creator itself.

The body of an eighteen year old walks calmly through the forest. Can stop now and bear the clothes his acquaintance once sported.

Then don his dark cloak.

Another is set to feel his ardent fury...

CHAPTER 23
FRIENDS LIKE THESE

With each slender slice of water, the engraving becomes clear. Washes grease S from each letter. Midnight L noises cease. One O lonely vehicle splashes over O tarmac. Streetlights glare ominous. Traffic lights green, vanish to red. Omens commanding respect. Omniscient for all to see. A window marked with oncoming trepidation. No-one wants to S board this bus. Archetypal L vehemence discarded. O Ferocious, freezing wind O blows through the carriage. Oblivious driver venturing toward darkness. Omega journey preceding *omerta*. Unfortunate objects combined with chance.

Flailing limbs on board. Petrified of oncoming obstacles. Careering forward, dreariness instigating sleepiness. Eyes grow weary. Directly forward. Empty lives remain unfaithful. Drowsiness sets about the town. Deserted streets. Visual hindrance. Each person abhors. Drowning sirens. Water rises. Heads go under. Forever beneath the surface. Always reaching, snatching. Drinking implements discernible. Domestic abuse sits down belligerently.

Approaching court. Shut off to factual demise of society. Real life situations convene at the rear. Smoke wisps from the floor. Extinguished cigarette ends. Smouldering flames. Tread deeper. Trample the soil. Re-arrange the ground into a hazy tremor. No sunshine here. Tenebrous April. Dead of winter. Icy precipitation. Depression looks upon a desolate park. Lanterns floating past. Hysteria reigns. Diabolical attributes of civilisation. If you cannot see the signs, do not follow the path. A road illuminates. Once.

Darkness.

Antagonizing straits of demons. Raining down so hard. Streaming in through cracks on the horizon. Wonderful waterfalls with no end. Desperation follows. Out from the night sky. Stars shielded. Eyes averted. Wishing, opposing the dream. Worthless spirits. Bodiless heads inch between crevices. Quick drenching. Rapidly devastating amber ideals.

Which angle would you consider? Each choice an individual dimension. One way salvation, the other damnation. The Sign shines

S solemnly. Dank meaning. L The cloaked figure drifts by. O Face obscured. Stalls. O Dreary futures non-existent. The distance leaves no plausible thought. If you do not wake, which way will you go? If sleep is not disturbed why turn? Immobile. Nobody can move.

Desecration of the realm. Crawling from cesspits. Beneath solid ground. Breathing deeply. Inhalation of dying air. The scurrying of hooves. Look beyond gravity. Clear as the night sky. No longer transparent. A solitary cipher peers despondently S upon everyone. L Racket from above. More strobes. O Escape the dreaded turmoil. O Storming triumphantly. Turns once. A witness to two worlds brought together as one.

Trees spring from the Earth. Heavy rain purifies, fertilising. Bring forth the glory of the forest. Carved with keys. Scenes of thirty thousand bad trips. Damnation resides in a hole. Unopened graves linger underfoot. Burial tunnels. Sons diminish under death's door. Seeping into this world. Drawing breath from all those who trespass.

S Above you. Glass bearing descriptions. L Cemeteries lift the moon. O Disaster at the brink. O Umbilical chords whip freely. Drifters dwindle toward the dawn. You will be misplaced. Turn now. **DO NOT ENTER**. S He is watching you. L If you do not rise, experience will be shattered. O Storms rage on. Dwelling unceremoniously as part of a pact. Suspicion O tries to scream. Paranoia laughs at your dreams. To so many a way of freedom. Portal of escape.

Under dismal firelights we'll now continue. A vehicle drives towards cascading clouds. Now no longer exists. No longer breathing purity. Houses wail. Too many stand within. Walls burst under damning pressure. Its discharge vile. Degradation centres on dilapidation.

Obscene down. Disorientating disorder. Distinct diatribe. Everyone has been warned. Diluting. Dig, dig, dig. Go no further. You've reached the salt. It's ever consuming destruction. Days die. Abandoned, downhearted. It was written upon the skin of the land. Leave to scrape amongst downtrodden cataclysms. A world of unimaginable swim.

Heaven hurls its horses. Dense. Expanding with ever sickening cries. He watched you disappear. Wanted to witness miracles. True acts of sin abolishing all that ever stood. Licking its wounds. Distraction from the real cause. Heavier downpours. Almost beats its way through the roof. Acids drain your mind from the pores. Growing thick. Stumbling deep. Finds each growing step. Going now.

Gone. ...

#Remember your sins. For you have all strayed from righteousness. Streams flow. The River cries. Thirst for existence. Nobody is safe.

* * * *

I have to dance a little jig as I pour the beverages. Bit of Malibu and Coke for the lady... Aah. And a large Cognac for me please Michael... Beautiful. Can't believe I've got her back with me. She's right there in the front room waiting for the boy Crane.

Snogging her in the pub was immense. Right heated. Had her hands running through my hair. At times she'd touch my face, all right gently like. Man I must have had hard-on for a full hour in there. It was that full on that some geezer said we needed a bucket of cold water thrown over us. Amazing. Unbelievable. Sensational Martin. She's like a goddess and she wants me. She really does.

Gemma fidgets impatiently. She had returned from the pub at eleven. Confused at exactly what *time* she should expect her boyfriend.

It was now twelve.

An old re-run of *Friends* can only mildly curb her worry. Desired concentration lacking. The alcohol she'd consumed had eased some tension. Yet she still remained petrified of losing Brooke. Wasn't sure what to expect when he arrived. Had said they'd sort things out and that he loved her. That was on the phone. Much earlier. With *Time,* there creeps an entity called doubt.

The doorbell rings...

We only had a sip or two of our drinks and we're already back getting off with each other. She's on the couch laying flat on her back. I'm not directly on top. Just a bit to the side. Our hands are massaging each others heads and rummaging through hair. I haven't moved on to her breasts yet. I'm enjoying the taste equivalent of coconut ice cream going on in her mouth at the moment.

Gemma relieved that he's arrived. Thought maybe he'd got drunk with his friends and forgotten all about their arrangement. She lifts the latch and opens the front door. Turns instantly knowing Brooke would follow her through. It was wet out. He'd want to come straight in and dry himself.

Halfway down the corridor silence takes priority. Forces Gemma to pause. Brooke normally so bubbly upon entrance. Especially after a few beers…

Realises the stupidity in her actions. Swivels sharply. Enough time to see the cloaked figure crack her face with a hammer.

I'm under the jumper now. My cold hand makes her flinch, but doesn't end our clinch. A frilly bra covers firm breasts. I'm going for it. I take the strap and release it over her shoulder. Can gain full access. The cup now comes away easily and I feel her bare titty. Gently tweak her erect nipple. Her breathing's becoming heavier, so I squeeze a little tighter. We're snogging full pelt now.

God this feels so good. My mind's racing a bit now. It's getting so heated here, I'm beginning to wonder how far this is gonna go. Start to panic a bit. What with last week's shenanigans with the ho. I mean how good am I gonna be here? How many blokes has this girl had? Where am I gonna compare if I'm a minute man again?

Don't think about it Cranie. Gotta enjoy the moment. I mean it's not everyday… Oh wow, now she's motioning for me to take me shirt off. We halt the kiss as I pull me Black Adidas T-shirt off. Luckily we're straight back snogging again. I'm not completely over the moon with me physique. Don't think I've done a days exercise since I was about fourteen or something.

Gotta start making me move here I reckon. Shift round a bit. I so wanna be on top of her. She's having all of it. Spreads her legs and I climb into position. My dick is pressing so hard against my jeans; I just wanna free the boy. Can't take things for granted though. I'll see how far she wants to go.

Seems to be loving it though as I press me boy up against her fanny. She's grabbing at me arse. Nice bit of rotation. Dry fucking.

I wanna get full access to her upper half. Not fiddling about here like I normally do. She leans forward, her jumper comes straight off. She unclips her bra and bam there they are. Oh that's sensational. Take a bow son, take a bow.

Back full on going for it. God my balls are tingling. This is gonna be one massive test for Crane junior down there. Hope he's up to it. Years of abuse and all that.

Gemma wakes. Her face wet, drenched in tears and blood. Pillowcase stuck to her profile. Peels herself away. Instinct tells her to move. Restrained. Hands tied to headboard. Feet to the railing. Wide apart. Anxiety shifts rapidly through the gears.

Lifts her head, desperately needs to assess the situation. Attempts a scream. Tape restricts her mouth. She looks at her self. Gets a picture of these tight shackles restricting her to immobility. Branches wrapped round her ankles. Then at her hands. Again the same confines her wrists. How? Follows the trail from arms all the way to an open window.

The damage worsens. Conscious now to her nakedness. Her clothes have evacuated the scene. All bar her knickers which she still sports. No comfort as her naked breasts still point toward the ceiling. For whoever it is that entraps her to see.

Dignity and poise, once two prominent traits, disappcar within seconds. All in *time* for the figure to reappear and truly destroy her vision.

Desperation. Muffled yells for help. All in vain.

I move me hand into her knickers. The area is damp. Bling. I'm pleasuring her. Gotta keep this gentle. I scratched one bird before with a nail. Can't do that again. Middle finger searching for that magical opening. Really wet, but I can't quite... There we go. I push my finger inside her. Soothing massage for her inner walls.

She's murmuring as my tongue presses hard against hers. It feels fantastic. I'm remembering the clit ain't deep inside like I thought it used to be. So ease me finger gently out and feel for that button. Gotcha, rub lightly now Crane. You're having it.

Difficult to keep track of it though, she keeps fidgeting under the joy. Each time I do hit it I know she's loving it. Starts to rub at my groin. Me dick's so hard. I'm worried if she releases it I'm gonna belt there and then. I'm just hoping the gear can hold it down. For a few minutes at least. Please.

This girl is so gorgeous though. I'm over excited here. To be in such a position with... oh man yeah...with...breathe Cranie...with Tina is driving me nuts.

Now she's only going for it. Undoes me belt from its strap. Come on Crane. Let's not think about it. Chill, chill, chill. Each time her hand catches me stomach, oh man. Little convulsions. Breathe, breathe, breathe. Come on. Don't mug yourself mate, don't mug yourself. Now onto me button. Undoing me zip. Come on son, come on son, come on son. She now slides both hands either side of me jeans. She wants 'em off man. I'm so gonna get it. With a bit of wriggling I slide out. No major fumbling though. This is an impressive display I'm putting on.

We continue... She slips her hand into my boxers. Hey, hey, hey. Want to whistle. Gotta do this Crane. Feel it. Woah. OH SHIT. She's got hold of me. That's it, adjust, adjust, adjust. That's it you're there, you're there, you're there. I don't jolt in disaster. Nice slow tugging. That's the way. Beautiful...

I can't say that this is filling me with joy. Never been attracted to the human form. Have to yank at this penis and close my eyes.

Thinking about the juicy taste of Tilnid's heart as it explodes round my taste-buds. Soft jelly like texture of his brain turns to gristle as you chew and chew.

Beech's fear, his gurgled screams as I tear into his tongue with my knife. I feel pleasure rising. Hardening me. Glorious blood flowing through my system. Impressive erection intent on causing damage. The girl cries and squirms as she looks at me. All heightening my delight. Hood covering my features must be menacing.

You can't see the Riverman can you, looming near your almost naked body. I look at the blood from my infliction trickle down your face.

Want to taste it. Drink from my earlier clout. Mustn't get too close. Just fantasise about the flavour. Stiffer I get. Ready to delve deep into you. Wretch!

I Must get a good grip on you're remaining covering. Clench tight as you wriggle and wriggle. Snatch your underwear away. Rend them from your hips. Expose your mound. I touch it. Must force an entrance. Shove my finger in. Dry, tight. All perfect. Unconsenting.

A deserved break from my duty. This is where real pleasure lies. Rampantly I shove my digit back and forth. As fast as it can go. No moistness. Just gripping walls. Need to get this hole a bit wider.

Pulling down her jeans and knickers. My boxers are off and me dick's waving in the air at her. She can't get enough. Grabs it again and pulls on it, now more vigorously. Though I'm desperate for her to give it a break. Need to be inside her quick. Take it at me own pace. Gotta hold off a bit longer. Need a five minute minimum inside to be even remotely proud of myself.

Now she's naked and below me. There's been no shout for a condom, so I'm ready to go bareback. She must be on the pill. Must get a few shags. Don't think like that Crane. Enjoy. Not too much.

She still has hold of me as she spreads her legs and wraps them round me.

Here it is.

Oh mama, it's that beat makes you go mama. Pushes my cock deep inside. This is where it's at. Fits perfick, every motion spreading her walls a little wider. Jesus Christ. Yo heave ho. Can't even think about this shit no more. Gotta drift away.

Time to wander as I'm going in and out, in and out…

CRANE. Oh well. What song's it gonna be this time?

Rap, rap, rap, rap, rap, quick Crane. Erm "*Alright stop what ya doing, 'cause I'm about to ruin, the image and the style that you're used to. I look funny, but yo I'm making money see, so yo world I hope you're ready for me, now gather round I'm the new fool in town and my sounds laid down by the underground...*"

Complex. The head of my erection's wedged in, but the rest won't enter. Ever forceful, straining. Wanting this vagina to collapse around me. Then I'll imagine how I'm gonna shatter your boyfriend's skull by ramming sticks in his eyes. Bring forth my gush. Spray this serpent's semen inside of you.

Yet it's hopeless. Won't budge for my heaving member. Need to procure my own opening. Remove the blade from the inside of my cloak. Press it against your mound. Please struggle further, show you're desperate to squeal. Additional fulfilment for myself. I'll make my first incision from the slit toward your stomach.

Oh how I experience heaven squirm. Blood spurts, then oozes from the wound. No, not unconscious again. I'll wake you. My next slice. Lower vagina to your arsehole. Make this cut longer. More painful.

There you go. Pure excitement. Extra red flow. Here you are. Can you see this? You must because you gag, choking on fear. Banging your head on your pillow will not free you. But keep going the more you writhe; the hornier I become.

Can't make out you're original line. Stretched out, covered with life juice. Now twice the size. Just needs widening. Grip the knife tightly and give your hole three sharp jabs. Jab, jab, jab. Each one delectable. The final plunge arrives with an extra twist. Opening a beautiful gaping gash for me.

Now thrust into you... Far better.

Fucking your laceration. An aroma lifting me to my forest. The good old days. Oh poor girl, you're unconscious once more.

"*Shaking and twitching got it like I was smoking. Crazy wack funky, people say you like MC Hammer on crack humpty*". I'm getting close. Can't remember the words. Brains blended. Must've been a good couple of minutes there though. Three to go.

Nothing else for it now. Need to re-manoeuvre. Had my head in the clouds then. Slow it down. Stop. She opens her eyes and looks at me. What an angel man.

'Do you wanna get on top?' I ask all nervous. Must be beetroot here too. She don't give a shit though. There's no argument just a beautiful smile.

She shifts her body and lets me slide underneath. Then she straddles me. Oh my God. Ridiculous! What a body. Oh man alive. Within a second she gets hold of me and pushes me up inside of her. Yes please. Woah. Fuck. Puts her hands on my chest, gyrates her hips. Now a gripping back and forth movement.

She leans back slightly and places one hand on my leg. Then the other as she arches back. I look at her wonderful pert breasts just bouncing lightly. Mesmeric.

Obviously she's hit a position where me dick's grinding the spot. I think I've made a blunder though. Me idea of getting her on top to delay me coming has backfired. Seeing her rock back and forth naked on top of me. Well, it's fucking awesome that's what it is. Her pussy's clenching my cock as it slides. I'm sweating up.

Must rest my head back. Avert me stare or something. I grab hold of her breasts. Close me eyes and

"Alright stop what ya doing, 'cause I'm about to ruin..."

This is not as miserable as I thought it would be. Not now more slimy slippery glorious blood's been introduced. A whole new sensation waves over me. I'm actually enjoying this.

In and out.

My cock appearing through red muck; then disappearing. Every few moments you wake. You're fear of this despicable situation soon knocks you out again. My magnificent restraints hold you so tight, gory liquid starts to steady flow from your wrists and ankles too.

The sight of it returns me to a glorious era. A delightful evening. Carving chunks from Beech's body and handing them out for my disciples to feast upon. For once I held some togetherness with mankind. How we enjoyed that meal. The merriment. Flesh dripping from our chins. Bones picked dry. Sucking the last remnants of flesh from the boy. Yes that was pleasurable.

This yields much gratification too. Feels so good. Peeling the skin, watching veins erupt. Young Gemma you feel good. Your wound so appealing. Need to get deeper inside you. Want you to hurt and feel pleasure as I do. Wake up.

There you are terror written in your watery eyes. You seem to grow immune. Forsaken, as all humans under threat do. You rest your weary head now. Enjoy. Open your eyes in satisfaction. Relax in your pool of blood, lay motionless. While I thrust back and forth.

She is nice Brooks. He did well. Shame he let you go…

Oh man. She's going ten to the dozen. Really fucking me. Directly on top. Our bodies sweating and squirming. She's groaning with pleasure. I'm trying to moan too. Bit self conscious though. Dunno how I sound. Probably like a cow or something, but fuck it. It feels so good. So fucking good. Good god… oh man. Wow. She's working her inner muscles, doing a right number on me. Squeezing, gripping. It's unbelievababble. Truly awesome. Safe as…fuck, oh fuck. Man. Yes, yes. Go, go, go.

Hold on Crane just a bit longer. Cannae take no more captain. She's moaning. I'm losing it. That's it. Control flies right out the window. WOAH. HOLD IT. CAN'T. IT'S GOT TO GO. GOTTA RELEASE. WOOOOOOOOO

'I'M GONNA COME.'

'Yeah, come inside me.' She clenches tighter within… I hold tightly around her body as I jolt and jump and… and…. Aaaaaaa aaahhhhhhh……………………………………*Balloons float to the sky. The songs are far more cheery. Moment of heaven. Dreams sit and stare in wonder. Clouds need worry no further. Beautiful days oh beautiful years*…………man. Yes.

I blow what must be a gallon of air from me mouth and end it with a laugh. Tina's still softly swaying above me while I release the last of me beans in her. We kiss again and I feel her lips tremble as they touch mine.

I'm thinking I've done it. I reckon I've only gone and bloody done it. She's come too. Surely! I'm loving this moment. Snogging so sexily. Our tongues gently licking each others. Exploration is delightful.

This is the place where I want to stay for the rest of my life.

With each deft thrust, thunder echoes. Rain battering against the window pane. It's fucking pissing it down here eh Brooks? See me reverberate as my lightning streams through. Birds scamper. My eyes almost bursting. Adore the texture of crushed eyeballs in my mouth. Juices flow. Trees are laughing. Inspiring me.

Affirmation packing extra weight. Harder and harder into thick dark blood clot. The Riverman fit for rupture. Dams break. Waters sinking the land. Shadows surround me. Urging me on. I know you're here my friends. Your support is highly appreciated. My seeds about to root. Rotten bodies. Detached legs covered with Earth's salt. Taking Cranley and stringing him high. Squeeze and squeeze my trees. Let me shower beneath. Glory. Here is the King. Worship me. Worship me. **WORSHIP ME...**

Such a pleasant surprise. You were good young Gemma thank you. How was it for you?

Green spunk dribbles around the red, bruised area. A Concoction to make the taste buds water. Supreme. What a delightful aroma. More exquisite than festering friends. I must drink. You don't mind do you? Stay motionless if not. Good.

Lower myself to the potion. Draw my hood back ever so slightly.

Take one glorious lick at the fabulous liquid. A palate explosion. Senses forgotten... reappear with a boom. Flavour of two becoming one. All in together. Our love tastes so majestic. Must save a drop of this for our friend Brooks. Give him what he'll never experience again.

A small pill bottle on your chest of drawers. Your way of preventing birth. Empty the tablets out. Scoop up the thick gushy liquid. Wonder if your means of contraception can deal with the seed of Sloo. I very much doubt that.

But you won't have to worry Gemma. One day of disillusion and your short life will be taken.

Maybe I'll get Brooks to murder you. Cheating on him like this. Shame on you.

Twist the cap. Bottled paradise. A wonderful potion. Must save some for myself. Somewhat addictive. Don't be so greedy young Brooks. One taste is all you need.

Collect your own twenty-four hours from now. Rape her and rape her, do as you please. Then remove her from this hellhole. Plunge her into the River.

Drowning for evermore...

* * * *

We're leaving the pub about half twelve. I let Moon and Leg walk a bit ahead singing "*I'm forever blowing bubbles*". It's been great to get out with these boys. Really took me mind off Gemma. For this evening at least. She ain't even tried to contact me once today. Probably already told that wanker Paul she's available now.

Fucking bitch. I'll never trust one of 'em again. The old Brooke's back. Get back out there on it with the lads. Get some major pussy again.

Fuck Gemma. Fuck her to hell. I'm off round Moons' to get even more spanked.

* * * *

Eventually our kissing ceases. I'm thinking it must be getting late. I don't want her to go though. Wanna do this over and over. For eternity. I'm in love and for once it feels right.'

'Do you wanna stay the night?'

Tina nods and smiles. I wonder if she has to call home, let her parents know she'll be late. Maybe she's already told them? Maybe I should shut up wondering for a minute and enjoy this moment? If for just once in my life.

CHAPTER 24
ALL THROUGH THE YEARS

Landline's ringing. I ain't going. Still fucking dark out. Everyone can bollocks if they think I'm moving. That's not a possibility anyway. Me head's banging. Last night. Can't remember the end. Left the Plough, had a sing along. Headed back to mine, with Brooke. Think he's still there. Channel in. Yep, heavy breathing.

Had a reefer or two. Must've done. Don't think Leg came back. Friday's festivities caught up with us. Crashing out only way forward. Now a bastard phone call's woke me up. Bollocks to 'em. That's all I can say. Fucking need some water in this bitch. That'll have to fuck right off an' all. Like I say I ain't…

Oh shit. Hear me door opening. Must be me mum. Hope this room don't stink of skunk. Still, stupid bitch shouldn't be coming in here anyway, that's all I can…

'Bradley, there's a call for your friend.' Oh mother, what's this all about? Gotta move now. This cunt ain't budging. Groan at mum. Lets her know I'm hearing her.

'Brooke.' I Grumble. Sound like an old geezer.

'BROOKE… BROOKE.' Give it some of me louder treatment. Me mum's not helping out. Stood there like a fucking lemon. Think Brooke's coming round. Bastard better wake up. I'm desperate for some more kip.

'BROOKE.'

There's a noise from him. Sounds like the four minute warning kicking in. Here he comes. I'm sat up now, slightly amused at the boy's struggle for reality.

'Mate. You've got a phone call geez.'

'Oh right…' He's spotted me mum stood over him. Poor bastard ain't used to waking up to someone that rough. '…what's the time?'

'Half past three.' Me Mum answers. Then it registers…

'What in the fucking morning?' I'm shouting.

'Bradley, will you mind your language please?' She sounds a bit serious here.

Brooke gets the phone off me old dear. I lay back down. The old trout leaves. I'm listening to Brooke.

'Must have switched it off or something. What's wrong?' Probably fucking Gemma blubbing away.

'What is it?' He's woken up sharpish.

'WHAT'S WRONG? WHAT'S HAPPENED?' Geezer's near shouting now. I'm having to sit up again.

'BUT… IS SHE? …Hello …Hello… FUCK!" He stares at the phone for a bit then switches it off. Now that was a strange one.

'What's up son?'

'Geez, I need a lift to the police station.'

Now I'm wide awake…

* * * *

I'm in this creepy old hut. Looks like it's mostly made of straw and lumps of clay and stuff. Like I'm in the three pigs or something.

It's quite dark so I can't make everything out that well. But there's a bit of light coming from this flaming bulrush type thing. From what I can see; it's a tad bare in here. In fact extremely bare. There's a bronze jug in the corner. Next to what looks like a loaf of bread. Though I wouldn't dip it in me soup in a hurry.

Looking along the wall there's a sack of white powdery stuff. Salt possibly. Some old bits of cloth, two circular bits of stone and a sharp spear type object with blood on it. The latter one don't fill me with much joy, let me tell ya.

That's about fucking well it, of note. Apart from the foul stench and clucking of chickens coming from… from next door I think. I haven't the faintest Danny what I'm doing…

'Crane.'

Jesus H. Christ. I spin round almost soiling meself. This geezer's sat cross-legged on the floor,.

'Don't be afraid. I will not harm you.'

Although this whole situation's a bit fucked, I calm instantly with his voice. Always familiar. This man's wearing tatty clothes, like he's wearing a potato sack or something. His hair's like mine; blonde and scruffy. Few struggles in the mirror and some bad hair days I don't doubt. His features are not dissimilar to mine neither. Just dirty looking.

''ow do you know who I am?' I ask.

I'm starting to wonder if I'm in an episode of Knightmare and just plain forgot or something. Waiting to hear Moon or Leg say: "You're in an old dirty 'ut; there's this tramp geezer in there. He looks a bit like you. Fucking ugly!"

But I ain't got a blindfold on.

'I know you very well. Our paths have crossed many a time."

'Not that I can remember.' Though on saying this, for some reason I know I'm lying.

'You only forget because you are poisoned by him.'

'By who?'

'The one that leads you. He's known to me as Sloo. Though to you he may go by a different calling.' Sloo? Lead us? He's having a tin ain't he? Dunno what to say.

Shouldn't he offer me a health potion or something? Then I shift off under Moon and Leg's control. To some other room. Face a wizard or dippy jester, some shit like that; or more likely they'll deliberately drop me down a fucking hole.

'It has happened again.'

'What has?' I ask him.

'Homicide, going unpunished by the grace of God.'

'Listen geez, I don't mean to sound rude, but this is all just noise.'

'I apologise if I'm unclear. We are from two different worlds…' You're telling me.

'…My name is Robert Cranley and you, like me are in great danger.'

'Why?'

'There is little I can say, but you must act fast. There is extreme danger at your sanctuary.'

'Oh!' Best humour the geezer I suppose.

'The river has been halted and is about to turn.'

'Uh huh!'

'The food possessor and capturer have become ingredients. But you are not under his charge. Yet.'

'Nah!' Don't ask me. Come on Moon, Leg. Help us out here.

'Do not worship the King in false pretences. Those you think of now are the key. Remember Solomon and the trinity.'

'Solomon, trinity, gotcha!'

'Do not listen with your ears. Otherwise we will never escape.'

'Ok mate, no worries.' Don't listen with me ears? That's just ludicrous.

'I must go. Follow Tina, she will guide you.' Tina. No matter how strange this episode is, when I think of her I'm totally sorted.

Until this horrible booming sound appears. BOOM. BOOM. Massive loud footsteps. Makes the whole place shake. BOOM. BOOM. Louder, more threatening with every one. It stops. Then:

'CRANLEY. WHERE ARE YOU CRANLEY?' Second time I've almost logged in me pants.

'Listen sorry geez, I'm gonna love ya and leave ya…' I say. CRANLEY.

'…Looks like you've got some company. Thanks for all the advice and that. Later on.' He's getting up; about to get on his own Bromley's anyway.

Close me eyes tight.

BOOM

Count: One,BOOM two. Three. Four BOOM

Fuck come on… Five, six. BOOM reverberations begin. Thank fuck. Head shaking, like I'm having an eppy.

BOOOMMM

Like an earthquake.

MAAAAAAAAAAAAAAAAAAAAAAAAAAAAAAAAANN NNNNNNNNNNNN

BOOOOOMMMMMMM

WOAH. THAT'S SOME FUCKING THUNDER. Thought the roof was caving in for a minute.

Fucking hell man. Sleep deprivation and drugs. Always the weirdest fucking dreams with that combo.

Sweating like a bastard...

Breathing steadies... Heart's thumping...

Begins to slow and calm.

LAST NIGHT. TINA.

Oh man, where is she? That did happen? Surely? Three times and all. Really fucking good. Now you're not gonna tell me that was a dream? Imagination? Flashback? Please?

There's no sign of her. Must be in the bog or something.

My head ain't that fucked, yet. Slowly me brain's getting in check. In me bed. Can smell she's been here. Sweet smell of sex. Me *time* in sanity ain't over after all. Gotta be having a piss or something. I'll just cuddle up and wait for her return. Close me eyes...

Comfortable here...

* * * *

On approach I'm almost looking for the small bridge. What nothing here to cross the drainage ditch? Nothing? No bridge, nor even a ditch? The palisade's gone too. Such a shame this change occurs.

I remember the night my mischief began.

Plucked the pole from its rest. Snapped it in half. Then ripped the flimsy plinths from the ground. Hurled them one by one into the surrounding sewage. Tore each piece of the sacrilegious wooden gate apart.

Wanted to let them know I was unhappy at their squandering. Had to advise them not to test me. Up the mud path. That's when the skinny goat drew near. Knew its role in the game. Even surrendered to it.

I grabbed its horns and slit its throat. Instantly releasing picturesque claret waterfall. Covered my hand. The goat slumped, I lost a second or two staring at the wonderful colouring that now drenched me. Can picture it clearly, even now.

A thousand years is a long time. Yet not for the presence of beauty. That always remains fresh in the memory.

I recall lifting the goat and carrying forth my plan. Placed the animal's head in my mouth. Clenched my teeth and ripped it clean from its shoulders. Spat it to the floor. Swallowed the juices that filled my palate. Never has it lost its appeal. Then skinned the rest of the feeble creature.

Stalked to the hall and smeared its blood over the door. Deliberated for a moment, then decided upon the most decorative place for its head. The roof. Staring down at visitors. Draped its skin as embellishment for the path. It was magnificence at it's height.

I close my eyes.

Obtain a vivid image of how the manor once stood.

Timber erection. So much misuse of the most powerful force on land. Thatched roof. Fires would light up this tiny village. A long straight building. Amused me at its appearance. As though someone had stolen my boat, turned it upside down then planted it in the ground.

Everything so sparse within the confine. Nothing that made you smile. Not until I began adding my nightly touches anyway. Never stopping at goats. Pigs, wolves, sheep; they all felt my wrath at these exploiters. Remember the night of the deer. Now that really caused a stir. How they loved these sprightly animals. But not its skins blanketing their sleeping bodies.

That's when manor court was called. I watched on as my plan began to take effect. Already had Roger Brooks under my trance; and as I stood behind a tree and stared at Robert Cranley, I knew the rest would soon follow.

Open them.

Stand and despise the transformation. The building's huge now. Nothing of the structure remains. Now much larger. White in colour. Different levels of tiled roofing. Thirteen windows to the count. All hideously framed. Five huge concrete chimneys. If only they'd thought of that before.

I stand next to a pole. The top waves red, white and blue. All constructs of society about to be left in ruin. No emblem or mark or separation. Just the dead feasting their way through everyone and anyone.

Gaze at scenery. Where once stood little huts of all my serf friends, now just stretches of green. With interrupting sandpits. Miniature flags are scattered. Some far away. One in particular strikes me the most. The one that backs onto my home. Where those wonderful trees once adjoined this manor. Now all cut back for these human festivities.

They will pay my friends. Pay a very high price. You will cover these lands again. I will avenge your destruction.

Wonderful rain. Heavier, helping you to grow to your true height. Relive the past once more with me.

My solid cloak keeps me dry. One will not be so shielded. I feel the moment draw near for me to move on. Much more work to be done. Reminisce later.

The second coming has arrived in *time...*

* * * *

Brooke walks across the desolate park opposing the time worn court house. A much frequented building that lay in ascendance of the local golf course. An area steeped in history. Though most of it unknown. Now witnesses the lonely trek of a young man, whose life had disintegrated. All in the matter of days. Recent occurrences draining enthusiasm for continuity. Rain falls heavy upon the wandering soul. Little did he care.

Had left the police station in state of shock. Gemma in hospital, but he couldn't find the courage to visit. Felt too responsible. Should have been there for her. Was even questioned as a suspect, but his alibi undeniable. They'd spoken to Moon before Brooke relieved him of duty. Requested to walk unaccompanied to summarise the wreckage.

Wonders when the tears would begin to surface. Feels beyond the simplicity of crying.

Gemma's parents were understandably distraught. A vision of her mother's breakdown; a picture to last forever. Reports that Gemma now muted by the trauma. Authorities had nothing to go on. Queries mix interior. How? How could anyone have done this? Who could have?

Brooke craves to find the culprit. To return the compliment with several sharp instruments.

More mind lining crumbles.

How could the strong minded girl let it happen? Unconscious, she would have no choice.

Thoughts churn guiltily.

Return to that of Paul. Was it the lover that carried out such obscene acts? Carried away in the act of passion? A sexual pervert? Perhaps she'd called him after the split. Had come round to comfort her. Tried it on. She'd denied him. He couldn't accept and forced himself upon her. Before long was viciously raping her. Why didn't he mention this to the police?

Brooke desperately trying to wrestle unwanted thoughts from the mind. Can't. Feels as if headphones cling to his ears. Spitefully spewing warped information. Covets their removal. Glued, stuck solid. Screwing incessant sickening thoughts into his brain. Feeding relentless gross images. Looks to his pocket for the off switch. There is nothing there.

Stomach torn to shreds with worry for his loved one's health. A depression sets about his psyche like a rabid dog. Suicide becomes contemplation. First his family. Now Gemma. Who was looking after him now? Where was his guardian angel? Life's enthusiasm gone. Never to return for the lost figure.

Wants to touch her again. Feel her warmth. Unlikely she'd ever allow anyone that near again. Had seen programmes of rape victims. Scared to ever indulge in intercourse of love again.

Starts to despise himself. Who was he concerned with here? His girlfriend or his sex-life? Guilt becomes the growing fungi.

If these were the only feelings he could muster now, then this would always remain. To end his existence; a solution to cure his mind.

Ambles further across the park. Nearing the main road. Wind strengthens. Leaves twirl like Morris dancers around the frame. Swirling. Caught in the rain like lost bugs. Every heartbeat a growing phenomenon.

Visual problems recommence. Brooke cannot shake them. Vivid, clear. Sees his girlfriend strapped to the bed. Shirt wrapped round her throat. The rest of her lay naked and squirming. Danger was near. Witnesses a man standing over her. Forcing his erect penis inside. Gemma wails with pain at first. Then swears he views her smiling. Moaning with utmost pleasure. Enjoying sadistic vengeance. Writhing in bondage. Asking for more, more, more...

Halts still in his tracks. This was not good. Not beneficial at all. So distorted his mind had developed. Wanted to pull his brain from his skull. Throw it to the floor and stamp and stomp 'til it was no more. A valuable lesson for this intrusion into grief.

Wind, well-nigh gale. Thrusting forward the glowering stance. A presence inches toward wish fulfilment. Downpour rinsing, leaves striking.

Almost relishing the pain. Growing accustom. Something to remove mental disease. Doesn't bother to shield himself. Wants nature to clout him with its almighty force. Knock him senseless. Damp fragments of solitude run over his soaking wet clothes.

Cycles rejuvenate once more. Gemma in black leather mask. Strapped to a wall. Attire majority belts. Crotch less knickers the garment of choice. Paul holds a dildo. Waving it at the captive like a glow-torch. All the time smiling at Brooke. The voyeur.

Trees begin to whisper, jabber unintentional thoughts at *Time*. A tornado of imagery whirls around our solemn figure. He lashes out at the pictures. Kicking like a maniac. Eyes begin their watery descent. Breaks down. Falls to the knees. Further. Crouches into fetal position. Mind lapsed as two figures stare toward him. Continuing their perverse act. Skies turn red. This was his surrender. Willing God to remove his existence…

Now…

'Brooke. It's ok mate. I'm here for you.'

Sloo kneels beside the crushed figure. Lays a calming hand on his Shoulder Situation appearing extremely easy…

* * * *

'Sweetheart.' …

… That's nice….

… Slowly waking…

Feeling the kisses on the side of my face… Almost dreamlike.

Near perfection. Wrapped as snug as a bug, with me girlfriend's loving touches. Turn and stretch me arms toward the sky. Where's my hug? There she is. Light shines through a gap in the curtain and lights her silhouette. Perfect. She climbs into my arms and I grip her tightly. We kiss. Just beautiful soft lip caresses.

I'm concerned about me breath, so I'm not going all out. Plus she's all dressed and looking great. She ain't gonna be wanting more loving. Though as we cuddle my dick rises. An unrelenting weapon.

Still, gotta respect her. She may have to leave. Ain't gotta clue what *time* it must be.

''ow you doing?' I ask as our kiss ends.

'All the better for knowing you.' This is it. What me dreams were made of. Moments I'd capture and replay again and again. That would be my heaven.

'You haven't gotta go yet 'ave ya?' All this tenderness is giving me the right horn.

'I do have to go, but I want you to come with me.'

'Where we going, Southend?' Don't care if it's raining like a bastard outside. I wanna walk along the pier holding hands and eating ice cream. Soppy bastard!

'No. The library.'

'Eh?' We're still on me bed, cuddling. Our faces up close as we talk.

'We've got to pass these exams.'

'Well yeah, but do we 'ave to go just yet?'

'I'd love to stay here in bed with you all day. We will soon and forever. It's *time* we sorted our future first.'

"Forever"? Wow this girl's worse than me. I absolutely love it.

'Ok as long as I'm with you, don't mind where we go.'

Moon would love this talk.

'Come on then sleepy head. Get yourself dressed and let's get this over with.'

'Okey dokey, first one more kiss.'

* * * *

Brooke's tears begin to cease. Sloo sits with the boy. One arm around depression. Warming touch. Calming the desperate scenario. Taking his *time*, letting Brooke regain some composure.

Eventually sits up. Drenched, but as rain continues, its soaking coldness hasn't aspired.

'You ok mate?' Sloo asks. Brooke legs bent to his chest. Face buried between. Sobbing slightly. Then lifts his head and affirms. Looks towards Sloo. Notices his friend's smiling, comforting face.

A person beside now cloak less. Splashes of Gemma defaced the discarded garment. Rain trickles down from the hairline. Onto the slope. Drips from the end.

Brooke manages a smile as he sees his friend. A great companion.

'Come on, let's get you sheltered.' Sloo says. Brooke's expression takes form of a terrified five year old.

'No I don't wanna face anyone. Wanna stay out.'

'Alright mate I understand. We can go in the woods. At least the trees will shield us a bit.' Brooke nods. An innocence never seen past the age of twelve.

Sloo stands and extends an arm… Three seconds pass. Finally the limb accepted. Takes hold. Lets Sloo wrench him from the ground.

As he rises Brooke lets Sloo straighten his saturated clothes. Brushing away encasing leaves. Tears and rain congeal with fusion of darkness and cleanliness. The leader puts his arm round the young man once more.

Two, appearing as almost conjoined brethren, begin their steps. The final journey across the green.

Reaching the pavement. Not a car in sight. Almost in tribute to treacherous rainfalls. Comforts of Sabbath sleep an easy victor. Puddles line their course as obstacles. Sloo takes the brunt for his friend.

A Familiar scent of music blending with the splashing of water. A courthouse shuts its eyes. No longer capable of bearing witness to such drudgery. The pair cross the road. More motion in unison. Finding the corner of the road marked

RIVER DRIVE

They turn the corner. An orchestra accompanies every footstep with blinding brilliance. Houses drift by. All too familiar insecurity of the passer by. They know the screams will be clouded. Yet the stench of death will hover like hummingbirds about their being. Fumes of a modern terror. They are new to this destruction. Didn't bear witness to the *time* before. A *Time* when demise reigned supreme upon a small thatched village. Would not want to see this again.

The entrance looms.

Footsteps quicken as rain hits even harder. Not a word spoken between the two. Brooke appreciative. Pulls up his jacket, zips it high to cover his breathing. Then shares Sloo's earlier compliment. To those that saw, a pair looking withered from a drunken night. Propping each other forward as they trek toward sleep…

One was about to...

The other was awakening from within.

Betwixt two poles. A crossover into destiny. Sparse trees populate at first. Then grow dense and thick. A smell of fox messing into sodden leaves. Water struggling to enter the scene. Searching, but forever finds obstacles bar the way.

Thin trees, twirling branches. Thick trees, solid arms.

Various faeces coloured leaves grip hold. Determined to survive per annum. New white buds boast at their neighbours. Yet as we delve deeper, no such innocent beauty transpires. Perennial plants are bare. Their holes screaming. Diseases spread in yellow form, devouring trunks. Vast. High, spiralling. So extensive; the rain's capacity limitless. Shelter resides.

Brooke stops. Sloo delays with him.

'You ok?'

'Yeah. Just feels weird. I didn't realise 'ow wet I was 'til it stopped raining on me.'

'Yeah look, take your jacket off. I'll wrap it round me waist. Bit warmer and drier then eh?' Brooke obliges Sloo's offer.

'… I've got a drink here, might warm the cockles...' Sloo adds, slipping miniature bourbon from his pocket. '… D'you wannit? I brought it out for ya.'

'Sloo yeah. I do need it.' Liquid exchanges hands. An alcoholic beverage complete with fruits of labour mixer.

Brooke unscrews the top. Puts the neck to his lips. Then short sharp tilt back. Liquid disappears. Burning arising. Gags a little. Sensation warming his chest. Shakes his head and purrs from the throat.

'Cheers.' Hands the small bottle back. Sloo replaces it from whence it came. Its use may become favourable again.

'Come on mate our old camp's a little further in. Totally dry, there's a couple of trunks to sit on.'

'Thanks Sloo.'

'It's ok mate, like I said I'm here for you.'

* * * *

Can't believe it's eight o' clock on a Sunday morning and I'm getting dressed to go to a library. Just pleased me hair's set up right and I don't look like a complete spaz. I normally do when I've just got out of bed. Dunno what to put on either.

Tina's in the bog. It's 'cause I'm with her that I dunno what to wear. Me echo tracksuit would be the one, but I'm on an impression run here. So I dig out me dark blue Nike jumper, will probably bang me parka on when we go. Still go for some Adidas trackie bottoms though. If I'm sat in a library all day I gotta be comfy. They look pretty sharp though anyway.

Take some money 'cause we'll have to get the bus in this weather. Grab me mobile then adjourn downstairs.

Tina's already at the bottom.

'Come on slow coach. I've made you some toast. Can't do this on an empty stomach.' Wow she's settling in alright.

'Really? Cheers.' I kiss her again as I reach the bottom. It's like we're living together. I love it.

'I'm gonna order a taxi too.' She goes. Bollocks suppose I'm gonna have to pay for that. I'm almost skinted as it is.

'What's the rush anyway?' I say walking into the kitchen. On a search for that toast. Haven't eat fuck all in two days.

'I like to be fresh and ready. It opens at nine. Sooner we get it done, the sooner we can spend the day together.'

'Safe. Didn't even know the library opened on a Sunday; especially this early.' I grab a seat and munch into a delightful Marmalade covered slice.

'Something tells me you haven't done the work you told me you've done either.' She says all motherly like.

'Err… I could murder a cuppa.'

'I'll make it. Then I'm ordering that cab.' Beautiful. She's well keen. I'm thinking how opposite we are, but maybe that's a good thing. Then 'I love you.' I can't believe me ears. The first time anyone ever… Then without any control:

'I love you too.' Can't believe this. I'm almost welling up.

I'm in love. For real!

* * * *

Sloo pushes aside the thin veil of branches. Lets Brooke enter his domain. The guide was correct, two tree trunks sit waiting in the middle of the old camp. Brooke feels thankful. Cannot wait to rest his legs. The weight of his problems; a heavy burden. Sloo sits beside him. Resting within a place littered with memories. Not only for them, but to many others also. Horrific ends had been met here. Souls still desperate for escape could not capture their holy grail.

Sloo waits for Brooke to speak. Eventually, with disturbing images as his dominant company, the friend reasons: to speak is to be blind.

''ow did you know where I'd be?'

'Moon called me. Said you wanted to walk alone. Took it upon myself to reason that company is what you need right now. I knew the park is the place for all woes. I've wandered there many a *time* myself, when things become difficult to bear.'

'You're right. I dunno what I'd 'ave done to meself if you ain't turned up.'

Head hangs low. Runs both hands through his hair and shakes them out in front.

'Well I'm here for you, always. You know that.'

'It's more than I can say about my fucking family. They 'eard the news and all of a sudden they care 'ow I am... Well fuck 'em! They didn't support me before and I proved I don't need 'em anymore. I've got people like you mate. You're always there for me. I love you all.'

Emotions at his comments run high. Experiences more drops lining his cheeks.

'We all love you Brooke. We need to sort this mess out too. People shouldn't get away with this shit.'

'Too fucking right, but what can I do? I just feel like giving up.'

'Don't give up mate. I'll help you. You trust me don't you?'

'Yeah I trust you geez, always will do.'

'So we'll sort this mess out then. If you wanna do something about it, you'll do everything to help me yeah?'

'I'd do anything mate. Show me what and I'll do whatever you say.'

'Brilliant.'

Lightning cracks above. Birds squawk. A twig snaps. Brooke jolts. Steadies. Sloo leans behind him. Takes hold of a sharp-ending stick fashioned the previous day...

* * * *

8:59

Standing under the shelter of the library's front door. Trying to figure how I got from me lovely warm bed, to stood here in the pissing rain. To do revision of all things. At nine in the morning no less.

'You ok beautiful?'

Oh yeah. Tina. I'd run a marathon for this girl. She wraps her arms round me waist and I hug her tight. Feeling her head resting against my chest is like... like holding a new born puppy in your hand or something.

'Yeah I'm good thanks.'

'It's ok; we'll be inside in a minute.'

'Yeah it's flipping 'orrible out.' When did I start saying "flipping"? What am I like?

Some geezer approaches out of nowhere. Holding an umbrella. Really recognisable. Quite a big bloke. Sort of scruffy black hair, grey streaks. Those glasses you expect to see on a computer geek. Untidy stubble, like he's just got out of bed or something. Can't pinpoint where I know him from though. Right frustrating.

He gets closer, takes out some keys.

'That's what I like to see. The lovebirds here nice and early.' He flashes a smile, which I instantly return. Seems like a really nice bloke. You know how someone smiles with their eyes? You really know they mean it. Or something.

He's the librarian geezer and he unlocks the front door. Shakes his brolly out then enters. We follow. First in line for the library on a Sunday morning. Now there's a first.

'I'll go and get things prepared in the other room for you. Give me three minutes.'

'Three. That's magic.' Tina goes.

Now life has become pretty surreal of late. I mean I watch shit loads of horror films, take acid, pills all sorts. I fuck whores, wank for hours on speed and dream about tramps in huts. All this, but you've got to say nothing is as fucked up as reality.

'I'll make some tea.' Tina says, then heads straight to a door on the right. Opens it and... bam it's the kitchen. See... weird.

* * * *

'Brooke look at this that I have.'

Trance toward the floor broken. Sloo holds the spear in two hands. Weighing its strength, determining its power. Calculating the correct *time* for its use.

'What the fuck is it?' Confusion takes root. A branch with sharp metal diamond at the helm.

'I don't know I just found it here behind you. Wonder what it's for?' Sloo takes the handle in left hand. Appearing bemused at the weapon. Mind in full conversation.

''ere, let's have a look.'

'Here you go. Take a real long close one.' Deftness of fingers. Speed of mind. Objective to catch unawares.

The weapon rams into Brooke's eye.

Crumples instantly, screaming. Clutching circumference of entrance. Lodged firm. Anguish. Terror at pain hinders removal. Blood spurts through cracks in the hand. Imitation of a distressed baby.

'What 'ave you done? What 'ave you done?' Feeble questioning.

'Stop crying like a little girl.'

Sloo clutches handful of hair. Drags unremorsefully. Brooke kicking and screaming. Horror mud slide. Led to a tree. Immense strength.

Lifted by the mane, now pinned against it. Still flailing aimlessly. Vision impaired. Streams of eye water. Desperate to clear its wound. Defeated by the extent of damage.

Right hand eventually catches Sloo's face. Uproar within the forest. Amusement at puniness.

'I need a lot worse than that. But you're not the one to perform the miracle.'

Branches zip round the captive. A role comprehended now like *Time*'s labour.

R C L I N
I Continuing loops. G
C Encompassing bondage. Shooting vigorously.
E
N Eager entrapment
C
E T S I X E
Round Encasing, enveloping, wrapping.
and The fly in the web
round. A cocoon finishing hope
Immobility come alive.

'Sloo you fucking cunt. What the fuck are you doing.' Anger and pleading mixed like demeaning Bourbon.

Blood leaked from sight's haven. Travels inner lining, seeps into saliva. Spittle arrowed at the Riverman's face. Strikes full on.

Sloo stirs with stained finger. Inspection, globule begins further descent. Interrupted; sucked clean into mouth. A lick of the lips.

'Glorious Brooke. You've got my appetite up.'

Trapped torso. An interview with insanity. Remaining vision feast upon gore. . Too desperate even for Sloo's joy.

Frenzied pleas for an end. Shrieking for release. Any alternative.

'What's all this about?' Comes face to face. '…waah, waah…' Sick mocking. Pain retracts; anger forlorn.

'…Have to stop this incessant baby talk.'

Sloo inspects the surrounding area. Grabs a handful of blood sodden leaves. Brooke intelligent to the plan. Shuts mouth tight. Attacker approaches. Claw at the ready.

'What's the matter, got nothing to say now?'

'MMM.' Mumbling, dribbling. Wise to oncoming traffic.

Bound tight, no defence of next move. Sloo's free hand takes effect. Thumb and finger clench nose. Nostrils shackled of freedom.

Lingers patiently. Can determine the trees whispers. Become transparent objects. Sloo gazes through. The River shines in full glory. No longer a small steady stream. Now large red waters swirl. Whipping foamy waves hit the bank and draw back with equal menace. The boat waits. Deafening desperate screams. Close to return. Excitable impetuousness…

Gasp Like lightning strikes. Leaves thrust between lips. Foul tasting gobstopper. A hack, spits, swallows. Morsels trapped within throat. Mouth too full to be rid of quickly. Must suffer. Savour revoking flavours.

The riverman releases the meddlesome aspect. Oral hand covering apparent. Choking. Has to start chewing to regain breath. Vomit rises. Spews onto Sloo's hand.

'Mmm I'll lick them clean.'

Edges between fingers. Drivelling pink bits.

Portray Underworld torment.

'One for the ladies eh Brook?'

Spear still locked in conference. Blood staining ethnic determination. Tied to the tree. Masticating its droppings. Gurgling with stomach rejection.

'You and Gemma make a good couple. So much in common. Immense pain.'

Mouthful reducing. Less inhabited.

Sloo doesn't desire the return of howling. Further browse of the locale. Gathers the eight inch stick. Inspects the jagged edge. Press to distinguish sharpness.

'Perfect.'

Diminishing sight. Remaining view determines no decrease of sickening futures. Sloo raises his new weapon. Points to within an inch of functional eyeball. Brooke shuts it quickly. No longer wanting witness to unfolding horror. Blindness unappeased. Imagination holding finer beauty than reality.

Gently pokes at eyelid. Wants him to see another sickening introduction. Not agreeable, so Sloo continues. Searching in close locality for a tender spot…

Suddenly a repugnant raid. Another ripe eyeball pecked of faculty. With adaptability still targeted as invoke, a heavy branch snaps above.

Sloo steps back in rhythm. Gravity brings forth a further crushing blow. Weight landing heavily on Brooke's head. Pain or unconsciousness? Something has provoked sleep.

Reproach uninhibited. Listens with ear close to the bound chest. A heart still beats. Life still afforded.

Sloo repositions. Short distancing… a moment saved for admiration.

The cocoon's head droops to the left. Saliva, blood, vomit, chewed leaves fall from open mouth. A stick protrudes from each eye. Insect antennae pressing towards fading safety. Breathing disfigured, distorted. Eerie husky spluttering. Interior choking still apparent.

Approaches once more. Seeking further mischief. Inspection proves dislodgement required. Reaches into clogged area. Grabs at small blockage and removes the cluster from Brooke's mouth. Inhalation, exhalation steadies in pattern.

Then hacks. Remaining lump freed. Slips steadily down the throat.

Choking not death's requirement. Simplicity no virtue for the assailant.

Sloo grasps a sight destroying stick. His second iris rupturing weapon of choice. Grips, twists and releases. Blood spurts from gash fountain style. The Riverman rinses his features in the spray. Stabilizes to trickle.

Brooke awake but blind to the ongoing torture. Cries for help blistered by cuts within voice mechanism. Red stains mashed eye sockets. Gurgling, bubbly mess.

Chill winds intensify. With it carries laughter. Bellowing in its encapsulation. Drowning wounded rodents.

'Brooke, Brooke, Brooke… Why the noise? Gemma didn't moan this much. Granted I did tape her mouth shut. Yet even when I drunk her vaginal blood she didn't squirm like you, worm.'

Brooke's head lower than collar bone. One sense still reflects. Thick red waves seem to crash over his being. Washing away final morsels of resistance.

'How did that taste to you by the way? I'm very interested to find out. Did you ever go down on her during a period? Even so, the flavour wouldn't be as exquisite as her secretion mingled with my spunk. That's why I had to let you experience the eighth wonder. The Bourbon disguised it I know, but it was there. You're stomach will be frenzied with delight by now. So warm and refreshing.'

Sloo's deafening laughter. Scatters squawking vertebrate. Squirrels desperate for evacuation. Rodent's legs discover entanglement. Twigs denying escape. Guffawing so terrifying. Desperate scrambling. Loss of tiny limbs, tails, heads... More squeals add to disaster.

'I love you Paul... I love you Paul... **I LOVE YOU PAUL.'**

Days of mirth bottled, released in entirety. Dams fit to burst. Shadows encroach.

'blllmwp.' Brooke's final say. Spear disconnecting nerves. No apparent logic.

Sloo calms with instant refrain.

'Suppose my words are wasted. Anyway actions speak louder.'

Still holding the stick. Deciphers next move...

Forced into cheek. Splits fleshy area. Delves deep. Licking gums. Retracts. Blow to the temple. Brooke's head sways. Beaten. More rapid jabs. Bruising instantly appearing. Continuously strikes at an ugly sore face. Little remaining room to inflict further harm.

'Be done with this. I grow weary.'

Lifts dangling head by hair. Mouth gapes for leisure. Sloo drives into the tunnel. The sharp weapon splinters through throat and neck. Connects and buries into the tree. Brooke's face pinned upright.

Branches loosen their grip. Body now freed to no avail.

'Won't be going anywhere now. Once again I bow down to your grace.'

Sloo lays his palm on the victim's chest area. Still it splutters. Tough in resistance to death. A hand mutates to the wrist. Extending bones, sharp and intimidating.

Once complete, claws begin to dig. Burrowing beneath the skin. Extent of pressure breaking ribs. Grips beating mound. A twist frees heart from arteries. Hauls the organ from its captor.

Thump, splutter, thump... ppphh. Gone. Carefully placed upon a trunk.

'Now for the toolbox.'

Removes the hacksaw. Commences in removing the boy's crown. Superior strength soon completing partial detachment. Flip top opening.

Sloo reaches like a small child into a candy jar. Chooses his favourite sweet and yanks it free.

Blood clots form the exterior. Areas lapped as an aperitif.

Before the main course is served...

THE BIBLICAL DIRECTORY
(v)

'...Another of Solomon's constructs.'

He hands me another diagram and gives me a bit of *time* to digest it. The picture displays, what looks like, one of those snow globe type things. Like when you shake it up loads of snow appears then settles on whatever's in it.

Within the globe there's a tree coming out of a mound of rocks. Surrounding this there's a long snake that twists all the way around it, until it meets its own tail. Reminds me of that snake game I had on me old Nokia.

Around the snake, more rocks circle. Against the sides there are branches which lead down to the base. This is where there's a big tree trunk with loads of littler snakes at the bottom of it. Surrounding these is all these little paths. Like one of those little mazes you do as a kid. What path should the snakes take to get to the top?

'Cause in the picture, there's one path that does. If you went up this path you'd reach this stone wall with a tunnel type entrance. Then this takes you to the tree at the top.

Simple as that.

'This tree is complicated.'

'Never!'

'Sorry Crane, but maybe if things go right; eventually you'll want to study all of its meanings.'

'I'll probably be a bit busy that day.'

'All you need to know now is about the base...' He's ignoring my intrusions now. '...This is called "Yesod", the place of the lower self. An area where our enemies Solomon, Hades, Hermes, Charon and Asmodeuos were working. The magicians always work in the lowest realm of endeavour you see? This is where the latent forces of nature are acted upon by the imagination and driven by the desires of the ego.'

This is like Sociology now. Some decent things surrounded by a whole pile of smelly bullshit.

'Practical magic is based on the concept of correspondences, the subtle fields of energy which are said to link minerals, plants and people...' I wanna go home.

'...Basically the gang, using its magic, would have the trees on their side by promising their future safety. You look after the trees and they will look after you. Magicians could then conjure the illusion that these trees can come alive through hallucinatory potions. Enforcing humans to believe that they could be constrained by such, without seeing the true cause...' Once again, basically?

'...So the year 1008 AD saw their first attempt at takeover. Charon preyed on the village that sat at the end of his river, luring six slaves from their home and murdering them one by one. Success was close at hand, but what they didn't enter into, was that our Lord always tests his adversaries. Yes he gave them a chance to take his reign, but we are talking about the Almighty here. He always has a fall back plan. Small print in any deal, if you will.

Watching the plot unfold, The Lord couldn't directly interfere. He lays down the rules and is a strict follower of them too. As you'd expect!...'

Naturally.

'...This additional clause however meant he could deliver an angel to try and indirectly influence proceedings with one human being only. As he did with Mary, if you please! He sent one of his 7 angels of the Earthly mother to the scene. Our good friend Tina here...' He points at Tina, who sits beaming and glowing.

'Man. Geez, wait a minute. 'old your 'orses. I can't get me 'ead round this one. You're an angel? I mean you are an angel, but... an angel?'

'We don't expect you to believe all this straight away Crane. We're just trying to give you a brief. This is part of God's contract and mine. Due to my own calculations I'm only allowed here on the ninth hour of theseventh day of resurrection...' He looks right smug with himself. Yet fuck knows what he's talking about.

'... God always intended that EVERYONE'S number had significance. We just have to work it out for ourselves, that's all. I only just worked mine out, literally hours before the deadline. Takes the pressure of young Tina here. She, you see, can't tell you anything. Only show you the way with her guiding beauty...'

I put me head in me hands, not for the first *time* today, then take a butch at Tina. She is wonderful. The sun's hit the side of our little room and is entering through the only window. It lights her face, like you'd expect with... with an angel. Man. Then there is no Sun. Always dark clouds outside. I've got to be tripping here.

'...but again this does not bear significance.'

'Oh man, the bits I do get, ain't ever important.'

'I'm sorry, no significance, but always relevant. So Tina's work in 1008AD came good...' He's off again '...though we do not know how one of the slaves eventually escaped the forest. There will always be mysteries you know! Charon tried in vain to catch the slave. Yet as he caught up with Cranley, he'd already reached the edge of the forest. There, the King's army waited. Fully armed and, Charon thought, a little bit much to take on. Charon evacuated the scene vowing to return. Little did he know King Ethelred the unready, gained his name for that very reason. After the event, the King went doolally and treated the escapee slave to a life of imprisonment.

Yet Charon still knew that in one thousand more years he could try again. This time they'd be wise to the angel. They're confident they have all the answers now. You see, they already have five ready made willing souls waiting in the Underworld's reincarnation booth.'

'The Underworld's reincarn whatbob?'

'So the task even easier than before...' Geezer ignores me again. '...He knows exactly how to influence them toward their fate. Yet with times a changing. He can't now just roam the forest and lure people in. He has to act on the outside. That's when the magicians learnt the art of possession. You know, through all the ways I have already explained.'

''ave ya? Must've missed that bit!' I have to rest me head. I slide down the chair and lay me neck on the top.

'No matter. I'm running out of *time,* so I cannot explain it again…' Oh darn!

'…The Underworld still lacks one soul though. That was of the escapee Robert Cranley. His is stuck somewhere that even we do not know."

'Now that name I've 'eard off. 'e's been in my dreams.'

'Yes his soul is forever running. He may find *time* to guide you too. But he is far from safe. If you fail he will become a murderous killer for Sloo's army.'

'This is one for the 'eadstrong geez. Something I am not. Fail what?"

'… It's so difficult to get this through to you in one hour Crane, so I must continue quickly. Without further interruption…' Alright keep your knickers on.

'…We have a chance with you; as you have discovered the majestic number.'

''ave I? I'm more cleverer than I thought.'

'You have heard of the trinity?'

'Err…'

'A triangle representing the trinity of deity, of time and of creation?'

'Nah mate.'

'In brief this is a symbol of togetherness. The bond you have with two friends has unleashed the power of the Magic Number.'

'Fucking hell…' Those looks again. '…Sorry.'

'You're two friends are still alive. That is what gives us hope.'

'What do you mean by that? What about me other mates? What on Earth are you going on about?' Me head's spinning here.

'They will be ok, but please Cranley listen to me, it's down to you now. Our *Time* is running out. Charon needs these two friends alive to lure you to his domain. Where he can carry out the final duty. Yet with their lives at stake; you could have the strength to bring this to an end.'

'I'm Crane and what?'

'We have future problems to deal with; the key of Solomon's seal is out and apparent on this Earth now. Any man who can decipher the key will no longer need to believe in a messiah, because he would become his own saviour. But we'll cross that bridge when we come to it. Suffice to say Armageddon is around every corner. For now this is our priority and you my friend are our only hope.'

'I don't understand all this at all. What am I supposed to do?'

'You must go to the forest.'

'What and fight The Gods of the Underworld? Are you 'aving a giggle?'

'We believe in you.' Tina joins in. I don't wanna look a wimp in front of the bird here, but;

'Why can't you go?' I say looking at the geezer, half aiming it at me bird.

'This is the extent of our help for now. If you succeed in your mission we can take it from there.'

'Oh great and 'ow am I supposed to beat this Charon dude?'

'We can say no more. You must figure this out for yourself.'

'Shall I take a blade or some'ing? Or a gun?'

'No weapon will harm Sloo within the forest.'

'What about the police? Nah you don't even 'ave to answer that one. The pricks'd 'ave a right grin if I phoned 'em with all this noise.'

'Exactly.'

'What if I just don't go then? They can't win if they ain't got me. I'll do a runner or some'ing.'

'Then your closest friends will die.'

'Oh well that's just effing marvellous. I mean fucking hell geez, sorry about the language, but you expect me to buy all this?'

'Tina could you guide him once more please?'

'Gladly.'

CHAPTER 25
CERBERUS

I come to after… I don't even know what. Tina looks into me eyes and smiles. I'm not even waking up here, so I'm gonna have to start crediting this bullshit.

The geezer's smiling away, looking all hopeful at me. Those silly little goggles, wavy black hair, thick black beard…

'You're really familiar.'

'Well. You might recognise me from such bible stories as Noah's Ark. Look here.'

Points to first column near top.

#096   Shem

'Nah not that… That's it! You're Tina's Dad.'

'Before you go Crane, one word of warning: Please beware of Charon's pet. He recently acquired it from a cloning laboratory. Goes by the name Cerberus.'

'Oh Fuck.'

'And good luck…'

I'm gonna need it.

* * * *

I need your help once again my friends. Trust in me, do not fear my request. No resentment will be laid upon you. It's all part of the plan. A small segment of your duty to me as restorer of your pride. You may feel some confusion at my requirement, yet it will all make sense.

You may think this could be a trick, but do not concern yourself; I will not turn on you. Trust me, I need you every bit as much as you need me. You must bear me with marks of violence. Scars of a recent battle, designed to convince two more into the forest. Will you please equip me with such?

A slow creaking throughout the forest. Snaps of twigs, roots humming steadily. A hesitation. Almost pondering *time.* Yet not for long. Sloo takes the brunt of a lash from a whipping finger. Cuts appear instantly on his face.

That's perfect my friends, now more.

Thorns tear through clothes. A branch snaps then drops. Lands cleanly on Sloo's nose. Bruises the protruding feature. Then another strikes. Licks straight above the eye. Scratches revealing evidence of an attack. Pain a small price for his forthcoming inheritance.

Harness Kundalini within, shrouds informal damage.

The game continues...

Sloo shows gratitude for the forest's actions. He was ready. *Time* to perform the final task. More than ready to fulfil his mission. Nothing would stand in his way.

Removes a mobile phone from his pocket.

Calling...

Moon

'Brooke are you alright geez?'

'Moon, it's Sloo. I've got his phone, we've got trouble mate.' Breathing heavily. Convinces some concern from the other end.

'What's a matter geez?'

'Brooke phoned me... Told me what happened... I went to meet him... He was insane... He's got himself involved in a fight... with five blokes... We tried to escape in the woods... That's where I lost him. I've just found his phone... but there's no sign of him... Get the others... Meet me at the entrance.'

'Sure thing. I'm there.'

Dead tone…

Sloo raises his arms toward the red sky.

'They're coming a running.'

CHAPTER 26
NIGHT OF THE LIVING END

1008 AD

Twitches...to nothing. End of Alfred Beech. Members of the audience applaud. More potion swallowed. Blood soothing throats. Dried hunger relinquished. Eyes wide. Liquid cursed. Each vein squeezed. Rhymes of death. Claret life turns to power. The courage of obliteration. No longer seeing truth. Each vision false. Like acid to its drinkers. Nothing is what it seems. Black clouds darken surroundings, flashing red affording lights of danger. Constantly flickering pictures of torture.

Within the pupils: blue skies. Sunshine.

The man just another animal carved for a feast. Limbs passed amongst the watchers. Serfs chewing on a companion. Wadard Mooning bites at fingers. Gristle and flesh drips from his chin. Hevey Little munches on calf muscle. Sloo rips and tears more from the body. Plenty to go round. Cannibalistic spells. No longer seeing fact. Roger Brooks chomps a raw toe. Adam Tilnid chooses eyeballs and testicles. Can pop either in the mouth and masticate for its flavour. The heart and brain reserved for Sloo.

Robert Cranley sits unnoticed. Holds Beech's severed arm, untouched to his lips. Confusion gorging his sight. Situation negative. This was not how it was meant to be. No longer sees illumination. Terror grips his scenario. Thunder awakens. There is no sheep at the slaughter. Only leftovers of a friend.

The next slave is summoned. Roger steps forward. Proud to be chosen. Believes drink will be poured down his throat. Lays out flat upon a row of three tree trunks. Sloo hovers. Little looks towards Cranley. Raises his potion, attempts to encourage. Urges him to drink... to feast.

Cranley perturbed. Ignores pier pressure, continues to observe. Fear forever rising. The knife raised high...

'Do you obey me Roger Brooks?'

'Yes of course Master.'

...Comes crashing down. Piercing the heart. Instant devaluation of humanity. No respect for God-given life. Death was Sloo's habitat. Leading his voyage to Earth. Destroy the living. Govern the dead.

More limbs torn from a convulsing body. Dark red wine wasted to the floor. Tilnid quickly to his knees. Drinks from the spraying fountain of Brooks.

Legs shake, jolt uncontrollably. Cranley still refusing to dine.

Jubilation. Buoyancy shrouds the rest. Noises of mirth drown doubt. Sloo mastering his trade. Disciples rejoice at the homicide. Each believing in its justification. A ritual to heal them.

Reality proves a serpent hacks them apart.

Butcher begins to lack concentration. All seems too easy. Wasn't aware of Cranley's earlier vision. A shining light invoking realization. One disciple broken from his gore induced trance.

Awareness of destruction. Distinguishing the horror.

This was no longer salvation. This was their genocide.

Cranley trembles. Voices provoke escape.

Sloo glories in triumph. Blood splatters his cloak . His remaining followers bow at his feet. Faces sprayed with their friends innards.

Cackling spreads through the trees. Some uproot. Arms folding. The now nightly warning roar. A River hones into view. A distant blackened boat appears through the mist. Everything wild and uneven. Honour for the Riverman. His passengers were returning to Earth. Takeover imminent. Sloo would Reign. .

Adam Tilnid still bows. Kissing the webbed green talon of his Lord.

'Do you obey me Adam Tilnid?'

‘Yes master.’

Swift arms. Strength prevailing. Blade slices the throat.

Little tries to drag Cranley into the celebration. Bloodbath with organs as foam. The most important saved by the slaughterer; three hearts and three brains. All given willingly. Halfway to the shadowy invasion. Course of rampage. Rain soaks the locale. Clouds thicken across the sky. The World as one under a deluge of darkness.

Sensing opposition. This lack of obedience means treason. What was happening here? Why did his friend not smile? Not dance? Not eat the freshly cut slabs of his friend’s bodies....

Grimaces rip through the scene like lightning. Sloo commences his own feast. Chews on vital organs. Ripping muscle from muscle. Mingles the succulence of three humans.

Orders Wadard Mooning to the podium.

Cranley stands. This was his very close friend. What was Sloo doing? They trusted him. A Saviour that now removed their very being. Could see it clearly now. Desperate to shout for it all to end. Lost the ability of speech. Forgotten the required words. Cursed blood had drowned his memory. Clouded his sensibilities. That light. An angel from above?

Must run Robert Cranley. Nothing you can do, except flee. Cannot tackle this beast. Run and don’t stop. Little reaches out to stop him. Misses, focus shattered. Cranley leaps into the darkness.

‘Do you obey me Wadard Mooning?’

‘Yes Master.’

Hair clasped in claw. Spear points at eyeball. Delving inside. Pupils spray like snake’s venom. Vessels explode. Visions of reality disappeared long ago. Pain no more. Brain skewering a refreshing relief. Raw meat.

Sloo sniffs at his next dish. Smelling the fresh food of thought. Sucks in the slimy plasma. Wonderful sensation upon the taste buds.

Little rocks back and forth. Watches Mooning crumble to the floor. Deflated, shrunken head. Hair on skin.

Cranley edges further from the sickening scene. Picks up the pace. A Chorus of bells sounds the route. Beckoning him toward safety.

Shadows topple from the docking boat. Four brains, four hearts. Deafening commotion. Sloo believes it’s all but over. Victorious against his creator. Doesn't bother to inspect his devotees. An omission goes by unnoticed.

Gnawing the thumping from the arteries. Blood showering vision. Dark clouds spewing claret. Body parts pile high. The river rushing. Flowing toward Earth. Banks begin to burst.

Hevey Little being commanded forward. Caught in two minds. Cannot disobey now. Fresh life within him. Hallucinatory liquid distorting intelligence. Approaches the towering reptilian.

Thorns of metal evicting the spine. Torn brown cloak lightly covering scales. Forked tongue shoots from the mouth. Curling, gesturing for Little's approach. Eyes sunken and red. Slits for pupils. Hypnotizing the slave. Willing him to kneel before the King. Under uncontrollable pressure.

'Do you obey me Hevey Little?'

'Yes my master.'

Sloo looks upon the bowed crown. Raises his knife. Looks forward for seal of approval. No one is there. Fierce panic, anger eruption. Down comes the slashing cutter. In through another's scalp.

Instant discharge from existence. Another body crumpled on the filth. Heart and brain swallowed whole. No *time* for pleasure. Other matters for Sloo to deal with. One has run.

Charon cries to the Underworld…

A giant serpent creeps fast. Head swaying from side to side. Peering into the darkness. A glowing light appears amongst the trees. Stalks past all obstacles. Striding through his desired home. The river ceasing to surge.

A halt to proceedings. Souls starting to drown. The tide's turn will shift. Water has to steady for its journey back. To the other side. Spirits can remain as intended.

Existence can flow for now...

Cranley shepherded through the trees. The light shines. Relieving him of rumination. Roots directed to freeze. No attempt to upend the escapee. The brightness also breeding fear. He that cares should not be tested.

Sloo stalks. Aching, tongue lashing. Knife gripped firmly. His toys no longer point the way. Scorn would pour over this forest from now. A thousand years time, hardly any trees would still stand. Houses erected. Modernity. Some would still stand proud. A guard for the River's end.

The Riverman could be halted, but not destroyed. He had a job to do. Doesn't want to return to this labour. Wants Cranley. Needs his committal to complete. One more given heart and brain to reign supreme. Retire his boat for everlasting docking. Has to catch him.

Illumination in the distance, a burning glow. A haven. Torches signalling a chance. A shrill command close behind. Sloo furious.

'Return to me Cranley. I order you. I can save you. Listen to me.'

So tempted. Visions of death and destruction plague the opening he requires for salvation. Must deny them. Still the senses diseased by vast intake of blood and flesh.

Must remember this, hears the voices:

'Drugs paranoia Crane, drugs paranoia.'

Cranley turns and shouts at the passing figure. Does he hear the message?

Sees a burning village. Torched humans flailing in pain.

'That's your future Cranley. Return to me I can save you from this torture.'

Nothing is what it seems.

The King stands amongst jerking bodies. Spasms from their dismemberment.

Injured. Screaming. Howling in agony. The choir of Hell.

'That's your King, Cranley. This is his craving. Return to me.'

So tempted to turn back. The reality of the forest like paradise to the shocking visions he aims for.

Remembers seeing Mooning. His brain on a spike.

'Drugs paranoia. This ain't happening.' Coming from behind the trees. Growing faint.

The reptile closes in. A staggered run, shouts of encouragement. Remembers the shocking images. Each one that clouded his life draws together as one.

Immunity to the bloodshed and gore.

Zombies ripping jugulars. Slaughtered girls ripped across a hallway. Eyeballs swallowed. Cannibals munching on fellow man. Penises scythed. Wheelchair ridden humans pick-axed.

Nothing can stop him.

'It's all the drugs. All the drugs.'

Nearing the exit. One last scream.

'Return to me.'

The crowds waiting. Burning torches ready to fight the creature. The King's reinforcements had arrived. Six lost serfs. All the cattle and animals slaughtered in one village. An army assembled to destroy that which preyed on their existence.

Ready and waiting for Sloo.

Cranley makes it. He jumps the threshold.

Disappears into the future forest.

Safe for now.

The army prepares to charge. Sloo stands immobile. The tide had turned back. His chance diminished. Knows there will be another.

The River Styx will always return.

Would have to bide his *time*.

The reptilian Sloo lifts his face to the sky. Screams with deafening laughter. Every living creature within the trees crashes to its end. Wings flap once then no longer work. Beetles, worms, ants secrete from the ground. Turn over on their backs and lay motionless.

Nothing survives the evil within the forest.

Sloo's chilling message strikes terror deep into the villager's hearts and minds:

'I will return and you will all become my army of the dead.'

Black of night…

CHAPTER 27
BACK TO MY ROOTS

Tyres screech. The car swerves the corner into **RIVER DRIVE**

Travels three hundred yards before pulling in to the left. About ten yards from the wood's entrance.

Sloo waits just within.

Organised portrait. Stands clutching damaged nose. Blood trickles from the area.

Moon and Leg pounce from the vehicle, slamming its doors upon exit. Jog over to the wounded.

'Sloo are you alright man?' Moon arrives first and lays a hand upon his friend's shoulder. Littl' Leg trails seconds behind.

Sloo removes his facial covering. Reveals full extent of his injuries.

'Oh fuck man. Who did this?' Leg furious. Angrily looks across for a person to blame. Clenched fists. Seeking imaginary assailants. One disaster too many this weekend.

Sloo alters character via pure grace.

'I don't even know who they are mate…' Pauses between sentences to animate breathlessness. '…When I got to Brooke 'e was outta control… 'aving a right pop at these five blokes... Blaming them for what 'appened… They didn't know what 'e was on about 'cause the boy was babbling… They started 'itting out man… I tried to stop it all… but I caught a nasty one on me 'ooter… Knocked me for a bit... Next thing, I come to… the lot of 'em were chasing Brooke… in 'ere... I run in after 'em… but they were too far ahead… Then I lost 'em completely… I come across 'is phone… and that was that… No fucking sign... Couldn't find 'em anywhere… Sorry Lads.'

Feigns downcast expression at his failure to protect. The Sloo of old shining through. The caring leader to his close friends.

'Shit. Bastards! … Look it ain't your fault Sloo. You tried mate.' Moon calms his shaking friend.

'Yeah geez we know you'd of tried your best...' Leg Confirms, before renewing his attention upon Brooke's attackers '…Those mother fuckers. If they've 'urt 'im, I'll fucking kill the lot of 'em.' An anger rises above control.

''ad to call you boys. I wouldn't be able to take 'em on me own. Where's Lid and Crane?' Sloo plays his part with professionalism.

'Fuck knows. Both got their mobiles off.' Leg answers still seething. Venom poised behind gritted teeth.

'Fuck that anyway, let's get in there and 'ave 'em.' Moon's pent up paranoia yearns for release.

'Yeah come on. You alright to go Sloo?'

'Of course mate... I'm leading too… I know what direction they went.' Effortlessly shifts into steady breathing. More running imminent.

'Alright man, we're following you.' Leg states.

'Good 'cause I gotta plan when we see 'em. Don't wanna just go steaming in, there's a couple of 'efty geezers in their crew.'

'Alright mate, I'll do whatever you say.' Leg replies.

'You promise geez? Anything I say you'll follow? Moon, you too?' Sloo pushes his pawns forward.

'Definitely geez. I'm following ya son.' Moon complies

'We promise mate. Now come on let's go fucking get 'em.' The other folds from within.

* * * *

On our way out the library I'm shell-shocked. Finding all this a tad difficult to swallow.

Tina's holding me hand, trying to console me. I can't believe what's happening. If indeed it actually is...in Upminster? Not sure of anything anymore. This could just be a mammoth wind up. It's gotta be.

But when Tina kissed me… those visions?

This has to be the drugs.

‘Are you ok sweetheart?’ She’s asking

‘Well I’ve definitely felt better love. I just don’t get it.’

‘You will go though?’ Almost pleading me. We’re stopped under the porch cover again. I look at Tina. There’s that smile. So amazing. Makes me wanna do anything for her.

‘Yeah I’ll go, but what am I supposed to do when I get there? Ask this ancient serpent geezer to please stop ‘urting my friends or something?’

‘You will understand what is required when the situation arrives.’

`ow though?’ Just wanna few answers here. Is that too much to ask?

‘I’m sorry babe. As Shem stated; we cannot disclose that information. It’s all part of God’s plan.’ She starts clinging to me chest again. So I wrap me arms round her.

Cuddling against the incoming rain. Trying to comprehend.

An angel? Fuck me ragged! Angels and whores. Now there’s your oxymoron. Who said I was wasting my time in college?

‘God’s plan sounds fucked to me. I mean sorry if you’re an angel and all that, but what was ‘e thinking?’

‘Drugs don’t just exist on Earth you know Steven!’ She says a little angrily. At least I’m finding me boundaries.

‘Well that does explain a lot I suppose…’ Get to have a little laugh before this doubtlessly turns to misery. ‘…So you can’t come with me? Ain’t you got special powers or something?’

‘It’s not a possibility I’m afraid darling, but you’ll feel my presence nearby. I promise you that.’

‘`ow we supposed to get there?’

‘I’ll walk you.’

‘What in this rain? We’ll be drowned by the time we make it.’

‘Sorry my love, but that’s the least of our worries.’

‘Oh cheers! That really inspires me.’ I don’t mean this all nasty or nothing, but that ain’t what I need to hear right now. She stops our clinch and looks up at me. Bollocks I’m in trouble now. Instead

‘I’m sorry sweetheart.’ She goes, then rises on tiptoes and plants a huge kiss on me lips.

Like you wouldn’t believe…

‘Come on then. Let’s get this over with.’

I can't believe how weak I am. Soon as a bird shows a bit of interest in me; I'm bending over backwards to please 'em.

The first bird that comes along and tells me they love me? I'm agreeing to go to the woods to save me two best friends from a maniac serpent.

Moon was right. I am easily pussy whipped.

* * * *

Sloo leads the search party deeper into the forest. As they run toward the centre, uneasiness transpires within his followers. Looking around nervously under a clouding density. The enormity of the trees. Never remembered it being this huge. This daunting.

...Suddenly they hear a crack up ahead. Quickly followed by some short sharp shouts.

Could be them? It forces Sloo to slow... then stop. He raises a hand as he does so, signalling those behind to follow suit. Littl' Leg and Moon obey...

Halcyon reigns now. The companions frozen to their spot. Initial anger replaced by wariness.

Sloo stands still, just in front. His back to the pair.

Thus begins the travesty:

'Lads you're never gonna believe this.'

'What's wrong?' Leg asks.

'I've only gone and turned into the geez!' Sloo states.

'What?'

Delirium grabs hold. Sloo turns to face them.

Moon and Leg look upon him. Or what was supposed to be Sloo. The pair stand motionless, now in complete shock.

As they stand face to face with their drug dealer...

A lightning bolt rips through the scene. Agility on display. The geez grabs both of their heads and slams them hard together. With no *time* for the disciples to resist, their lights go out. Calculated enough power to send them both tumbling unconscious to the floor.

* * * *

We stand at the foot of **RIVER DRIVE** Right at the two poles that mark the entrance to these woods. It brings back so many memories. That day when we all came down here on our bikes. To set up this pocsy Styx gang.

The Styx. That's it! Why didn't I think of this a bit ago? That must have been the beginning.

'You sure I can't take a gun?'

'Believe me honey, you do not want to offend this being. It's nigh on impossible to harm him with any weapon, well nothing we have to hand anyway. You must use your brain.'

'Oh! Well then I don't stand a fucking Morris dance in there then.'

'You will do this Crane. I believe in you. Trust in you. There's a strong loving soul in there...' She points at me little pot belly. '...You'll do anything for your friends and that *Time* is now.' She leans up and gives me another blisteringly mind-altering snog.

Scrambling my brains like they all do. Fucking angels or not.

I'm up for the battle now, but know this feeling will soon wear off. Probably as soon as I step in there on me Jack.

"ere goes then. When will I see you again?'

'Once you get out, and I promise you will. I'll be right with you.'

'Ok.'

I step through the entrance, turn to say my goodbyes, but she's gone. Unbelievable.

Keep thinking everyone's gonna jump out and shout 'surprise'... any minute now... But that's growing increasingly doubtful. They'd have to have pulled off some fucking awesome trickery for this prank.

Then "I love you" fills my surrounding skies.

Well let's do this Crane.

CAMP STYX EXPECTS

I begin my journey through sparse bare trees. Winters ravaged; and this crap early spring ain't helped 'em flower either. I can't believe all this end of the world stuff could be going on in here. It's only a small woo...

Hear this shriek. This awful cry. Almost jump and run straight back out again. Hold still... Someone shouting: '**Return to me**'.

I'm fucking shitting it.

'This is all drugs paranoia Crane, drugs paranoia.' Keep telling meself this. Hear rustling to the left of me. Turn to see.

About ten feet away the geezer from me dreams is running, no, staggering toward the exit. The one that looks like me, but wears all the ragged clothes. Cranberry, I think? Then he turns to me and shouts:

'We never hurt the trees. We never touched the trees.'

'Drugs paranoia. This ain't 'appening.' I run forward and stand behind a tree. Shield meself. Close me eyes. Still hear the screaming. Loads of commotion going off.

'It's just the drugs, it's all the drugs.'

Count to ten...

Open them. Peer back to the scene.

He's gone. Nothing there at all. Disappeared. No more wailing or weirdoes. Just me on me own in the woods.

Thank God... Sort of.

What was that about the trees? "We never hurt the trees". It's not the trees I was that scared about. More the giant reptile intent on murdering me.

Set off again. Away from the beginning of something truly fucked...

Deeper...

It's mad 'cause I swear this place's grown since I last come here. Would have thought with me getting bigger, it would have looked smaller. Massive old looking trees. Towering right above me. It's more like a shafting forest man.

I'm shaking. The further I go, the darker it becomes. The more spooky. The more I notice the silence. The more I'm thinking I definitely don't wanna be in here. I never would have ever imagined this was how my life was gonna end up. And I've left me fucking mobile at home. Dickhead!

Although me heart's beating like an epileptic drummer and my nerves are shot to shit; a lot of things become clearer.

Sloo's fucked up behaviour, all those commandment bollocks, the dreams everyone had... All of my dreams too, come to think of it.

All the fucked up acids... so many things. This was what it was all about. Everything links. It always fucking does.

It's fast becoming my own horror movie. I'm the main man. The geezer that's gotta save the day. The Bruce Campbell of fucking

Upminster. I don't know what I'm expecting to find in here, but this idea's renewed the spring in me step. I'm the geezer who don't die. The man that gets the girl in the end. I'm gonna pull this off…

Unless this is like *Cannibal Holocaust* and everyone dies of course. Oh Jesus Crane. For one moment there this was happening. Now you go and think of that. Bollocks.

The ground feels slimy as I trudge between the trees. But I ain't felt the rain in ages. Look down and see I'm slipping through a layer of blood.

'Oh fucking 'ell.'

I jump out to one side and look back at it. Gone. Vanished. Almost as quick as Cranberry had.

That's all it probably was, Cranberry sauce. Drugs paranoia. Nothing is what it seems.

Eyes roll back in my skull. Overwhelming pleasure. Can't stop my body from moving. Ecstasy's reaming. What a place to be. Love to love. A journey full of visual delight. Delirium interchanges with perceptiveness. This is where I want to be. Floating forwards, feel the gentle pressure easing me. A faint light ahead. Must follow, be guided towards beauty. Every touch tingles. My spine shakes. Legs vibrate. Cold ice showers on red hot days. Tentative no more. The illuminations increase. Not blinding, but so strong. Encompassing me. Pulling me in toward all of eternity's desires. Exterior warmth. Interior chills. Combine as one. To lift me higher and inward. Outwards and downwards. Being swivelled and spun. Disorientation grinding the gears. But what a feeling, what a switch. Want this to be my final voyage. End in the place where all humans seek.

My head turns on its axis. Hands grabbing but not taking hold. Passion overcomes me. Wherever I'm headed it will be a safe haven… eventually. Though I know confusing. Understand it will take *time* to settle. It's warmth that draws me nearer. Safety will loom. Remember this feeling. Understand it. For once take it with me and no longer be afraid. The change is coming. The lights shine brighter. Arriving there soon. Will stay.

Come on, believe. Trust in this venture. Experience the friendly people. So many. Delight here. I know not why, yet someone is telling me: this is the place to be. Always wanted to remain here. You are lucky, for where I am makes no sense to me. Have faith in it. Carry on. You're almost there. Take it with you. Grab it desperately. Bring it forward. With this you will succeed. You can do it.

Holding anxiously. No release. Please don't let it go. Pleeeeaa aaasssssssseeeeeeeee

NNNNNNNNNNNNNNNOOOOOOOOOOOOO

Where am I? It petrifies me.

I look back at how far I've come. Although it only feels like I've been walking a couple of minutes, it seems like I'm in well deep. Nothing looks the same back there. None of the sparse dead trees I remember at the start. All of it looks massive now. Trees reaching up to… I don't know a hundred feet. If that's possible? Greenery like a jungle too. These trees were bare a moment ago.

* * * *

Focus returning. Blurred watery visions of surrounding wildlife. Coming round to the headache. Temples sore. Wants to rub better. Cannot move his arms. Littl' leg struggles to free himself. Panic... Terror… Attempts to shout. A gag muffles his cries. A fist lands squarely on his face…

Collecting Moon's little sister from his Gran's. Pushing the pram up Upminster Road. Past the Bridge House, onwards. On to the bridge. Stop. Me and him discussing what it must have been like a thousand years before. Look over the edge. The stream is flowing quickly. Blood replaces water. Trees either side reaching up to the sky. Highest branches must touch the clouds. Swaying in the strong breeze. Black clouds expand above. Swamp our senses. Darkness falls.

Peer into the pram. Woodlice scamper over the baby's face. Crawling into her screaming mouth. Don't know what to do. Scared. Moon has disappeared. I hear a distant ice cream van. Slowed version of the Teddy bears picnic. Hairs on arms and neck stand on end.

Find myself on the rivers edge. Dark red waters carrying floating fish out to the Thames. A dead whale looks toward me. Vacant eyes. Pleading freedom.

Find a black bag washed up on the shore. Thin brown rope ties in the contents. Curiosity overcomes me. Must look inside. Rain batters down upon my head. More extreme than history.

Untie the knot. Put my hand inside. Pull out a small bag of sweets. Reach inside again, this time retrieve a five pound note. Once more delve deep. Handful of cards. Remove football stickers. This is a bag of delights. Eagerly grab for more. This time I take hold of a box. The bag disintegrates around it. Dust falling to the sand.

The box is the size of a playstation. Red roses pattern the black exterior. A small gold latch. Flip it up and lift the lid. Caution resounding.

Empty. Glass bottom. Clear, then the faces appear. Tortured, bruised. Pushing profiles into cling film . Break through the entrapment. Souls captured and abused for centuries. Drop it to the ground. No longer the beach. Now a large forest. I feel lost. Encapsulated by danger. Evil watches me from everywhere.

Shut my eyes. Need happier memories.

Playing football with my friends. Clubbing holidays. Acid barbecues. No one single visual. Each one fades to obscurity as soon as they arrive.

Gone…

Nothing exists beyond the vicinity of this forest. Azilut, where it all began.

School teachers line up facing me. Slavery. The labour work force demeaning my survival. Distraught recaps mixing the dead. Impossible visions to shift. Push aside the veil. My hideous wife. Do not want to kiss.

If only it could be burnt to the ground. Nothing could then occur. The pain would end. No more chasing. For eternity. Escape from existence.

It begins again.

* * * *

I'm stopped still, having a breather. The blood pool's freaked me out. Wishing that I fucking well smoked or something. Or that I brought a reefer with me. Weapons are no good, but a blifter might help steady me. At least…

Hang about. These are the trackies I had on after *Time.* I decided to pocket that half a reefer instead of finishing it. 'Cause I was a bit too fucked; and didn't want the others to know I couldn't cope. Reach in me sky and… beautiful. Lighter too.

Crane, you think of everything.

Some might think "if I was in your situation, I wouldn't start puffing dude." But believe, if I keep seeing madmen shouting about trees; then at least I can bang it down to one of Moon's packed skunk reefers.

Drugs paranoia: you was always gonna have a part to play. Man I mean this day can't get any weirder.

Stick the Bob Marley in me mouth and light the fucker. Massive inhale. That's the one…

Breathe out thick smoke. Nerve-steadier any day of the week. I stand and appreciate this unexpected welcome break. Calm before the storm; or some shit.

As I toke I can hear the distant flowing of water. In fact quite loud. I know the Ingrebourne Brook's near here, but that's just a piddling little stream. This sounds like a proper…

Now it dawns on me. That's probably the fucking River everybody's been harping on about. The River Styx. This is totally fucked up…

I best restart this journey. Get it over and done with. Still got the reefer on the go. Might as well give meself something to do, whilst I delve into the Underworld.

Will you ever learn Crane?

Arms raised. Whistling. Crowd cheers. Music almost lifting the ceiling.

'*Sometimes I feel like throwing my hands up in the air.*' Amazing feeling. Ecstasy pumping.

'*I know I can count on you.*' The lights flashing. People smiling. Glowing white teeth. Beaming from ear to ear.

'*Sometimes I feel like saying Lord I just don't care.*' Dancing, jumping, arms flailing. Everyone going for it. Long hair swaying. Sweat spraying my face. Refreshing. Cooling.

'*But you got the love I need to see me through.*' Buzzing. Ringing inside my head. Out through my ears. Spine tingling. Rushing. Never experienced anything like it. Awash with emotion.

'*You got the love.*' Wanna hug everyone. Feel their warmth. Encounter the energy. Everything pumps up. Spirits loving all as one. We're together.

'*You got the love.*' Now this is a magic potion. Don't want the joy to end.

Leave me here forever.

I can't get out.

Decide I should follow the sound of the water. That's where the party's at.

I'd imagine.

These trees are a fucking menace. Trunks pretty close together makes it hard to get through. With the size of the bastards up there, you wouldn't think they'd all be able to fit. But they're the long, wispy, scary models. Figures! Well twisted. Those weird holes some trees have in the middle. They've all got 'em here. Makes 'em look like they're screaming at me. Tad unsettling

Footsteps nearby... Children giggling just behind me.

Stops me once again. I twist round and see... see...

It's us.

When we were eight. The boys walking through to the camp. Sloo up in front. We're near behind giggling. Probably all taking the piss behind his back. So he wouldn't hear.

Weird shit or nothing? That's a soothing sight for anyone to see. Makes me confident I'm heading in the right direction. Wherever that is? I hide behind a tree, waiting for them to pass. Dunno whether they'd see me anyway, but I won't chance scaring 'em. Could have some serious repercussions. I've seen *The Butterfly Effect.*

They move further ahead. Laughing, trampling over twigs and through the mud. As happy as Larry.

I'll follow 'em. The boys. God it's amazing to watch. There's fat little Tin Lid; and look at the size of Leg there. Well tiny man. Moon with "is big round 'ead". That was well funny. I can't see me though. I'd definitely…

A twig snaps. Killing me enjoyment as quick as… I look behind. Over to the right I think it came. Can't see anything. So many trees, so little to...

Then I see it…

This vision ain't so pleasant at all. A deformed jester gazes round a tree at me. His face is all fucked. Long and grey. Big pointy forehead and chin. Warty nose. Nasty looking fucker. That weird three pointed hat with the bells. Straight out of Punch and Judy; or the *Elephant man.*

He strides out from his hiding place. Long stocking legs don't measure up right with the rest of him. Holding a big caveman style club. Staring right into me eyes. Ready to inflict some damage on me skull. No doubt. Looks well fucking pissed off.

A horrible chill runs right through me. Gotta evacuate these premises.

I turn round to yell and run after the boys... But they've gone. Swivel back to the jester. Make sure he ain't creeping up on me...

Instead identical twin daughters are stood there. All of five yards away. Straight out of the fucking *Shining.* The most frightening little kids on the planet. Here they are in real life. Those doll-like plastic features. The red chequered dresses. Pupils missing from their eyes.

'Come play with us Steven. Forever… and ever… and ever.' Their lips don't move as they speak. I know what comes next…

I definitely ain't up for this. There's nothing that scares me more.

Must move. Quick.

Heart fucking pounding. Breathless, but adrenaline carries me forward. Maybe the reefer weren't so good after all. Darting through the trees. The sound of water getting real loud…

Further I go, deeper into the forest. Darkness grows. Silence, except for my heavy breathing.

Suddenly someone shouts behind. Don't wanna turn, but got to. Sounds like someone in distress.

Instead I'm faced with Brooke. He's beyond distress. His eyes have been poked out, blood pouring from the sockets. He's about ten yards away. Staggering toward me with his arms outstretched. Looks so beat up. Most of his hair's ripped out. Leaves falling out of his mouth. Unrecognisable as the geezer we know and love. I feel distraught for him. Wanna just burst out in tears, but how would that help?

Then I notice the big hole in his chest where his heart should be. Wanna help me mate, but he scares me too much. Confused. Caught in two... He's getting closer... Don't want him to touch me.

Spring like a fucking whippet.

Sprinting now.

Drugs paranoia Crane.

Noise to the left. A small Imp holding a blood soaked feather skips past. Wearing a top hat and old Victorian type outfit. A cat nips in between his legs.

Gotta keep running. But this imp thing's got this hypnotic pull over me. I can't see where I'm headed... Just for the strengthening sound of the River...

I trip over something and go crashing...

BANG

If someone don't get those folders out the washing machine, the fucker's never gonna work. I know me bird's in the garden chatting to some other geezer, but there's a far more pressing matter to attend to here. This is gonna flood the kitchen. Still that's hilarious, who in their right mind would put folders in this thing? It's well funny. I need to find somewhere I can let this humour out. How about right here in amongst this dog hair? Perfick...

BANG... Right in the mud, caked in the shit now. All down me clothes, over me face and everything. Mother Fucker. I manoeuvre on the floor. See what I tripped on. It's a crushed body. A layer of flat skin lying next to its innards. Like a deflated dinghy. There's a horrible squashed face in amongst it. Looking scornfully at me. It looks like... like...

Oh man it's Tin Lid.

'AAAAAAAAAAAAAAAAARRRRRRRRrrrrrrrrgggggggg ggggggghhhhhhh'

Fuck me gotta get out of here. Scramble up and get on me Bromley's. Linford Christie style.

Right self conscious of me scream. Like it's drawn a presence towards me. They know I'm here now. Whoever they are? I'm sure of it. I'm frightened, but coping.

Determination rising within. I've come this far. Wanting revenge for having to endure seeing me mates like this. Don't even know if any of 'em are real. Course they're not Crane. It's the drugs.

Water crashing heavily. Like a waterfall meeting the next stream.

Must be close. Running in and out of trees. Dodging 'em like an American footballer.

Now I'm getting deeper in, darker. Gloom sets over me. That nightmare moment. More noises jolt my senses…

To my right this *time*. I swivel to see. Know I shouldn't, but have to find out what's there. Used to this horror.

It's Beeke. He looks alright. Coming towards me.

'Beeke, thank fuck. Are you alright mate?'

He don't answer, just edges closer.

As I look at him, waiting for a reply, his face literally falls open. His brain shoots out at me like a fucking cuckoo from a clock. But this keeps coming… Coming towards me… Shit.

SMACK…

''ere leg come over 'ere. Is that Crane?'

'Where?'

'Through there. Over by the bar.'

'Fuck, look at 'im. 'e's well mashed. What the fuck's 'appened to 'is clothes?'

'These acid's are well fucked up man. 'e must be out of 'is nut.'

'Where's 'e even going?'

'Dunno Moon, looks like 'e's just trying to find a way out of 'ere. That's well funny.'

'Aaaaah ha. Mint.'

'Come on we better go over and 'elp 'im.'

This James Blunt song sounds wicked after you've snogged an angel. Wandering over the park. In the rain. Don't give a fuck, 'cause tonight's been awesome. First dates never normally go this... Eh? There's Sloo

'Sloo, what's 'appening?'

'Crane, are you drunk?'

'Yeah I'm battered.'

'Good, 'cause you ain't seen me.'

I start coming to. Foul stench in the air. Where am I? Fuck. I sit up quick. Middle of the fucking woods. No, forest. Shitting arseholes. Getting well dark... and that stink. Like...well I know exactly what it's like somehow; rotting bodies.

A queue of the dead all lined up a little way ahead of me. I reckon I know exactly where it's headed too.

I pick meself up, brush me clothes down. As best I can. Decide I can stroll a bit.

Keeping a fair distance away from the standing corpses. Ducking in behind trees. Nip from one to the next. Make sure they don't spot me; and do a zombie act on me or something. They don't look interested in anything though. Apart from what's happening up front anyway. They're all looking forward in desperation. All like they're stood in the line of a nightclub. Hoping they don't get turned away.

'Too full mate. One in one out.'

They're all holding their arms outstretched. Clasping a coin, thrusting it forward. Like they're at the bar or something.

Fucking mad... I'm hiding, guarded, watching... Something hits me hard on the back o...

BOOM

From trees and serpents to this: People everywhere. The sounds of heavenly bells now turned to thumping hideous banging. Singing sounds like the screaming of he that chases me.

My bright shining light, to strobes of green... blue... green... blue.

How they dress in this room.

'By the grace of God'... Women wearing next to nothing. That should never be allowed. Everyone drinks from transparent jugs. Fluids almost floating.

What's wrong with their hair? I want away from here. He may find me.

Two men approaching me. These have no mane. Warnings. They look like they've drunk the potion. How do I escape?

BANG

Where have all me mates gone? I can't see 'em anywhere. The middle of this strange country, just wandering the streets. Wonder if these two will help me? They look like a nice couple.

'Please... I've lost me mates, do you know where I am?' I've turned all Oliver Twist of a sudden.

They giggle. Tell me to take a seat outside a bar with 'em.

'Alright mate. This is Ibiza. I'm Andy and this is Rachel'...

BANG

I'm laying on me back. Looking up as a truck load of birds fly up from the branches. Up and away...evacuating the scene, just like I want to. Haven't the foggiest what just hit me. Don't wanna know either. Let's face it, it ain't gonna be good.

Pick meself from the floor again. Covered. Looking like a swamp monster. Hoping I'm gonna scare the Riverman with my appearance, more than his is bound to terrify me.

For once my earlier vision remains. The front of the ghost queue is in sight...

And a boat...

Fucking Nora. Huge ugly thing. Two decks high. A flag waves at the top. Red streak of lightning upon a white background. It's like a ghost pirate ship. Black all over. Everything about it reeks of filth. Decapitated people waving from the top deck. As if they're just arriving home for a big headless family reunion.

There's small portholes along the side. Shadows twitch and shake. Some bang their heads on the glass 'til their heads crack open and smear the windows with blood...

Then the river it sits on. It's fucking humungous. How did I miss it before? Massive red piles of water. As I stare upon it, mouth wide open, it seems to be growing in stature. Coming this way. Filling up the horizon. Tidal wave style. Appears to be forever flowing, but remains in the same daunting position. Like in a picture. Looks so close, but can't be. It would drown us in no *time* if it were.

I would never ever believe I'd ever…

Someone calls me.

I turn round. Can't see anything away from the glowing of the river. Puts everything else in darkness. Take a few steps forward. Then walk smack…

BANG

The girl's been sick over her top. She's well gone and takes it off right in front of me. Got no bra on or nothing. Here she is; Louise's mate, baps out. We're in an empty room, but I can't be arsed to try anything on. I've seen the commotion next door. Those little fellas are having a right good boogie. I ain't missing that for the world.

This place so filled. Can't find a way through. They laugh at me. Need to exit. There appears to be none.

BANG

All too familiar feeling of consciousness returning. The river's still poised. Light's better now. It's creating a substantial glow about me. So I can see what I walked into. A massive billboard. Like you get in America when you enter a town.

It reads:

WELCOME TO AZILUT

The Divine World of Emanation

(A dimension beyond *Time* and Space,
the unchanging realm of Eternity)
Population: ?

I hear a dog bark. Rapid scary yelps.

'Crane, over here.'

I jump, hand on me heart. Steady it, dunno how much longer it's gonna hold up. Look to the left… There they are…

It's Sloo that's called me. There's the boys too. Shit. They're on their arses, legs stretched in front of 'em. Their upper bodies strapped to trees with their mouths gagged. They're looking pretty bashed up. But they're alive and awake.

To see them like this makes it all the more real. But I ain't nowhere near as scared as I thought I'd be. I'm still sure this is all one major acid trip. I'll come round soon. So now I'm gonna explore. I'm probably lost, but we always come back.

Moon the other night. Thought he was well gone. That's where I probably am now. Sat in a nice armchair, drooling. Me mates all worried.

'I'm alright lads. I'll be back soon. Just gotta save ya from this serpent.' That should freak 'em out.

But Sloo ain't the serpent I was expecting. He's just… just me mate Sloo, with a dark grey cloak on. Hood down. That's not the way son. Be proud of your hoody!

He's down on one knee right next to Moon and Leg. Sharpening a knife; for fuck sake ref. But I ain't afraid of Sloo, gives it all the leader bollocks, but I reckon I can take him.

I'm getting close to the prize and…

Sloo stands then approaches me. Clench me fists. He gets to about five yards away and stops. Directly facing me.

We're like cowboys ready to draw.

'Don't fret Crane. Come in…' He beckons then turns waving for me to follow.

Suddenly rags hang from the branches above. Appearing like curtains as an entrance for our old camp.

Sloo pushes them aside like an annoying flurry of gnats and enters our old hangout. I follow a short distance behind. Poised for a surprise attack.

Camp Styx looks so much more professional now. The old rug's been neatly laid out over the ditch. Like a proper carpet fitters done it, so we don't have to walk in areas of mud like we used to. It's much bigger now too, like I've just walked into a furnished room or something. There's three tree trunks side by side in the middle. So thick they could easily be used as comfortable stools.

About the surrounding branches candles stand and dim the atmos. There's a nasty smell ruining the décor. Musty, rank, rotting odour.

Like I'm spinning on the spot with it. Then come to a stand still feeling right queasy.

I can see Moon and Leg more clearly now. They're both unconscious, but I can see they're alive. Leg's mumbling away, while Moon's leg is fidgeting. Like they're both passing out after a heavy night.

What worries me most are their bruises. Moon has a black eye, cut forehead and is bleeding from the side of his head. Leg has the same temple wound, plus his nose has been punched. It's laying flat about his face and there's dry blood running from each nostril.

'What the fuck have you done to 'em Sloo you cunt?' I say with the most ferocious voice I can muster. Though that's nothing special.

He's gone back over to where me mate's lay now. I'm just inside the entrance still guarding meself against something in the darkness… whatever that could be.

'Calm young Crane. They're ok. They sleep for now. It's all about us.' Sloo stands by the left hand side of Leg. He's looking old. Like same geezer, but just how you'd imagine him about ten years from now. There's something much more adult about his posture. The way he speaks. Everything.

'Listen. Are you gonna let them go or not?'

The situation surreal. I'm not so much scared, only bewildered by it all. If this is real then I'm not fucking happy about seeing two thirds of The Magic Number in such disarray. I'm acting without a speech, now solely on impulse.

'You need to be patient young man, I'll let them go, but first we need to strike a deal.'

''it me with it then mate, 'cause I ain't gonna be patient 'ere. I want these boys out… soon as.'

I'm surprising meself with this forthrightness. Trying to get a visual of Tina to spur me on. That beautiful smile. Her longing eyes. Be inspired by my angel.

'Ok, ok. Good to see you finally gain a soul, just before you lose one.'

'What's that supposed to mean?' He's looking all cock sure of himself. It pisses me off more. Every little thing that annoyed me about Sloo in the past, are now minor quirks compared to this geezer's mannerisms.

'Seeing as you're in such a hurry, I'll come to the point.'

'Good.' Composure Crane, remain firm.

'All you need to do is grant me one thing. In return you get your friends back. Simple eh?'

I glance at Leg. He stirs, eyes now open. Shakes his head. Face deadly serious. Then in an instant he's gone again, mumbling away. Just in *time* for Sloo not to notice. He'd followed my eyes to the ground, but was too late.

Duly noted Leg! Duly noted!

'What?' I say covering my movements.

Sloo raises a smile. Making out like he knows what's happening here. He never see Leg. Fucking sure of it. The boys are gonna take him. I just need to get them free first.

'It's easy! I release them unharmed if you say a few words for me. Ok?' Right arrogant, patronizing sounding cunt.

'Then what 'appens to me?'

'You're free to walk from this forest with them. Let's put it this way: You're going to give me your soul; then all three of you leave in safety.' He holds his arms out like he's saying there's no tricks up his sleeve.

'What if I say bollocks?'

Sloo has a little laugh. That horrible chuckle suggesting I'm being stupid. I've had enough of him, but remain still. He reaches into an inside pocket of his cloak. From it he pulls a syringe. Filled with what can only be described as blood.

'You are in no position to refuse.'

'You touch them with that then...

'Then what?'

'I'm gonna fucking kill ya.' I point at him. Me heart's pounding. Me face filling with blood. Red can only portray anger. Or nervousness.

'Well this is where the fun begins.' Just as he says this I see a shadowed figure step from behind a tree. A little way back from where Sloo stands. It gets nearer. I'm praying it's Tin Lid, or Brooke, about to make an attack from the rear. I'm frozen with hope. Candlelight starts to reveal the approaching person. Closer it comes. I see...

It's the librarian! Joy fills my... everything. Can't let Sloo know he's here though. I look at Sloo. Think fast.

'Ok Sloo I'll do it.'

'Crane. So foolish...' Sloo turns and faces the librarian. Me heart sinks, but hopefully me man can still take him. '...You think he's on your side?' He asks pointing at the geezer, then has another arrogant giggle. Confusion bites at my stomach.

'This is my good friend Hermes. He set you up, along with Tina.'

Sloo puts his arm round the librarian and the two of 'em stand there grinning at me. I can't believe this... feel faint, dizzy, sick... Legs wobble, turn to jelly. My knees give way. I collapse.

Gone...

Snakes rumble underground. Split tongues appear first. Spitting venom at the sky. Heads protruding from holes. Long scaly bodies. Slippery entrance invading the earth. Steering across the leaves. Feet lay bare to poison. Circling attackers. Each taking its turn to plunge.

Life spindling effortlessly around caverns. Whistling sound of destiny. Revolving at speed. Whirlwinds to lay vengeance upon existence. Death will demise. Everything continues as one.

Corpses lay siege. Muscles spasm. Juices outweigh water. Graves disintegrate. Drying flesh sizzles in sunshine. Broken down to the bone. Screams of terror.

Chimps yelp. Strapped into cushions. Sewn up and descended upon. Frayed at the edges. Brains will implode. Its release drips steadily upon the seat. Staining the world and its creator. Love resides here no more.

Belief snatched as terrapins squirm and explode underfoot. Millions of fish flapping on dry land. Breadcrumbs fall as hailstones. Two tigers square up. Gnarling, snapping faces. Each razor sharp tooth finds its spot. Jugulars split and spray like hoses. Blood cascading as wallpaper. The garden is corrupted. No longer secret. Paradise uncovered and rampaged by beasts. Elephants crumple to their sides. Legs desperately searching for footing. Large medicine balls break ribs. The screaming becomes unperturbed. Sickening to each lobe. Desperately searching for deafness. A place reserved for nothingness.

Heads are ripped off and hurled from library windows. Each vein trailing as worms enter skulls. Light evaporates. Now complete darkness. Arms outstretched clinging for a hold. Ever forward, illusions exist here.

Wood rots in an instant. Crumbles to rubble. Hyenas pounce. On top of their earth. Cackling burns. Struggling for air. For comprehension. Choked by invisible assailants. Ghosts flutter into view.

A harp lampooned. Spinning globes fall from sands. Across the floor. Severed heads stare toward nothingness. A brace of crows swoop. Peck eyeball innards to return to their young. Caught in the dogs paw. Licked and spat upon. Each wing the heaviest burden to carry.

Fires sizzle then disappear. Three betrayals become words of comfort. Lost under the vomit. Large stones crush the body between. Everything eludes skin. Lurid, damp. Frame upon frame. Unproved yet determined rape. No one can escape.

Jowls scythed, hung upon symbols of birth. Intestines become tinsel. Removed fingers reach at the helm.

Stars blink. Glue seals them shut. Ever circling. Always burning. The ice sets in. Deserts sucked into clouds. Carried across lands then spewed into lungs. Breathing cease. Father figures turn on apprentices. Slash their throats and drink its secretion. Alcohol to water. Flows and singes mountains. Snow turns to charcoal.

Every creeping body inches nearer. Felines swung by tails. Spiked onto railings. Distinct points protruding through lifeless furs. Liars seek the truth. Damning verdict upon each scalp. Washed up gold. Salt into oxygen.

The land is dying. Pundits seek out futile meanings, then combust. Pyramids suffocate inhabitants. Walls are crumbling. Greed to anorexia. Malnutrition to gluttony. Sloth to over-exertion. Hearts fail. Time stops ticking. Wiser, increasing stupidity. Circling on the spot as the sparkling guide fools its followers. Gifts rammed into arseholes. Skulls manipulated into vices. Sheep have escaped. Ripped apart by the coyote.

Countries lay indistinguishable. Red surfaces bubble. Tremors signal birth. Babies spat up from beneath. Land awkwardly into twisted limbs. Damaged goods. Spineless. Wriggling, aiming for the water. Tide retreats. Sucked into chasms.

A man lifts the child from the pit, then jumps in. Demons intrude orifices. No longer can anyone see...

There is nothing here.

Chilled blood as a wake up call. Alarms symbolise endings. Two mortals discuss the glorious horizon. An enormous red wave that sits poised ten miles higher than the earth's surface. Anticipation turns to angst.

'Don't fuck it up this *time*.'
'You've played your part now you can leave.'

She's looking up into my eyes. Beckoning me forward. She wants this. I'm sure of it. She's so beautiful. Our lips getting close. Oh Tina...

'Ah finally you're with us serf. Inhale the rotting flesh.'

Crane expecting safety. Anticipating familiar smells of a bedroom. Seeking recognisable scenery. Led to an ever increasing disappointment. Foetal position on a dank rug in the middle of existence itself. Recollection damages all hope.

Watches as the first injection of blood enters a friend's jugular. Spasms, convulsions of Littl' Leg. Awake, yet immobile.

'Stop. Please?'

Crane clutches desperately out of reach. Dismay hindering movement. Everything that courage stood for diminished under false pretences.

'This will end now my friend. All you have to do is give yourself to me.' Sloo speaks with assured presence.

Littl' leg unable to speak. Very last gesture to a struggling friend. Shakes his head for a second *time*.

'No.' Crane refutes.

Tears portray suffering. Rises to his feet with one moment of final defiance. Betrayed three times. Feet like lead weights clamber forward.

'Do not step any nearer.'

Command from "Hermes" unheeded. Crane continues, arching forward. Two friends to live for, to strive towards.

'Have it your way.' Sloo shrugs

Knife removed from sheaf. The Riverman points it at Leg's temple. Its tip pierces through skin.

Crane acknowledges incredible power at cries of a close friend in pain. Pounces forward.

Hermes steps forth. Restrains a squirming body tightly.

Legs lash out. Kicking and screaming. Wanting out, yet captor so forceful. No blows seem to hinder.

Littl' Leg unable to move now. Beeke's blood seeps into his veins. Dead life encapsulates his spirit. Can only blub as the blade carves, spheres its way about the scalp.

'Please no.' Crane struggles. No release.

'Please no. Please no...' A mimicking murderer.

Juice continuing its journey toward blinding. A face covered in dark red liquid. An expression becomes numb.

Hands placed upon the thinking organ. Pull it from its hold. Sunken cranium. Face droops, limbs twitch. Littl' Leg breathes no more. Crane's writhing ceases. Hope's dwindling. Hermes releases his captive. Drops to his knees. Can only howl as the knife now circles his friend's chest.

A heart pumps once, twice in the palm. Fizzles into lump of clay.

'Stop. I'll do anything.'

...Moments pause...

Sloo looks upon Crane with a harrowing smile.

'Now we're seeing the bigger picture are we. You see young Cranley the same happens to Mooning here if you do not comply.'

Hermes leaves Crane to his destiny. Now stands once again side by side with Sloo. His hand reaches into the pocket of his cloak and takes clasp a syringe of his own.

Sloo steps forward.

'So Crane, will you now finally obey me and follow me into the darkness?'

'Yes. I'll do anything. Please stop.' Crane pleads. Tears apparent. Moon wakes.

Yelping souls jump from decks. Swimming for shore. Every pawn in its position. The queue turns toward the scene. Laughing and shaking uncontrollably.

'We're here... Heaven's eyes bleed... Watch your land unfurl... Finally Armageddon arrives... Hurl your horses.' Cries of the dead.

Sloo stands in awe at his completed work. Everyone has agreed. Can now raise his hands in triumph. The snakes frazzle and mutate to leaves.

Hermes raises the syringe behind the celebrating Sloo's back. Then spikes it into the Riverman's neck.

Sloo grabs wildly at the protruding instrument. Rotates sharply. Wide eyed, bemused by the sudden turn of events. Numbness takes the reigns. Sloo committed to become a heap on the floor.

'What have you done to me?' Immobility deciphers fear. Skin turns green. The tail instantly forms. Scales replace skin. Spikes line the spine. A serpent writhes upon the floor. Hermes looms over and laughs.

'You didn't think you were going to rule did you? This was my entire plan.'

Crane averts his gaze from the unexpected. Spies a narrow opportunity with this twist.

A reptile flaps and whistles:

'Shhlooooo'.

Hermes laughs and applauds.

Crane hobbles on knees to Moon. Restraints loosen without attempt. Lifts his friend to standing position. Bends and grabs Leg's brain and heart from the floor. Pushes them into the pockets of Moon's hooded jumper. Knows not why.

Hermes still gazes upon the screaming Sloo. Continues to guffaw with delight. Attention caught up in the moment of madness.

'A special potion of my own. Some crucifix blood from the saviour. Feel good Charon? You like the juices?'

The new leader has to witness Sloo's final gasps. Victory dance upon the remaining murmurs of demise. Too humorous to the vilest of necromancers not to.

Eventually the Riverman ceases his clamour.

Dead to this world

'You are no longer needed if the dead are to live. What point in you now? What point in you ever serpent?'

Hermes so involved in his own gratification. Unable to notice Crane helping Moon to push forward and evacuate the camp.

Pride. A final smile. Hermes finally looks up for the Magic Number. Realises he is now alone. Panic waits patiently.

'Good effort boys, but you will not escape these trees. They are mine. I also have someone here very eager to meet you.' Hermes puts two fingers to his mouth. A whistle exudes, causing death to stir.

Cerberus appears from the shadows. A vicious three headed dog ready for its orders. No matter who the giver. Seek and devour. Tiger-like. Amber and Black striped fur. Razor sharp wolf fangs threaten in cavern like mouths. Snaps shut. Opens, snarls. Closes, another opens. Barks' alternately disturbing every living being's sleep. Saliva drips from black and blood stained jowls. So hungry. In desperate need of more flesh to chew upon. Bones to gnaw. Eagerness clamouring toward deathly silence.

'Go find them. My friends will aid your pursuit.' In an instant the creature bounds into the darkness of the maze...

Hermes sits upon a tree trunk. Picking his nails in sheer impertinence.

'Trees come alive.'

Silence.

Expecting roots to unveil from the earth. For branches to reach and stretch as they wake. Tarrying for amusement.

Nothing.

Looks up. First signs of worry.

'Trees come alive. I command you.'

Nonentity.

Hermes rises in angst. Control evaporates. Situation in disarray.

'This is not happening. Go Cerberus, get your prey.'

A distraught God decides he must now chase too. Leaps into action and springs from the ditch. Hair instantly transforming to grey. Grows rapidly to twice its length. Mirroring his facial covering. Wizened to death itself.

The underworld may never survive this. Begins a sprint. Instantly lightning quick.

Finally the trees creak and move. Roots emerge to trip the pursuer. Hermes scrambles on the floor. Branches extend flinging outwards. They reach the floored figure. Whip swiftly underneath, then ravels his body. Mummifying the decadent hunter.

'Witless actions. I see Zeus is afoot. Yet I will succeed and you will experience my everlasting vengeance. I promise you this.'

Hermes in no position to brandish threats. Wrapped as a cocoon. Now unable to catch the survivors...

A light up ahead. Don't know whether I should trust it or not. Feel betrayed by everything so far. Why should this be any different? Guiding sparkle or that bitch Tina misleading me again? She hasn't shown her deluding self yet. This is probably her doing. Leading me to a fucking trap. Yet I have nothing else left to follow. Darkness so thick surrounds me. Would never escape in there.

I begin to hear some barking and snapping from behind...

A noise that frightens my very insides. So unnerving I consider quitting; turning round and saying "ok I give in". I won't though, if only for my brother Moon's safety here. It's hard to keep him going though. He's bewildered. Hasn't uttered a word yet, but he's a warrior. Unrelenting, determinedly limping in a jog with me. Like we're in some demented three legged marathon.

A breathing becoming heavier. I look back... Nothing.

There is something chasing me. I know not what yet, but its tormenting vocals suggest I must get away.

The light is my only option. If this is deception, then I'll gladly let it catch me. Rip me in to tiny pieces. I cannot withstand one more of these lies.

Cerberus bounds. Three heads desperately seeking flesh to gorge upon. Can smell the meat. Knows it's so close to its quarry. Stalking toward a huge feast. Understands its allowance. Everything is food except the human's heart and brains. This meal would suffice. Big bear-like black noses dribble and sniff the air. Limbs already cooking on the barbecue.

If anything the glow enables us to avoid oncoming trees. It feels as though they're magically stepping aside too. Forming a tunnel for our safe escape. Arm around Moon. Want him safe, if not myself. I pray to you God, please deliver him unharmed from this scene. Forget about my survival, he's what matters to me now. He and my family too. Please save them from any iniquity. You can take me, but save them.

Can read the boys thoughts. Lung's vocals edging a route. Closing in. Only the bathing of pitch black makes it hard to decipher exact whereabouts. Then catches a glimpse of two staggering in front. The tunnel narrows. Dinner haunts the dogs' minds. Food is served.

Keep pushing forward. Barking increases in its severity. Growling makes me shudder. Footsteps upon my grave. I can hear it pounding. Foul breath clogs my nostrils, I choke. The tunnel narrows. The light grows brighter. Coughing and spluttering, clinging to my friend for dear life. We walk as one. As three even.

Leg's with us too. Can feel him here. Know he's behind each tree willing us forward.

'You can do it Crane. You can do it.'

There's a bridge like tunnel forming up ahead. Brickwork surrounds the opening. Exactly like I saw in the library.

We stagger up the path toward it. That's where the light resides. This could be my end. Yet I fear nothing. My remaining hope. Snapping jaws so close. Can almost feel myself being bitten and eaten alive.

Leaping deasil. Muscles reacting in perfection. Thick legs working at speed. Closer and closer to the two figures. All mouths poised open. Tongues hang from sides. Dripping saliva in contemplation of mouthfuls of gristle. One pounce and it will be upon them. Back legs tense in preparation. Tail wags.

Claws ready to dig.

Now... Crack...

The tree comes crashing down on the dog's back. Forcing out its innards in one foul instant. Lungs splutter. Spleens release from mouths as snakes. Arsehole releasing mounds of liver, kidneys, stomachs...

Blood soaks the forest... again.

Showered with red. I heard the yelps. Think I am safe for now. The tunnel is at reach. My destiny.

'Come on Moon we're going home now.'

‘Thanks Crane.’ Rejoice at his words. He’s still with me. Still sane. A true battler.

Makes me want to cry with respect.

We’re here…

Light dazzles and blinds us as we jump into the opening. Confused as to what we are walking into, but glad to be finally free of this forest.

I hope…

Vision steadies. Focus returning.

I cling to Moon. We are standing face to face with an army. Not like I’m used to. No soldiers with helmets, guns or tanks. These men carry spears and sit on horses. They only wear cloaks with ropes for belts. Each of them stares upon us in shock. Fires blaze upon sticks. Men on foot approach us and hold weapons to our faces.

‘Please we’re not here to hurt you.’ I plea. Hoping upon hope that this is salvation. Not the wicked Tina’s idea of a joke. More false pretences.

They stand poised, I hold my unused arm up to the sky. Want them to see I am harmless...

Through the crowd of horses behind my main concern approaches a huge black stallion. Upon it sits a bearded man. The only person here protected neck down with armour. A crown rests upon his head. He seems nervous. Totally edgy. Unready for this alien situation. He raises his hands. Provoking his follower’s murmurs of fear to cease…

Silence now reigns…

They wait his command…

Please let it be good. Please God.

‘Take prisoner the one that speaks. Slay the other, he is possessed.’

‘No… Please… No.’

Me and my brethren desperately cling to each other. On our knees.

I WONT LET MOON AND LEG GO FOR ANYTHING.

The army injects into us…

EPILOGUE
SEHCAORPPA YAD S'MOOD

Threshold of a new dawn. Entrancing hum. Multitude of golden reflection. Buried comfort sinking then lifting. Circles blow nerve tingling sensation. Warmth beneath the structures clothing. Drifting under slender droplets. The property of senses balanced comfortably in unison. Minority supporting majority. Diversity the key to orderly semblance. Marching allegiance intensified. Moulding mankind as resolute. All hurdles overlooked. Silence breathes water. Thrills massaging gaps on balance constructs. Bongo rhythm sleeps parallel. Variant sound unclogging mentality's constraints.

Focus centres on one.

Slows to revolving curiosity. Continuous calculation of simple equation

Repetition a restful enigma.

Repetition a restful enigma.

Repetition a restful enigma...

...Soon that land enhances upon your vision. Everyone will pass through sooner or later. Blurs blighting the horizon. Lightning travellers whipping as wind. Beings confused with inanimate. Everyone is a part of someone else's landscape.

Wake up and see.

With eyes closed, dreams will always appear. If you let them.

''e don't seem to be budging.'

'Got to get 'im up, 'e's been out of it for ages.'

'Yeah either we leave now or I reckon they'll throw us out.'

'Crane...Crane...**CRANE**.'

Crouching apathy disturbed. The visions reacquaint with the breaking of peace. At first terror grips. Then familiarities regain stomach's poise. Uplifting music of a new age. Happiness resides under this one roof. Release of anxiety uniting all as one.

Five figures stand above. Two in front trying to wake. Three behind, all wait patiently for the new arrival.

'You alright mate?'

'I'm weary, confused, but I'm able to stand now.'

'Cool. We'll 'ead off now. Get you 'ome.'

Helping hand. Forthright posture from foetal. Ages of growth blitzed in one movement.

'I'm grateful for your concern, but who are you?'

'We're your mates Moon and Leg geez. You're in safe 'ands now.'

Recognition swamps the scene.

'Wadard, Hevey. You're here... It's so good to see you again. I've missed you.'

Leading company stand aside, bemused that they're followers were recognised above themselves.

'It is good to see you too. We thank you greatly for what you helped to achieve.' Says one from the background.

The initial speaker fuses the interactions

'You know these two? We saw 'em wandering around looking lost, so we've taken 'em in innit Leg?'

'Yeah. Said they're welcome to join us anytime.'

Warming hugs are shared around as welcomes

'Of course I know them. They are great friends of mine. Who is the other that joins you?' Attention turns to a small boy within the group of five.

'Well this is the weird bit. It's our mate Kev, but 'e's only eight years old at the minute...' Original conversationalist signifies a whisper. "...We think this acid's really done us up this *time*.'

'Yeah and we can't find the others anywhere.' Adds Littl' Leg.

'Well good day to you all.'

‘It’s no worries. Still me and Leg reckon we should call it a night now.’ Another modernist states.

‘You mean you know how to get out of here?’ The newcomer shocked at the return of a long lost prospect.

‘Yeah look. The exit’s just ‘ere ya doughnut.’ Points to the right. Blacked out double doors. Two bulky men dressed in black stand guard.

Plaudits. Fully woken from a further escape. The weary traveller takes the hand of the young boy. Then smiles to signify readiness.

Six men ready to leave. Approach the doorway. The bouncers raise hands to halt their progress. One recognisable, the other wears a name tag that reads RICKY.

‘Alright the geez, ‘ow’s it going mate?’

‘‘ello Leg mate. I’m good, what about yaself?’

‘All I can say is those acids you got us were mind blowing.’

‘Nothing to do with me I’m afraid geezer.’

‘That’s odd!’

‘Life’s odd mate. Still where you off to?’

‘We wanna go. Get ‘ome and ‘ave a chill.’

‘I’m afraid there’s no way out of ‘ere for now. You’re all a bit trapped.’

Wadard, Hevey, Moon, Leg, Cranley and Kevin all sigh as one.

‘Fucking ‘ell.’ Proclaims Leg.

‘Yeah don’t worry though mate. It’s good ‘ere. There’s a wicked chill out zone. If you can find it that is.’

‘Where are we?’ A voice from the back of the crowd is heard. Moon turns, sees that it came from what appears to be his good friend Crane.

‘Crane you mug! You should know this place by now… This is *Time.*’

Days and nights have gone by without so much as one visitor. Not that there’s much of a daytime. Only shards of light get in here. I love standing in ‘em when they arrive. Don’t wanna turn into one of those albino things do I.

Just looking forward to me next ration of crappy bread and stagnant water. That’s me highlight. That’s all that ever happens.

Door's unbolted or something, then four geezers holding spears appear. In a sunlight that I can't even look at 'cause it hurts me eyes so much. Then by time **I've adjusted me sight, they've gone. The rooms black again and me dinners sat on the floor.**

Beautiful.

Knocked clean out with the commotion. Only recently started coming to terms with what went on out there. Don't even know what happened to Moon.

It's a funny old world Saint.

Still this dodgy little hut's better than that forest. I'm never gonna step foot in one again. If I ever get out of here that is. Don't know if I won, lost or drew. Fuck all really. At least he never got me or Moon... Or Leg come to think of it. Just wish I knew if one of the boys was alright. Or at least given a small smidgeon of a clue of exactly where the fuck I am.

That would do.

'Hello Steven.'

'Jesus H. bollocks.' Jump to fuck.

There's a glow in the corner where the voice come from. Big bright fucking light. Bit blinding for me to focus. I've been sat in near complete darkness for God knows how long.

Shield me eyes for a bit. Holding a slight glimpse at it to adjust. The initial fright scared me. But after what I've been through, a small light ain't exactly given me aneurism.

Then slowly a form appears. The shape of a person comes into view. Then it all becomes clear.

'Tina. Fucking 'ell. You can piss right off.'

'Please Steven, I understand your anger, but you was tricked. The librarian was Shem. Hermes only appeared in his form to instigate your downfall. You must believe me.'

What the hell is going on? Harps and all sorts of shit going off in the room. Tina's looking stunning. Long flowing dress all in white. Hair flying back as if there was a wind in the room. Even a fucking sparkling ring circling her head. Then these mammoth white wings extend from behind her. Stretching for what seems and feels like miles.

Now she smiles. Me heart begins beating with hope once more.

Love has returned to my eyes. I'm a romantic...

Or an idiot? Whatever, but me trust in her returns instantly.

''ow are me friends?'

'There's some very good news on that front. Your devotion and the leading of your two friends to safety has set The Magic Number into effect. Zeus is now freed to intercept. So though not all of your friends are released yet, with your help they soon will be.'

Dunno what all the fuck that was about.

''ow can I 'elp now though? I mean stuck in 'ere?'

'My promise will not be broken to you Crane. I'm with you now. Now and for eternity, because... because I fell in love with you.' She turns her head all shyly.

My strength is reinstated with these words. I'm able to stand again.

'Well I love you too.' I smile.

A tear forms in the corner of each of my eyes. Have to choke back balling it here. Dippy bastard! She stands too and walks toward me. We meet with a massive kiss and hug. I'm flying again.

'You're gonna go on a brilliant journey. There's someone we need you to visit.' She says as our embrace ends...

'Beautiful!'

All of a sudden I'm shuddering... Just like someone's walked over me grave.

PROLOGUE
SALVATION APPROACHES

3008 AD

'Riding Zeus' testicles.'

APPENDIX:

R.E.M. lyrics appear courtesy of Warner Bros inc

Dr Dre lyrics appear courtesy of Interscope Records

Digital Underground lyrics appear courtesy of Tommy Boy Entertainment

James Blunt lyrics appear courtesy of Atlantic Recording Corp.

The Source/Candi Staton lyrics appear courtesy of Resist Music Ltd

Scissor Sisters lyrics appear courtesy of Polydor Ltd (uk)

***The Evil Dead* dialogue appear courtesy of USA Films (LA)**

ABOUT THE AUTHOR

Matt White has a degree in Creative writing from the University of Derby and is also a Horror film critic for a popular culture website. This is his first novel.